TRIANGLE CLASSICS

ILLUMINATING THE GAY AND LESBIAN EXPERIENCE

And the Band Played On
by Randy Shilts

The Autobiography of Alice B. Toklas
by Gertrude Stein

The Beebo Brinker Chronicles
by Ann Bannon

Bertram Cope's Year
by Henry Blake Fuller

Borrowed Time/Love Alone/Becoming a Man
by Paul Monette

A Boy's Own Story/
The Beautiful Room Is Empty
by Edmund White

Brideshead Revisited
by Evelyn Waugh

The Celluloid Closet
by Vito Russo

City of Night
by John Rechy

Dancer from the Dance
by Andrew Holleran

Death in Venice
and Seven Other Stories
by Thomas Mann

Family Dancing
by David Leavitt

The Family of Max Desir
by Robert Ferro

Giovanni's Room
by James Baldwin

The Lord Won't Mind/One for the Gods
by Gordon Merrick

The Lure
by Felice Picano

The Naked Civil Servant/How to Become a Virgin/
Resident Alien
by Quentin Crisp

Nightwood/Ladies Almanack
by Djuna Barnes

Olivia
by Olivia

Oranges Are Not the Only Fruit
by Jeanette Winterson

Orlando
by Virginia Woolf

The Picture of Dorian Gray
by Oscar Wilde

The Price of Salt
by Patricia Highsmith

Rubyfruit Jungle
by Rita Mae Brown

A Single Man
by Christopher Isherwood

Skinflick/Gravedigger/Nightwork
by Joseph Hansen

The Sophie Horowitz Story/Girls, Visions and Everything/
After Dolores
by Sarah Schulman

Stone Butch Blues
by Leslie Feinberg

Surpassing the Love of Men
by Lillian Faderman

The Well of Loneliness
by Radclyffe Hall

What Is Found There/An Atlas of the Difficult World/
The Fact of a Doorframe
by Adrienne Rich

Zami/Sister Outsider/Undersong
by Audre Lorde

THE LORD WON'T MIND

ONE FOR THE GODS

THE LORD WON'T MIND
ONE FOR THE GODS

GORDON MERRICK

QUALITY PAPERBACK BOOK CLUB
NEW YORK

THE LORD WON'T MIND

For Didine

"I say, if it's love, the Lord won't mind.
There's enough hate in the world."
—*Mrs. Sapphire Hall*
Harlem, 1940

"HE'S COMING IN A WEEK," C.B. said, laying the letter down beside her breakfast coffee.

"I suppose he's wildly good-looking," I said. No, not I. *He* said. He. I will not associate myself with the things I have to tell. If I must intrude occasionally, it will be from the distance of time and change. Charlie Mills has nothing to do with me.

"I suppose he's wildly good-looking," Charlie teased his improbable grandmother.

"I've never made any secret of liking handsome young men." She smiled roguishly, a roguish smile in a face that remained invincibly impish in spite of her elaborate and rather old-fashioned style. She derived not from the twenties but from a more gracious Edwardian era. "But you must admit, I also insist on their having some wits. Yes, he's very — no, not handsome — but very attractive in his way. In your way, really. You're enough alike to be taken for brothers by the unobservant."

"Are you trying to say I'm not handsome?" he protested with a playful show of indignation.

"Not really what we'd have called handsome in my day. I've never said you were. But very, very attractive, my dearest." Again the roguish smile, a flirtatious tilt of the head. Charlie felt himself melt with delight. Her accent was self-Anglicized with broadened *a*'s and well-shaped *u*'s from which emerged occasionally an unexpected echo of the South. She lifted a scrap of lace handkerchief and twirled it once in the air as if conjuring the future. "We must take him in hand. You're just what he needs at this stage — someone to look up to, someone who can offer him understanding. He gets none at home. Imagine being a general's son! Imagine being packed off to West Point! It won't do. His tastes are the same as ours. Books. The theater. You must take him under your wing for the summer."

"But he's only a kid."

"Pooh. Three or four years' difference. Nothing." Her hand remained suspended in midair as if she held all the elements of the situation firmly fixed before her. She invested even her smallest effects with drama. He adored her. "In England, he'd be considered a finished gentleman. Why, men are already launched on careers at his age. Look at the poets."

"That may be true in England, but it isn't here." He couldn't understand his elders' habit of dismissing three or four or even five years as being of no consequence. It made all the difference in the world. This Peter Marshall or whatever his name was couldn't be more than eighteen at the most. Callow, all knobs and knuckles with nothing matching anything else, probably smelly, no matter how good-looking. The prospect failed to please. "He just won't fit with any of my crowd. He'll be too young for any of the girls."

"I don't think we need worry about girls for the time being. I want him here for you. I can count on you to stir him up, draw him out. He's like Sleeping Beauty. He needs only a kiss to wake him up."

Charlie threw his head back and laughed to cover a blush. "Really, C.B. Aren't you getting things mixed up? Surely you want a girl for that."

She flicked her handkerchief at him playfully. "Don't be dense, my dearest." She picked up a small silver bell and rang it briskly as they rose from the dining table. The sharpness of her perceptions sometimes struck him like a blow in the stomach, quite taking his breath away, even though she seemed an innocent in many areas. She couldn't say the things she said if she weren't. Nevertheless, he was glad for movement now.

It was hot outside, but here in the big dark rooms of the old summer house, with every window guarded by a great white mushroom of awning, they remained crisp and comfortable in their smart summer clothes. I remember it was hot all that summer, although none of it has anything to, do with me; nor will my memory always be reliable. What year was it, in fact? Had the war already started? No, it must have been the last summer of peace. The last summer Charlie spent with his grandmother. He hadn't always spent his summers with her. Although he would have been happy to forget it, he had more immediate family — mother, father, brother — living outside of Philadelphia, whose conventional provincial life dealt death to his soul. As long as he could remember, C.B., as unique, original, unclassifiable as the initials that made her nickname, had embodied the glittering alternative of the great world. She had disposed conversationally of his mother some years before. "There's no point in denying the fact that your mother is my daughter," she had said to him once. "That doesn't mean that I'm obliged to like her." It had suddenly made life enormous, trackless, frightening, but boundlessly exciting. Needless to say, C.B. was a widow. It wouldn't have surprised him to learn that she had murdered her husband. There was mystery enough, but so far murder had not been hinted at.

Mystery? It pleased him to think of her as mysterious, although there was nothing really to justify the epithet, except that he didn't know anybody like her. This house. Why had she chosen to spend her summers in the rather obscure grandeur of Rumson, New Jersey, rather than in, say, one of the stylish Long Island resorts? It had the look of old family property, but she had acquired it only ten years ago, just at the beginning of the Depression, when Charlie's parents were deciding they couldn't afford to keep their New England summer cottage. He didn't think of her as more or less rich than other people; she was the way everybody should be: money flowed from her effortlessly, without being mentioned. All his formative years had been lived in the gray shadow of the Depression; she was the only person he knew who continued to bask in the bright light of ease and prosperity. While his parents' friends were leaping out of high windows, she maintained her two imposing establishments (his childhood impressions of her apartment in New York had endowed it forever with the vastness of Versailles) as if nothing had happened. Others grimly discussed Hitler and such uncongenial places as the Sudetenland; C.B. projected a vision of marching heroes and flashing banners when she referred to the impending war. All her causes and interests were cloaked in glamour.

Peter, whose last name turned out to be Martin, received the full treatment in the week that preceded his arrival. He was apparently some sort of cousin. The South was populated with C.B.'s vague relations. They all paid an annual visit to New York that in turn became an annual visit to C.B. From time to time, she pounced, extracting from their unpromising ranks a son who struck her fancy. Peter was the latest in a long line, but the first with whom circumstances permitted Charlie to be involved. He expected the worst, but somewhere in the back of his mind an insistent hope lingered.

"I'm going to put him in the little room next to you," she announced at lunch. "I want you to be near each other so you can make friends quickly. Young men like to burn the midnight oil. You'll be quite on your own up there together, with nobody around to bother you."

"I hope we don't hate each other on sight." The prospect of a friend-in-residence was undoubtedly appealing. Except for the constant joy of her company, he found the summers with C.B. a trifle empty. The country-club life, the enforced companionship of young people with whom he had little in common except age, made him restless. There was no opportunity for the sexual adventures that had been for years the core of his existence. He thought of his childhood visits to C.B. in the city, when he would find the closets piled high with gaily wrapped presents, impromptu Christmases whose memory still made him tingle with delight. It was like her to make him the gift of an ideal companion. When he thought of the difference in their ages, though, his hopes dimmed.

"It's going to be perfect. When I saw him this winter I knew you were made for each other." Her laugh was irrepressibly youthful. "I sound like a silly matchmaking old lady."

"You sound as if you were planning a marriage." Charlie forced a laugh, suddenly self-conscious at having put it so succinctly.

"Friendship is much more important to a man than marriage," she said with a wave of her hand. "A man can never be friends with his wife. The English understand it so well — their men's clubs. That's where an Englishman's real life is lived. I'm so glad you've never been silly about girls. So many men your age become total bores over them."

"Oh, well, that's just kid stuff," he said, relaxing into his most worldly manner. Her attitude toward girls had always relieved him of the necessity of inventing romances. His mother pushed them at him and plagued him with anxious leading questions so that he had always to be on his guard to conceal his indifference. "What about your precious Peter?" he asked, tackling the question that had been uppermost in his mind since she had confirmed his

10

imminent arrival. "How do you know he's not going to be a bore about them?"

"He's not that sort at all. He has great delicacy of feeling. It's the first thing one sees in him."

There were moments when they achieved such perfect understanding that he felt himself drawn giddily close to total self-revelation.

"I know exactly what I hope you'll accomplish," she said, drawing circles in the air with her finger as he drove her to the hairdresser in the little sports car she had given him. She was dressed all in white and wore a rakish straw hat that lent extraordinary chic to every tilt of her head. "It's too late to save him from West Point. The die is cast. What he needs is an ideal that'll help him resist being swallowed up by the military mentality. Once he's known you he'll never accept the second-rate."

"Goodness. Is that the effect I have on people?" Charlie asked with a chuckle.

"You have so many splendid qualities, my dearest. Knowing you is bound to be an important experience for anybody with dawning perceptions. The fact that you've finished college and are about to embark on a career will give you an enormous influence over him even if there's no great difference in age. Oh, yes, we'll rescue him from the General."

Charlie laughed again. "You really are a born conspirator, aren't you?"

"Women are so useless. I'm no exception, but at least I've had the opportunity to help some talented young men make the most of their lives. I don't claim any credit for you, my dearest. I've simply had the pleasure of watching you turn into the fascinating person you are. I admit you've frightened me at times. You have almost *too* much talent. Your acting. Your painting. Of course, making a career of either would have been out of the question, but it's a relief to know that your life has taken its final direction. I've looked forward to the years that are beginning now."

"Me too, so long as we don't really have a war and everything's turned upside down."

"We mustn't think about it. Thank heavens, there are always strings to pull. I understand that if there *is* a war, some of the most interesting jobs will be right in New York. You'll be absolutely stunning in uniform."

11

He executed a racy left turn, displaying his skill for her admiration and marveling at his good fortune. Nobody he knew had family like C.B. — gay, clever, still attractive, generous, devoted, and incapable of a critical word. He couldn't imagine what life would be like without her.

"One thing about West Point," she said over after-dinner coffee. "It's not far away. If you really do hit it off together, as I'm sure you will, he can always come to us for weekends. We can take him to the theater and get his mind off tanks or machine guns or whatever it is they talk about at West Point."

"I just hope he's aware of how lucky he is to meet me," Charlie said lightly. He could no longer pass the room that awaited the visitor without indulging in fantasies about the days that would follow its occupancy. He and Peter were very alike. Could she have been so insistent on that point without meaning something by it?

THEY WENT TO MEET HIM at the station in the towering old Packard C.B. kept in the country. "You can't miss him," she said, remaining in the car while Charlie and Henry, the Negro driver who doubled as butler, were dispatched to wait on the blistering platform. "I've told you, he's about your build and very blond."

The train, pulled by a clangorous steam engine, was a long one so that Charlie caught his first glimpse of the arriving guest from a considerable distance. He was coltishly lugging a battered suitcase. Young. Much too young. His keyed-up interest died. They approached each other, they identified themselves, they exchanged a perfunctory handshake. It was over. The summer was to be like any other.

He left the backseat of the car to C.B. and the new arrival and sat in front with Henry. He was mildly impatient with the effusive warmth that marked C.B.'s welcome. They had barely started on the homeward trip before she exclaimed, addressing Charlie, "Now, tell me. Don't you agree with me? Isn't he utterly charming-looking?"

Charlie turned to face them. "Now, stop it, C.B. You're just embarrassing him. We can see for ourselves how beautiful we both are."

12

His eyes encountered Peter's and started to move on but were held by the clear blue innocence of the boy's regard, openly responsive, with none of the guarded defiance with which young males generally eye their own sex. He smiled, and Peter smiled in return before quickly looking away. C.B. had been right, he admitted to himself. Handsome was too strong a word. He was beautiful in a just barely formed way. His eyes were big, his nose slightly tilted, his mouth full and soft, but there was strength enough in the line of the jaw and the curve of cheekbone. His golden hair frizzed slightly at the sides and fell in a smooth wave across his brow. His neck was smooth and strong. Charlie's eyes dropped to the boy's hands, and he experienced a surge of sharpened interest. They were big but not clumsy, with long, strong fingers. He felt an impulse to hold them, to feel their grip. His glance shifted automatically to the crotch. The swell of the trousers was promising but inconclusive. He became aware of the beating of his heart. The clothes were responsible for the unhappy first impression, he decided. A plaid shirt was all very well in wool, but it wouldn't do in cheap cotton. Proper clothes would add to his maturity. He might even pass for twenty-one.

Charlie remained twisted around, facing the two in the backseat. He allowed himself to express his interest by asking friendly questions of a casual sort, but he was careful to divide his attention with C.B. When they drew up under the trees in front of the big old frame house set on rolling lawns, he helped her out with courtly solicitude, although he was hoping to make this a moment of decisive contact. He turned from her as soon as he could and was in time to put his hand on Peter's shoulder before he moved into place beside C.B. The boy shot him a quick, gratified, slightly questioning look. He gave the shoulder a slight squeeze. It felt solid and well muscled. He noted with satisfaction that he was a shade taller than the newcomer. "Leave your bag," he said. "Henry will take care of it. We'll get you settled after lunch."

He was keenly alert for some sign of recognition from the boy, a look, a touch, but Peter only smiled and nodded and moved on, leaving Charlie with the feel of bone and sinew in his hand.

They had long, mild drinks in the rich gloom of a deep veranda. Charlie was determined now to dazzle, and since he and C.B. were a formidable team, they had no trouble reducing Peter to charming, helpless laughter. They engaged in wild flights of nonsense, scatter-

13

ing their shared knowledge of books and plays and people along the way, but Charlie was careful to modulate their performance to carry Peter with them. Peter revealed a lively mind and although a slight air of reticence clung to him, he was able to hold his own.

At lunch, the two youths sat opposite each other and now their eyes met constantly. Charlie made no further effort to share him with C.B., although for her sake, he tried to keep some check on his response. To her, he would always be slightly aloof and superior, the wooed, never the wooer. When he caught Peter's eye, he charged every look with significance without quite giving his hand away. If Peter recognized this as flirting, he gave no indication of it. His regard was open, admiring, untroubled, with no trace of the extra awareness that Charlie was eager to provoke. Of course, the eyes didn't necessarily tell the whole story. He might be the sort Charlie had encountered not infrequently who took the outcome so completely for granted that he felt no need to underline it. That he might remain insensible to Charlie's intentions was another possibility, which shook his natural self-confidence. He felt as if he might commit some frightful indiscretion if he didn't soon get the boy to himself.

He knew that he had only to muster a little patience. It was C.B.'s invariable habit to retire to her rooms for the afternoon, immediately after coffee. The small room next to his own more spacious quarters on the top floor was waiting. The thing would take care of itself.

Soon after they had returned to the veranda, C.B. announced, "You two adorable creatures must have a thousand things to talk about." She rose and went to Peter and held both hands out to him. He stood to receive the benison of her undisguised approval. "I'll leave you in Charlie's capable hands. I'm sure he'll do you the honors."

Charlie rose too, suddenly daunted at the thought of being alone with Peter. "Come on. We might as well go on up and see your room."

They passed through the house and mounted the stairs together. In the first-floor hall, C.B. hugged Charlie's arm. "We'll have a long talk about everything later," she said to him and hugged his arm again and was gone.

"Come on. It's up here," Charlie said. He gave Peter a brisk tap on the back and started up the next flight. His heart was beating rapidly. He didn't dare look at the boy at his side. Only his duties

14

as a host made it possible for him to speak naturally and maintain a surface equilibrium. "That's my room," he said, standing in the upper hall. "Your room's here and that's your bathroom down there. There's nobody else up here so you'll have it all to yourself." His voice seemed to echo in the big, dark, suddenly silent house. He felt not just that they were alone, but that they were totally isolated from the world, existing only in each other. He pushed open the door he had indicated as Peter's and stood aside to let him pass.

Here again, on the threshold of the bedroom, he hoped that the boy might reveal himself in some way, but he let the opportunity pass and simply entered. Charlie followed and put his hand on his shoulder once more as they inspected the room. Then, shifting his hand to the base of Peter's neck, he retreated into comedy as he conducted an elaborate tour of the modest quarters, discoursing on the electric fan, the window, the bedside table, and the books upon it. Peter laughed easily, but although he was held now in what was very nearly an embrace, he remained quite contained within himself. Charlie was suddenly oppressed by the difficulties inherent in the simple situation. All he wanted was to know. If it wasn't going to work out, he would forget about it; but it would be too stupid to discover weeks from now that Peter had wanted it too, had been waiting only for an unequivocal move. At the same time, he couldn't imagine risking a rebuff. He had had no experience in seduction. There had been at least an easily detected complicity on those occasions when the advances hadn't been made by others. He had never considered himself a fairy or a pansy or any of the other words bandied about contemptuously by his contemporaries and himself. His sexual activities with other boys were a natural extension of the play he had been introduced to at school. He had always assumed that in due course there would be a girl and marriage and the usual developments of adult life; it simply hadn't happened yet. By sixteen, his had been widely proclaimed the second biggest cock in the school and he had not been challenged thereafter. He felt quite sure that now he would have qualified for first place, although at the time he had refused to measure himself against the winner, whom he had found inexcusably ugly. His spectacular equipment had given him a certain sexual arrogance; he expected people to want to go to bed with him and to find it a not ordinary experience. He could more readily attribute Peter's careful neutrality to shyness rather than disinclination. A hand brushing by accident against the crotch would tell him all he wanted to know. Perhaps if they fumbled together with the suitcase he would have his chance.

"Here," he said, relinquishing the boy's neck. "Let me help you with this thing."

"Oh, lord." Peter swung the bag up and dropped it on the rack provided for the purpose. "I don't need help with that."

Check. There was nothing more he could accomplish here. Retreat was indicated to plan more definitive tactics. "Look, why don't you unpack and then come on next door when you're ready? Wear anything you like. Shorts would be fine. We may want to go to the club later." In order not to break the tenuous contact established between them, he gave his arm a little squeeze and smiled into his eyes. "Don't be long."

"No, it'll only take a minute."

Charlie went to his room and stripped off his clothes and hurried to the bathroom. He smelled of the tension he had been through. He showered thoroughly while he considered abandoning his project. Yet the eyes had been telling him something — if not offering an invitation, at least hinting at assent. Peter couldn't have looked at him as he had if he weren't susceptible, even though he might not yet be aware of it himself. C.B. had chosen him with unerring taste; it was too perfect not to work out. He longed for a friend, here under the same roof with him for the weeks to come. Affection expressed physically made friendship so complete and binding. The thought of it suffused him with a piercing sweetness. Only the achieving of it promised to be a ridiculous bore.

He must find some way of getting him out of his clothes. Perhaps he could manage something at bedtime tonight. He looked down at himself, stirring now with his thought, and smiled. Wait till Peter had a look at that.

He finished his shower and powdered himself and splashed himself liberally with cologne. He was combing his hair, a shade less blond than Peter's, when he heard tentative knockings at the door and his name spoken.

"Come in. I'll be right out," he called. He gave himself several long-practiced caresses and then twisted the towel around his waist and went out. Peter was already seated, but he sprang up and hitched up his pants with awkward charm and stood with his head back, slightly defensive, as if prepared for flight. He was wearing a white shirt and shorts that suited him much better than his traveling clothes.

16

In the filtered light of the big room he looked golden — golden hair, golden skin. Charlie's breath caught at his beauty. The way his shorts were bunched at the crotch suggested that under them he was wearing some sort of jockey shorts that held him strictly confined. Charlie started toward him. He was aware that the heavy swing of his sex, partially aroused, must be visible beneath his towel and he waited for Peter's eyes to be drawn to it, but they remained unwaveringly on his eyes. He stopped just out of reach of the boy, feeling the wide gulf between them that remained to be bridged somehow.

"I was hot. I took a shower. So how do you think you're going to like it here?"

"Very much. It's a wonderful place. C.B. is fabulous."

"She is. She's wonderful." He gazed into the eyes that were level with his and only a few feet away, eyes softened by long lashes so that they seemed to melt into his, yet remained tantalizingly, maddeningly unflirtatious. It wasn't safe to go on gazing; things were happening under his towel. He found his voice. "By the way, how old are you? C.B. doesn't seem to know."

"Nineteen. Practically twenty, really. My birthday's in August. I lost a lot of time at school when I was a kid. We were always moving around."

"Well, hell, that explains it. I knew you couldn't be all that much younger than me. Just a little over a year's difference. Has C.B. been going on at you about how much alike we are?"

Peter smiled. "She has mentioned it."

"I hope you don't mind."

"Mind? Why?"

"I mean, being told you look like me."

"Gosh no. You're terrific-looking."

Charlie's throat tightened. If his damn towel would drop off, if the two or three scraps of cloth covering Peter would vanish, they would know each other and there would be no more problems. He attempted laughter. "Well, thanks. The same to you. A mutual admiration society. Hey, I know what." He turned and strode to his desk, finding relief in activity. This was going to be a fairly obvious play, but better that than to go on wondering. He could imagine it rapidly becoming an obsession. He wasn't used to being at such a disadvantage with anybody; if he could satisfy himself that there was no chance of anything happening between them, he could dismiss Peter as just a pleasant enough guy to have around.

17

He fumbled in the drawers and found a tape measure and turned back with a smile. "Before I get dressed, let's see how much alike we really are. Come on. I think I'm a little taller than you. Of course, not when you have those things on." His eyes traveled down the long, smoothly fleshed legs to the big feet strongly molded by sandals.

"I can take them off," Peter said simply with a smile and a shrug, going along with the game. He stooped and unfastened the buckles and kicked them off. Charlie's heart accelerated as he watched this small prelude to stripping. He went to Peter and took his arm and moved him to the door and backed him against the jamb. Now that he had an excuse for touching him, he was less fearful of betraying himself. He inhaled the smell of him, fresh and scrubbed and faintly animal. He lifted his hands and straightened Peter's head, carefully avoiding his eyes but letting his fingers linger in the silk of his hair. He flattened the shoulders and felt the firm muscles of Peter's chest under his shirt. He dropped his hands to his hips and adjusted them. Here, he was within inches of his goal, but he could take his time now. Touching Peter in this way dissipated somewhat the potent mystery of his body, and Charlie's nerves eased.

He placed the end of the tape on the mark and gave Peter a little pat. "OK, I've got it."

Peter moved out, and together they measured the distance to the floor. "Right." Charlie gave the tape to Peter and took his place, still avoiding his eyes. Standing flat against the door brought his sex thrusting forward beneath the towel, but Peter took no visible notice of it, nor did his hands explore as Charlie's had. He simply placed the tape and nodded. They measured the jamb once more.

"I thought so," Charlie said. "But the difference is damn little. Barely a quarter of an inch. OK. Take off your shirt."

"My shirt? What for?"

"So we can do our chest measurements."

"Oh, sure. OK." Peter remained noncommittal and placidly cooperative. He unbuttoned his shirt and pulled it off. Charlie stood before him with the tape, inhaling once more the smell of soap and fresh linen, his vision filled with the boy's nakedness. He was superb — wide-shouldered, slim-waisted, smoothly muscled, hair-less.

"You've got quite a build," Charlie said, openly admiring him. This was permitted.

"If it's anywhere near as good as yours, I'm satisfied."

"The mutual admiration society. Well, come on. Let's get on with it." He was still able to be brisk and matter-of-fact, but it required all his control to refrain from taking the golden body in his arms as he moved in close to make the measurement. Peter stood before him looking touchingly attentive and willing. Willing for what? Charlie still wondered if he had an inkling of where this was leading. Willing only to have his chest measured? Peter raised his arms away from his sides. Charlie slipped the tape around him, and as he lifted it into place he ran the backs of his hands over his nipples and felt them contract and harden. Something was going on behind that untroubled exterior. He marked the tape with his thumb and showed it to Peter. "OK, my turn." He handed over the tape and lifted his arms, all his nerves alert to the contact of Peter's hands. If desire was stirring in him too, surely some hint of it would now insinuate itself into his fingers. Peter's hands moved nimbly, scarcely touching him until they joined the tape on his chest.

"Practically the same. Maybe a hair more," he reported. He laughed briefly. "That is, if you had any hairs."

"Fine. Now, you'll have to undo your top button." Peter did so, revealing the secret little coil of navel in the flat stomach. Charlie eased the top of the shorts down as he circled his waist with the tape. So close now. He had never wanted anybody so much in his life, nor gone to such lengths to conceal it. "Twenty-nine. That's about what I should be. I'm beginning to think we're the same person." He allowed his hand to press against Peter's as he returned the tape. His mind was whirling, but he could see no reason to postpone the next move. There could be nothing suspect about getting rid of the towel that was bunched around his waist. On the contrary, it would seem foolishly modest to go on hiding behind it. The moment had come. If Peter could get through this without any loss of composure, he would give him up as hopeless. He gave the towel a tug and dropped it from him and stood boldly, confidently naked. His sex was extended to its fullest limits before actual erection, prodigious but blameless. He had walked through locker rooms this way and had felt all eyes on him. He thrust his hips forward and lifted his arms slowly and sought his eyes, coming as close to an outright offer of himself as he dared. Peter's eyes met his with a curiously stricken look — pleading for a further clarifying move? Appalled at Charlie's advances? And then Charlie saw the

19

long lashes flutter against his cheeks as Peter lowered his lids. He saw the color rush to his face. Peter lifted his hands hesitantly, perhaps reluctantly, and there was a tremor in them as he fumbled with the tape. He had trouble getting it around Charlie's waist; he seemed unable to complete the circle against his abdomen.

Charlie laughed with growing certainty and anticipation. "Hey. Come on. It's twenty-nine, isn't it?" Peter nodded dumbly, without lifting his eyes. "Wait a minute," Charlie exclaimed. "We've forgotten something. We ought to see if we can wear each other's hats." He was backtracking deliberately, giving himself a moment's respite before making the irrevocable move. He retrieved the tape and took a step closer, directing his body so that his sex brushed against Peter's hand. The hand shot away as if it had been scalded, but he saw Peter's mouth and throat working as if he were having trouble swallowing and a pulse in the base of his neck began throbbing visibly. As he placed the tape around the golden head, it was without design that his sex kept nudging Peter's thigh. He wasn't going to be able to play this game much longer.

"Plenty of room for brains in there," he said rather breathlessly.

Peter took the tape and moved back slightly and to one side. His eyes seemed no longer to focus properly. His face was drawn, his breath rapid. As he lifted his arms Charlie saw sparse golden curls in his armpits. A single pearl of sweat was rolling down his ribs. His fingers trembled against Charlie's brow as he announced the result.

"Good," Charlie said, struggling to maintain the hearty tone he had used throughout. He moved around behind Peter. He didn't want to be caught with an erection until Peter had definitely committed himself, and he knew he couldn't hold himself down much longer. "You're going to have to pull those shorts lower," he ordered. "It'd be simpler if you'd just take them off."

"Well, I—" Peter mumbled.

"It doesn't matter. Just so I can get the hip measurement." Nobody could say that he had insisted; he had stuck to the rules he had laid down at the beginning.

Peter unfastened something, and the rich curve of his buttocks slid into view. Charlie's sex instantly swelled and rose heavily before him. He had to step back to give it room.

"Talk about slim hips," he said to steady himself. "I'm afraid you have me there." He felt terribly exposed, fearful that Peter might turn and see him. He checked the position of the towel on the floor. He could always grab it and run for the bathroom if it turned out that he had misjudged his companion after all. He took a deep breath and made an effort to steady the trembling of his hands. Peter was gripping his lowered shorts. Charlie slipped the tape against his hips and led it around along his lower abdomen until his hand encountered crisp coils of hair. He paused, pretended to straighten the tape, fumbled skillfully, retrieved it with a quick flip of his lowered hand. It encountered a hard knot of sex contained in the shorts. He expelled a long sigh of relief as the knowledge of victory burst over him, and felt no longer exposed but proudly prepared. His sex surged up in complete, straining erection. He completed the measurement quickly, but instead of following the routine they had established, he said, "While I'm at it, I might as well see about this." He slipped a hand within the shorts and grasped hot, hard flesh. He pushed at the elastic, freeing Peter's sex, and it sprang up and burst its bonds. Peter uttered a gasp that was almost a cry, but he didn't move.

"I can't help it," he muttered thickly. "Your touching me and—"

Before the staggering fact of Peter at last revealed, Charlie thought for an instant that he had been surpassed. A quick glance for comparison reassured him. It was more slender than his and an inch or two shorter, just the way Charlie would have wished it, big without threatening his supremacy. He laughed exultantly.

"Don't worry about helping anything," he said with laughter in his voice. He moved around so that they were facing each other again. "Look at me. Anyway, we have to be like this if we're going to measure everything properly. That's part of the whole thing. Look. We're tremendous."

Peter kept his eyes averted, his mouth working. "What's the point of measuring? I'm not as big as you are," he managed finally.

"That's nothing. I've never met anybody who was. You damn nearly are. There's probably less difference than you think." To ease Peter's evident distress, to relieve him of self-consciousness at the start, he maintained the pretense of cheerful, scientific detachment. He crouched down, and Peter's sex leaped and quivered before him, the head as taut and smooth as ripe fruit. He ran his tongue over his lips and opened his mouth, but checked himself. He would wait another moment before any direct love play. Everything that had happened up to now could be written off as a physiological accident, without erotic significance. Peter still hadn't made any

21

overt move. He pulled down the shorts and scanty underwear and lifted each big foot in turn to disentangle them. He applied the tape to the leaping sex, allowing his hands to become cautiously caressing and making no attempt at accuracy. It became as rigidly immobile as steel under his touch, and he saw the boy's knees begin to tremble. He straightened and handed over the tape, his thumb on the mark, giving him an extra inch. He took Peter's arm and guided him around and backed him up, their sexes playing against each other as they moved, and forced him gently down on the edge of the bed. "There," he said, "you can get at me better that way.

As Peter sat uneasily on the edge of the bed and leaned forward with the tape, Charlie swung his hips slightly so that his sex struck Peter's cheek and brushed down across his lips. Peter's eyes closed, his mouth dropped open. He looked as if he were going to faint. Then he flung himself back on the bed with a great cry as he was gripped by the paroxysms of orgasm. His hips thrashed, his sex leaped up with a wild life of its own, his arms beat the bed, his whole body was shaken by the spasms of an enormous ejaculation. Charlie stood over him, amazed, close to orgasm himself. At last, with a groan and shudder that ran through his whole body, Peter lay still.

"That's marvelous," Charlie said wonderingly. "It's really sweet. I hardly even touched you."

"I couldn't help it," Peter murmured in a stricken voice. His eyes were closed, he lay inert and spent. "I don't know what's the matter with me."

"I can't see anything the matter with you," Charlie said with happy laughter. "I almost came myself." Peter's legs were trembling. Charlie briefly hugged the feet against his chest before he lifted them and swung them onto the bed. The small act of possession brought him close to orgasm once more. He picked up the towel from the floor and stretched out beside Peter. He wiped Peter's cheeks where he had splashed himself, his neck, his shoulders, his chest. The head of his sex was lying in a little pool formed by his navel. It had shrunk slightly, but as he wiped it, it sprang up again into full erection. Charlie chuckled at the lively response. All that trouble and the crazy kid had been dying for it the whole time. Shy. Probably not much experience. He wondered if his tastes were fixed. He let his eyes roam appreciatively over his conquest. He looked rather slight in his clothes, but there was so much of him, all of it beautiful. Charlie had

22

known him less than three hours, and he already felt a potential intimacy between them that seemed to fill all the corners of his life. He glanced at the closed eyes and then ran his hand down over his chest and made a ring of thumb and two fingers and encircled the rigid sex. He ran his hand down to its base and encountered the crisp curls that had been his introduction to the secret area. He gathered the balls into the palm of his hand and watched the skin pucker and tighten. Peter's whole body was alive to his touch. His own sex was aching with the prolonged tease he had subjected it to. He hoped Peter wasn't the sort that just wanted his own off and was indifferent to his partner.

He tossed the towel away and slipped his hands under Peter's shoulders and helped him pull himself up completely onto the bed. As he did so, he put his mouth on a nipple and nuzzled it with his lips and tongue. Peter cried out ecstatically and his body jerked in his arms. Charlie lifted his head and looked at him with a flash of comprehension.

"Haven't you ever done anything like this before?" he asked. Peter rolled his head on the pillow in negation, his eyes still closed. "My God, I can't believe it. With your looks, I should've thought everybody would be falling all over themselves after you."

"I was afraid to. I don't know. I wouldn't. I thought it was wrong."

"There's nothing wrong. It's great."

Peter opened his eyes. Tears were in them, and a reluctant, ambiguous plea. "Have you done it before?" he asked.

"Well, sure. Hundreds of times."

"How did you know I was — Did you know it was going to happen with us?"

"I didn't *know*. I thought it might. I hoped it would."

"I guess I did too, from the minute I saw you, but I tried not to think about it. You're going to have to show me. I don't know how to act. You're going to have to teach me everything."

"That won't be any great hardship," Charlie said with a chuckle. "Just do anything you feel like." He lowered his head and put his mouth on Peter's. He met with closed lips, but he ran his tongue along them, inviting entrance. Peter's mouth opened slightly, their tongues met, and then their mouths were devouring each other and they were seized by a storm of lust — legs thrashing, arms gripping, their bellies and chests writhing against each other, their sexes, hard

23

columns of flesh, lifted in an insurmountable barrier between them. Charlie ran his hand down Peter's back, encompassing the full smooth curve of buttocks. He slipped his hand between them. Peter's hips were agitated by brief thrusting spasms, and the muscles of his buttocks quivered in welcome of the invasion. He wrenched his mouth from Charlie's and threw his head back, his chest heaving, his breath coming in gasps, his mouth open, uttering moans of ecstasy.

"That feels good?" Charlie asked against his ear.

"Oh, yes," he gasped. "Everything you do feels wonderful. I don't know what's happening to me."

"Just a minute." Charlie gave his nose a little kiss and sprang up and went to the door and locked it and turned back to the bathroom. He emerged with a tube of lubricating jelly. Peter watched his approach, his eyes wide and transfixed on his swaying sex. Charlie dropped onto the bed and squeezed jelly onto his hand and applied it between Peter's buttocks, a finger exploring tentatively. Peter's hips lurched forward and his muscles danced as Charlie urged his finger deeper.

"What are you doing?" Peter asked, his eyes staring with blind acceptance.

"I'm going to do it with you like this. You told me to teach you everything."

"Can you? I mean, it doesn't look possible. You're so big. Will I be able to?"

"Of course," Charlie assured him with a smile. "It's supposed to be better, the bigger it is. It might hurt a bit at first. I'll stop if you don't like it."

"No. I want everything. I don't care if it hurts."

"OK." He urged him over onto his stomach with a loving pat and lifted himself and straddled Peter's thighs. The golden head, the delicate profile partially crushed against the pillow, the wide slightly bony shoulders, unmistakably male yet touchingly vulnerable, the smooth, slim flanks, the buttocks yielding richly before him stirred him so intensely that he felt close to tears. He had never had such beauty given so totally into his possession. He anointed his sex liberally, as always slightly in awe of it and anxious.

"Now just relax," he warned gently. "It shouldn't hurt if you relax." His own breath began to labor as, guiding it with one hand, he slid his sex between the buttocks, and his body was in turn

24

wracked with a great shudder as he felt the head make its first penetration. He paused to recover himself and then began to force a long, slow entrance. Peter's hips lifted to him, trembling, his muscles working hungrily to hasten the union. He uttered a groan of pain and pleasure as he pressed backward and lifted himself on his hands. Charlie's hands were on Peter's buttocks trying to control his straining efforts. "Take it easy, baby," he soothed him. "It'll hurt if you go too fast."

"It hurts," Peter cried. "It feels as if you're tearing me apart. I don't care. Go on. Do it." Peter lifted himself upright on his knees, and Charlie dropped back on his heels. Peter was whimpering and uttering brief, strangled sobs, but he bore down hard, his hips rotating as he sought to impale himself completely. Charlie withdrew slightly and then bore implacably into him. The sobs became uncontrolled, but something seemed to give way and they both cried out as Charlie felt his full length plunge into him, bringing Peter down onto his lap. The sobs were transformed into choking laughter, and Peter uttered another cry as his head fell back onto Charlie's shoulder and he abandoned himself to the leaping flood of another orgasm. Charlie's sex was gripped by the spasm, and he felt a thrill of astonished pride that he could provoke such an instant and conclusive response. He saw Peter reach for the towel and then saw little more as he felt his whole being flow into his sex. He raised Peter so that only the head remained at the lip of the entrance, and then pulled him close so that his sex surged through Peter in one huge thrust.

"Oh yes," Peter moaned. "It's unbelievable. I can. I can do it." He took the initiative, repeating the movement, his hips working with abandon as he explored the pleasures of this unknown exercise.

When Charlie felt himself being brought to the limits of his control, he lunged forward and flung Peter down so that his head was resting on his folded arms and then took final, overwhelming possession of him. He adopted his own rhythm, submerging Peter in his will and desire, driving always deeper into him. The force of the onslaught met with no resistance, and Peter's cries came in unison with his own as frenzy seized them and they rushed headlong together toward an unimaginable climax. At last, Charlie uttered a great shout, Peter echoed him, there was a split second of unbearably exquisite promise, and then all of him dissolved in bursting release as he toppled over and lay heaving on the boy in a tangle of arms and legs. They remained still, in a mindless stupor of fulfillment, as they slowly recovered their breath.

"Did you come again?" Charlie asked finally, his lips moving against Peter's cheek. After his triumphant possession of the boy, speech felt flat and inappropriate.

"Yes, with you. The other times were nothing."

"Good. I wanted you to. I thought you had."

"God, yes. Are we — I mean, is this something we're supposed to just forget about?"

Charlie's mouth shaped a kiss against Peter's cheek. "Forget about? We're going to spend practically the whole summer together, remember?"

"Are there lots of other people around you do it with?"

Charlie laughed briefly. "You've got the damnedest ideas. Of course not."

"*Have* you done it with lots of other guys?"

"Oh, well, it depends on what you mean by lots. It was never like this."

"And girls?"

"A couple. Forget it. I tell you, it's never been anything like this."

"You mean you'll only do it with me now?"

"Nobody else. Promise." Charlie laughed once more, this time softly, with unfamiliar tenderness. It was an easy promise to make since there was nobody else around who tempted him.

"That's wonderful. Is it true what you said, that you've never met anybody bigger than you?"

"Yes, but that's just the way it's happened. I'm sure there're plenty of guys who are bigger."

"I bet not. I got the champion right at the start." He laughed with a sunny gaiety that delighted Charlie. His heart lifted with happiness. The initiation had been inevitable and carried no guilt with it; Peter had obviously just been waiting for the right person to come along. He had never encountered a less inhibited partner, and this was just a debut. He felt at peace with himself. He gave Peter's cheek another kiss. "Come on. We better get cleaned up." He made a move to withdraw, but Peter gripped him.

"No. Don't go. I want you there always. I can't believe it. Charlie Mills, the guy I've been thinking about for months, here, like this. I'll never let you leave."

"That'll present certain problems."

"Will we be able to sleep together at night?" Peter asked, with a return of the shy anxiety that had edged his voice before.

Charlie's voice caught as tenderness swelled up in him. "Of course. Do you think I'd let you sleep in there alone? We're going to be together now, baby."

"I think I'm losing my mind, I'm so happy." Peter relaxed his grip with a deep sigh. Charlie withdrew slowly and then pushed himself up and sprang away from the bed. He caught a glimpse of blood and other matter on himself. This was always a moment he had never reconciled himself to, but he had trained himself to limit his revulsion by moving quickly, by washing blindly until most of the traces were gone and he could give himself his full attention.

He went through his routine and returned to find Peter seated on the edge of the bed with the towel across his lap. His eyes widened at Charlie's nakedness, and he clutched at the towel.

"I've made an awful mess of the bed," he said.

"I'll take care of it. You go take a shower."

Peter went, holding the towel close around him. Charlie pulled off the bedspread and rolled it up and threw it into a corner. He went out to a hall closet where towels were stored and brought back a fresh supply. He was dressed when Peter reappeared, still draped in a towel.

"Where are we going?" he asked with averted eyes.

"I thought we'd go for a drive."

He went to the end of the bed where Charlie had laid his clothes and put them on with awkward modesty. He communicated a sudden shyness that was an almost palpable barrier between them. In a moment, he was ready and Charlie went to him and put a reassuring hand on his arm. Some guys turned all moony and romantic; others became speechless with shame. He hoped Peter wouldn't do either.

"Come on," he said.

Peter turned to him, his head back, his eyes full of anguish. The hair was damp on his brow, he smelled of soap again, his lips worked in an effort to speak.

"It's all right, isn't it? I mean, you're not sorry?" he said.

Charlie's heart dissolved. "Sorry! Good lord. It's wonderful, baby."

"Yes, call me that. That makes everything right." Their mouths met and opened to each other, their bodies locked, Peter uttered a whimper of longing assuaged. Charlie pulled himself back with an effort and gave Peter's cheek a little slap.

"Come on. I'm supposed to be showing you the town." He was deeply stirred by the boy in a way he instinctively resisted. He felt threatened by unknown depths. Of course, he reasoned with himself, Peter was probably just carried away because of its being the first time. He had doubtless been the same once himself. He couldn't remember. He would set an example, calm him down. It was, after all, just harmless fun.

As they left the room, Peter took his arm. At the head of the stairs, he dropped behind and put his hands on Charlie's shoulders as they started down.

Charlie shrugged them off. "Cut it out," he said. "Somebody might see us."

"Oh, yes. I forgot. I feel as if we're the only people in the world."

They went down through the silent house and out onto the shaded drive where Charlie's little convertible was parked.

"Hey, is this yours?" Peter asked as they got in.

"Yes. Well, actually it's C.B.'s. She keeps it here for me." Charlie started the car and set it in motion. Being out of doors, going through the familiar maneuvers of driving, Charlie was restored to his accustomed sense of normalcy. The fact that they had held each other in their arms, kissed, known passionately each other's bodies gave them as a pair a special mysterious awareness of each other, but it had no extension into everyday life. They were just good friends, going for a drive on a hot summer afternoon.

"Do you think C.B. will know what's happened?" Peter asked.

"With us? Heavens no. She could never even dream of it."

"I'm not so sure. She's said a lot of things that didn't mean anything to me at the time. Almost as if she'd been planning it."

"I know what you mean, but you don't understand. It's hard to explain. She has a sort of romantic — well, ideal. It's all involved with young men, watching them develop and all that. She has no use for females. I don't think she ever thinks about sex."

"That may be. But there's something else. I felt all along as if she was preparing me for something. She has a way of putting ideas in your head and then watching to see how they work out."

"She has that, all right. They usually work out the way she wants them to. She's fascinated by you. She's decided to make you one of her projects. I'm supposed to sort of draw you out and broaden your experience." They glanced at each other and burst into roars of laughter, sharing youth's joke on its inexplicable elders.

"You've certainly made a good start," Peter said.

"I'm not so sure you're not going to broaden mine."

"Oh, you've obviously done everything. I might as well tell you — I've always longed for something like this to happen, without quite admitting it to myself. Does that mean I'm a fairy or something? Not that I really care so long as it's with you."

"You're no more a fairy than I am," Charlie said sharply. "It's something that happens to everybody."

"Well, you know more about it than I do. But I don't think that's really the way I feel. Anyway, I don't care. I feel so damn happy. You have a job waiting in New York, don't you?"

"Yes. Publishing. In the fall. I was supposed to be there now, but C.B. arranged everything." He drove through a tunnel of trees past big, old-fashioned properties like C.B.'s. He turned into a street with shops. "This is the town, what there is of it. We might as well go look at the ocean. Then I'll take you to the club and introduce you to the gang."

"Are you going to live with C.B.?"

"No, she's found me a little apartment. She doesn't think men should live with their families. It's one of her ideas."

"It sounds great. I wish I knew what I was going to do."

"You're going to West Point, aren't you?"

"Oh, that's the idea. But I'm not. I'd rather shoot myself. C.B. wants me to go to Princeton. Did you like it?"

"It was all right. But I've never much cared for school. I always wanted to get it over with and get out and do things."

"Me too. Except I don't know what I want to do."

"I do. I know just what I want to do, but for God's sake don't tell C.B.; I'm going to be an actor. The job is just an excuse to go to New York. Broadway people have seen me at Princeton. They think I'm good."

"An actor! That's amazing. I suppose that means you'll be a big movie star. I wouldn't like that."

"Why not?"

"Everybody after you. Too much competition." Peter put his hand in Charlie's lap and grasped his sex. It responded immediately. Charlie shifted in his seat to ease his trousers.

"Don't worry," he said. "I'm not interested in movies. That would kill C.B. I want to work in the theater. I don't think she'll really mind if I'm a success."

"Why should she?"

"Oh, she has ideas about what's proper. I once wanted to be a painter, but she talked me out of it. She was probably right." His sex continued to grow under Peter's hand.

"Well, you obviously have talent. I haven't. It makes a big difference."

"You could have. You just might not have discovered it yet."

"I doubt it." He interrupted himself with laughter. "But I guess today proves there's a lot I haven't discovered yet." He unfastened buttons and grasped Charlie's sex and eased it out. It sprang up, and the head hovered near the wheel. "Golly, it's even bigger than I remembered. I thought I must've imagined it."

"Do you want me to kill us both?" Charlie protested. Being naked and erect out of doors in broad daylight brought him immediately to the verge of orgasm.

"You just keep driving. You said I could do anything I felt like." He leaned over, obliging Charlie to remove one hand from the wheel, and ran his tongue along the length of the sex and took the head in his mouth. Charlie's loins were rocked by the shock of it. He knew he should stop him, but the daring of it thrilled him. His size had always inhibited oral play, exposing him to teeth, but now he felt only the moist, smooth warmth of Peter's lips and tongue. Peter's head moved against his chest, surely visible to the whole world, as his mouth demonstrated its extraordinary capacity. Charlie felt his eyes closing, his hand slipping from the wheel. His free hand gripped the back of Peter's shorts and he made a furious effort to concentrate on the road as the power built up in him, making his jaws clamp shut and his legs stiffen. His hips were convulsed, every muscle seemed to lock as he exploded into the avid mouth. They both uttered stifled cries. The car swerved, but he recovered control. Peter's shoulders contracted, he retched once, but he held the sex in his mouth until Charlie's final spasms had subsided. Then he rested his head in his lap.

"Was it all right to swallow it?" he asked, his lips brushing against the dwindling sex.

"Yes, sure."

"I thought it might make me sick." He kissed the sex with lips and tongue and gentle teeth and lifted it back into the trousers and buttoned it in. He gave it a squeeze and sat up.

"Actually, it's supposed to be good for you," Charlie assured him.

"You taste wonderful. It *is* something people do, isn't it? I mean, with the mouth? I've heard of it."

"Of course. Only nobody's ever really managed to do it with me before."

Peter's face lighted up as he turned to him. "Honestly? That's marvelous. Did I broaden your experience?"

They laughed. "Jesus. You're really something."

"I can't go to the club now," Peter said.

"Why?"

"I came again, naturally."

"You're incredible. How many times does that make?"

"I don't know. I come automatically when you do."

"And a few times when I haven't."

"That was just the beginning. It won't happen anymore. What do you call it?"

"What?"

"This." He gave Charlie another squeeze.

"Oh. Cock, I guess. I don't like most of the other words."

"I want to see your cock when it isn't hard."

Charlie felt it stirring again. "I don't see how you ever will if we go on like this," he said dismissively. This was somehow going too far; he felt once more that he was being drawn in too deep. He wanted suddenly to get away from Peter for a while. He had to be with other people, see himself reflected in the familiar faces of the boys and girls who offered and demanded no more than simple companionship.

The road he had taken came to an end among sand dunes and he turned the car without stopping. "That's the Atlantic Ocean. We can look at it some other time. I have to go to the club. I left my racket there yesterday. You can wait in the car. I won't be long." He accelerated recklessly.

"You don't have to hurry for me," Peter said. He removed his hand from Charlie's lap. "It'll dry."

They said no more as the landscape flashed past. The club was all trees and lawns and tennis courts. Charlie parked the car and slid out from under the wheel. "I'll be right back," he muttered and was gone, walking fast. He was free. He breathed deeply. His sex finally subsided to its usual dimensions. He hitched up his trousers and felt complete in himself and self-sufficient. He went first to the locker where he kept his tennis racket and took it out. Then, no longer hurrying, he went on up to the big porch that served as a social center. He found Anne and Harry and Belinda having lemonade. They were all members of his crowd, and he was greeted enthusiastically and urged to have a drink. He ordered a lemonade from a passing waiter and sat with them. They resumed their chatter, he was included in it, he joined in dutifully. Before his lemonade had arrived, he had had enough. The day, which had been touched with wonder and joy, had become intolerably ordinary. Their jokes seemed flat and childish; when he looked at Harry nothing happened in his eyes, Anne's schoolgirl flirtatiousness was a silly bore, and Belinda's attempts at weary sophistication were simply ludicrous. When the lemonade was served he took a few long gulps of it and put some money on the table.

"I've got to go. C.B. has a sort of cousin staying with us."

"Family. How too utterly sick-making."

"It's not that kind of family. Actually, he's about our age. You'll be meeting him. He's a good guy."

"Good-looking?"

"Of course. C.B. says he looks like me."

They all made suitable noises of mockery and pain as he left them. He felt guilty at having left Peter so long and was eager for a fresh glimpse of him. When it came, he was stunned by its impact. All the muscles of his face lifted, something happened in his chest, and he began humming a tune. Peter looked terribly alone and there was strained anxiety in the way he sat. Charlie felt the tender protectiveness welling up in him and spreading into his arms so that he wanted to hold him. When Peter saw him approach, his face was transfused with delight, dazzling and undisguised. Charlie handed him the racket as he slid in beside him.

"Well, that was quite an experience," Peter said. "I didn't know it was possible to want to be with somebody so much."

"Did you miss me, baby?" He put his hand on Peter's knee. Peter brought his legs together and gripped it.

"God, it kills me when you call me that. I'll say I did. It's frightening."

"I got stuck with some stupid kids."

32

"Are we going home now?"

"Yes." Charlie already had the car in motion.

"Thank goodness," Peter said fervently.

Charlie parked the car in front of the house, and they got out. Peter's shorts were stiff and wrinkled. Charlie handed him the racket.

"Carry that in case we run into anybody." They entered the house and climbed in silence to the top. As soon as they reached the safety of Charlie's room, their arms encircled each other and they exchanged a long, breathless kiss. Charlie was the first to draw back. "Come on, now. Into the shower with you," he ordered.

"Can I use your bathroom?"

"Sure."

"Will you take a shower with me?"

Charlie looked at him and smiled. "If that's what you want to call it. We'll probably drown." They both undressed, Peter with his back slightly turned. He held his shirt awkwardly before himself when he was done. Charlie stood unconcernedly naked before him. He saw Peter's eyes go to his sex. He looked down at himself and laughed.

"You see? You're not going to get your wish all that easily."

"It's wonderful I do that to you."

"Come on. Let's see what I do to you."

They went into the bathroom and turned on the shower and stood together under it. They were totally absorbed in each other. They soaped each other more than was strictly necessary for hygienic purposes but as their roving hands grew more purposeful, Charlie called a firm halt.

"It's time to get dressed. C.B. expects me every evening at six. Anyway, we've got the whole night ahead of us. I've never been worn down by sex yet, but then I've never been with anyone like you before."

"I've got a lot of lost time to make up for," Peter giggled.

Charlie noted with approval the playfulness, an emulation perhaps of his own carefully imposed casual approach. Peter allowed himself to be dispatched to his own room. Charlie dressed. He was almost finished when Peter returned. Charlie's face fell. He was wearing a seersucker suit that was shapeless and baggy, his saddle shoes were scuffed, his tie was twisted, and his collar was too tight.

"You've got to pay more attention to the way you dress," he scolded. "You don't do yourself justice."

Peter blushed. "I was hurrying. Anyway, my family doesn't give me much money for clothes."

"Well, what's the point in our being twins? Come on. Take all that off, and we'll dress you properly." Peter stripped down to his jockey shorts while Charlie went to his closet. He had an ample wardrobe, largely provided by C.B. He went through it selecting things he thought would suit Peter. "We didn't get as far as our feet, but they look about the same. Try these." He handed over socks, trousers, shoes, shirt, and light silk jacket as Peter put them on. "C.B. doesn't insist on ties for dinner. Try this scarf."

When he was finished, Peter stood self-consciously, an expectant little smile playing around his lips.

"My goodness." Charlie surveyed him with possessive pride. The clothes made him an extension of himself, his creation. He felt an identity with him so close that they might have been wearing each other's skin. "I certainly wouldn't let you out of my sight when you're looking like that."

"Am I all right?"

"You sure are."

They laughed together, their eyes swimming deep into each other, and left the room and went down to C.B., touching hands secretly while the coast was clear. She threw up her hands when they appeared on the veranda.

"Good heavens. What a stunning pair." She rose and took each by the hand so that they were obliged to stand shoulder to shoulder, and looked searchingly from one to the other. She nodded her head with satisfaction. "I was right. You are very alike. I thought I'd been mistaken at lunch. Stunning. Come. Let's have a drink."

She released them and went to a table laid out as a bar. She favored fanciful concoctions. Charlie drank little, and Peter refused anything when asked. "Oh, come, now." She turned to him with a winning smile, a hostess so concerned for her guests' well-being that it would have been unthinkable to resist her. "You must have something. A man looks so comfortable with a drink in his hand."

"All right. I'll take anything you're having."

She turned back to the bar. "Where's my grenadine? It must be in the cupboard in the dining room. Dearest, would you get it for me? Henry's out watering the hydrangeas."

Recognizing that the request was directed at him, Charlie went. As he was crossing the living room, she pattered up behind him and took his arm. "I had to talk to you," she said in conspiratorial tones. "I don't know what you've done to him, but I've never seen such a transformation. Just since lunch. He has so much more poise. And such style. Are those your clothes? What a brilliant idea to dress him. His little things are so sad. He obviously worships you. Don't discourage him. I know how hurt one can be at that age."

"There's nothing to discourage. He's very nice."

"Then you do like him? I'm so glad. You're a dear. Thank you for being kind to him."

"He's not as young as you think," Charlie said, a defensive note creeping into his voice.

"Isn't he? You're both supremely young. It's the best life will offer you. Take advantage of it. It doesn't last forever, unfortunately." She made a rueful grimace and hugged his arm to her generous bosom. "We must outfit him. That college shop in the village has quite good things. We'll develop his clothes sense so that he won't be able to bear the sight of a uniform."

Charlie laughed. "I don't think you're going to have a very tough campaign. He's already told me he hates the idea of West Point."

"You see? You're already exerting an influence. Now that he's met you, he'll want to go where you went. If only we'd taken charge of him sooner."

"You're losing your touch, C.B."

"How could anybody guess that he would blossom in an afternoon? We may work something out yet."

In her preoccupation with Peter, her grip on his arm was growing uncomfortable. He freed himself discreetly and leaned over and kissed her on the forehead. "You'd better get on with your plot. Don't you want me to get your grenadine, or was that just an excuse?"

She looked up at him with a beguiling tilt of her head and laughed. "I couldn't wait to find out if you really liked him."

He laughed with her. "Well, I do, so you don't have to worry about that." She made everything so easy.

They returned to the veranda hand in hand. Peter rose at her entrance. Charlie's eyes dropped to his crotch with pride of possession, and he thought of the night that awaited them.

"Darling Peter, I haven't asked you yet if you don't think he looks like me," C.B. said.

Age and familiarity had obliterated C.B.'s face from Charlie's mind so he was always slightly embarrassed by this inevitable question. How could anybody say? When he thought of what she looked like, an overall impression came to him: impish and vaguely simian, prominent nostrils, a long upper lip, the luxuriance of wiry gray hair that sprang vigorously from her brow. As a child he had always been fascinated by her complicated arrangement of her hair before she had had it cut short. "I might as well warn you there's only one acceptable answer to that question," he said. "Though why anybody should want to look like me is a mystery."

"Fishing," C.B. chided him.

"I'll say," Peter joined in unabashedly. "He knows perfectly well he's the best-looking guy any of us know."

"Ah, there's a young man with discernment. He is, isn't he? Now I suppose I'll have to withdraw my question." She returned to her bar and resumed the preparation of drinks.

"No, I can see a resemblance," he continued with enthusiasm. His eyes sparkled at Charlie behind C.B.'s back. "All my family says you were the most attractive girl ever to come out of Alabama."

"You're a perfect dear. Here, my dearest, give this to Peter." Charlie took glasses from her. Peter's fingers caressed his as he handed him one. He acknowledged it, looking into dancing eyes, even though he knew he shouldn't encourage this sort of public play. C.B. went on, "Conventional good looks are meaningless without magnetism. That's what makes you two so irresistible."

"Charlie certainly is. Everything you said about him is true."

Charlie flushed. He was stunned by Peter's outspokenness, but apparently he and C.B. understood each other. She was beaming when she brought a drink and sat with them. "I knew you'd appreciate him. Did he introduce you to all his friends at the club?"

"No," Charlie interjected, glad for a change of subject. "We got to talking upstairs, and then I drove him all around and there really wasn't much time for the club."

"They have a treat in store for them. You must have some tennis tomorrow. Didn't somebody tell me you were good at it?"

"Pretty good," Peter admitted. "But I'll bet Charlie's a champion. He looks as if he would be."

"He's very good at everything he does."

"The champion." A sudden gust of laughter burst from him. It was contagious, and C.B. joined in. After a breathless moment, Charlie did too.

When Henry announced dinner, they all rose and C.B. moved in between them and took their arms. "I was going to say the Three Musketeers," she said as they proceeded to the dining room. "But I suppose I'd have to be Porthos, and I'd really rather not."

Their talk ranged over a variety of subjects under C.B.'s guidance. They laughed a lot. Afterwards, once more on the veranda, Peter grew increasingly silent and withdrawn. Charlie tried to catch his eye repeatedly, but he avoided the contact. He wondered if he could have said anything to upset him. His longing to be alone with him made an agony of the necessity of sustaining the conversation with C.B. At last, she rose.

"I must drag myself away. I've loved every minute of it. Thank God for the young. They keep the rest of us alive. I suppose I should stir myself and have some people in, but give me time. I'm selfish. I want you both all to myself at the beginning."

Charlie stood immediately, and Peter followed suit. "We might as well all go up," Charlie said. "Peter's had a long day."

Once more, they traversed the lower floor and mounted the stairs together. At the first landing, C.B. kissed them both and walked briskly off down the hall. They continued up the stairs. Peter took the last few steps at a run and, when Charlie reached the top, seized him and covered his face with kisses: eyes, cheeks, forehead, mouth. His arms tightened around Charlie's neck and he held him in a tight embrace.

"It's been so horrible," he breathed into his ear. "Not being able to touch you. Not even being able to look at you the way I want to. I don't see how I'm going to stand it."

"Did you feel it, too?" Charlie gripped his waist. "I thought you were mad at me."

"Oh no, no. God, no. Never." Peter's mouth fluttered over Charlie's face again.

"You were going great guns at the beginning. I wouldn't have known what to do if C.B. had been saying those things to me about you."

"Oh, that was easy. I was just saying the truth."

"Make sure you don't ever say too much of the truth. I guess we'll get used to it."

"There's something else I've got to say." He lowered his head and rested his forehead against Charlie's shoulder. "Now. I must. I'm — I don't know what you're going to think, but I can't help it."

37

His voice had dropped so low that the sound of his mouth forming the words was louder than the words themselves. "I'm — I'm in love with you. I didn't know it could happen with two guys, but it has. There's no doubt about it, no matter what you say. I'm just — completely madly in love with you."

Charlie had been through this with others and it had always intensely embarrassed him, but now he found that the declaration made his heart sing. He circled Peter's waist with his arms and held him closer. "What if I'm in love with you too? There's nothing wrong with that."

Peter lifted his head. The light rising from the stairwell shadowed it with anguished beauty. "Isn't there? Doesn't it prove what I said — that I'm a fairy or a queer or whatever they call it?"

"Stop saying that," Charlie replied savagely, but remembered to keep his voice down. "We're friends, aren't we? It's perfectly natural." He was sure there was a distinction to be made. The Greeks had made it. They recognized the passionate love that occurred between men as opposed to the serious everyday love of man and wife, based on childbearing and so forth. He lifted Peter's chin and cupped it in his hands and said more gently, "Go get ready for bed and stop being silly. I'll be waiting for you."

"What about the clothes?"

"Keep them. C.B. knows I've given them to you. Go on." He gave Peter a little push and turned toward his room. He took off his clothes and hung them up as usual, refusing to give way to the joy that surged in him, that urged him to fling everything at the ceiling. He went to the bathroom and brushed his teeth and anointed himself with cologne. He gathered together towels and the tube of lubricant and was just coming out when he heard light footsteps and Peter appeared in the door. He was wearing striped cotton pajamas from which arms and legs protruded by a foot or more. Charlie threw his head back and laughed. This was the way he wanted it to be — silly and fun and relaxed. "What are you supposed to be dressed up for?" he demanded and laughed some more.

"Well, I—"

"You better take a quick look at me. This is the way you've been wanting to see me, thanks to that sexy costume."

Peter took a step forward and stared. "It's amazing," he said. "Nobody would believe it can get so big. Talk about sexy. It looks so damn powerful, even like that. The champion."

38

"All right now. Take those things off. Not here. We might forget them. I don't want anybody to find them in here."

Peter left obediently and Charlie completed his preparations, placing everything within easy reach. In a moment Peter returned naked, holding his hands in front of himself as a clumsy and inadequate screen. Charlie pulled them away.

"You're beautiful, baby. Can't you understand that? Stop hiding yourself. You like to look at me, don't you?"

"God, yes."

"Well, then, what's wrong with my liking to look at you?"

Peter gave his head a little shake, his eyes wide and wondering. "I just can't believe that any of this is the same for you as it is for me."

Charlie took a step toward him, he slid his arms around him and pulled him close, and their mouths opened to each other. Charlie backed him up and they fell onto the bed on top of each other, grappling with each other, arms and legs intertwined, hands clinging and exploring, moaning and crying out and shouting with laughter in an exultant prelude to union.

After the first tumult of their lovemaking, when Charlie had washed, they lay side by side flat on their backs, their heads touching, their hair tangled together on the pillow. After a while, they talked.

"Do you understand now, baby?" Charlie asked. "It's the same for both of us."

"I guess I'm beginning to believe it. Anyway, I know what I'm going to do. I've thought about it all evening and now I know."

"What do you mean?"

"I'm going to New York with you. I never had any intention of going to West Point, but now it's impossible. I can get a job. It doesn't matter what. I'll cook for you and clean for you and be with you. That's all that matters."

"But what about education and all that?"

"What difference does that make? There'll probably be a war — my father says there's going to be and he ought to know — and then what? At least I'll be with you."

"You mean, you'd live with me and — uh, well, the apartment's pretty small."

"If it's as big as this room, I can't imagine wanting anything more."

"It isn't actually, but that doesn't matter." He felt that he should resist the proposal and was astonished to find so little resistance in himself. He simply couldn't quite grasp it. He wasn't accustomed to thinking in terms of the future; three months seemed a long time away. He didn't even know if they would still want to have sex together. He had had relationships extending over a year or more, but actual contact had been intermittent and interspersed with transient adventures. Peter was suggesting that they should actually live together like — well, they would really be roommates. There was nothing unusual about that. He had always longed to be grown-up and on his own, but now that the fact of it loomed before him, he found it intimidating. To face the world with an eager lover at his side made the prospect much more cheerful and gay. As he turned the idea over in his mind, he sought the hand at his side and pressed it.

"It's the only thing we *can* do," Peter said. "Can you imagine shaking hands and saying good-bye in a month or two? You do want me, don't you? I wouldn't be any trouble to you."

Charlie lifted himself onto an elbow with a chuckle and rolled over slightly so that all his body was pressed against Peter's. "It's a fabulous idea. We could fix up the apartment together. Do you really know how to cook? I think you save money if you eat at home. Hey, it's exciting." He ran his hand over Peter's chest and down to his navel to grasp his sex, which stood erect to the summons. Peter looked up at him with shining eyes.

"Can we tell C.B. tomorrow? I want to tell everybody. It's like getting married."

"Good God, no. We can't tell C.B."

The light went out of Peter's eyes, and they widened with apprehension. "Why, doesn't she like me? Does she suspect something? Did she say anything when she went out with you before dinner?"

"Of course not. She's mad about you. You can see that for yourself. But — well, she has very firm ideas about college, for one thing. She wouldn't approve of your not going on with school. We've got to work out the practical details. Maybe you could take some courses at Columbia or somewhere. That might make it all right with her."

"You care a lot about what she thinks, don't you?"

"Well, sure. She's always been the most important person in my life. Besides, she's going to give me an allowance at first. She says

40

I've got to live like a gentleman and all that. It's something I have to take into consideration."

"What if she *is* against it? Would you still let me come?"

"Of course," Charlie said impatiently, but he was unable to imagine himself in opposition to C.B. "We've just got to figure out the right way to put it to her." To forestall more questions, he fluttered his fingers along Peter's sex and brushed the silken curls at its base. The hair was so fine and delicate that the feel of it sent a shiver down his spine. He gathered the balls into the palm of his hand. Peter's eyes turned dreamy with pleasure.

"When I told you I was in love with you, I was afraid you wouldn't have anything more to do with me," he said. "I had to tell you, before we could decide all this."

"It's all decided, baby," Charlie promised him.

"It's fabulous. We're going to live together. I always knew there was something that would make life make sense."

Later, at Peter's request, they lay with their shoulders hunched up, propped on their elbows, their sexes riding side by side along their bellies to illustrate the difference between them.

"Are you sorry mine isn't bigger?" Peter asked.

"Bigger? If it were, it'd be bigger than mine, and that isn't allowed."

"I should hope not. Hey champ, you've done it with lots of others. Is — is mine—?"

"You can take my word for it, it's a lot bigger than most guys, if that's what you want to know. So don't start running around trying to check up for yourself."

Peter burst into laughter. "Would you be jealous?"

"No," Charlie said with a cold flash of anger. "I just wouldn't ever speak to you again."

Missing the steel in the voice, Peter laughed again. "Imagine me even looking at anybody else when I have you."

Charlie rolled over abruptly and slid down and lowered his head to Peter's sex. It was not his favorite erotic exercise and he knew by experience that he was incapable of equaling Peter's prodigies, but he was driven by a sudden necessity for this additional act of possession and by an instinct to demonstrate the equality of their desires. He ran his tongue around the sex and Peter's whole body leaped at the contact and he let out a shrill cry. Peter's hand was tugging at his hair as he opened his mouth wide and took the head.

Further effort was ended by the violent contortions of an immediate orgasm. The warm liquid filled his mouth and he tasted its sweetness as he drank it in grateful communion. He remained where he was, nursing the sex with his mouth in the convulsed aftermath, amazed at the tenderness swelling within him, at the richness of the reward. When it was over, he pulled himself up reluctantly. Peter lay with a forearm flung over his eyes, his mouth open, his lips tremulous. Charlie kissed the side of his face and murmured with playful reproach into his ear, "I thought you weren't going to come without me anymore."

Peter's mouth worked before he spoke. "I tried to stop you. Oh, God, just thinking about it almost makes me come all over again. When I first knew I wanted you that way, I thought I'd lost my mind. I never dreamed you'd do it to me."

"I tell you, baby. It's the same." He stroked his hair. "Next time, do you want to be the one to do it — the other way? I mean, with us the other way around, you inside me?"

Peter dropped his arm and looked at him with stunned eyes. "No. Oh, no. It wouldn't make any sense. I want you inside me all the time. You having me. You — is it all right to say fuck? You fucking me. That's what it is, isn't it?"

"Sure. That's what it is."

"I want you to fuck me always. Never the other way around. I want to be the best fuck you've ever had so you'll forget all the others."

"Good lord, do you think I've ever had anybody like you before? You're fantastic."

"Am I? The way you make me feel, it's as if my whole body were made for you."

"Do you want me to fuck you now, baby?"

"God, yes."

And again...

"Haven't you really ever been in love before?" Peter asked. They lay on their sides facing each other, arms and legs intertwined. Peter was tracing Charlie's eyebrows with a finger.

"Not the way I feel with you. Oh, I suppose once, long ago. The last year of school. With the captain of the football team, of all people. We didn't discover it until Graduation Day. That is, I didn't discover he felt the same way, and then it was a bit late. We met once after we'd both started college, but it didn't work out."

42

"Met how? Tell me."

"He took a room for us in New York. I remember I had to sell some books to pay for the trip. I went up from Princeton and he came down from New Haven."

"Golly. You actually did that? Why didn't it work out?"

"Oh, I guess we'd both worked it up into such a big thing in our minds that it was bound to be an anticlimax. It just wasn't any good."

"Did you suffer a lot?"

"Suffer? Why? It just happened and that was that."

"I'd kill myself if anything went wrong with us."

"You're crazy. My crazy baby. How do you know you'll even like me a week from now?"

Peter lifted his arms in the air and wriggled his body in closer against Charlie's, making a deep animal growl of lust and longing in his throat. He dropped his hands on Charlie's shoulders, still growling, and kneaded his neck with strong fingers and ran them through his hair. "I know," he said, smiling into Charlie's eyes. "I love everything about you. Your looks, of course, your huge cock, but lots more than that. I love everything you say, I love your voice, I love the way your lip curls here when you smile." He put a finger on the spot. "And that's just the beginning. That's just the first day. Think of all the other things I'll find to love. Golly, when I got out of that train this morning and saw you, I knew something tremendous was happening. Darling, dearest love, dearest, beautiful lover, precious love, my champ." The words poured from him in a gentle croon as if they had been locked away for years, saved up for this occasion.

Charlie had always shrunk from endearments. There was something ridiculous and distasteful about men calling each other "dearest" and "darling," but Peter was somehow, apparently, an exception. The words were undeniably sweet on his lips. Charlie warned himself not to be beguiled into reciprocating. "That's enough of that," he said. "You'll hate me in the morning. I suppose we ought to be thinking about sleep."

"Oh, no. Not yet. There's still so much I have to find out about you."

So the night passed. They went back and forth to the bathroom, sometimes they showered together, somehow eventually they went to sleep without knowing they had done so. When Charlie woke up, the first pale morning light was in the window. His eyes made a slow, drugged inventory. The golden head was nestled in the hollow between his shoulder and chest. A leg was thrown across his, and Peter's sex thrust up hard against Charlie's thigh. A hand was clinging to his own sex. His arm ached, but he was so enchanted by what he saw that he scarcely noticed it. His chest was suddenly bursting with happiness, tears pricked behind his eyes, his throat tightened. A sob that was also laughter burst from him. He ran his finger down the tilt of Peter's nose and across his lips. They stirred in the motions of a kiss. My boy, my lover, my baby, my love, he thought, so befuddled with exhaustion and happiness that he didn't know his mind was singing a litany of treacherous endearments.

THE SUMMER HAD BEGUN. They quickly established a routine, with the club and Charlie's room as its centers of activity. They played tennis, at which they were closely matched. They swam. Invitations to parties accumulated, and there were weekly dances at the club.

Despite Peter's indifference, Charlie insisted that they should take an active part in the social life of their age group. Peter was a welcome addition; they lived in the midst of laughing, playful youth. This communal life stimulated their passion. Aside from the long nights they shared, Peter was always ready with sexual improvisations whenever they found themselves briefly alone. In broad daylight on a deserted beach, at night, on the grounds of the club, in the guest room of a neighboring house where they were attending a supper party, he celebrated his adoration of Charlie's body, finding in these dangerously public acts a sort of public sanction of their love. Charlie was an enthralled and enthusiastic partner, but at the Saturday night dances, he insisted that they should go their independent ways, attaching himself to girls, dancing and flirting to the exclusion of everybody else in a continuing need to assert the normalcy of their situation. Peter quickly came to loathe Saturdays.

In the first few days, C.B. made good her promise to outfit Peter. They all went in the stately Packard to the local shop and bought slacks and summer jackets and shoes and shirts and various accessories.

"Nobody's ever been so wonderful to me," Peter said on the way home. "I'm going to stay with you forever."

C.B. took his hand. "Darling Peter. You can't imagine what pleasure you give me."

"Hey, champ. You hear that?" The nickname was an endearment he could use with impunity in public. He used it constantly. "I'm going to live with C.B. We'll let you come for dinner every now and then."

Shopping had been a hot business, and they raced upstairs to change for a quick swim before lunch. A colorful beach robe was one of Peter's acquisitions, and he flung it over his shoulders. Charlie carried one like it. They encountered C.B. crossing the wide entrance hall on their way out. She stopped and threw up her hands in a characteristic gesture of admiration.

"What a glorious color you're both getting. I can see heads turning as you two walk down the beach. You look more alike every day. I'm soon going to find it difficult to choose between you. You're both such superb specimens. Which of you do you think has the better physique?"

They both began to speak at once and looked at each other and laughed. Peter eyed the swelling pouch of Charlie's trunks, amazed not for the first time that he was allowed out in public. Only the blind could fail to be aware of his majestic dimensions. He was both proud and jealous of the display. He wondered what C.B. thought of it.

"I'm stronger than he is," Charlie asserted.

"Ha. I very much doubt it," Peter countered.

"We'll have to battle it out. We can set up a ring on the lawn and sell tickets."

"And risk spoiling your lovely faces?" C.B. protested. "Not on my lawn." She looked from one nearly naked youth to the other. "You're very powerful-looking, my dearest, but you've never had Peter's grace. He's so exquisitely made, without, of course, the slightest trace of effeminacy. Heaven spare us effeminate men." She turned to Peter and took his hands. "I think I'd have to award the prize to you, my darling."

"The champ bites the dust," Peter exclaimed with glee.

C.B. moved from him to Charlie, prepared to offer him a conciliatory embrace. He saw it coming and gave her cheek a quick peck and moved away. She had always been prodigal of caresses, but for reasons he couldn't quite define, perhaps because of the intense physical life he was sharing with Peter, he had become sensitive to all such contact. He was beginning to find C.B. too insistent. He gave Peter a quick jab. "Come on, dope."

Peter jabbed him back and danced out of reach. "Watch who you're hitting. We haven't sold any tickets yet." Charlie went for him and they rushed from the house, sparring and romping and shouting with laughter.

C.B. stood for a long moment looking after them when they were gone, a thoughtful but not dissatisfied smile on her lips.

THEIR ROUTINE WAS DISRUPTED a few weeks later on one of the Saturdays Peter had come to hate. The announcement was made by C.B. after lunch, when Henry had removed the empty coffee cups from the veranda. (Its repercussions were to echo through their lives, though at the time it seemed only a small domestic crisis.)

"We're to be without a cook for the next few days," she said, looking over her shoulder and putting a finger to her lips. "I've been dying to tell you. It seems we have a great singer in our midst." She twinkled with contained mirth.

"Really? Who's that?" Charlie asked, responding to her high spirits.

"Sapphire, if you please. Mrs. Hall, as I think we must call her from now on. She's to have an audition with the Metropolitan Opera on Monday morning." She uttered a peal of laughter.

"No, seriously," Charlie interjected, laughing with her. "What's she up to?"

"Ah, that remains to be seen. I understand the darkies so well. I pretended to take it all absolutely seriously. 'That's very nice, Sapphire,' I said. 'How long have you been interested in an operatic career?'" She erupted once more with laughter. "'I'se always sung in de church. Mr. Otto Kahn, he say I got a big future. That's what he say.' She was very severe with me. I'd made her sit down. There's nothing that flusters them more than treating them as equals. Mr. Otto Kahn! I suppose she's read his name somewhere in the paper."

"And you're letting her go?"

"Of course. They're like children or very nice animals. It's a scientific fact that their craniums are smaller than ours. One must humor them up to a point. Since she isn't taking Henry with her, I presume she intends to return. I can't wait to hear all about Mr. Otto Kahn's reaction." She and Charlie laughed together some more. "There's the dance tonight. You two had better go early and have dinner at the club. Rosie can manage something for me."

Later, when the boys were alone, Peter returned to the subject. "Darling, why does C.B. think it's so funny for Sapphire to be a singer?" he wondered out loud.

"Oh, I suppose she knows it's all just a fake."

"I don't see why it should be, necessarily. Lots of Negro singers have started out as somebody's cook. I don't think she should laugh at her."

"Naturally, she doesn't laugh at her to her face," Charlie said with a dismissive tone. He didn't like criticism of C.B., and he was accustomed to Peter taking conversational directions from him. "You heard her. She said she treated the whole thing completely seriously."

"Yes, but — well, I know Negroes too. They're not necessarily like children."

"Oh, come off it. She's letting her go, isn't she? Lots of people would've made a big stink about it."

"Yes, I suppose so."

The brief conversation left a little cloud between them that dinner at the club did nothing to dispel. Peter loved any new experience with Charlie, and dining out tête-à-tête with him was a major one, but it was Saturday and it didn't turn out as he had hoped. Peter had come to feel that if they could get through Saturday without disaster, they could count on another week of perfect harmony. They were surrounded by people from the moment they arrived. Charlie table-hopped, and others returned the visits. Peter had acquired many admirers of his own without being aware of it; nobody really meant anything to him except Charlie. Together they proved a powerful magnet. As the meal was ending, Peter pressed his knee against Charlie's. "Let's go look at the tennis courts," he said. The line had particular significance for them; it referred to the time they had indulged themselves on the lawn.

"Don't be silly," Charlie replied curtly. "I have a date with Betty Pringle." He threw down his napkin and was gone.

Betty was a pretty girl in an ordinary, rather doll-like way, but she was a good dancer and had a reputation for being fast; that is, she was said to be willing to neck and pet more boldly than most of the girls. As the evening progressed, Charlie found himself devoting all his attention to her. The dance floor was soon crowded and other youths frequently cut in on them, but he returned and she welcomed him with giggles, accepting him as her special date for the occasion. When the music was slow, she pressed herself against him in a way that immediately aroused him. He knew that she must feel it. They danced, they paused for cold drinks, they danced again. He caught glimpses of Peter from time to time, but whenever he seemed about to approach, he took Betty by the arm and led her back to the floor.

They were dancing a slow tango and she clung to him; Charlie responded more positively than ever. She made an extra little pelvic movement, acknowledging him. He broke away and smiled down at her.

"What about going for a drive," he suggested.

She looked up at him, all innocence. "Do you think we should?"

"Why shouldn't we?"

"It *is* getting awfully hot in here. Dance us over to the door. My mother's here somewhere."

When they were out, she took his arm primly. "We mustn't be gone long," she said. He ran her across the lawn to where the car was parked. They got in and he started off with a roar. This was part of the club-dance ritual, as familiar to him as the feel of the wheel in his hands, yet he was aware of change, of growing up. A year ago they would have kissed perhaps and played with each other a bit with their hands. Now he knew that anything might happen. His sex told him there was nothing wrong with him; he could play this game as well as any guy. He made no attempt at conversation, but let her fill the silence with chirpy little remarks such as, "The stars. They're so beautiful!" and "I love to drive fast at night."

He drove out along the ocean toward the deserted beach he and Peter had been frequenting. When he reached a point where they were unlikely to be disturbed, he turned in among the dunes and stopped. He switched off the lights and casually put his arm around her shoulder and pulled her to him and kissed her. She didn't resist. Her mouth felt small and pursy after the soft, rich generosity of Peter's. He lifted his hand to her breast in a conventional caress. She made a quick movement, and he found himself holding a small bare breast. He started to cover it tactfully, but her hand urged his head downwards and he bent his head and took the nipple in his mouth, feeling it pucker as he did so. She slumped lower in her seat and placed his hand between her knees. He ran it up under her dress along her thighs, encountering obstacles as he did so, stockings, buckles, straps, and reached the warm moist emptiness of her crotch. He ran his thumb along the edge of some undergarment, stroking hair. She quivered under his touch, writhing and uttering small gasps of pleasure.

"You can do it with your finger if you want," she whispered.

His sex was caught in a fold of his trousers and was becoming intensely uncomfortable. He lifted his head. "Just a minute," he said, and put his mouth once more on hers. He withdrew his hand and busied himself with his own needs. The buttons were stretched taut, but he managed to undo them and work himself out of the tangle of clothing. Freed, the whole hard length of him rose between them and he felt genuine desire. Perhaps she would let him really have her. It would be wonderful to drive it into her, there where it belonged. The thought made his breath catch and his heart race wildly. His hand was trembling as he found hers and lifted it and placed it on his sex. There was an instant of stunning contact, and then she pulled her mouth from his and screamed. Briefly, he took it as a tribute, but she screamed again and began struggling frantically with the handle of the door.

"Oh, you — you — you filthy—" She was gasping. "Oh, you made me — you made me touch it. That thing! You made me touch it. Oh—"

He leaned across her and grabbed her hands and held them. "What's the matter with you? What're you trying to—"

"Don't you touch me. Help! Go away. Take it away from me." She tried to fight him off. Her voice rose to a shout. "I'll tell my father. He'll take you to the police. He'll have you thrown out of the club. You dirty — Help!"

"Stop yelling, you silly fool. There's nobody around for miles." He held her wrists in a hard grip. He wanted to break them. Her bare breast hung from her dress. Her skirt was gathered around her thighs. She was disgusting. His momentary bewilderment was replaced by searing rage. He would crush her. He would destroy her. Girls were all alike. They didn't know what they wanted, unless it was to make a fool of you. They lifted their skirts, they bared their breasts, they screamed if anything came of it. They didn't give a damn about male needs. The last time, What's-her-name had made such a fuss that he'd been unable to keep an erection. The other time, it had been rape. That's what they really deserved. These thoughts flashed through his mind with the speed of hate. He held her wrists and wanted to make her scream with pain. His voice was hoarse with rage when he spoke. "Go on. Tell your father. I have a few things to tell him myself. What am I supposed to touch? A hairy pee-hole. That's supposed to be wonderful. 'You can do it with your finger.' God. Talk about filth."

As he spoke, a wail rose in her throat until it broke into sobs and she seemed to shrink as her body was shaken by them. He released her wrists and rearranged himself in his trousers and buttoned himself up. The hand that had been under her skirt felt contaminated. He didn't like to touch himself with it. As her sobbing continued, his composure returned. He had given her a little of what she deserved. He began to feel a small glow of satisfaction.

"OK, Miss Hairy-pee-hole. What shall it be? Shall I take you home or back to the club?" Her sobbing redoubled in force, and he almost laughed. "Considering the condition you're in, I guess it'd better be home." He started the car and turned and headed back. Her sobs slowly diminished and died. He was aware of her adjusting her bodice and straightening her skirt. They continued in silence until he reached inhabited streets and pulled up in front of her house. She opened the door.

"Don't you ever dare speak to me again," she said shakily. "I'll get back at you if it's the last thing I do."

"Well, if I'm not supposed to speak to you, I won't bother to say good night. Go on. Get out. And don't try stirring up any trouble. I can talk too, remember."

She slammed the door. He chuckled as he shot the car into gear and sped off toward the club.

He went first to the lavatory and washed his hands thoroughly and removed a smudge of lipstick from his cheek. Then he went out to look for Peter. The dance was on the wane. There were fewer people about, which simplified his search. Peter wasn't dancing. He wasn't in the bar. He wasn't in any of the public rooms. He wasn't on the big brightly lighted porch. Charlie went down the steps that led to lawn and the tennis courts. He passed under trees into deep shadow. It occurred to him that Peter might have gone home, but even as he thought it he rejected it as extremely unlikely. Peter wouldn't leave him unless he was sick. He heard voices off to his right, and he veered in their direction. In a moment, he recognized Peter's voice. He slowed to approach more cautiously. He made out two forms seated on the grass under a tree. He was only a few yards from them when two heads turned, catching the light.

Charlie swung around and started back, almost running in the direction he had come from.

"Charlie," Peter called. There was the peculiar tremor of delight that was always in his voice when he spoke his name. Charlie speeded up. He circled the building and leaped into the car and was off. His thoughts and feelings were in such a tumult that he couldn't sort them out. His throat ached. His eyes were burning. He gripped the wheel, his muscles straining, as if it offered him his only hope of salvation. Even after he had parked the car in front of the house, he remained in the same position, clinging to the wheel. He had recognized Peter's companion. The one member of the club whom everybody referred to openly as a "pervert." A man whom mothers warned their sons against.

He became suddenly conscious of time passing, and he flung himself out of the car and raced into the house and up the stairs to his room. He started to lock the door, but changed his mind. Not that he wanted to see Peter again. He could rot in hell. He tried to undress but couldn't. He wanted to lie down, but the empty bed repelled him. He paced, all his body feeling stiff and unmanageable. His muscles were tensed to the breaking point. He wanted to let out a great roar of pain and fury. Nervous tension expressed itself in blinding rage. Jesus Christ. Why should this sort of thing happen to him? That goddamn girl. He had let her off too easily. He should've really frightened her so she wouldn't dare talk. God knows what the bitch might accuse him of — rape, indecent exposure, anything. Nobody would pay any attention, but word might get to C.B. And Peter out on the lawn with a queer. If he discovered that they had so much as touched each other, he would kill him. Kill him. Kill him for making him feel like this.

He heard a car below, and his heart leaped up and began to hammer painfully against his chest. He remained motionless, listening. He heard the car stop, the gentle closing of a door, footsteps on gravel, and then nothing until there was another flurry of footsteps before his door and Peter burst into the room.

"Why did you—" he began, and then stopped as he saw Charlie's face.

"Did your boyfriend bring you home?" Charlie demanded with a sneer.

"Oh, darling—"

"Stop calling me that." He took a quick step forward and hit Peter hard across the face with his open hand. Peter rocked with the blow, but remained standing defenseless before him. "I've had enough of this whole thing. You can have Jimmy Harvester. Did he give you a good fuck, or was it the other way around?"

"He understands about us, which is more than I can say for anybody else."

"Understands about us? Jesus Christ. So you had a nice heart-to-heart talk, did you? Just you two girls together. You dirty little pansy. Goddamn it, I won't have you blabbing about things that concern me."

"They concern me too."

"Do they, now? Well, they won't concern you for long. You're leaving here tomorrow. Do you understand? C.B. will be interested to hear about the friends you choose for yourself."

Peter's face worked. For an awful moment, Charlie thought he was going to cry. He made a visible effort to pull himself together, a remote look came into his eyes, and he turned and walked out, leaving the door open behind him. Charlie stared after him. So that was that. If he came crawling back asking for forgiveness, he would really let him have it. His hand still tingled from the blow. He went to the door and started to close it, but left it slightly ajar. He could see the light under Peter's door across the hall. He undressed, but instead of going to bed as he had intended, he put on a dressing gown as if he were expecting company. He went to the door. The light was still on. With Peter there, nearby, he found that his mind was beginning to work more clearly. What exactly had he been so angry about? Peter had been out in the dark with Jimmy Harvester. That was enough. But what if they had just been talking? Outrageous, but not really sufficient grounds for making him leave. The thought of his not being here left him with an emptiness so profound that he shook his head and put his hand out to a chair to support himself. There was nothing he could tell C.B. that would make his leaving reasonable, so it was out of the question anyway. He had no intention of going to him, but if he came back, as he was bound to do, he wouldn't be quite so belligerent.

He went to the door again. The light was still on. What in hell was he doing? He paced, staying near the door. Thinking back, he had to admit that Peter hadn't betrayed the slightest trace of guilt, not even when he had first come upon them. "Charlie." The call was in his ears, eager and welcoming. Perhaps he should go see what was going on across the hall. If he waited much longer, Peter might go to bed and — That was all over now, at least for the time being. He wasn't going to have a boy calling him "darling" all the time. He gave a tug to the cord of his dressing gown and peered around the door. Then he pushed it open and walked quickly across the hall and entered Peter's room without knocking.

He was wearing the clothes Charlie hadn't seen since the day he arrived. His suitcase was open on the rack, and he was putting something in it. He looked up without surprise or any other emotion.

"What in hell are you doing?" Charlie demanded.

"Did you want something?"

"Yes, I did. I want my clothes," Charlie said, hastily improvising. "But what do you think you're up to?"

"I wasn't going to steal your clothes. You told me to leave. I'm leaving."

"You're going to go marching off into the night? You really are a total ass. How would I explain that to C.B.?"

"You'll manage. It'll probably have something to do with the friends I choose for myself."

"Oh, of course. Why don't you call Jimmy Harvester and ask him to rescue you? The damsel in distress. Jesus." He strode across the room and seized the suitcase and flung it upside down onto the floor.

"That's pretty stupid." Peter picked it up and replaced it on the rack. He began to gather up his belongings. Charlie grabbed the suitcase again and hurled it across the room. "Now listen," Peter said. "You'd better get out of here. This is still my room." He took Charlie's arm in a strong grip and started to lead him toward the door. Charlie seized him in a headlock and began to force him to the floor. Peter wrenched himself free. Charlie went for him again. They struck out at each other, hurting but careful not to do any real damage. They grappled. They were evenly matched. They broke free and hit each other and grappled again. A chair was overturned. Peter slipped and Charlie was on him. He wrenched himself free again and backed to the end of the room. They were both panting.

"You better stop," Peter said. "C.B. will hear us."

Charlie was held by the cold challenge in his eyes. There was none of the soft, familiar yearning in them. He looked competent and manly and dangerously purposeful. "Will you stop this idiotic business of clearing out tonight?" he asked.

Peter started to speak, his eyes went dead, the strength seemed to drain out of him. "Yes. I'll do anything you say," he replied dully.

"Well, you might as well start by telling me what went on with Jimmy Harvester." Thrown off balance by this easy victory, Charlie was barely able to maintain a severe and uncompromising manner.

"Nothing. You disappeared and I was wandering around and Jimmy started talking to me and we went out and sat under that tree."

"Did he try any funny business?"

"Oh, darling — I'm sorry. I won't say that anymore. No. Maybe he intended to. I don't know much about that sort of ... thing. He asked a lot of questions about you, and I told him I was in love with you just to make sure he wouldn't get any ideas. He was very nice."

"Oh, for God's sake. Don't you understand you can't have anything to do with people like that?"

"No, I don't understand. I don't understand why you're so angry."

"He's a queer, for God's sake. Everybody knows it. From now on, I don't want you to have anything to do with him."

"I thought I was leaving. What difference does it make?"

"Oh, don't be so silly. I lost my temper."

Peter's expression didn't alter. He started slowly toward him as if moving in a trance. His eyes wavered. "You've got lipstick on your neck." He gasped and his face crumpled and he flung himself onto the bed he'd never used and burst into tears.

Charlie stood over him, rubbing his neck. Unlike Betty's tears, these gave him no satisfaction. He shrank from the pain they caused him. A flood of tenderness and longing swept over him, making his knees feel weak. He sank onto the edge of the bed, a sob in his own throat, and put his hand on Peter's shoulder and began to stroke it. "Don't, my baby. Please don't," he murmured.

54

Peter shook his head on the pillow. "Oh, God, I'm so in love with you. It hurts. It hurts so damn much, sometimes."

"I won't let it. Honest. Never again, baby. I'm sorry. Please. Please, my love."

A bubble of laughter escaped through the sobs. "You've never called me that before."

"Sure I have. At least, I've thought it often enough. My darling lover."

Peter rolled onto his back and seized his hand and held it to his mouth. Then he lifted it and rubbed it across his eyes. He heaved a deep shuddering sigh and was still. "Oh, God, let's fight some more if this is what it's like after." He opened his brimming eyes and smiled. Charlie leaned over him and kissed him on the mouth, his tongue lingering on the full, soft lips. He drew back, and their eyes met and sank deep into each other.

"Come on, darling," Charlie said, no longer caring about the words he used. "Take those damn clothes off and come back where we belong." He ran a finger over Peter's cheek and stood. His sex surged up out of the folds of his dressing gown. Peter swung his legs over the edge of the bed and laughed.

"That's what I like about you. You're so modest. Come here. Give me that." He took it in both hands and put it in his mouth. Charlie pushed his fingers through his hair and tugged gently.

"Not like that, darling. I'm dying to have all of you."

Peter released the sex with a little smack of his lips and laid his head against Charlie's belly. "God, yes, me too," he said.

Charlie waited while he shed his clothes and then took him in his arms and put his mouth on his and moved him out the door and across the hall. Their coupling was a breathless act of reconciliation, so highly charged emotionally that it was quickly done. When Charlie had returned from the bathroom, they lay together, Peter's face snuggled into Charlie's armpit.

"Have I told you how much I love your armpits? I didn't know anybody could have beautiful armpits, but you have. The hair is so sexy, just like around your cock." He ran his tongue over it and giggled when Charlie's muscles contracted in response. "Tell me things. I don't really understand much about homosexuality and all that. If anybody had told me a month ago that I'd be begging a guy to shove his cock up my ass, I'd have killed him. Please don't mind me saying it like that. It helps me to understand to say it straight. I

55

hardly ever stop thinking about having your cock inside me there or in my mouth or somewhere. I don't think it really matters much that it's so big. I love its being big because it is. If it were any bigger or smaller, it wouldn't be you. The thing is, I can't imagine loving anybody who didn't have a cock, so I guess that makes me a queer. I know it's awful and I don't know how it happened and I probably should shoot myself or something, but with you it just seems right. I'm nuts about being fucked by you and you like to fuck me, so I can't see how it's wrong."

"If everybody felt like that, what would become of the human race?" Charlie intoned the question in a schoolmasterly fashion.

"The human race is doing all right. Anyway, everybody doesn't feel like that, although I don't see how anybody could resist being fucked by you. Golly, what bliss. But I still don't see the difference between us — or me, at least — and Jimmy Harvester. Tell me about that."

"It's so obvious, darling. He's such a swish. And the way he goes around ogling all the young kids."

"Yes, we're not like that. But then we couldn't be, as long as we're together. But there are things — about myself, I mean. I'm beginning to notice fellows' baskets. That's what Jimmy calls crotches. I never let myself before, but I do now. Not that I want them or anything. It's just out of curiosity, to compare them to you. Most guys look as if they didn't have anything at all. There just isn't any comparison. I'm so proud of it — as if it were mine."

"It is, darling." Charlie became aware of using the word too frequently. Saying it gave him an odd little thrill, and he warned himself against it.

Peter put his hand on the subject of conversation and held it. "Mine," he repeated contentedly. "Jimmy says you might be bisexual. It seems some people like both. It just depends on who they're with. Thank God you're with me."

"But that's just what I've been telling you." Charlie was briefly tempted to tell him about this evening, but found there was nothing about the episode he wanted to remember. "We'll both probably want to get married someday, but that has nothing to do with this."

"I'll say it doesn't. I can't imagine it. Jimmy says there's lots of guys like us in New York, living together as if they were married. That'll be wonderful."

"We'll be roommates. Why do you have to say like being

married?"

"Oh, well, think, darling. I'm so proud of us — of being in love with you and you saying you love me. I hate having to hide it. It doesn't make any sense. Why should you hide something that's so perfect? It'd be wonderful to be somewhere where it didn't have to be a secret. Jimmy says it's a whole different world."

"Jimmy, Jimmy, Jimmy."

"You don't want me to admit being a fairy, do you?"

"Of course I don't. It's — well, it's not normal. And it's not true. I ought to make you do it with a girl."

"You wouldn't mind? You minded my even talking to Jimmy."

"That's the whole point. He's a queer. I don't want to have anything to do with queers, and I don't want you to, either."

"Would you do it with a girl now — I mean now that we're together — if you had the chance?"

"Well, sure. Why not? Except that most girls make such a big thing of it that it's not worth the bother."

"I guess I wouldn't mind. No, that's not true. I'd mind horribly, but not as much as if it were a boy. The only way I'd do it with a girl is if you were with me."

Charlie's sex, which had been responding lazily to Peter's hand, bounded into full erection. He felt Peter's slide up along his flank. "You have the nuttiest ideas," he said.

"Well, it's a fact. I don't really want girls. I never have. When I was a kid, when I used to — you know, masturbate — I used to think vaguely about boys I knew. That's something I've never admitted even to myself. It was never girls."

"You've just started late. That doesn't mean you're queer. You'd never actually had anything to do with a guy."

Peter laughed. "That's the sad truth." He pulled himself up onto his knees and threw a leg across Charlie and straddled his thighs. "Look at me now." He lifted Charlie's sex and held it against his own. "Golly, look at us. Who'd want a girl? I'll never forget when our cocks first touched each other, when you were doing all that measuring. I've never asked you. Did you start measuring on purpose, to—" He interrupted himself with laughter. "To seduce me?"

"Well, sure, I guess so," Charlie said grudgingly, obscurely resenting being reminded of it.

"If you'd only known. When you first put your hand on me, when we were getting out of the car, I almost passed out. Oh, God, darling. I'll always be faithful to you. I'm yours. You were crazy tonight to think anything could happen with Jimmy. You did think so, didn't you? There'll never be anybody else. I *want* to be faithful to you. I have to be faithful to you. That's all there is." He held their sexes together again with both hands. "Like that. Together."

Charlie stretched voluptuously and arched his back so that his sex towered over Peter's. He dropped back flat on the bed and put his hands around Peter's, all of his attention concentrated in their joined hands and the hard flesh they held. The wounds of the evening were healed. "It is amazing, isn't it? About us," he said.

THEY PRESENTED RADIANT FACES to C.B. at a late Sunday breakfast the next day. She asked about their evening and they offered a well-edited account of it. They had been sitting for some time when Henry entered from the hall to announce a telephone call for C.B.

"Just find out who it is, Henry. I've told you. Oh, well, never mind. I'm finished here. Excuse me, my dears." She rose and left them.

The phone was in the hall. "Yes," she said into it.

"Mrs. Collinge? This is Willard Pringle. We know each other."

She found the voice common. "We have perhaps met," she admitted.

"Now don't start getting high and mighty with me. I have a thing or two to tell you. It's about that boy you have with you, your nephew or grandson or whatever he is. Young Mills. I had a good mind to come over there and thrash him within an inch of his life, but Mrs. Pringle talked me out of it. We have to protect Betty. That's our first responsibility."

"I presume you don't intend me to follow the ramifications of your family life. What are you trying to say to me?"

"By George, I'm telling you what that young whippersnapper did to my daughter. Attacked her. Exposed himself. He's nothing but a degenerate, a low — there aren't words to describe him. I won't have him contaminating the purity of our young girls. You're going to withdraw him from the club. If I hear of him being there again or coming anywhere near my daughter, I'll take steps you'll regret. I don't want to subject Betty to any more of this nastiness, but I have my duty as a father."

"I don't find this conversation suitable for a gentleman to have with a lady," C.B. interrupted coldly. "I will report it in the proper quarters. I have nothing further to say to you, sir." She hung up and waited a moment and then picked up the phone and made a call of her own. She found the president of the club not at home but already presiding over his bailiwick. She called him there.

"Bruce? This is Armina Collinge. This *is* a rather odd hour to call, but I want to see you."

"What a delightful surprise. It's always a pleasure to see you, dear lady."

"Dear Bruce. I'm afraid it's a rather tiresome business. Shall I come along now?"

"By all means. The whole family's here until lunch. I'll be looking out for you on the porch."

She hung up and returned to her place at table and rang for Henry without sitting. "I'm going to have to go out for a little while," she explained to Charlie and Peter. Henry appeared and she turned to him. "Bring the car around please, Henry. I'm going out."

"What's it all about?" Charlie asked with an almost imperceptible shading of apprehension.

She looked at him with a tilt of her head. "Nothing, my dearest. Really nothing. I'll tell you about it when I get back. I must go get ready."

She left them again. When she came back, she had completed her costume with a rakish hat and was carrying a tightly furled pale gray silk parasol to match her silk suit. She was jeweled; she glittered discreetly. They had taken advantage of her absence by spreading the Sunday papers over the table and were engrossed in them. They looked up at her entrance. Peter whistled.

"You're really going to knock their eyes out," Charlie said.

C.B. laughed. "You're both outrageous, trying to turn an old lady's head. Why don't you go somewhere more comfortable? Rosie should clear away here. Are you planning to go to the club this morning?" The small beat of silence that preceded the question gave it a certain weight.

Charlie felt it. He looked at Peter questioningly. "I don't think so. I wouldn't mind a swim."

"Fine," Peter agreed.

"Will you go to the regular beach?" C.B. asked.

"No, let's go out where the breakers are big." Peter always chose their deserted beach where they could romp about naked, with plenty of time to grab their trunks if anybody was sighted.

"Splendid," C.B. approved. "Then I'll see you at lunch. I'm afraid it won't be much more than a picnic. Perhaps we should take it out under the trees. That might be quite gay." She left them with a swirl of gray silk.

The majestic Packard deposited her in front of the club porch. Henry handed her out, and Bruce Munger was waiting to welcome her at the top of the steps. They greeted each other as old friends. He was an ample, genial, courtly man.

"I know why you've come," he said. "I had a call from Will Pringle after you'd called. I guess we'd better talk in private. Let's go up to the office."

They mounted the stairs and skirted the deserted dining room and entered the rooms where the club's business was conducted. They, too, were deserted except for a younger man, who rose from behind a desk as they entered. "Ah, Dick. You know Dick Baird, Armina. This is Mrs. Collinge. Charlie Mills is her grandson."

"Grandson? I thought it was nephew."

C.B. leaned gracefully on her parasol. "There was a time when people found it difficult to believe that I was a grandmother. They mistook my daughter for my sister." She lifted her head jauntily. "I wasn't always scrupulous in correcting them. The error has persisted."

"Not surprising," Munger said. "I still don't find you convincing as a grandmother."

"Flattery always came easily to your tongue, Bruce."

"Well, I'll leave you," Baird said. "I'm taking those announcements about the cabaret up to town tomorrow and having them run through my office."

"Don't go, Mr. Baird," C.B. commanded. "You're a member of the Board, I believe. I'm glad to have a witness. I wish to make this an official visit." She swept over to one of the chairs grouped around the desk and seated herself. The two men followed her and sat. C.B. flicked one of her gloves with distaste. "I've just received an unspeakably insolent telephone call from a man called Pringle. I know your requirements for membership these days aren't as strict as they might be so long as people pay their dues promptly, but it appears that in this case you've been too lax."

"Oh, well, Pringle's all right. A bit of a rough diamond, perhaps."

"I don't choose to associate with rough diamonds, Bruce. He's made unmentionable charges against my grandson and since he's made an issue of his membership in the club, I insist that you obtain a written apology from him by tomorrow morning or I'll demand a public airing of the whole disgusting affair."

"Well, now, Armina, I daresay there's been a misunderstanding between the young people. Youngsters have a lot more freedom than they did in our day. Sometimes it leads to difficulties."

C.B. squared her shoulders and sat very straight in her chair. She tapped the floor with her parasol. "I've brought Charlie up to be a gentleman through and through. It's inconceivable that he should be guilty of misconduct under any circumstances."

"I'm sure you're right, He's a fine lad. I wish I'd had his looks when I was his age. I'll bet he has lots of the girls swooning over him."

"That may well be, but I can assure you that Charlie has no interest in this wretched Pringle child, nor in any other girl at the moment."

"Now, Armina, I don't think we can be too sure of that. We menfolk are always capable of being susceptible to a pretty girl."

"I find your manner frivolous, Bruce, in view of the fashion in which this Pringle person spoke to me. Am I to count on you to produce an apology, or do you wish me to demand a full hearing before the Board? I'm sure Charlie can produce witnesses to disprove whatever filth this person may invent."

"Now, that surely won't be necessary. I think I can put it to Pringle that he'd be well advised to climb down."

"I hope so. My first impulse was to resign from a club where such a man could be a member. If I did, I'm sure I wouldn't be alone. The world is changing, but there still remain those with certain standards who won't be bullied by the Pringles among us. By tomorrow morning, then?"

"Yes, that seems fair enough."

"Can I count on you, Mr. Baird, to second Bruce's efforts?"

"Yes, indeed. I don't know what the story is, but I know Pringle is apt to be a bit of a firebrand. We don't want the club's atmosphere poisoned by gossip."

"Very well. You don't have to see me out, Bruce. Stay and set the wheels in motion." She rose, and they sprang up. She bowed to them both with a proud but charming tilt of her head and tripped out on neat and dainty feet.

"My word," Baird said when she was gone. The two men looked at each other and laughed. "She seems to have a rather peculiar idea of the way young gentlemen behave with girls."

"She's an extraordinary woman. I think Will bit off more than he could chew when he tackled her."

"Nice clean-cut-looking kid, the Mills boy. What's it all about?"

"Randy young devil. Have you noticed him? Hung like a horse, to put it plainly. From what Pringle said, my guess is that the girl had hot pants for him and then balked when he produced it for her. He should've let her have it anyway. Serve her right."

"What's the next move?"

"Let's tackle him together. He doesn't want to start a lot of gossip about his own daughter."

"I know his partner well. As a matter of fact, the bank is holding some of their paper."

"I don't think he'll give us any trouble. Not when he understands just who he's dealing with. Armina Collinge is not one to accept halfway measures. She'd blow the whole club apart if it suited her purposes."

"I've always been fascinated by her, but I've never seen her under quite such full sail, if you know what I mean. My wife's from the South, you know. She says there was some mystery about her husband's death. There's supposed to be a bit of the tarbrush there, too."

"That's pretty generally true of those old Southern families, isn't it? I might as well call Pringle."

CHARLIE AND PETER, dressed again after their swim, found C.B. on the veranda reading the Sunday papers. She lowered her lorgnette as they joined her and gazed up at them.

"My bronze gods. I've been waiting for you. Let's have a drink. I need one. I've had a rather harrowing morning."

"Well, come on, tell us about it," Charlie demanded, with the same almost imperceptible apprehension. "Where've you been?"

She laid the papers aside and rose and went to her bar. "I didn't want to go into it until I'd straightened it out. It doesn't matter now. As a matter of fact, the phone call I had this morning was from a deplorable man called Pringle."

"Oh, for God's sake." Charlie flushed. He felt Peter's eyes on him. After the first contraction of his heart, he recovered himself. She had said she'd straightened it out. "What in the world did he want?" he asked almost casually.

"He was quite incoherent — common men always are when they let themselves go — but the gist of it was that you'd upset his daughter in some way." She turned and held out glasses to them.

"But what did he say? Upset her how?" He had to know what Pringle had told her; he couldn't allow her to think that he'd actually done any of those things. He took the glasses and carried one to Peter without meeting his eye.

"Oh, my dearest, you don't suppose I'd allow such a man to go into particulars." Her laughter tinkled disdainfully. "I know, just as Peter does, that you're incapable of doing anything low or questionable in any way."

"It's ridiculous," Peter joined in. "He was being very nice to her. We were together the entire evening."

"I knew you would have been, my darling." She carried a drink back to her chair. "I quite understand it. Charlie was nice to the poor little thing, and she went quite out of her mind with fantasies about him. I suppose one mustn't be too hard on her. We've both seen how irresistibly charming Charlie can be. It's unthinkable that he could ever be guilty of grossness or cruelty."

"I did take her home," Charlie pointed out. He was sufficiently experienced in deception to know that it's wise to keep outright lies to a minimum. "You weren't with me then."

"Oh, that," Peter agreed hastily. "That was nothing. Ten minutes at the most. Just time to take her to her house and come back." Charlie noted the falsehood; Peter was apparently determined to provide him with an alibi.

"That would be useful to know if anything were to come of this," C.B. approved, "but it's all taken care of already. I simply went to Bruce Munger and told him that if I didn't have an apology from the person by tomorrow morning, I would insist on a full hearing before the club Board. I knew I could count on Peter as a witness."

"What did Mr. Munger say?" Charlie asked.

"He agreed that an apology was quite necessary and correct. I put it into his hands. I think I can let the matter rest there. But I do think you'd better avoid the poor girl in the future."

"I should hope so. The whole thing is absolutely nuts." He looked at her with gratitude, knowing that he needn't have worried. He could always count on her, no matter what difficulties might arise. Still, he'd feel better when she actually had the apology in her hands.

As far as C.B. was concerned, the subject was apparently disposed of and she didn't refer to it again, but Charlie could see that Peter was still brooding about it. When he and Peter returned to their room after lunch, they didn't pull their clothes off as they might normally have done but wandered about restlessly, ill at ease and constrained.

"All right, champ," Peter said finally. The use of the public name in private marked a distance between them. "You might as well tell me. Did you — well, did you fuck her?"

"Oh, for God's sake. I might have known it. Now you're going to grill me. No, I didn't."

"Then what's it all about?"

"We were just fooling around the way kids do and she started screaming and I told her to shut up and took her home."

"I see. Then you would've fucked her if she'd let you?"

"Sure. Why not? It happens between guys and girls."

"I suppose it does." He knew that there must be more to the story than Charlie was telling, but he didn't particularly care about details; he believed Charlie's account of the basic facts. The experience of love was so new to him that he had no fixed convictions about fidelity and related questions. He knew he shouldn't even think about competing with girls, and yet he was determined to do so; he fiercely wanted Charlie for himself. He had no firmer grasp on the future than Charlie had. He knew simply that as long as life continued as he knew it, he would have to be with Charlie. His own fidelity was an imperative, regardless of what Charlie did, even though in the last few weeks he had become aware of the attractions of other young men.

"Thanks for lying for me," Charlie said grudgingly, after a silence.

"Oh, that." Peter shrugged. "I loved doing it. If you ever need to be rescued from a sinking ship or anything, just let me know. That's the sort of thing I dream about."

"Crazy. Then what's the matter, baby?" He came and perched on the arm of the chair where Peter was sprawled and ran a hand over his hair and gave his shoulder an impatient little shake. Now that it was sorting itself out, he wasn't sorry to have been the subject of a small scandal with a girl; it was the best advertisement of his masculinity. If C.B. had gone to Mr. Munger, there would be gossip — about him and the girl, not about some other thing. He tugged Peter's hair. "The whole thing with Betty was just stupid."

Charlie's tentative satisfaction came through as smugness; Peter felt helpless against it. "I think it was. I guess it's obvious I wish it hadn't happened, not that that matters to anyone."

Charlie put his hands on his shoulders and squeezed them. "That shows how much you know about it. I wish it hadn't, too."

Peter looked up quickly. "Do you?" He looked at length, amazed at having won this much of an apology, and then smiled slowly and lifted his hands to Charlie's. "Then that makes it all right."

The events of the night before and this aftermath were solidifying and defining their relationship. To Peter, Betty was a warning. If his idol was flawed, it was all the more important for him to be at his side, to defend him from danger; he sensed instinctively that Charlie's refusal to accept the nature of their relationship could lead to serious trouble. He hadn't attempted to analyze his own whole-hearted acceptance, but if he had, he would have encountered special circumstances: the taboo on sex in any form at home, so that guilt would have been apportioned equally to all acts he might have committed, an intolerable burden, which in effect mitigated guilt; and his deep angry antagonism to his father, the General. He knew his father would be appalled by the road he had chosen, and this confirmed him in it. He already looked forward to his finding out, but not until he was twenty-one, so there could be no legal complications. He could imagine himself being slapped into some sort of reformatory school.

He gripped Charlie's hands for safety and was aware that needs and demands of his own were emerging. All their talk about going to New York together had remained singularly amorphous because of Charlie's edict against discussing it with C.B. He was suddenly determined to take practical steps.

"I'm going to write Columbia this afternoon. Right now." He

pulled himself up in the chair and propped his elbow on Charlie's thighs. "We've got to find out about night courses and fees and all that stuff. Even if I don't actually do anything about it, we've got to know what we're talking about when we talk to C.B."

"Well, I've been thinking more about that, too, of course. I don't see why we necessarily have to tell her. You have to go home first, anyway. I don't see why you can't just come back to New York and move in, and we'll see how things work out."

"But you say it has to be all right with her because of the allowance and everything."

"Well, sure."

"Then we have to tell her. I know damn well she wouldn't like it if she found out we'd planned it all behind her back."

"Well, we can't do anything till you get the stuff from Columbia, anyway."

"No, of course not. But then we'll tell her." Peter was aware that Charlie had made no effort to get him to write. At such moments, he had only to look up at the level, slightly upswept, somehow devilish brows, the deep blue eyes, the mouth, which seemed always to be slightly smiling, for all doubts to be suspended. Charlie was all the joy and beauty a human being could be. He leaned down and kissed the strong hand resting on his arm.

THE NEXT DAY, the apology arrived, routine was restored, and Sapphire returned in the evening. On the following morning, after breakfast, Peter was delegated to collect their swimming trunks from the line in the kitchen yard while Charlie went upstairs. Peter was gone a long time. He entered Charlie's room twirling the trunks in his hands.

"Where've you been all this time?"

"Did you miss me, beautiful?"

"I did. What were you doing?"

"Talking to Sapphire about her audition. She really had one. She told me all about it. She's nice. She's so simple about it. It was at the Metropolitan, but not *for* the Metropolitan. It's some show in the fall Otto Kahn's putting money into. The joke will really be on C.B. if she turns out to be a star. You'll be a star, too. You and Sapphire starring on Broadway. How about that? And me? Well, stars have to have secretaries. That's two job possibilities right there. Except Sapphire has Henry, so I guess I'll have to settle for you."

Charlie laughed at his nonsense and pulled him close. "You'll have to settle for me, all right. Tell Sapphire to lay off." He studied the face before him, aware of the change in Peter just since the fight the other night. He was growing less sensitive, less solicitous, tougher, brighter; the sweet docility was fading. On the whole, Charlie approved; he felt more air around them.

An anxious little frown creased Peter's brow. "She said something peculiar. You won't like it, but I'd better tell you. She said to tell Mister Charlie if he did anything he didn't want his Granny to know about, be careful of Rosie. She says she's a spy."

"What's that supposed to mean?" Charlie smiled and shrugged. "C.B.'s right. Negroes are crazy. Didn't you ask her what she was talking about?"

"No. I didn't think I'd better."

Charlie's smile vanished and his eyes stared with alarm. "You mean — good God. Spying on us here?" He released Peter and looked distractedly around the room. "I'm always careful about the towels and all that. You haven't been forgetting to muss your bed?"

"No. Always."

"Well, there's nothing here to make anybody suspect anything. If she wants to stand outside the door and listen, let her. C.B. wouldn't believe her."

"I don't guess anybody would. All that whooping and hollering and squealing."

Charlie turned and hurried to the bathroom. He came back with a little shake of his head. "Everything's in order. It always is." He stopped and looked at Peter. He approached him slowly and stood close to him and lifted his hand to his face, running a finger lightly over it. His eyes had grown intent and searching.

"Uh-oh. Now what?" Peter asked. "Why're you looking at me like that?"

Charlie continued his scrutiny. Then he stepped back and to one side, still looking. "I'm going to do your portrait. I get so excited looking at you that I wasn't sure I could, but I'm beginning to see you now. Let Rosie spy on that."

"Golly, what a fabulous idea. I can't wait to see how you work."

"I haven't got oils here, but I've got all my drawing stuff. That should settle it if anybody's wondering why we spend so much time up here. I'll do a portrait, and we'll give it to C.B. from both of us."

"From both of us. That sounds good. Darling, why is C.B. called C.B.? I've never known."

"Oh, it's an old joke. Her maiden name was Barton. Armina Barton Collinge. A.B.C. Some friends of hers were kidding about it and she said, 'I'd rather be C.B. than B.C.' It stuck."

Peter laughed. "That sounds like her."

"Come on. Let's have a swim. We're going to be busy."

They were out of their clothes and into their trunks in a moment. As they were leaving the room, Charlie said, "Listen, don't tell C.B. you spoke to Sapphire about the audition and everything."

"Why not?"

"She wouldn't want us being pally with the servants. She prefers to handle them herself."

"Well, I hope she's nice to Sapphire about it. It's so important to her, even if she is an animal."

"Of course she will be, silly. She's wonderful with them."

"I know. I was just talking." He hugged Charlie's arm in his, but Charlie shook him off.

"Look out. Somebody might see us."

Charlie started on the portrait that afternoon. As a preliminary, he confined himself to rough sketches, and Peter reveled in the bliss of being the focus of his probing eyes for hours at a time. He had never felt so totally possessed. Charlie continued with his sketches in the days that followed. When he felt that he was ready, he worked all one afternoon on the finished drawing. At last, he let Peter see it.

"Holy mackerel," Peter said with awe after studying it in silence for some minutes. "I'm beautiful. Why hasn't anybody told me?"

"I have," Charlie said briefly, holding the portrait up.

Peter looked at him and back at the drawing. He studied it line by line and saw love in it more explicit than anything he had ever dared hope Charlie would express in words. The muscles of his jaw tensed. "Yes, you have. I'm trying not to bawl like a baby." He slammed his clenched fists onto his knees and stood up. "What do you expect after this? I'd crawl all the way to New York on my stomach to be with you."

They carried the portrait down to C.B. before dinner. Charlie made the presentation. "It's from both of us. We thought you'd like to have it."

She studied it through her lorgnette. "How absolutely superb! So that's what you've been up to. What a glorious surprise." She rose and went from one to the other and embraced and kissed them. She held it out and looked from it to Peter. "It's so absolutely you. You really are a beautiful creature, my darling."

"Don't you think it's good?" Peter demanded, bursting with admiration. "I think he's fantastic. To be able to do that in a few hours."

"He has great talent. I discovered that years ago."

"He has. He did some sketches before he did this final one. They're all marvelous."

"This is superlative. It has such feeling and understanding. You should be a proud subject."

"Don't worry, I am. I had no idea I looked like that. You should let him do you."

"Never," she said with a smile and a tilt of her head. "I'm afraid he took to drawing too late for me to be committed to posterity."

"That's ridiculous. It would be beautiful. We should make him work. He ought to be doing something with it."

"He will. It will always be a fascinating hobby, a source of interest all his life. Winston Churchill paints."

"But why just a hobby?" Peter insisted.

"What else could it be?"

"Well, he could really work at it. You know, be a painter."

"Oh, my darling," she said with a tinkle of laughter. "I'm afraid you haven't acquired much worldly knowledge. Can you see Charlie starving in a garret in Paris? That's not really his style."

"No, I guess not. But you wouldn't let him starve."

"I daresay I wouldn't, but that really isn't the point. Surely you understand. Charlie would never accept being helped on a course he knew I disapproved of."

Her expression didn't alter, her rich dramatic voice rang smoothly, but Peter felt the ice in her admonition. It froze him. "Oh, well, I suppose it's because I don't do anything in particular very well," he said, in retreat. "When I *can* do something, I never want to stop doing it." His eyes flicked to Charlie, and he suppressed a giggle.

"A talent can so easily become a burden. Unless one has genius. Everything, of course, must be sacrificed to genius. But genius makes its own rules. A talent is simply a little specialty that cuts one off from a full experience of life." She turned to Charlie, who had watched the subtle clash with alarm for his friend. One didn't cross C.B. She held out the drawing. "You must tell me how you want it framed. If it can't be done properly here, I'll have to wait till New York, but I do so want it now."

They discussed the question at length before dinner. Later in the evening, Charlie suggested, apropos of nothing in particular, "Let's all go to the movies tomorrow night."

"Tomorrow's Saturday," Peter reminded him dutifully.

"You'll surely want to go to the dance," C.B. pointed out.

"Not necessarily. It gets to be a bore if you go every week. Let's the three of us have a party."

It was a triumphant moment for Peter. Saturday was no longer to be feared.

INSPIRED BY THE SUCCESS of the portrait, Charlie decided to go on with his sketching. He started by taking his sketchbook with him whenever they went out, but working conditions weren't always satisfactory.

"I'm going to do you the way I really want you," he said to Peter one afternoon in the room. "All of you, naked."

"Hey, feelthy pictures," Peter exclaimed.

"Go on. Take your clothes off." Peter complied and stood before him expectantly. "Oh God, I'd better get going quickly or I'll never get anything done. Go on. Just walk around naturally. Yeah, like that. Good. Hold it."

He was quickly absorbed. He had Peter wander about, and when he struck an attitude that pleased him, he called, "Hold it," and went to work again. He discovered a new excitement in the aesthetic exploration of Peter's body. It looked freshly formed, offering small unexpected angularities. The golden head was set on a long, strong neck. The shoulders were wide without being top-heavy. The muscles of the chest were sharply defined planes. The line from shoulder to narrow hip flowed smoothly, richly completed by the full curve of buttocks. The sex in repose, only faintly blurred by golden hair, was gentle and discreet, a soft vertical stroke with a suggestion of neat, closely packed spheres nestled behind it. The

70

legs were long and straight with slightly knobby knees that delighted Charlie's drawing hand. The hands and feet were solid, finely articulated accents to the extremities. He drew him from every angle — standing, sitting, sprawled out on the bed. Through his intent eyes and his busy hand, he absorbed the body into the emotive core of his being. It was so totally satisfying aesthetically that he was unaware of the risk he was exposing himself to.

"Come here," he commanded. "I want to do you with a hard-on."

Peter went to him, and Charlie lowered his head and shaped the buttocks with his hands. The sex sprang up eagerly, long and slim and very straight, before he could take it in his mouth.

"Yes. Can you keep it that way for a while, baby?"

"Ha. The trick is not letting it be that way all the time. You looking at me like that. How about me? A month ago I was creeping around clutching at towels. You're turning me into an exhibitionist." He struck a pose. "Go on, do me like this. Only add a little, will you? So it looks more like you."

"What a dope. It wouldn't be nearly as pretty if it were any bigger. There's such a thing as proportion. I just want to get you the way you are."

When he had explored the graphic possibilities of the erect sex, he called Peter to him and completed the play with his mouth. Peter's quick orgasms had given his mouth a mastery it had never had before; he received the leaping essence hungrily, possessively, claiming it as his own.

"You keep breaking my law about not coming without you," Peter said ruefully.

"An artist's privilege."

Together they studied the results of the afternoon's work.

"I'm certainly pretty sexy," Peter said. "No wonder you're mad about me. But God, darling, you're so damn good. It's incredible. I still can't understand why you haven't been doing anything with it."

"I don't know. C.B.'s right. It's a pretty grim life." Charlie shrugged off the acute pleasure Peter's appreciation gave him. "When I've really got you down, I'll do some more finished things."

"Listen," Peter broke out excitedly. "Can't you do one of yourself? Like that. You've got to. I've got to have one."

"I don't know. I've never thought of it. The mirror in the bathroom is probably long enough. I don't see how I could work and have a hard-on at the same time, if that's what you mean. The

71

two don't go together."

"I could help with that."

Charlie laughed. "Come on. Let's see." They went into the bathroom. Charlie studied the light and the mirror and tried a few tentative poses. "I might manage it. There's just room. Yes, I could trick it." He stood experimentally with his left hand on his hip, the right lifted to an imaginary easel. "I can make this hand look as if it's resting on something. OK, I'll try it tomorrow."

"It'll be sensational, except that you probably won't be able to get it all on one sheet."

THE ATTEMPT WAS POSTPONED by the arrival of the material from Columbia. Everything else was momentarily forgotten. They were amazed at how cheap it all seemed. They pored over the catalogue, working out a possible program of courses.

"You know, a lot of it sounds damn interesting," Peter said. "I might just go ahead and do it, if it doesn't take up too much time away from you."

They discussed at anxious length how the project should be presented to C.B. Peter would undertake explaining it to her as if it were entirely his own idea. Sharing the apartment appeared to be the stumbling block.

"Once I've told her all about it, can't you just offer to let me live with you?" Peter asked reasonably.

Faced with the hard fact of it at last, Charlie knew that that was precisely what he couldn't do. Ever since his brother had developed a scientific bent and had grown up serious and rather humorless, all C.B.'s passion for shaping personalities had been largely concentrated on him, elevating him to the position of prince consort, the rare spirit who could truly share her exquisite visions of life. She was glad for him to be friendly with Peter, but she would account it as a kindness, a condescension. It would be making too much of Peter to suggest that they should live together; it would have to come about as a happy accident. Even as he recognized this, he was aware of a suspicion, buried deep within himself, that he was a fraud. He really didn't feel as clever, as original, as infallible in his judgment of literature and art as C.B. maintained he was. His sex

72

was tangible evidence of his superiority in one field. His art might have provided the prop on which his character could have developed, but C.B. maintained that a gentleman should be a dilettante, savoring the best of all that the world had to offer. There was only C.B.; he needed to see himself constantly reflected in her approving eyes to preserve intact the insecure structure she had created. Even with Peter, he was constantly on guard not to be found out.

"I really don't see why you shouldn't just come and move in," he said after a moment's pause to give the appearance of reflection. "It's so much simpler that way."

Peter's expression clouded. He didn't want to leave any loose ends. "Well, if you think so. God knows, I don't want to do anything that would put C.B. against me. She can be very helpful with my family. They think she's Mrs. God. Even my father is impressed by her."

"Well, then, let's concentrate on the Columbia part of it. The rest will just work out naturally."

When they were dressed for the evening, Peter went to Charlie and put both hands on the back of his neck and gripped it hard. "If you'll just tell me it'll be all right no matter what she says, I won't be so scared."

Charlie pulled him close. "It'll be all right, baby." He kissed him lightly on the lips and they went out, their arms around each other.

Peter waited until they had started dinner before he plunged in. "I need your advice, C.B. I've been talking to Charlie, and he says you can tell me what I should do. You know I can't stand the idea of West Point."

"I've thought about it so much and wanted to talk to you about it, but I haven't been able to see my way clear. You, an Army officer. Such a waste. Your father is mad."

Peter hurried on, offering Columbia for her consideration.

"Columbia? I can't see that that would be much better. It draws its students from all the slums of New York."

"Yes, but it's rated very high scholastically. Isn't that true, Charlie?"

Charlie had withdrawn from the conversation and was concentrating on his food. He shrugged without looking at either of them. "Yes, sure. Quite a few fellows at Princeton were going on to Columbia for graduate work."

Peter shot him a grateful look that was wasted on him and continued to elaborate, mentioning getting a job, going to night

73

classes.

"I see you really have been thinking," C.B. said when he paused. "You make me feel as if I've been rather defeatist about it. I would so love to take you on. Princeton is the obvious solution. You deserve the best. Shouldn't we start there and see if we could work out some scheme to foil your father?"

"Oh, no," Peter blurted out. He hurried on. "Well, you know yourself, Dad would never allow it. But if I'm on my own, if I'm not asking anything from him, there's nothing much he *can* say. I'm much older than I ought to be already, to be starting college. A couple of more years can't make any difference."

"And would you live at the university?" C.B. asked.

"Oh, no. I couldn't afford that. I've got to find the job first and then find a room somewhere that's convenient." His heart ached as he said it.

"That's probably just as well, considering the sort you'd be thrown in with," C.B. said. "Fancy your having thought it through so far. I don't like the idea of a squalid little room somewhere. But the rest, how very exciting. You do delight me. Nobody can say I put you up to this. Well, we must plan. What do you intend to do if your father actually forbids it?"

"I don't see what people can do when they forbid something. I mean, he can't take me by the neck and shove me through the gates at West Point. He can cut me off without a penny, but I'm ready for that."

"I can see I've been nurturing a rebel in my bosom." She sparkled with mischief. "You're absolutely splendid. I suppose you've talked all this over with Charlie."

"Well, only a little. All the stuff from Columbia just came this morning. We've been going over it this afternoon."

"And all this time, I've been thinking of it as a lost cause. Of course, one thing springs to mind. I'm not one to meddle, but would you consider sharing the apartment with Charlie or would that be inconvenient? It's tiny, but men seem to manage. Needless to say, it's entirely Charlie's decision."

Peter choked and was seized by a tremendous fit of coughing. Charlie shifted violently in his chair and almost knocked over his glass of iced tea. He didn't dare look at Peter for fear he wouldn't be able to keep a straight face. He looked at the wall and when he was sure he had himself in hand he looked at C.B. She was looking anxiously at Peter.

"Are you all right, my darling?" she asked. He nodded. His face was scarlet.

"I guess it's a possibility," Charlie said judiciously. "Well, sure. I guess it's all right with me. If Peter doesn't mind sleeping on that sofa thing that turns into a bed."

"How very good of you. I must say I'd feel better about this whole scheme if you could look after him. You've become such good friends." She turned to Peter. "What do you think, my dear?"

He roared with laughter. Tears glistened in his eyes. "I don't mind anything," he said when he could speak. "It'd be wonderful."

Charlie caught his eyes in a neutral stare, warning him not to overdo it. C.B. beamed at both of them.

"How delightful. You make me feel as if I'd contributed in a small way, though I'm sure you'd have thought of it for yourselves once you began to really examine the possibilities."

"Then you mean it's all right?" Peter demanded breathlessly. "You approve of the whole idea?"

"Approve? It's far from perfect, but I see what you mean. The General could make it rather disagreeable for you if it were obvious that you were getting help. I'm inclined to think of it as making the best of an unfortunate situation. At least it's a start. We'll see what it leads to. Next year, you'll be twenty-one and then perhaps I'll step in. You're not the first person to have to work for his education. I suppose some people would even say it's good for you, although I've never believed in putting obstacles in the way of the young. I should have taken charge of you long ago, but I wasn't allowed to see as much of you as I wanted."

"Dad probably thought you'd spoil me."

"And so I should have. If one doesn't spoil the young, who *is* one to spoil?" They all laughed.

"I'll write tomorrow and resign my appointment," Peter said, seeming to age visibly as his happy confusion passed and he faced realities. "I'd better write Mother so she can sort of break it to Dad. He'll probably have a firing squad waiting for me when I get home."

"I'll write to her too," C.B. promised. "I know she'll understand, but she'll have to cope with the General. Poor thing. She's used to it."

"You're so wonderful, C.B.," Peter declared with conviction. "I didn't believe you'd be actually against it, but it's so wonderful to know that you think it makes some sense."

"I'm inclined to think there's a great deal of sense in that lovely head, my darling. You can depend on me to help out whenever you need it. I must admit, I've always rather looked forward to seeing the General meet his Waterloo."

Peter rocked with laughter. "You're absolutely wonderful."

They spent a cheerful evening discussing the courses Peter would take, the sort of job he might find. Charlie was careful to stay more or less out of it, imagining the circumstances if Peter had been simply Peter, C.B.'s latest acquisition, and acting accordingly. When C.B. finally released them, Peter raced to the top of the stairs and waited for him. He seized him and pummeled his back.

"Oh, darling. Oh, *darling,*" he exclaimed in a whisper. "It's fantastic. I couldn't believe my ears. You're right. She's really wonderful. And you were so funny just sitting there as if it didn't really matter to you."

"I told you it would be all right."

"Yes, you did." He dropped his hands to Charlie's crotch and gathered up the sex and did his animal growl. "I'm never going to worry about anything again. We're together. It's fate. There's nothing anybody can do about it."

Charlie took him by the scruff of the neck and led him into the room and closed the door. "There. We can talk. I'm sorry I had to put on that act. I thought it was better that way. You know how happy I am too, don't you?"

"Of course, darling. I just couldn't hide it as well as you did. Darling, darling, darling, dearest. There. Those are some of the words I didn't say all evening. Do you really have a sofa that turns into a bed?"

Charlie laughed. "Sure. I had it at Princeton. I've sent all my stuff from Princeton to New York."

"What about your real bed?"

"It's big enough for us," he said, smiling into Peter's anxious eyes.

"Thank goodness. You made it sound so convincing that I thought I really was going to have to sleep on the sofa. It was the one thing that worried me. I wish we could take this bed with us. I'll never forget it. It's the best bed ever."

Charlie laughed and reached out to him and began unbuttoning his shirt. "Let's avail ourselves of its hospitality."

THE ETERNITY OF SUMMER had suddenly shrunk to barely a month, which still seemed eternity enough. Neither of them could imagine an end to the golden days and the enthralling nights.

Charlie would have forgotten about the self-portrait, but Peter insisted on it. It required some intricate timing and they laughed a lot while he was doing it, but he managed a drawing in which all the elements were pulled together and balanced by the imposing sex. Charlie knew it wasn't as good as the things he was doing of Peter, but Peter was enraptured by it.

"On paper, it really doesn't look possible. Only, I know it's true. Can you mount it somehow so it won't get damaged? I can hardly frame it and hang it on the wall."

Charlie made a cardboard cover for it and Peter hid it away among the discarded clothes in his locked suitcase. Charlie was equally careful with the growing pile of his studies of Peter. He chose as his hiding place the bottom of a drawer filled with mothballs and some of his old winter clothes.

By chance, he went to the drawer one morning to see if one of the sketches he had done the day before was as good as he thought it was. He pulled it open and started to reach in and remained with his hands arrested before him, paralyzed. One end of the sheaf of drawings was exposed. He knew he couldn't have left them that way; he was always careful to cover them completely. His scalp tightened and his mouth went dry and his hands felt numb. Somebody had been looking at them.

He managed to force his body to function once more and reached in and pulled them out. Here was incontrovertible evidence of his passion for Peter expressed in anatomical detail. His heart began to race and there was a roaring in his ears. His mind began to hammer at him that it couldn't have been C.B. She couldn't have looked at them. C.B. had too much respect for his privacy. It was the sort of thing that might happen at home; his mother was always looming up silently in his room, hovering over him, opening his letters by mistake. Not C.B. Never C.B. But if somebody had seen them and described them to her, the disaster was just as complete. What if

Rosie — what would a simple woman like Rosie make of them? His mind was trained to react quickly in perilous circumstances, and it immediately began to fabricate a story that would cover him. He began to fill in details, discarding some, substituting others. It was reasonable. It would stand up to interrogation. He invented dialogue for Rosie and tested his story against it. He had taken all contingencies into account.

He went through the drawings with fingers that still fumbled uncontrollably and made a selection of six or eight in which Peter's sex was not shown or only faintly hinted at. He pushed the rest back under the clothes and carefully covered them and closed the drawer. He wanted more time to think, but he knew it had to be done now; there was no time to lose. He hurried for the door. Peter was entering as he went out.

"Wait. I'll be right back," he said as he brushed past him. He ran down the stairs and found C.B. in the gloomy living room sitting at her desk writing letters. He went over to her, holding the drawings conspicuously under his arm.

"Have you seen Peter? It's about time to go to the beach." His voice was working right. It sounded perfectly natural.

She hastily removed the pince-nez she wore for writing and looked up at him. "I thought he went up with you. What have you there? More drawings?"

"What? Oh, yes." He looked at them as if he had forgotten he was carrying them. It was an accomplished performance. "Some things I've been doing of Peter. It's good practice and he's a damn good model. Life-class stuff. Want to look at them?" The muscles of his arms seemed to lock as he offered them, but he had to get through this step if he was to achieve his purpose.

"I'd love to, my dearest." She took them and put them in front of her. "Lovely. Lovely. Brilliant," she commented as she turned them over. "You're right. He's a splendid model. You're getting better every day, my dearest."

Seeing them spread out in front of her, exposed to her gaze, made his head roar again. There was nothing wrong with them, he told himself desperately. Everybody knew that men thought nothing of being naked together. His heart seemed to have crowded into his stomach. His entrails heaved. He felt as if his whole body would collapse under the iron control he was exerting over it. All his muscles were engaged; he had to say the next part easily and lightly. "It's a funny thing. I have a bunch of drawings upstairs that a girl gave me who was at that life class I went to a couple of years ago. They're — it's hard to describe. They're not improper or anything, but she always got things a little wrong. The proportions are distorted. The general impression is sort of weird. The thing is, somebody's had them out."

"Really?" she sat back and looked up at him. He was watching her closely. The slightest oddity in her expression would be capable of demolishing his control. He met her gaze and prayed he could survive this moment. She looked only mildly interested.

He managed to make his shoulders shrug. "It doesn't matter. I'd practically forgotten I had them. They were shoved in with some old sweaters and things. I found they'd been moved the other day." His mind raced. Was that an error? Would Rosie report that she had found them yesterday evening? It couldn't matter.

"Perhaps Peter ran across them."

"No. He'd never look in those drawers. Never mind. I wouldn't have kept them, but it seemed wrong somehow to just throw them away."

"Yes, rather cruel with somebody else's work, although I've never been convinced of the propriety of a girl working with a nude male model. I suppose one of the darkies thought she ought to turn out your drawers. I think Rosie is inclined to be a bit of a snooper."

She hadn't indicated by the faintest twitch of a muscle that she was in any way upset or even curious. If she had heard anything, she must have found his story convincing. If a report were brought to her now, she would be prepared to dismiss it.

"Well, I might as well go find Peter." He gathered up the drawings and made his departure, revealing nothing of what was going on inside him. His pace accelerated as he left the room. He made it to the foot of the stairs. He stumbled against the newel post and gripped it. He thought he was going to vomit. He breathed deeply and waited for the heaving of his stomach to pass. Never, never, never, his mind repeated. He could never allow her to have the faintest suspicion of the things that had taken place upstairs. If there was ever even a possibility of her discovering them, Peter would have to go. He couldn't bear the thought of her catching him in an impure act, let alone an abnormal one. He must always remain her ideal, for his sake as well as for hers. As his strength returned, he found himself trying to think of an absolutely secure hiding place. If he couldn't find one, the drawings would have to be destroyed. At last, he was able to mount the stairs.

As he recovered, he was able to assure himself that he had got through it quite successfully, but something still gnawed at the back of his mind, some wrong note, something that didn't quite fit. He was halfway up the stairway when it struck him. He put his hand out to the railing for support as his legs failed him again. She had talked about nude male models. How had she known? He hadn't said anything about male nudes. All of his body began to react once more while he insisted to himself that she couldn't have kept such a straight face if she really knew anything. The drawings of Peter had been spread out in front of her; it was a normal association of ideas. That was the only possible explanation. His legs steadied under him, he took a few deep breaths and continued up to the top floor.

After consultation with Peter, he gathered together all the drawings and locked them up with the one of himself in Peter's suitcase, which in turn they locked up in a cupboard in the guest bathroom Peter rarely used. Sketching was permanently abandoned.

T IME WORE AWAY their remaining days. Soon, they could no longer talk of "almost a month." It was weeks, and when there were no longer fourteen full days, they lost the comfort of the plural.

They stopped at the drugstore in the village one day to let Peter buy some toothpaste. When he came out and they had started off, Peter asked, "Darling, why do so many people refer to you as C.B.'s nephew? Mr. Haines just did."

Charlie had always been aware of this deception of C.B.'s and had accepted it as harmless coquetry but it embarrassed him to have to explain it to Peter. It made him feel ashamed for her. He shrugged. "Oh, it's just an old misunderstanding. She doesn't bother to set people straight."

"It's a lie, really, when she doesn't. It's hard to think of C.B. lying."

"She doesn't, in any real way. She couldn't possibly. It's against everything she believes in."

"I know." He remained silent for a thoughtful moment and then shifted in his seat, underlining a shift of mood. "Do you realize how many days it is today? I don't see how I'm going to stand it. If only

I could just stay and then we could all go to New York together."

"You insist on having birthdays. C.B. promised you'd be home for it and things are tense enough already with your family. She couldn't let you stay. It'll only be three weeks."

"Three weeks. Golly. I wish you hadn't told me that story about your football captain. You might as well be prepared for great gooey love letters every day. I'll try not to be too awful, but I've never written a love letter. They're apt to be wild. Please don't mind. You've got to write me, you know."

"Of course."

"Every day?"

"Twice a day if you want, baby."

"Oh, darling." He leaned forward and kissed the hand on the wheel.

"Stop it," Charlie warned roughly. "People might see."

Peter drew back quickly. "OK. We're not going to be apart for three weeks. Everything's lovely. There's just going to be a sort of a little blank in there somewhere and then we'll be in New York together."

All their talk was of New York now, the apartment, furniture, whom they would see, what they would do. Peter resolutely limited his references to the impending separation, and Charlie was grateful to him for it. He had dreaded a succession of increasingly tearful scenes. The days sped by, spent almost exclusively in each other's company. Suddenly, Peter's departure was upon them.

T HE LAST NIGHT BEGAN very much like their first. They were unable to sleep, unable to leave each other alone, unable to have enough of each other. Sometime during the night, Peter said, "There's just one thing I ask of you. Please God, take care of yourself. Don't let anything happen to you. That's all. I'm not going to talk about it anymore. You're my life. You know that."

Charlie suddenly rolled over onto his stomach and was seized by madness. He bit the pillow and pounded it with his fists. He was making a strange noise in his throat. Startled, Peter stretched out beside him and put an arm around his shoulders.

"Oh, darling. Please," he begged as the strange seizure continued. "What is it?"

Charlie's head lifted and swung from side to side. "I can't stand it," he cried in a strangled voice. "I don't want you to go."

"Oh, darling." Peter nuzzled his neck. He was immediately close to tears. "How do you think I feel? I've done my best not to show it."

"I just can't stand it," Charlie cried again. He butted his head into the pillow and his fists flailed. His whole body was shaking so violently that Peter flung a leg over his to quiet him. The strange whimpering noise rose in Charlie's throat.

Peter hugged him closer. "Please, darling. Don't. It's the same for me. God, how wonderful. Please, my dearest." Responding to the urging of their bodies and the pressure of Charlie's hands, Peter found himself on top of him, belly down, sprawled on Charlie's back. His sex was cradled in the cleft between Charlie's buttocks, his arms were locked around his heaving shoulders. The buttocks were working, trying to grip Peter's sex. Then a feverish hand was on him, spreading lubricant between them, seizing his sex, guiding it. As Peter realized what was happening, he was torn by a great cry. "Oh, God. It's not possible. I can't," he sobbed. He felt his sex entering the beloved body, sliding deeper into it. Charlie's hips lifted, and Peter's body lunged forward in total penetration. He uttered a hoarse shout.

"Oh Christ! I don't believe it. Jesus Christ! Please." Gripped by instinct, incapable of thought, he performed a few long experimental thrusts, stunned at the power they generated in him, and then he felt himself beginning to dissolve in an orgasm. He fought it. His hands were tangled in Charlie's hair, his teeth clamped on his shoulder. The wave mounted and crashed over him. He felt himself bursting into Charlie, all of himself streaming into him in great demolishing jets. Charlie's hips heaved, his hands gripped Peter's buttocks, drawing them to him. Their bodies leaped and writhed in unison. When Peter finally relaxed his grip on Charlie's hair and their breathing was more normal, he let his whole weight flow over Charlie's body. Even as he had performed the act he had felt something basically alien in it, but the thrill of it had filled him with intimations of an exuberant mastery of life unlike anything he had ever known.

"That's really it," Charlie said at last. He seemed to speak out of a deep peace. "That's all of it. You've got to come back to me. We're all one now."

"If it never happens again," Peter murmured, "it's — well, if it's at all the same for you, I want you to fuck me more than ever, always. I'm beginning to understand things, darling. All to do with making you happy."

"You do. So beautifully. It's incredible to feel you inside me. You'd better let me up, my sweetheart."

Peter pulled away with a moan and rolled over onto his back. Charlie's hand was immediately on his chest.

"Don't move. Just lie there. I'll take care of everything."

He leaped up and was gone. He returned with washcloth and towel and tended Peter, who appeared to be dozing. When he was finishing, he felt Peter's eyes on him. He looked up and his lips parted to take a quick breath at the unabashed love he saw in their limitless depths. Peter rolled his head slowly back and forth.

"You've given me everything. I thought I was doing fine an hour ago, but I didn't even exist."

"We're all one, darling," Charlie repeated gently. "Come on. You've got to wash. I came all over the place. I've got to change the sheets."

"I know. I'm lying in it. I don't want to wash it off."

"Come on, my baby. We'll take a shower together. It'll be all right if we wash it off together."

Somehow, they managed to dress when morning came. They exchanged a long kiss at the door and were almost back in bed together. Peter broke away. "I know. We've got to stop. I'm not going to be able to look at you again, so — so long. Be seeing you." He hurried out of the room.

Somehow, they were able to face C.B. over breakfast, they were all in the car, they reached the station, the train pulled in, Peter was gone.

"We're going to miss him," C.B. said in the car on the way home. "However, I will enjoy having these last few weeks just with you." She took Charlie's hand and lifted it to her lips.

Dazed, bereft, he snatched it from her. "Look out. Somebody might see us," he warned.

She looked at him with astonishment and then burst into youthful laughter. "Why, you act as if we were a courting couple."

His face was burning. There was nothing he could say that wouldn't make it worse. He managed brief laughter. "That was pretty silly," he said. He returned his hand to her, and she gathered it to her bosom so that his slightest movement would have become an unwanted intimacy.

Soon AFTER LUNCH, telling himself that he might as well get the first letter over with, Charlie wrote to Peter:

Peter — baby—
It somehow just doesn't make sense writing it.
At lunch, C.B. said, "What an utter charmer. I'm going to miss him. How nice to think we'll all be together again so soon in New York." She took the words out of my mouth, except that I might have expressed it a bit more strongly.
·The house seems very strange without you. I don't think I'll spend much time in it for the rest of my time here. I guess I'll go over to the club in a little while and sit around. How exciting. I'm looking forward so much to New York that maybe I can get through the next few weeks in a trance. I'm not looking forward to tonight. I've never been really drunk. Maybe I'll bring a bottle up here and try it.
I'm dying to hear how everything is there and how your plans have been received and everything. I know nobody can change your mind so I'm not really worried. Don't forget to try to get a rug from your mother. We really need one.
I've been through the drawings before I locked them up for good and picked out the most prim and proper one and I've pinned it up near the foot of the bed where I can see it from everywhere. It's not the one I'd like to put up, as you can imagine. I'm looking at it now. To an expert eye, it's not really all that prim and proper because it keeps moving.
I'll keep you posted about everything here, but I don't suppose there will be much to tell you. I'm discovering that being in love isn't all fun. I'd better not write any more now. God, last night was wonderful, except for thinking about today. Write soon,
                                        Your champ

Charlie's letter crossed Peter's first:

My love—
I could go on saying that about nine hundred and seventy-six times, but I guess it might get monotonous for you. It's worse than anything I imagined. I've been without you

for one night and it's absolute torture, it seems like six months already. I haven't done myself for years, old Late-Starter Pete, but I sit around thinking about you and you've seen often enough what that does to me. So I have to do something about it and it's awful and such a waste because you're not here.

I know one thing. You've taught me how to laugh. It's amazing. I go around roaring like a hyena, and my dismal little brothers and sisters think Big Brother has finally lost his marbles.

I thought the picture was going to be such a big help, but every time I try to look at it I start bawling my head off so I've had to lock it up again. I don't guess I'm making much sense, laughing one minute and crying the next, but that's the way it is. I think about your football captain and it scares me so. It really did happen to us, didn't it, my darling, my dearest, my big lover? It isn't something that we're just going to build up in our minds and then find out it's no good? You've got to tell me it can't be like that. I keep thinking maybe I shouldn't write you at all, I shouldn't even think about you — ha ha — and then when we're together again it would be as if we hadn't been apart at all. Don't you dare think anything like that. I'll die if I don't hear from you all the time. Maybe it'll be better when I actually have a letter from you.

It seems my father isn't speaking to me. I'm allowed in the house just to humor my mother, and the sooner I leave the better. So I've Sacrificed All for Love. Thank Goodness. Mother is really being very decent about it. She says she has a rug we can have. Also some fairly lousy silverware. I'll bring it for the servants.

How is this for a love letter? It turns out that a love letter is just saying what you think to someone you love. I love you more than anybody has ever loved anybody ever. I'm thinking about your cock and having it inside me. I'm thinking about you having my cock in your mouth. I wish we could do both at once. That would be something. I don't even dare think about night before last, because it was too incredible. I want you all inside me and me inside you so we couldn't tell where one of us began or ended. I want you so, it kills me. I want you to call me baby. I'm not going to sign this so you'll have to guess who it's from.

From HERE ON, memory grows erratic. The past is people moving against a vague background of events. The physical background comes in flashes: sunlight filtering through trees, surf breaking on a beach; that was at the beginning, then dirty snow piled up in a city street, a bar, a room. Was somebody running for President? Was there a war on? Well, yes, a World War broke out in Europe about this time, but we scarcely noticed it. That would come later. What was running on Broadway? What courses did Peter take? When did the draft start? How long did Charlie work for the publishing house? I don't remember. I could look it all up, but it doesn't matter; let the anachronisms fall where they may. The people are there, impervious to time, passionately acting out their lives while the world moves dimly around them. A short stretch of dirty New York street on a hot September afternoon fills the mind's eye.

Peter arrived ahead of time. He stood beside the entrance to a dingy medical appliance shop, two battered bags and a roll of carpet at his feet. At his right, the marquee of El Morocco stretched out to the curb, looking astonishingly shabby in the harsh afternoon light. Peter's face was drawn and anxious. His wide eyes scanned every approaching pedestrian and flew from taxi to taxi as they roared toward him from Lexington Avenue. He kept looking at his watch and chewing the knuckle of his forefinger. He had been standing there for fourteen minutes when a taxi swerved in to the curb and stopped in front of him. He was so busy covering all approaches that it took him an instant to see Charlie climbing out of it. Their eyes met, they exchanged a smile, and then Charlie was busy extracting luggage from the cab and paying the driver. Peter didn't know whether to shout, or to leap in the air, or to burst into tears. He was trembling violently all over. The taxi pulled away, leaving Charlie standing in a small island of luggage.

"Hi. Will you help me with this junk?"

Peter lurched toward him and grabbed the two biggest suitcases and dragged them across the sidewalk to his. Charlie followed with the rest. He dropped it all together and took out a key and opened the door beside the entrance to the truss shop. It was on a spring and they propped it open with a bag as they trundled everything into the hall. Charlie went past the staircase to the back of the hall and opened another door.

"It's back here," he said. Peter grabbed luggage again and rushed it all back. Charlie helped and, when it was all in, closed the door behind them. Peter flung himself on him and crowded him back against the door and covered his face with kisses. He was still trembling from head to foot and uttered odd little noises. Charlie held him tight for a moment and then eased him away and chuckled. "Take it easy, baby. Somebody's supposed to be here any minute to do something about the stove."

Peter took a grip on himself and let him go. The worst was perhaps over. "Never again," he said. "I was just barely able to get through it. From now on, I'm not budging. You're just as beautiful as ever. I didn't imagine that."

Charlie put his hand on his shoulder and gave it a careless squeeze. "Come on. Don't you want to see our nest?" They were standing in a narrow entrance hall. Ahead of them a door gave into what appeared to be a fairly spacious kitchen. He gave Peter's shoulder a little push, and they entered a room to the right. Furniture was set aimlessly about in it, some of it still wrapped in brown paper. At one end were two windows that opened onto a tree in a littered yard. At the other end, there was an arched area that was big for an alcove but small for a room. It was very hot and smelled of fresh paint.

"This is it," Peter said wonderingly. "We're going to live here. I mean, golly, this is life."

"We've got to decide where everything goes. I wanted to get it all ready for you, but the lease only started yesterday. The furniture's just arrived."

Peter wasn't interested in the furniture. "Tell me things," he said. "What's it been like for you?"

"Oh, lord, I've missed you, but that's all over. We've got work to do. Let's get these windows open."

Peter moved obediently to a window. The sense of momentousness that he felt should belong to the occasion was definitely missing. His heart contracted. The barely suppressed fears crowded in on him from their precarious confinement. He lifted the heavy sash with numb fingers. Hot air stirred around him.

87

"I've just come from C.B.," Charlie said from the other window. "She expects us for dinner tonight. She's dying to see you."

It was a bitter blow, but Peter wasn't surprised. As much as he wanted to see C.B., he had been looking forward longingly to their first meal together in their own place. Naturally, C.B. took precedence. The realization of a dream could be postponed. He said nothing.

"You have an appointment tomorrow with some man about a job," Charlie went on. "I really start work tomorrow, too. I've been in a couple of times already. It's going to be all right, I guess."

The glory was dimming minute by minute. They were together again, yet Charlie's manner contained no hint of the momentous experiences they had shared. It couldn't be like this. Charlie moved out into the middle of the small room. Peter couldn't look at him.

"Now then. Where shall we begin?" A bell rang and Charlie went out into the hall and pushed a button. Peter heard the door open.

"Come about the stove," a rough voice said. "Where's the missus?"

"There isn't any missus," Charlie said. "The stove's in there." Charlie came back into the room and they wandered about, fingering the furniture. There was an occasional bang from the kitchen. In a few minutes, the man appeared in the doorway.

"She's fixed. A couple of guys, huh? Well, it's happening all over. Sweet." He leered grotesquely and lumbered out.

"The son of a—" Charlie exclaimed and strode into the hall and slammed the door. He reappeared looking indignant.

Peter stood without moving, slackly, close to tears. That was all that had been needed to finish things off. "All right. You might as well tell me," he said. "What's wrong?"

"Well, that son of a bitch—"

"I don't care about him. I mean everything. I tried not to build it up in my mind. I couldn't, really. It was so big to start with. What's gone wrong?"

"Gone wrong? What are you talking about? Oh, for God's sake." He laughed with a touch of exasperation. "Are you thinking of Eddie again? I've told you, it wasn't anything like it is with us. We were all set before you left. It hasn't changed."

"Hasn't it? Do you really mean that?"

"Oh, baby." Charlie went to him and put his hand under his

chin and kissed him on the mouth. "Darling baby. No, it hasn't." Peter took a long, gasping breath and shook his head. "I'm sorry. I'm a dope." He threw his head back and laughed. "You see? That's my hyena laugh. Isn't it frightening?" He put his hands on Charlie's crotch and held the sex and growled. "That's what I wanted. What've I been waiting for? I was so bowled over seeing you that I didn't know what I was doing. I guess all I could think about was piling into bed with you. It was sort of a shock discovering there wasn't any bed to pile into."

Charlie put his hands over Peter's and pressed them to him. "Wait till tonight, baby." They smiled into each other's eyes. A little thrill of anticipation ran down Peter's spine. The sex was heavy in his hands.

"Yes. Well, then, let's get this place in operating order." They threw off their jackets and ties. Peter laughed again for no particular reason. His spirits lifted, the strains and terrors of separation receded into the background of his memory. They pushed furniture around. It was all solid, some of it handsome, the rest serviceable.

They placed Peter's rug. As they went about their chores, they kissed frequently and put their hands on each other. Peter worked fast, hoping that there would be some time to spare at the end of the afternoon, but they were still at it past the hour when they should have been getting ready for C.B. They showered hurriedly, catching glimpses of each other's bodies as they passed back and forth to the bathroom, but not daring to pause for fear of missing dinner entirely. They pulled on their clothes and permitted themselves a parting kiss. Peter took a final glance at the bed, now in place and ready, before they went out. It was getting cooler. They crossed over to Park Avenue and walked uptown in the glittering night. Peter was inclined to take Charlie's arm at crossings, but Charlie shook him off.

"We've got to be careful. You saw what happened this afternoon."

Peter couldn't see that it made any difference in this anonymous city, but he complied. He felt blissfully alone with his love, eager to proclaim the joy they shared, but keyed up by the presence of people.

They were admitted to C.B.'s apartment by an unknown Negro. After the impersonal opulence of the building, it was like stepping into another age and another country. Here, all was old and burnished and delicate, creating an immediate atmosphere of grace and ease. C.B. was waiting for them in a large living room that looked as if it ought to give onto tree-shaded lawns. She flew to Peter and enveloped him in silks and lace as she embraced him extravagantly and kissed him. Diamonds scratched him. She held him at arm's length and welcomed him ecstatically.

"My darling. Darling Peter. At last. We've longed for you so. We've talked of nothing else for three weeks. You've captured both our hearts. How incomplete we'd have been if things hadn't turned out this way."

Peter quite forgot his disappointment about dinner in the intoxicating warmth of her greeting. She pattered off to the bar cabinet, chatting all the while.

"I've made a special reunion drink for us. We have so much to talk about. You have an appointment with Bryan Wilcox tomorrow. He's the head of the firm and doesn't generally interview applicants for messenger boy, but he's very much interested in you. Poor darling. It doesn't sound very glamorous, but it's a start. At least you'll have a little place of your own to go home to, and Charlie to discover New York with. You've seen the place. It's absurdly small, but you'll be happy together. Whenever I begin to worry about you, I remind myself that anything is better than West Point. Don't you look smart in city clothes! And you haven't lost any of that glorious summer tan. I want you to come here whenever you're at a loose end. You'll meet interesting and attractive people. When you have your job settled, we'll see if you need a little extra pocket money. I think we'll have a splendid winter. Well, here's to all of us, my darling, my dearest. I am so fortunate to have you both."

The evening passed with swift gaiety. When they were once more in the street, Peter's feet were ready to race for home.

"Let's stop somewhere and have a drink," Charlie suggested, sounding very adult to Peter.

"Oh, OK. Do you think they'll serve me?"

"Of course. You look as old as me, and I haven't had any trouble for over a year."

They crossed back to Lexington and went into the first bar they came to. Peter ordered a beer, Charlie a whiskey. Despite Peter's hunger for them to be alone, the small occasion confirmed them as inhabitants of the city. They could walk into a bar, the night was theirs to dispose of as they wished, they were their own masters.

"She's amazing," Peter said, thinking over the evening. "You know, the things she says, you'd swear sometimes she knows all about us."

Charlie's eyes flashed to him. "Don't ever think that." He enunciated each word with emphasis.

"Oh, I know. If she really knew, she probably wouldn't be so open about it. Still, I love it. It makes you feel as if she's on our side."

"Time to go home," Charlie said as he finished his whiskey.

Peter laughed softly and struck his forehead with his fist. "I just can't believe it. Time to go home. Just you and me. It's absolutely incredible."

Charlie started to pay, but Peter intervened. "Please. Let me. I've never bought you a drink. I've never bought you anything. I'm going to get rich and buy you thousands of things." He paid, feeling very adult in his turn, and they went on their way.

When they reached the truss shop, Peter moved ahead. He had his own set of keys, and he pulled them out proudly. "You did it the first time. It's my turn now."

He unlocked the outer door and stood back to let Charlie pass and then ran ahead and unlocked their own door. "Isn't that something," he said as he closed the door behind them. They switched on lamps, and the room sprang up around them. It looked settled and comfortable and snug. Peter moved in close beside Charlie and put his arm around his waist and hugged him. "It's beautiful. I don't know what I've done to deserve this. Aren't you sort of stunned?"

Charlie laughed. "A bit, I guess. And yet it seems so natural, somehow. I keep thinking what it would've been like if I'd been doing all this alone. I don't see how I ever could've thought of it."

Peter hugged him again and turned shining eyes to his. "That's nice. Of course, it's different for me. It's all just happening out of the blue. I feel sort of as if I were just being born."

"You make a fine bouncing baby."

They laughed, and Peter moved around to face him and held him close and kissed his mouth, astonished by the taste of whiskey. Charlie put his hands in his hair and pushed him away. "For God's sake, let's get out of these clothes."

They flung clothes from themselves and Charlie ran to the bathroom and returned with towels and the tube of lubricant.

"Oh, oh, oh, oh," Peter murmured, his eyes fixed on Charlie's swaying sex. Then they were in bed, tangled with each other, their mouths open to each other, their hands searching avidly for the loved, remembered places. When the first urgency had passed, Charlie slid down over Peter's body and took his sex in his mouth and welcomed it. Then he lifted himself to his knees between Peter's legs and sat back on his heels. They smiled softly at each other. Peter's lips moved in some unknown prayer or song of praise.

"Give me the stuff," Charlie said. Peter did so and started to roll over onto his stomach. Charlie stopped him with a hand on his thigh. "No," he said. He applied the lubricant to them both.

"What are we going to do?" Peter asked, his eyes adoring and puzzled.

"I've been thinking about you." Charlie pulled him toward him and lifted his legs and put them over his shoulders. He guided his sex with his hand and entered him. He slowly worked the hips closer to him. When they were completely coupled, he bent over and took Peter's sex in his mouth.

"Oh my God," Peter moaned. He flung his arms out and clawed the sheet with his fingers. He lifted his hands and covered his eyes. He reached out and put his hands on Charlie's face and felt for his sex where it entered Charlie's mouth. "Oh my God. Oh my GOD," he shouted, as his body thrashed about in the grip of orgasm. Charlie waited until he had received it and then he straightened and threw back his head and in an instant reached his own climax with a joyful cry. He toppled over onto Peter's willing body.

They lay, one on top of the other, breathing heavily, still loosely linked. Peter bore with rapture the whole warm abandoned weight of his love, his own body lifting to melt into Charlie's. He felt consumed, absorbed, penetrated, possessed beyond the possibility of his own identity's survival. It was an oblivion he had sought and dreamed of. When he was finally able to speak, he said, "You make the bad times so wonderful. I could've stayed away from you for six months for that. Well, not really. Nothing can make up for even one day without you, but you get the general idea."

"You said you wanted it. I was pretty sure it would work. It probably wouldn't with most people. It's because your beautiful cock is just the right size."

"I never really cared before, but now — thank God. Thank God for every inch of it."

92

THE NEXT DAY, Peter was given a job. He became a runner on Wall Street, but he was placed under the protective eye of the head of the firm and there was talk of advancement as his studies progressed. His hours were short because of his classes at Columbia, and his pay was proportionately short, too. Peter didn't mind; he hadn't the slightest idea what money was for. He had time in the afternoon to shop, clean the apartment, and get dinner started before Charlie came home. Peter kept careful accounts and scrupulously paid his share. He loved keeping house for Charlie. It was understood that the rent was Charlie's responsibility. Sometimes, when they were feeling particularly grown-up, they had a drink before dinner, but neither of them very much wanted it. Then there were the long glorious evenings.

It was quickly established that Sunday was more or less reserved for C.B. They slept late and made love luxuriously all through the midday, but by late afternoon they were handsomely dressed and ready. She conducted a sort of salon in the big living room, which evoked generations of moneyed permanence rather than the smart, showy instability of the city. She presided, a shade too grandly to promote casual informality, too intelligently to permit boredom, over selected gatherings of young professional men, with an occasional female attachment. The drinks were neither notably good nor plentiful, but the young men came, handsome and well dressed, publishers, journalists, an exceptionally favored actor, a Congressman's executive assistant, sometimes the Congressman himself and his wife, some out of a sense of sharing in a more gracious past, more out of real devotion and sometimes gratitude to C.B. There were never more than six or eight at a time, so good talk was the rule. Peter found these occasions rather awesome and confining and didn't shine. He and Charlie usually stayed on for dinner, but this was never taken for granted. Invitations were duly issued in advance. They both dropped in on her at odd moments during the week when she could be irresistibly playful and winning. This was the way Peter preferred her. Charlie lent himself wholeheartedly to the Sunday ritual.

It was very nearly the married life that Peter had looked forward to, but there were flies in the ointment. Charlie announced one evening that he had been obliged to accept a dinner invitation from one of his superiors for the next day.

"It seems it's a great honor when they invite you. It's more or less part of the job to go. It's their way of grooming you for promotion. I think that's what they call it."

"That's great. It's important for you."

"Not really. I'm not going to be there indefinitely. In another week or so, when we're finally settled and you've started night school, I'm going to start calling people about the theater."

"That'll be really exciting."

Peter considered filling the empty evening by calling the Congressman's executive assistant who had given him his card and asked him to do so, but decided against it. He was pretty sure he knew what the Congressman's executive assistant had in mind.

T HEN CLASSES STARTED, and everything changed. There were no more dinners with Charlie, no more long evenings. He had just time to give Charlie a welcoming kiss when he returned from work, and then he had to be on his way. More and more frequently, Charlie didn't come home to receive it. When Peter got home, Charlie was sometimes asleep, sometimes not there. On the latter occasions, he would sit with a textbook propped in front of him, struggling against sleep, frequently losing the battle. Charlie would help him fumble his way into bed. When he automatically initiated the gestures of love, Charlie would kiss him and hug him and say, "We're tired, baby. We'd better go to sleep."

Whenever there was time, Charlie told him all about his doings, the Princeton classmates he had encountered, the senior editor and his wife with whom he was becoming real friends, the important theatrical director who had preceded him at Princeton and the agent who had seen him there, both of whom held out hopes for the immediate future. There was mention of a girl called Hattie he had met somewhere. There was another mention of her, and another. Hattie became a presence.

"Listen, baby," Charlie said one evening as he was coming in and Peter was going out. "I'd like you to stay away tonight until eleven-thirty."

"Stay away?"

"Yes, not come home. It's only an extra hour or so. Hattie

wanted to come over and cook dinner here tonight. It's better if you're not around. I don't want her to get any ideas about us."

"You mean, she doesn't even know I exist?"

"Well, not exactly. There's just been no reason to mention it."

"Has she been here before?"

"Of course not. I'd have told you. She just got this idea she wanted to cook dinner for me. She lives with her family."

"Are you planning to do anything with her?"

"What do you mean?" He caught Peter's eye and added, "Certainly not."

"I don't care about anywhere else. But not here. I couldn't stand it."

"Oh, for God's sake. Stop being so damn morbid. You're going to be late."

Peter nodded distractedly and gathered up some books. Charlie grabbed him as he passed and kissed him. For an instant, all of Peter's body flowed to him, then he pulled himself back and left.

Shortly afterward, the bell rang and Charlie went to the door to admit Hattie Donaldson. She came whirling in with an armload of groceries. "Don't try to take them," she cried. "I'll drop them all. Where's the kitchen? Ah, here we are. It's all mostly from the delicatessen, but I'm going to do something delirious with the steaks."

"All that's supposed to be for two of us?"

"I never know how much to buy of anything. You can have the leftovers for breakfast. How about a drink for the cook?" She had a face of wondrous eccentricity. Her features included enormous, mocking, protuberant eyes, a nose like a blob of putty that looked as if it had been added as a facetious afterthought, and a wide mouth that filled her whole face when she laughed, which she did frequently — crowing laughter, conqueror's laughter, with a hint of warning. She was of average height, but very thin, all arms and legs attached to an angular skeleton. The Donaldsons, of whom there were many, were important in the cultural and philanthropic circles of the city. She had the supreme self-confidence of belonging, of having always moved in the centers of power. She dressed to accentuate the eccentricity of her looks, with fanciful hats and a great deal of jewelry. She unburdened herself now of an impressive collection of accessories: bag, hat, scarf, gloves, a couple of rings. "Strip for action. That's my motto. Do we eat in here?" she asked, indicating the kitchen table.

"Why not?" Peter always set up a card table in the living room, with candles and all the trimmings. The change of locale was appropriate. Peter would be pleased.

"I'll find everything. Out with you. I don't give away my secrets. One must guard one's assets." She crowed with laughter as he left her.

Listening to her clattering about in the kitchen, he realized that this was somehow the most intimate thing he'd ever done with a girl, more so even than a sexual exchange. Perhaps she would turn into "his" girl. He would be glad for a name to drop for C.B., and Donaldson was an impressive one. C.B. would be bound to find her above average, a manifestation of his cultivated tastes, even though being a girl would be a strike against her.

"You can come back now," she called after a reasonable interval. "How clever of you to live next to El Morocco," she said as he returned. "So convenient. Shall we go over after and dance?"

"Listen, I'm just a very junior editor making my way up in the world."

"I have money. That's no problem."

"Fine. As a matter of fact, I've never set foot in the place."

"Oh, you must. It's so awful. I love it. Wait till you see the palm trees. They're hysterical."

They sat down to foie gras and a bottle of wine, followed by the steaks, which involved mushrooms in some sort of sauce. After, there was asparagus with hollandaise and some exotic preserved peaches.

"It's fabulous," Charlie said, dazzled by the richness of the fare.

"Don't ask which is mine and which came out of cans. That's one of my secrets."

When they were finished, she asked, "Is there a drawing room? I think it's so important to have coffee in the drawing room. It's one of my principles."

"Of course. The drawing room awaits."

"I do hope you don't expect me to cope with all this," she said, looking suddenly helpless as she surveyed the littered kitchen.

Charlie laughed. "Certainly not. You've done more than enough already. It was wonderful. The servants will take over."

She brightened. "Lovely. Here. Take cups. Sugar. Coffee will be served in a moment."

96

When she had poured it, she surveyed the little room. "Nice. Ever so masculine. The bed's a bit conspicuous, isn't it? Shouldn't there be a discreet curtain?"

"I haven't been entertaining ladies much. I suppose you're right." She studied him for a moment with great mocking eyes. "I wonder why you haven't made a pass at me yet."

Charlie was taken aback, but managed not to show it. "Am I supposed to?"

"I'm a girl. I'm rather funny-looking, but all the bits and pieces are in the usual places. Men generally make passes at girls."

"And what do you generally do?" Charlie's sudden anger came out as cool sarcasm. "Tease them and lead them on and slap them down when it pleases you?"

"Oh, dear. Is that what girls have done to you? I suppose we all are the most terrible bitches." She laughed, but turned instantly sober. "Of course, I'm quite different. I'm an actress. Actresses *must* lead rich emotional lives."

She said this with such intensity that Charlie flung up the first defense that came to mind. "Actually, this isn't much of a place for making passes," he said loftily. "I have a roommate. He might come in at any moment."

Hattie's glance slid to the bed. "A roommate? In here?"

"He sleeps here," he said, indicating the sofa he was sitting on. He blushed and turned his face away, reaching for a cigarette. The business of lighting it gave him time to recover. "He's a cousin of mine. Just a kid working his way through college. It was C.B.'s idea."

"I think it's too glamorous, your being C.B.'s grandson. I'm dying to meet her. My family thinks she's mad."

"How so?" Charlie asked, pleased at having skirted the question of Peter so easily.

"Some story. I don't remember exactly. Something about her having practically kidnapped some young man. There was a frightful row with his family."

Charlie chuckled. "That sounds like C.B."

"Is she a lecherous old lady?"

"Good heavens no. She just likes to have young men around. She takes an interest in their careers and all that sort of thing."

"Sounds like sex to me. But nobody ever knows anything about their own family. If you'll let me meet her, I'll give you a complete report."

"Fine. Anytime you like. We always go on Sunday."

"Who's 'we'?"

Charlie blushed again. He cupped his chin in his hands, covering his cheeks. "Oh, the usual group. C.B.'s circle." She had an uncomfortable knack of crowding him into tight corners. He counterattacked. "How come you always call yourself an actress? You've never done anything."

"I've done heaps of things. I've just done eight weeks of summer stock."

"I mean professionally. Were you paid?"

"Hank Forbes thinks I'm great," she countered, referring to the distinguished director from Princeton who had promised to help Charlie.

"Hank thinks I'm pretty good too. That's something we have in common."

"Oh, you. You'll never be an actor. You're much too grand."

"Me? Grand?" he asked, laughing, not displeased with the epithet.

"You're frightfully grand. Otherworldly. Unattainable. You'd never communicate."

"That's not what Hank thinks. He says something may be coming up for me very soon."

"Oh well, Hank's probably after you. That's one of the problems a girl has to face in the theater."

"What's that supposed to mean? I can't imagine what you're talking about."

"You can't? Some imagination. I told you you'd never be an actor."

"You're ridiculous," he said with a dismissive shrug and she crowed over him. She was tough. She fought back. She wasn't all cute and coy like most girls. It was the thing that had first struck him when he met her. He felt a resilient comradeship growing up between them of a sort he had known before only with other males. Except for her lapse about passes, sex had been agreeably absent from their preliminary contacts and he had no wish for it to be otherwise.

"Did you mean it about going to El Morocco?" he asked.

"Of course. I was just waiting for your roommate to burst in on our illicit tryst."

Charlie glanced at his watch. It was not yet eleven. "I never know when he's apt to come in. We see very little of each other."

"But you say he sleeps there. I feel as if you'd been sitting on him for the last hour."

"Oh no. You'd have seen him. He's real enough."

"Is he?" She crowed over him again as she rose to prepare herself for the nightclub next door. When they parted later under El Morocco's marquee, gleaming expensively in artificial light, it had been agreed that she would attend C.B.'s gathering the following Sunday. She refused his offers to accompany her home. She was a working girl and rejected gallantries reserved for the weaker sex. Despite his insistence, Charlie approved this attitude. She wasn't going to be a nuisance. When he went back to the apartment, he found Peter, heavy-eyed, finishing up the dishes.

"Oh, lord, baby. You shouldn't have done that." He took a dishtowel out of his hands and kissed his ear. He felt guilty.

Peter offered him a wan smile of welcome. "I didn't mind. I wanted to wait up for you. It was one way of staying awake. It looked as if you had quite a meal."

"It was terrific. She's a good cook."

"Why did you eat in here?"

"She seemed satisfied. Nobody but you would take all that trouble with the card table. I told her about you."

Peter brightened and his eyes filled with pride. "Did you? I don't suppose it really mattered. I'm glad, anyway."

"Come on, baby. You're tired."

HATTIE TURNED UP at C.B.'s strangely bedizened, looking like a child dressed up in her mother's clothes. Her crowing laughter soared above all the others'. When she had identified Peter, she devoted a great deal of attention to him.

"I think one can safely say she's extraordinary," C.B. said over dinner with Charlie and Peter. "Not at all what one would expect of her family. They're unmitigated snobs, like all New Yorkers who have the incredible good fortune to know who their grandparents were."

"I like her," Peter said. "She makes me laugh just to look at her. Not in a bad way. She knows she's funny-looking and plays up to it. I thought she was marvelous."

Charlie said nothing, choosing silence as the most provocative course.

"She's a deep one," Hattie pronounced of C.B. when she met Charlie for lunch in a midtown restaurant a couple of days later. "That report will have to be postponed. There's only one thing I'm sure of. She's madly in love with you. But I'm beginning to think that's true of everybody. Me. Peter. You're having an affair with him, aren't you?"

"Me? An af— What in God's name are you talking about now?" he demanded, outraged and blushing furiously.

She gave him a mocking stare. "You do get strangely dense whenever it's a question of gentlemen climbing into bed together. It does happen, you know."

"I suppose it does. I've never thought about it. I don't know anything about it."

She laughed at him. "If I were a boy, I'd know *every*thing about it. It must be so deliciously easy. No fuss about babies and all. You do disappoint me. An affair with Peter is definitely indicated. Why not admit it?"

"There's nothing to admit. I tell you, I don't know what you're talking about. Why don't you just drop it?"

"Oh, so grand," she said lightly. "Very well. I'll have to worm it out of Peter."

"You leave him alone." His voice was savage with menace. "He's a perfectly decent kid. I won't have you upsetting him with your dirty innuendos."

"All right, all right," she said, maintaining her mocking tone but shaken by the revelation of violence in his voice. "You can keep your secrets if that's the way you want it."

"I trust you'd never talk that sort of stupid nonsense in front of C.B."

"What a terrifying thought. Actually, though, if she thought it would keep you out of the clutches of a girl, she might not mind the idea."

"Oh really!"

It wasn't until later in the afternoon that Charlie had calmed down sufficiently to become aware of her declaration of love.

He got home ahead of Peter that evening. When he switched on the lights, the first thing that caught his eye was a letter in Peter's handwriting among the books on the desk. Thinking it might be for him, he gave it a closer look. "Dear Jimmy." He turned away, hesitated as he made the connection, turned back, and picked it up and read it.

Dear Jimmy,

You asked me to let you know how everything is going, so here I am. Everything is fine, more or less. I'm with Charlie, which is all that really counts. I'm not completely sold on life in the Big City. When you talked about guys living as if they were married, I guess I saw myself bustling around the house in a little apron. It's not like that at all. I have this lousy job and it's in and out of subways all day long and rush rush rush. The real trouble is these night classes I'm taking. Before I started them, everything was wonderful. We had all our evenings together, and it was heaven. But Charlie has his job, of course, and I'm out practically all day until ten or eleven at night so we almost never see each other. Of course, we always sleep together, so I suppose I shouldn't complain. I'm seriously considering giving up school. God forbid my education should get in the way of my love life.

I'm as much of a sex fiend as ever. Probably more so. That's part of the trouble. Of course, Charlie's cock is huge. I've been meaning to measure it to find out exactly how big. It must make a difference. I guess when you get used to having something like that all the time, you miss it all the more when it doesn't happen so often. It still happens pretty often. If I weren't such a sex fiend, it would probably be all right. We've discovered this fantastic new

The letter ended there. Charlie crushed it into a ball in his hand and started to throw it away. Instead, he dropped it onto the desk as evidence. He went to the kitchen and poured himself a stiff drink. His hands were trembling with rage. Of all the dirty, disgusting, stupid drivel. It had gone too far. Hattie at noon and now this. Peter must have lost his mind, describing his cock and the rest of it. He felt like beating him, pounding some sense into him. Phrases from the letter kept running through his mind. They made him sick. He drank the drink fast, standing in the kitchen, and poured himself another. He went back into the living room, his eyes drawn to the letter. He wanted to rip it to shreds.

The drink began to take effect. His emotions smoothed out. The urge for violence receded. He would have to explain it all over again. Their making love together was just a phase. The words of love they exchanged were harmless so long as they kept the whole thing in perspective. Basically, they were simply good friends. Everything else was a sort of accident, something that might or might not happen, certainly nothing to dwell on and talk about to others. If Peter would see it for what it was, they could go on having a wonderful time together. Otherwise — well, there was no otherwise. Of course they would go on. He didn't deny that he wanted it and would continue to want it until life took some new turn and they passed quite naturally into another phase. Apparently Peter needed to be slapped down from time to time to keep him from getting carried away. His mind revolved slowly around these thoughts until he heard a key in the lock. He drained off his drink and put the glass behind the lamp and assumed a grim expression as he faced the door.

Peter came to a full stop when he saw him, and his face lighted up. "Hurray. You're here. I was hoping—" He stopped and his eyes widened and his shoulders slumped as if a weight had been dropped on them. "What's happened now?" he asked.

"If you're looking for your letter to dear Jimmy, there it is. Jimmy Harvester, I suppose."

Peter turned and went to the desk and put down his books. He stood looking at the crumpled paper. "I wondered where I'd left it. It looks as if I'll have to write another one."

"You're damn right you will. 'Charlie's cock is huge.' Good God Almighty."

Peter threw his head back and looked at him. "Well, isn't it? You're the tape-measure expert. You say it's pretty special. I certainly wouldn't know."

"But you'd like to find out for yourself. Is that what you're getting at?"

"Oh, darling." A little laugh escaped him, and his body shifted into a more relaxed line. "I don't care if everybody has a cock three feet long. I just want yours. I'm so proud of you. I like to talk about you. God knows, I don't get any chance to. I've got to keep it all bottled up."

"I see. Another little girlie heart-to-heart. And what about this great new discovery we've made?" He seized on what to him was

102

the least likely interpretation of the unfinished sentence. "I suppose you were going to tell him all about how we make love together."

Peter straightened defiantly. "Well, what if I was? What's wrong with that?"

"Oh, for God's sake. Don't you understand anything about privacy?"

"Privacy? Boy, do I ever. I understand so much about privacy that sometimes I want to go running out into the street and start shouting, 'I'm in love with Charlie Mills.' That's how much I understand about privacy. Don't you understand? I'm bursting with it. There must be people around who take it for granted and don't think it's awful. Why can't we see them? No, we can't see anybody. I'm supposed not to even exist. I'm a dirty secret. You have friends. You see them all the time. Not me. I'm not allowed to know who half of them are."

"At least, they're decent normal people, not some cock-crazy kid."

"*Me* cock-crazy? What about your—" He stopped and his jaws clamped shut. He lowered his eyes and turned back to the desk. He picked up the crumpled letter and began to bob it about in his hand like a ball. When he spoke again, he sounded as if he were making himself a speech. "No, I'm not going to do it. It hurts too much. Why should I try to say things to hurt you too? I don't want to hurt you. I want to love you." He tossed the letter away and turned back to Charlie. "OK, I'm cock-crazy. I admit it. Why can't we admit I'm a homosexual, too? I see people all the time who talk about it. They don't think it's strange. I don't care if you don't want to be, so long as you let me go to bed with you."

"Listen. Once and for all, I don't want to hear any more of this homosexual crap. I see queers all the time, too. Sometimes they follow me. We're not like that."

A little smile twisted the corners of Peter's mouth. "I'll say we're not. But I probably would be if it weren't for you. Golly, if I saw you coming down the street, I'd certainly follow you."

"Stop talking like that."

"I'm sorry. But do you realize I'm twenty years old and I've never had anything to do with anybody but you? In my whole life? It's the way I want it but it's pretty shattering sometimes."

"Why not just accept things the way they are? It's all this talk that's so unhealthy. Writing letters, for God's sake. If you were the raging queer you claim to be, you wouldn't be satisfied with me. You'd be out picking up guys all over town."

Peter shook his head. "I'm in love with you, Charlie. That's what it's all about."

"And I love you. I've told you all along, there's nothing wrong with us loving each other. It's wonderful. If you just wouldn't turn it all queer."

"I don't want to. I won't write any more letters, if that's what you mean. You know I never have any secrets from you, don't you? I was going to let you read it if you'd wanted to."

"I'm sorry I did. I just want to forget it."

"I'm sorry." He stood contritely in front of Charlie for an uncertain moment. Then he kicked a hassock out into the room and sat facing him. He took off his jacket and threw it onto a chair in back of him and loosened his tie. Charlie studied the flow of muscle under the shirt. "Listen, darling. Can I quit those damn classes? It's not queer to want to be with you, is it?"

Charlie looked into the eager face, open, trusting, lighted with love. His proximity made him want to reach out to him, touch him. "Of course not," he said. "I certainly wish we could be together more. It was a hell of a lot nicer for me when we could have dinner together. But you can't quit now. It's part of the whole bargain. Later, things may change. Maybe I'll get something in the theater. Then we couldn't have evenings together. If I get into a hit, maybe you could quit your job. We'd have all day together."

"You mean you'd keep me?"

"We could call it a loan. It doesn't matter. Two can live as cheaply as one. Everyone knows that."

Peter rested his forehead on his hand. He shook his head. "Oh, darling. You think of the damnedest things." He lifted his head and shook back his golden hair. "I almost wish you hadn't mentioned it. Now I won't be able to think about anything else." He laughed exultantly and leaned over and untied his shoes and kicked them off. "I'll be your valet. How about that?"

"If I really get a break, there'll be lots of things you can do. I talked to Hank Forbes again this afternoon. He says he's going to make an appointment for me with somebody. He's being very mysterious about it."

Peter drew off his socks and wiggled his toes. "Is Hattie in on it, too?"

Charlie made a little face at the mention of her name. "Not that I know of. Listen, baby. Hattie thinks something's going on between us."

Peter started to pull off his tie, but stopped in midgesture. "She does? Why?"

"Oh, feminine intuition. Who knows? It's nothing. But if she starts hinting around with you, for God's sake be careful."

"When would she? I'm not apt to see her." He flung away the tie and started to unbutton his shirt.

Charlie looked at the strong throat emerging from the collar and followed the movement of his long fingers as they moved down, exposing smooth skin. "No, probably not. But just in case, be damn careful you don't say anything she can make something of."

"Don't worry. I suppose she's in love with you, too." He pulled the shirt out of his trousers and peeled it off. Light fell along his shoulders and modeled the muscles of his chest. He undid the top two buttons of his trousers and ran his hand over his abdomen. Charlie's fingers closed on an imaginary pencil as his eyes followed the line of neck and shoulder down to the straying hand. His vision was dazzled by beauty.

"Who cares what she is?" he said. "Go ahead. What are you waiting for? Finish undressing."

Peter looked at him and then stood up and dropped his trousers and shorts and kicked them off. His sex slanted off at an angle in partial erection.

"Come here."

Peter stepped forward and his sex rose to complete its erection. Charlie took his hands and pulled him down to him and gripped him between his legs. He drew him close and held him for a long moment, his heart pounding, his head bowed over the golden one.

"God, I'm nuts about you," he said, speaking into the golden hair. "I really am, you know. You. Peter. My love. Sometimes it seems too much. I want so for it not to be bad."

"How can it be bad? There's just you and me. Nobody else. Don't let there be anybody else."

A FEW DAYS LATER — a week? a month? who knows? — the faithful Hank Forbes called again. This time the mystery was resolved. He had arranged for Charlie to do a reading for Meyer Rapper's new play. No, it wouldn't be possible for Charlie to see the script in advance. The part wasn't long, but had one or two nice scenes.

Unable to prepare in any other way, Charlie spent the next couple of days talking to Peter about Meyer Rapper, about the likelihood of the play being a hit, about what they would do when it was. Rapper was at the height of his success, his last three plays had each run for over a year, the boy who had played the juvenile in the one before last was already a big Hollywood star.

He tried not to think about having to tell C.B. He assumed that being actually cast for a Broadway show would be so thrilling that he wouldn't care who knew. In his mind, he eliminated the time lag between casting and triumphal opening, so that he could appear before her as a successful member of the profession. Who could fight a *fait accompli?*

The reading was set for noon at a Broadway theater. Charlie arranged for an early lunch hour and told a few lies to cover himself in case it took longer than he expected. On the way to the theater, he stopped at a bar and had a drink, which, on an empty stomach, made him agreeably drunk. He entered the stage door two minutes ahead of time, his nerves taut but under control, feeling that he had a date with destiny. It was bound to work out, it had to work out, he had always been told that his future was assured in the theater.

Two youths were lolling in the dingy corridor, both rather cheap-looking, Charlie thought, dismissing them as potential rivals. He brushed past them, aware of being given a long, careful scrutiny, and went to an old man in shirtsleeves sitting in a sort of cage.

"Meyer Rapper, please," he said.

The old man glanced up at him. "Oh, yeah. You're up for the part of Johnny," he said without asking his name. He picked up a typescript from a pile at his side and opened it at a marked page and handed it over. "They'll call you when they want you."

"Thanks." Charlie's eye ran down the page until he came to the stage directions: "JOHNNY ENTERS." He stood by the cage and read. The scene ran for three pages to "JOHNNY EXITS." It was apparently a youthful love scene with comic intent. Accustomed to playing big parts, such as Hamlet, at school, Charlie could find no clue to the character in the colorless dialogue. He read through it several times. The girl had a couple of rather cute lines, but Johnny remained a total nonentity. He felt a strange tingling in his legs, and the palms of his hands were moist. What was he supposed to do with it? He

106

turned pages, looking for more of Johnny, but his eyes were beginning to fail him. He went back to the scene indicated and read it again, trying to hear his voice saying the words. He found that the lines were written to be spoken, running easily and naturally against the girl's lines. His optimism revived. It could be a nice little scene. Come on slow. He would have to make himself slightly gawky. A bit of business where the girl laughs. He was just exiting to applause when a voice said, on an interrogatory note, "Charles Mills?"

He slapped the script shut and pulled himself up and saw a man in a rumpled sweater standing in a doorway in a thick wall. He stepped forward. "Yes," he said.

The man looked at him without interest. "You Mills? Come along." He turned, and Charlie followed him into the dark area of the wings and out onto the stage. A single bare bulb hung in the middle of it, lighting elements of a living-room set. Charlie was accustomed to walking onto stages. He moved well and with authority. He could have been back at Princeton. Except this was Broadway. This was the way the big hits and the big stars were born. A chill ran down his spine, and his knees began to tremble. The man in the sweater stopped and turned to him, holding an open script in his hand.

"Page forty-six. You've had a chance to run through it?"

"Yes. Can you give me an idea of what the character is like?" Their voices sounded conspiratorial in the empty theater. Charlie became aware of two figures sitting in the middle of the orchestra. He was careful not to look at them. He shifted on his feet and got his knees under control. He wished he had had another drink.

"We're casting to type," the man in the sweater said. "Just read it as it comes. Ready?"

"Sure. I guess so." He lifted the script and found the page. He was pleased to see that his hands were trembling only slightly. The first line was his and he read it. He couldn't hear his own voice. A cue was thrown him, and he read on. All the little effects he had been planning were forgotten. There was no opportunity for movement. The girl's lines came at him in a mumbled monotone. They were getting toward the end of the second page when a voice called out, "Fine. That'll do." The shock of it ran down his legs and into the soles of his feet. He dropped his hands to his sides and looked out into the dark auditorium and then at the man in the sweater. The latter nodded toward the wings. Charlie turned and started off slowly, wondering whether he should ask for Mr. Rapper, explain that he was Charles Mills, that Henry Forbes had sent him. He became aware of movement in the auditorium and glanced out and saw a man approaching down the aisle. Charlie hesitated and then saw who it was and stopped. The man came down to the rail of the orchestra pit and leaned against it looking up at Charlie with a smile of great charm. "I'm Meyer Rapper," he explained unnecessarily. Charlie knew him from a hundred photographs — the swooping hairline, the Mephistophelian features, the elegantly tailored figure. He seemed to glitter with gold. "Hank's told me about you. That was very nice. I'd like to go over it with you again."

"Well, thanks." Charlie broke into an ecstatic grin.

"That's it. That's exactly it. That's just the way I see the boy. We've got other people waiting now. How's my schedule, Herbie? Can I work Mr. Mills in this evening?"

"You're having dinner with Charlotte Harris," the man in the sweater said.

Charlie was thrilled by the casual mention of the great name.

"Ah, yes, Frankenstein's mother. Well, perhaps later. Could you meet me after the theater, Charles? Say eleven-thirty at my place? I'll give you some supper."

"Yes, sure. Anytime you say," Charlie agreed.

"Splendid. The Waldorf Towers. Just ask for me. They'll be expecting you."

Charlie had no recollection of leaving the theater. He found himself in the street. It was a crisp, clear day with a wind blowing off the river. He wanted to leap in the air, he wanted to burst into song. Wait till he told Peter. Nobody else. It was bad luck to talk about it until it was definite. But what could go wrong? "That's the way I see the boy." Meyer Rapper had said it. Meyer Rapper was his own director. He was in. There remained the problem of C.B., but she would be fascinated once she got over the first shock, especially if he was with a big star like Charlotte Harris. He wondered how much notice he would be expected to give at the office. He would have to get all the dates straight with Meyer Rapper this evening. Once he started rehearsals, Peter could quit his job. C.B. wouldn't necessarily find out about that. Life would begin to really make sense. There was no reason why he shouldn't call Peter his secretary. He could introduce him everywhere that way. In the theater, such arrangements were common and accepted. It was all too fabulous, too incredible, too marvelous to be quite taken in, and yet it seemed to him that he had always known that this was the way it was going to happen.

Peter telephoned him at the office and received a guarded version of the news so that he was waiting with whoops of joy when Charlie got home.

"I'm not going to class tonight. I don't have to, do I? I've got everything for dinner. Including a bottle of wine. Oh, darling, this is the best day ever."

Charlie told the story of his midday rendezvous over and over. Peter plied him with questions. They weighed every word of the deathless dialogue with Meyer Rapper and agreed that there was nothing left but to sign the contract. After dinner they rushed into bed for what Peter described as a "luck fuck." He was delighted with the expression and repeated it with roars of laughter.

"Look at me," he said later. "In bed with a big star. Oh, lord, the whole world's going to be madly in love with you and you're mine."

By eleven they were both dressed again and ready to go. Peter accompanied him to the Waldorf Towers, and then they walked up and down Park Avenue, killing time. When the moment came, Peter gave his arm a secret squeeze.

"OK, darling. I'll be praying. Hurry home. I'll be waiting for you."

Charlie went in and pronounced Meyer Rapper's name. He gave his own with brisk authority, feeling almost like the big star Peter insisted he already was. He was bowed to the elevator. He walked down a long corridor and rang at the number indicated. He was admitted by a uniformed manservant, who took his coat. The apartment was overwhelmingly opulent. Charlie had always moved in comfortable surroundings, but this was his first experience of the fabled world of celebrity and he felt suddenly underprivileged. This was the way it should be. Everything he had known was drab by comparison. Meyer Rapper was standing in the living room waiting for him. Charlie was struck once more by the glitter of gold. Great windows behind him looked out onto the sparkling city.

"Ah, there, sport. I've been looking forward to you after a harrowing evening with that great lady of stage and screen, Miss Charlotte Harris. What'll you have to drink?"

Charlie asked for a whiskey, and they sat side by side on a sofa. "I know you want to talk about the play, and I won't keep you in suspense. Bad for the digestion. Frankly, it's not much of a part, but it has a couple of showy little scenes. People would see you. It could lead to Hollywood."

"I'm really not much interested in Hollywood," Charlie said. This line, which he had always offered in one form or another as evidence of his dedication, now sounded fatuous.

"Let me give you a word of advice," Meyer Rapper said. "Take success where you find it. With success, you're your own master." He waved his glass at the room. "This is success. It's extraordinarily agreeable. You're very good-looking, but you have something much more rare. You have class. Ty Power has it. Have you seen him? He's already becoming a big star."

The manservant wheeled in a table set for two. Meyer Rapper rose. Charlie found that the suspense had in no way diminished. Had he been told he could definitely have the part? The tenses seemed wrong. Perhaps there were implications he was missing.

"I hope you like smoked salmon. It's lox called by another name, but smells as sweet. Bring your drink. Unless you'd prefer wine. Champagne perhaps?"

Charlie declined and joined him at table.

"Hank gives very good reports of you. I make it a rule to hire untried actors whenever I can. It's one of the rewards of having a free hand, finding youngsters, starting them on their way. I'll have you read for me again when we've had some nourishment. I thought you did very well today."

The smoked salmon was followed by lobster in a rich cream sauce. Charlie began to get the uncomfortable impression that he was being toyed with. Meyer Rapper remained tantalizingly oblique. The definitive word had not been said. His mind was bursting with questions, but he had little chance of inserting a word into the easy flow of the playwright's monologue. When they had eaten, the manservant replenished their drinks and rolled the table away. Meyer Rapper crossed the room to a desk and returned with a copy of his typescript.

"The play's about rich people on Long Island. You look the part. Onstage, you'll look younger than you actually do. I want it full of youth. The boy is in love as only the young can be. I want it to be incandescent. It's all in that breathtaking smile of yours. Of course, we can't have you grinning all the time. We'll have to find ways to convey it. Will it make you self-conscious to stand? I can get a better idea that way."

Charlie stood with the typescript in his hand. When ordered to, he read. Meyer Rapper fed him cues from memory. He went all the way through the scene this time, and when he was finished Meyer Rapper nodded. "You could do it. It needs work, of course, but Hank was right. You have a lovely quality." Meyer Rapper paused and his satanic features sharpened as he went on, "Now Charles, I'm afraid you'll have to learn right from the start what a sordid business the theater is. I want to go to bed with you."

Charlie's knees sagged. He almost dropped the script. He stared at Meyer Rapper without seeing him. Surely he hadn't heard correctly. "What?" he said faintly.

"You're quite free to say good night and go now."

"But what about the play?" Charlie was amazed that he was able to speak.

"I'm sorry to make it sound so cold-blooded. But my analyst would never speak to me again if I went into rehearsal with this situation unresolved. I might easily have a breakdown. It wouldn't be fair to my backers."

"But you say I'm right for the part."

"At my office, I have a list of at least a dozen youngsters who could do it just as well. They have an advantage over you. I don't want to go to bed with them."

Charlie was outraged by the unfairness of the proposition. If he had seized him and kissed him, if he had waited till they were sitting together and groped him, acquiescence might have been possible, but to have the terms stated so baldly denied him any choice. To accept would be outright whoring.

"What would Hank say if he knew about this?" Charlie asked, to give himself time.

Meyer Rapper smiled his charming smile. "We have few secrets from each other in the theater. Hank warned me not to expect anything. He needn't have bothered. One has only to look at you to see that you can't be bought."

"Then why did you have me up here? What's it been all about?"

Meyer Rapper's smile turned faintly melancholy. "One is egotistical enough to hope. You might not have found me repulsive."

"But I don't. It's not that at all. I just don't go in for that sort of thing. I mean—" Charlie thought of Peter. He thought of all that this meant to both of them. What difference did it make if someone handled his body? "I mean — Well, if we got to know each other, if

111

it just sort of happened. I mean, who knows what might happen?"

"That's exactly the risk I can't take. It wouldn't be convenient for me to fall in love with you. I doubt if I would be a demanding lover. Once would probably suffice. My analyst would take charge thereafter."

"It just isn't possible," Charlie said helplessly. It was inconceivable that he could lose so much by saying a few simple words. Why hadn't the man taken him by force? Why hadn't he put him in a position from which he couldn't extricate himself without looking ridiculous?

"Of course not. As I said, it's not much of a part. If you really want the theater, you'll undoubtedly have better opportunities. Perhaps our friend Hank will give you a start without asking anything in return, although I don't believe it for a minute. Let this be a lesson to you. We live in an ugly world, and the theater is a particularly ugly part of it."

"So that's that?"

"I should think so. I've enjoyed very much looking at you. If you'll permit me one more word of advice, stick to publishing." He rose and took the script from Charlie and escorted him to the hall. Charlie's coat was waiting for him. Meyer Rapper shook his hand, smiled with great charm, and closed the door on him.

Charlie wanted a drink. He wanted lots of drinks. He couldn't bear the thought of facing Peter. There was no way of presenting the story without feeling dirty or, worse, stupid. Nobody had been interested in his talent. He had been only a body to be bargained for. Why hadn't he beaten them at their own game? He could have let Rapper do whatever he wanted to do. He wouldn't have had to respond. He could have signed a contract and spat in his eye. The thought of going to work at the office the next morning filled him with desolation. He had been so nearly free of it. If only Rapper had given him time to think. Even as he wished it otherwise, he knew he could never have submitted. He went into a bar on Lexington Avenue and had two drinks in quick succession.

As soon as he saw him, Peter knew it had been a disaster. "Oh, damn, damn, damn," he said as he took his coat. Charlie staggered slightly as he made his way to a chair.

"Give me a drink."

"Sure, darling. Right away. I guess I'd better have one too."

Charlie told his story and held out his glass to be refilled.

"The shit. The dirty shit," Peter exclaimed with fury. "I'd like to go beat the hell out of him. I'd kill him. Who in hell does he think he is, even thinking he could put his dirty hands on you. I wish you'd socked him one."

"I probably would have if he'd tried to touch me."

"Thank God he didn't. The lousy fucker. With you of all people. To try a thing like that. I really could kill him."

Charlie had a third drink. When he had finished it, he couldn't move. Peter had to undress him and put him to bed.

A LTHOUGH HE MADE a determined effort to erase it from his mind, the episode continued to nag him in the days that followed. He couldn't help wondering whether it could have happened to anybody or if Rapper had somehow detected in him a flaw, a weakness, a tendency that was there to be exploited. He tried to surprise himself in an effeminate gesture or falling into an unmanly pose. He listened to his voice for similar signals.

He had no taste for telling Hank Forbes what had happened, but when Forbes called again he had obviously heard the story from Rapper. "Don't be too upset. These things happen sometimes."

"Well, I hope they don't happen to me. I don't go in for that stuff." He said it in the slightly toughened accents he had adopted, and was glad of the opportunity to forestall any notions Hank might have been nurturing.

"Well, fella, I'll keep my eye out for you. I'm sorry there's nothing in the script I'm supposed to be doing next. Tell Hattie to give me a call."

He began to see more of Hattie; they became almost nightly companions. She took him to meet some of the more immediate members of her family, and he was cordially received. She cooked dinner for him more and more frequently, and they became an established couple at the bars where they went to see theater people. She knew everybody and believed in constant exposure to further her career. He grew to rely on her cutting him off from the men who were obviously attracted to him. She saved him a lot of trouble. If Rapper had known about her, in the way that more and more people did as their names were linked, he probably wouldn't have dared to make his proposition. He never told Hattie the true story; he made up something about not being right for the part. Hattie heard all about it, of course, from Hank Forbes and thought him insane to have lost such a chance, but she never said anything. She had learned he had limits beyond which it was not wise to stray.

At her suggestion, they started to rehearse a scene from a Barry play, so that, as she pointed out, they would have something to do if they ever had a chance to do an audition together. It was, of course, a love scene, and at one point they were called upon to kiss. After they had rehearsed it awkwardly several times, Hattie burst into hoots of laughter.

"Oh, really. Let's get it right. How *do* people kiss, anyway?"

They stood in front of each other. Charlie shrugged. "Like this, I guess." He drew her to him, and their mouths met. She felt almost dangerously frail in his arms, as if she might break. She opened her mouth and eagerly explored his with her tongue. His sex stirred in response. He broke from her as it risked becoming obvious. The mockery was gone from her face, and it glowed softly, uncharacteristically defenseless and vulnerable.

"OK?" he asked.

"Much better," she said with a return of mocking laughter, which failed to completely obliterate the effect Charlie saw he had had on her. She was ready for him to carry it further. He had no intention of doing so; it suggested too many complications. Peter would never forgive him if anything occurred between them here in the apartment. If she were like all the others and there was some unpleasantness, even C.B. might find the Donaldsons rather a handful. It was something to hold in reserve, evidence of his masculinity.

Peter frequently found them together when he came home from class. He quickly lost his first enthusiasm for her. She had ways of making him feel an intruder that went unnoticed by Charlie. As far as Charlie was concerned, they were all good friends. That was the way he wanted to think of them; at times, he came quite close to convincing himself that there was little difference between his relationship with Peter and his elected role as constant escort to Hattie. His self-consciousness had extended to Peter; he reverted to his former caution about the use of endearments. He never said "baby" except in moments of extreme intimacy. He saw effeminate mannerisms growing in Peter every time he moved, and he bad-

114

gered him about them. Once, he brought him close to tears by calling him a "silly little queen."

Peter found C.B. a great comfort. She was the link with the magical summer days of discovery, an assurance that the bonds they had forged then were indestructible. She enjoyed talking about Charlie as much as he did. They indulged themselves freely.

"Is he still seeing a great deal of Hattie?" she asked one day when he had dropped by in time to have tea with her.

"Yes," Peter admitted without enthusiasm. "Practically every day."

"I wonder if he might be getting serious about her."

"Oh, no." He brightened at being able to make the denial. "Nothing like that. They're just pals. He takes her around to all her theatrical hangouts. They're rehearsing a scene together." Realizing that this might give her ideas, he added, "You know, he's helping her prepare it. She wants to have something to do at auditions."

"I see. You know, of course, that it was one of the greatest frights of my life when I discovered a few years ago what an extraordinary actor he is. It seemed inevitable that he would want to go on with it."

"I wish I'd seen him. He really is all that good?"

"Extraordinary. Such magnetism and authority. I hadn't the slightest doubt he would be a great success. That's what was so frightening."

"I don't understand. Why are you so opposed? It wouldn't be like starving in a garret."

"Oh, my darling. The life. So sordid. All very well for poor little Sapphire. I'm delighted she got a job in her show. But Charlie has so many gifts. I've always wanted him to use them all to make a really worthwhile life for himself."

"But I should think the only way to use a talent like you say he has for acting is to be an actor."

China clashed against silver as she set down her cup. This was dangerous ground he had dared tread once before and again he felt the ice of her disapproval. "Is that the sort of advice you give him?" she asked, with a tolerant smile.

"Oh, C.B.," he protested with flustered laughter. "You know he doesn't need any advice from me. You know Charlie. He just sails along and everything falls into his lap."

"Are you suggesting that he still entertains some thoughts about the stage?"

"Of course not. I mean, you'd know as much about that as I would. He always talks to you about everything."

"That's the way it has always been. We've always talked to each other, even when he was tiny."

Peter's laughter was genuine now. "I can't imagine him being tiny. But that's just it. He'd never do anything without talking to you first. You're the only person who has any real influence on him."

"I hope you're right, my darling."

He detected lurking doubts. Thinking of Charlie, wanting to prepare the ground for him in some small way, he dared add, "You know I am. It's just that if he ever did have a chance to do something in the theater, I hope you wouldn't think it's too awful."

"I think I'm a better judge of that than you. I know the world." She pushed the tea table from her. "You've depressed me, my darling. I had thought that that danger had been disposed of once and for all. You've given me a great deal to think about. I'm glad, at least, that you think we have nothing to fear from Hattie."

"Absolutely not. He was maybe sort of fascinated by her at first, but now they're just friends."

"I'm glad. I don't find her really suitable. You know, I'd like to feel I could count on you to warn me if this theater thing should ever crop up again. Perhaps I shouldn't. Male solidarity. You're a faithful creature. In your eyes, I daresay, Charlie could never do any wrong."

"That's the way you feel about him too, isn't it?"

"He has needed guidance, as the young always do. Perhaps he still does. We shall see."

He was obliged to leave before he had quite succeeded in re-establishing the loving flow of understanding between them that was the basis of his devotion to her. He knew he had blundered badly. Next time, he must avoid anything controversial, follow her lead, say only the things she wanted him to say. He didn't report the conversation to Charlie.

Soon after, a day came when C.B. called Charlie at his office. This was not in itself unusual, but her tone was — as was the urgency with which she asked him to stop by on his way home from work. He went, curious and uneasy, but with no real presentiment of catastrophe. When she rose to receive him in her living room, all his guards were immediately alerted. Her kiss was ominously restrained. She flicked a scrap of handkerchief at a chair.

"I don't think this is an occasion for offering you a drink." She sat very straight, her hands on her knees. Charlie sat opposite her. She looked him gravely in the eye. "Peter was here earlier. What I have to say is very painful to me. I think the sooner it's said the better. He has confessed his love for you."

At mention of Peter's name, Charlie's heart leaped up violently and now the room reeled. There was a roaring in his head. His face felt numb. He found himself gripping the arms of the chair. "What?" he gasped.

"Does it come as such a surprise to you?" She continued to fix his eyes with hers.

"I just don't know what you're talking about." He felt his cheeks burning. He didn't know how he could meet her level stare, but his practiced controls took charge and he managed to face her. His mind whirled and clung to a single formula. Deny it. Deny everything. Deny.

"I'm afraid he left no room for misunderstanding. He seemed deeply troubled, and naturally I asked him why. He confessed that he was in love with you — criminally in love with you. He made no attempt to equivocate."

"He must have gone out of his mind. Did he suggest that I — that we—"

"He made no suggestion that anything improper had occurred. I wouldn't have permitted him to, in any event. Is it possible that you've had no inkling of this?"

Charlie drew his first easy breath. The question gave him all the opportunity he needed to save himself. He thought of the drawings. She had obviously never known anything about them. He had always known that her innocence would bar her from any real understanding of the things she often seemed to be referring to. "How could I have any inkling?" he protested, reminding himself that innocence would be conveyed more effectively by bewilderment than outrage. "Do you suppose I'd have allowed it to go on? I still don't understand exactly what he said."

"Just what I've told you. I prefer not to repeat it. He seemed to reproach you for not sharing his unspeakable passion."

"Sharing it? I don't know anything about it." The scene that must have occurred between C.B. and Peter was beginning to come clear to him. Peter must have been carrying on about not ever seeing him. C.B. would take this to mean that he had rejected him. It wasn't as bad as he had feared, but there was only one way out. He thought only of protecting himself with C.B., not of the consequences for Peter. "As you know, I've — well, I've been pretty involved with Hattie lately. I've hardly seen Peter for the last month."

"And the poor soul has been consumed with jealousy. I suppose that must be the way of it. It did strike me that he wasn't quite himself. It's been obvious how devoted he was to you. I understand all about Platonic love, but the other — the physical — one cannot think of it."

"Certainly not. It's absolutely impossible. Are you sure he meant it that way? Are you sure he wasn't just hysterical or something?"

"His words were 'I love him in every way possible. Passionately. The way men and women love each other.' He insisted on it, as if he were proud of it."

"Oh, for God's sake." Charlie passed his hand over his eyes and steeled himself. "Well, there's nothing to be done about it. He'll just have to go."

"Poor tortured soul. I confess I can see no alternative. It's so terribly sad. I can't help feeling somehow responsible."

"Don't be silly, C.B. Nobody's responsible. He's just gone out of his mind." As his initial terror passed, anger grew in him. He would never forgive Peter for this. He had given him enough warning. That he could have even hinted to her of the acts they performed together filled him with loathing for what they had done. Only her unquestioning belief in him had saved him from being incriminated. He would throw him out. Even if he had to wait till Peter came home from school, he would throw him out tonight.

"He's doubtless not well mentally," C.B. said. She continued to sit very straight, her little slippered feet side by side under the hem of one of the flowing garments she favored for the house, her hands in her lap. "But the fact remains that I brought you together, you were kind to him as a kindness to me, I gave this New York arrangement my blessing. I don't know what I can write to his mother."

Terror constricted his chest once more. The thought of repercussions appalled him, with the consequent public discussions, the risk

118

of his part in it being misinterpreted. The thing must be buried quickly and without trace. "Why should you write anything? I don't see why you should have anything more to do with it."

"Naturally, I've forbidden him ever to enter my house again. He left me no choice. But if the poor creature is sick, he must be cared for. One has that responsibility."

"You'd better let me talk to him. Not that I even want to see him again. But I can find out more about it than you could. Then you can decide."

"As you wish. Oh, my dearest, I'm afraid you're fated, as I have been, to be disappointed by people. We idealize them and they rarely live up to our expectations. I've never spoken to you of your grandfather. You've perhaps found it odd. I know your mother is inclined to be sentimental about him."

"She's always said I'm like him."

"You're not!" She spoke with sudden, jolting vehemence. "George Collinge was a drunkard and a beast. I was young and very foolish. He induced me to elope with him. My parents closed their door to us. I soon learned that theirs was not the only door that would always be closed to Mr. Collinge. I would never tell anyone the things he did to me. The things he did to your mother are another matter. He beat her. He beat her in drunken rages because of some childish prank or because she was making too much noise, as children do. When I found her one day with her mouth bloody and swollen, I warned him that if it ever happened again, I would take her and leave. He knew I could ruin him utterly. Fortunately, he died very suddenly."

He stared at her, transfixed. Her voice throbbed with a passion he hadn't known she possessed. She lifted her handkerchief and brushed nightmares from before her eyes. "I could never give myself to another man. The hurt that can be done the young is incalculable. Yet I have survived. I wonder if I could have lived these last years without you, my dearest. The sensibilities we share make ordinary intercourse with others often painful and destructive. You will have to learn, as I have, to be self-sufficient. One must test others in fire before one finds the rare spirit one can trust. I've had to learn it with my own daughter. I suppose I should regard her attitude as a tribute to my success at protecting her from the horror of the past, but I've never forgiven her for taking her father's part against me."

Charlie was stirred by the drama of her speech, but it left him strangely disturbed, as if something in it had eluded him. Why had she chosen to tell him about his grandfather now? The general point she was making was clear enough, but he felt somehow that there should be something more. "I don't think she's ever done that," he said hesitantly. "She's just always talked about how charming and handsome and talented he was."

"Well, now you know the truth. You're a great consolation to me, my dearest. I can't forgive myself for exposing you to — to the sickness that Peter has brought into our lives."

"Please don't worry about it. I'll get rid of him right away. It's not going to be pleasant, but I might as well get it over with. If I go now, I'll just catch him before he goes to school."

"Perhaps that would be best. How sad for it to end like this. I was quite smitten by him. I don't often make such mistakes with people. Come see me tomorrow if you can manage it. Or call."

She rose, and he stood beside her. They walked arm in arm to the door, she hugging his arm to her in the way he had found overinsistent at times, but which he welcomed now as a blessing. He was overwhelmed by the miracle of his escape and hated Peter for nearly robbing him of this irreplaceable support. If his control had failed for an instant, he would be crossing the room alone, banished forever, in unnameable disgrace.

When he got home, rage gathering in him, he found Peter standing in the living-room doorway with books in his hands. His greeting lacked its usual exuberance. He avoided Charlie's eye. "I was just going. I'm late already."

Charlie stood in front of him, breathing heavily. "You've really torn it this time."

Peter glanced at him and looked away. "She's told you, has she? She didn't waste any time. I hoped I'd be able to tell you myself." He turned and went back into the living room and put down his books. Charlie followed. "All right. How much did she tell you?" Peter asked.

"Everything, I hope," Charlie said with barely contained violence. "You just couldn't resist another heart-to-heart, could you? It's a wonder you didn't tell her the size of my cock."

Peter winced. "Please. Tell me what she said. I've got to know her version of it."

"What do you mean, 'her version'? Did you talk to her, or didn't you? It seems you told her you're madly in love with me. You may have told her we've been going to bed together for all I know, but that's one thing she didn't grasp."

"'Didn't grasp'?" Peter looked up incredulously.

"No. Didn't grasp. Some people don't, you know. All she understood is that you're passionately in love with me, you want me physically, and you're upset because I don't respond as much as you'd like me to. A lovely story. Just what you'd expect your best friend to tell your grandmother."

Peter shook his head with bewilderment. "Did she tell you how it all started?"

"Of course. She said you seemed upset, and she asked you what the matter was, and you confessed, as she put it."

"But that isn't the way it was at all." Peter took a step toward him. "Please, darling. You've got—"

"Don't call me darling," Charlie shouted.

Peter bit his lip. "Please. Please listen to me. You wouldn't be angry if you knew how it happened. Not with me."

"Oh, wouldn't I? We'll just see about that. Go ahead. Tell me how it happened."

"Well, I dropped by as usual. She was particularly nice to me. She said she'd been looking forward to a talk. And then all of a sudden, she just threw it at me. She said she knew all about us. She said she knew we were very much in love with each other. She said I should feel free to talk about it."

"You're stark raving mad. She could never have said such a thing."

"But I tell you, she did. You can imagine how I felt. I was staggered. I was going to put on an act, but before I could pull myself together she said she wanted to understand it better. She practically begged me to tell her about it."

"Oh, for Christ's sake. I don't believe a word of this, you know. You're just wasting our time."

"But darl— Honestly, champ. You know I don't lie to you. If I'd been idiot enough to just blab it all out, I'd admit it. I'll admit it might've happened the way she says if I'd been drunk or delirious or something. But it didn't. She was perfectly natural and nice about it. She made me feel she really wanted to know about it, so I started telling her that it had been a bit difficult because of us both being so busy and everything. I told her I missed not seeing more of you. That's—"

"Just like that, as if we were having a little problem with our marriage. Jesus."

"But I tell you, that's the way *she* was talking about it. So that's when I told her it was probably different for you. I said that for me it was everything, but that you needed other people and thought I made too much of it sometimes."

"Sometimes!"

"Then she said, 'I assume you're speaking of your physical love for Charlie.' She didn't sound shocked or anything. So I said, of course. That men could love each other the same way men and women love each other. That's when she dropped the ax. She said that of course she could never receive me again and threw me out. I didn't know what hit me. There'd been absolutely nothing to give me any warning of what was coming. I've never been so horrified in my life when I realized what had happened. I almost couldn't get home I was so sick about it. You've got to believe me. The whole thing was just a trick."

There was a silence. Peter stood poised and suppliant, his eyes blazing with truth. Charlie looked at him and started to speak and then stopped and took a few paces around the room. He ran both hands through his hair and gripped his head. He flung his arms out.

"It doesn't make any sense," he exploded. "A trick to do what? What's it supposed to accomplish?"

"That's pretty obvious. It all makes horrible sense to me. I'll bet she's known all along. She suggested our living together, don't forget. If we'd just been seeing each other, she wouldn't be able to do anything about it. But no. She has us where she can watch it grow and when she thinks the moment has come, she can move in and kill it."

"If that's what it is, she's certainly succeeded."

"Don't say that. What did you say to her? How did you take it?"

"I denied it, of course. I said I didn't know what you were talking about."

"Of course. Did she believe you?"

"She acted as if she did. Why shouldn't she? Unless you said things you haven't told me."

"No. She could've taken everything I said as being just about me. I assumed from the way she talked that the sex part was taken for granted, until she asked that question. Even that she phrased so it didn't necessarily include you. No, she's got it fixed so she can believe anything she wants to believe."

"Fine. Except she's not like that. Why should she do this now? If she knows anything, she's known it all along. She's maybe thought of us as loving each other in a Platonic way. She said so, just now. She's always adored you. Why should she want to get rid of you all of a sudden?"

"I'm pretty sure I know that, too. We've talked about you and the theater. She suspects you're still interested in it. Not from anything I said. The other day, I made the mistake of saying I didn't think it was such a terrible idea. I know I shouldn't have. I could see it happening — she doesn't trust me anymore. She thinks maybe I'm encouraging you."

"Oh, Christ. You can't shut up about anything, can you? But what's that got to do with our being in love with each other? You have it all so much on your mind that you misread the first simple question she asks about our being friends or something into an invitation to spill the whole works."

"Misread? Is it possible to misread, 'I've known for some time that you and Charlie are passionately in love with each other'?"

"Yes, it is, goddamn it." He felt bested by the quiet conviction with which Peter had made his case, and his anger boiled up. "She doesn't always use words the same way we do. She has her own interpretation of certain things. Can you imagine what it would do to her if she believed that something had actually happened between us? There's no use talking about it anymore. You've got to go."

"But that's just what she wants. I wouldn't be surprised if she used me as bait right from the start, to test you. Well, now she knows. I don't think she'll be introducing you to any more pretty boys in the near future."

"God, you have a dirty mind. She doesn't know anything. She knows that a nutty kid has said a lot of romantic crap about me. And she knows I'm getting rid of you."

"Is that the way you left it?"

"You're damn right. Do you think I can go on living with a queer who goes around telling everybody he's in love with me? Good God Almighty. I'm going to have a drink." He brushed past Peter without looking at him and went to the kitchen. Peter followed and stood in the doorway while he fixed himself the drink.

"If you're going to throw me out, I'd just as soon you'd do it sober," Peter said.

"I can have a couple of drinks and still be sober."

"Well, then, maybe I'd better have one, too." He joined him at the counter. Charlie was amazed at his composure. He had expected tears by now. He took several long, parched swallows. He still found the effects of liquor unpredictable, but it always began by easing tension, softening emotions.

Peter felt the change taking place in Charlie, and all his love was released to flow out to him. He couldn't take the talk of leaving seriously. They had to get through this somehow. "Are you expecting Hattie?" he asked.

"No. She had to see somebody. I was glad. I told her not to come by later." His voice turned bitter and self-lacerating. "I was going to stay home and wait for you. We haven't made love for two nights. That's the sort of thing I'm beginning to sit around and think about. It's another reason you have to go."

"It sounds to me like a reason for staying. Oh, God, darling, all this is so horrible. I know we have to do something. I've known that ever since it happened. Can you imagine what the last few hours have been like? I thought about killing myself so we wouldn't have to go through this. Maybe I would have, if I could've thought of some way to do it. I hoped that when you talked to C.B. it might turn out to be not as bad as I thought."

"Well, it didn't."

"No, of course not. Since this is the way she wants it. I'm out, and she has her beloved Charlie all to herself."

"You're just asking for trouble if you go on talking like that."

"All right. Forget it. What are we going to do? Can't you go to her and tell her you've talked it over with me and it was all just a big misunderstanding? I was just talking about theory or something. About the way people are. I didn't mean that I actually had any special feeling for you. I'd do it if you could persuade her to see me again."

"You know what you said to her. Do you think it would work?"

"No, because she wouldn't let it. But at least we could try. If you're right about her, it would have to work."

"I *am* right about her, and it wouldn't. She's perfectly clear about what you said."

"Well, then, why not just tell her I've gone? What's wrong with that? She's not going to come around and look. She's never come near the place."

"It's impossible. She'd find out. She'd find out from your family to begin with. She's planning to write to your mother."

The color drained out of Peter's face. He put out a hand to Charlie and withdrew it. He shook his head. "Oh, no, darling. She mustn't. Don't let her. You've got to stop her."

"I'm certainly going to try to. I don't want this turned into a big thing with everybody whispering behind my back. I think I can make her see it that way."

"Thank God. It would be awful. Do you know anything about laws? Could they come and take me away? Maybe I'll have to disappear. No. Listen. I know what we can do. I'll write my mother right away. I'll tell her I've moved. I know a couple of kids at school who'd let me use their address. You can tell C.B. the same thing."

The scheme sounded so feasible that Charlie was compelled to take time to pour himself another drink before he could answer. He felt trapped. He wanted to yield, but he knew that the only way he could remove the taint, the only way he could look C.B. in the eye and feel worthy of her, was to make the final break, to remove all possibility of any further revelations. He took a sip of his freshened drink and waved the glass at Peter. "It wouldn't work. What if they don't like the idea of your moving out on your own? What if they decide to come and check up for themselves? It would all come out. Then we really would be in a mess. They might as well find us in bed together."

"It needn't be like that. I can fix it. I can arrange it so that everybody will know what to say if anything comes up. I could even leave some of my things there to make it look convincing."

"You seem awfully friendly with these kids."

"They're all right. They're just a couple of guys who live together. They'd understand."

"It's too risky," Charlie said curtly. "I won't do it."

"Well, what *are* we going to do? Are you just going to sit there and say I have to go?"

Charlie's heart began to pound as he felt the storm gathering around him. His fist clenched on his glass. He wasn't sure he would be able to speak. "That's exactly what I'm going to do," he said. The kitchen was suddenly too small. He strode into the living room. Peter was at his heels.

"You can't do it. She's killing you. Maybe it doesn't matter about me. I'm probably not worth much anyway. But look what she's doing to *you*. She's killed your family, your own mother. She's killed your painting. She's killing me. Wait till you see what she does to Hattie if you go on seeing her. Boy, then you'll see some fur fly. But all it adds up to is she's killing you. You're too good. You're too wonderful. I won't let her do it."

"Oh, Christ. You've got her on the brain."

"*I've* got her on the brain? Can't you see what she's doing to you? She's turning you into her pet possession. You'll end up a cipher. I won't let her."

"I don't see there's much you can do about it."

"There's plenty I can do about it," Peter shouted. "I'll go to her and tell her you've been fucking me for months. *And* throw in the size of your cock if she wants proof."

"So now it's blackmail, is it?"

"Oh, no, God, darling, I don't know what I'm saying. You know I'd never do anything bad to you. But you've got to stop doing this to us."

"It seems to me you've done all the doing."

"You need me, darling. I don't mean to sound conceited, but I know you so well. You need me as much as I need you."

"I need you. I need Hattie. I need C.B. I sound pretty helpless. Goddamn it, I *don't* need you. I don't need anybody. I'm fine by myself."

"Oh, darling, everybody needs somebody. There's nothing wrong with that. I'm not saying anything against you. How could I? You're perfect as far as I'm concerned. But please, darling, dearest, please make sense with me. You know I'm no good without you."

"What shit. When you say things like that it's all the more obvious you have to go."

"But I can't go, darling. Go where? This is the only place I belong. This is ours."

"Is it? I haven't noticed you paying the rent."

"Oh, don't." He put his hands to his head as if he had been struck. "Don't do it. Stop it. This is us. This is all I have. Charlie?" He stretched out his hands to him. Charlie moved away from them.

126

"Let's just cut out the theatrics, shall we?"

"But you said it. We're all one. That means forever. It has to."

"Forever! What's that supposed to mean? People leave each other every day."

"Do you want another boy? Is that what this is all about? Has something been going on I haven't known about?"

"Oh, for Christ's sake. You really do have a dirty mind. *No, I don't want another boy.*"

"You will, you know, if I leave. I can't stand it, but you realize that you will, don't you?"

"No, I don't realize anything of the sort," Charlie roared. His anger now was clear and steadying. "Just because that's all you can think about doesn't mean everyone's the same way. I've had enough of it. I just can't take it anymore."

Peter studied him for a long moment, his eyes full of love and confidence, which slowly gave way to alarm. Charlie struggled to meet his open gaze without flinching. "You really almost think you mean that, don't you?" Peter said finally.

"Now we're getting somewhere. What more do you want to convince you? Shall I pick you up and throw you out in the street?"

Peter spoke very quietly, as if he hadn't heard him. "You'd let me go in there and pack my bags and go? Now?"

Charlie felt himself consumed by the great eyes, but he could no longer meet them. "That's exactly what I mean," he said.

"I don't believe you."

"Why don't you try it and find out?"

Peter nodded as if in a trance and turned. Charlie watched him withdraw. Gripped by anger, he felt a flush of triumph pass through him. He had won. Peter moved slowly back through the alcove toward the closets. Halfway there, his body suddenly went rigid. A terrible cry was torn from him. He flung himself onto the bed, and his whole body was shaken by wild, animal sobs. He sounded as if he were surrendering hope, reason, life itself. Charlie's scalp crawled. He fled the sound, careening through doors, into the kitchen. It was less agonizing there. He bowed his head against the refrigerator, trying to close his ears to it. He flung back his head and put his hands over his ears. He seized the bottle and his glass and poured himself another drink. By God, he would not give in. He would not go to him. Another drink would make it all right. It had to stop eventually.

He was pouring himself another drink when it did. It took him a moment to become aware of the silence. He cocked his head in the direction of the bed and moved slyly toward the door. He staggered slightly and steadied himself against the jamb. Silence. Had he gone to sleep? After a moment, he heard a sound that he identified as the closet door opening. There was a thump. Packing at last. Still, there'd been a lot of wild talk this evening. Better keep an eye on him. He swirled his drink in his glass, swaying gently. Then, making a great effort to hold to a straight course, he walked rather stiffly into the room. He didn't look into the alcove but sat where he could keep an eye on everything without appearing to do so. Peter was indeed packing. His movements were erratic, with long moments of total immobility. Charlie thought of the last time he had packed. He mustn't let himself be tricked into interfering again. No matter what he said, no matter what he did, he must let him get on with it.

The silence began to bother him. He allowed himself to take a more direct look, at the risk of meeting his eye. Peter was dropping things into the bag without seeming to know what he was doing. He looked totally withdrawn into himself, expressionless. The moments of immobility seemed to be moments of vacant reverie. What was he thinking? He almost wished he were still crying. That would be understandable. That would tell him what he was feeling.

When the bag was full, Peter stood over it for a long minute, his body slack, not seeming to know what to do with it. He closed it finally and pulled it off the bed and came out and dropped it beside the hall door. Charlie felt his heart race wildly. Don't say anything, he warned himself. Just one bag so far. Peter wasn't ready to go yet. If there was some final point to make, he had time.

Peter straightened and stood looking down at him. Charlie buried his face in his glass. He began to tremble. Suddenly Peter's shoulders hunched forward, his mouth opened, and the terrible sobs came again as he doubled over and beat his forehead with his fists. "I don't — I can't—" Strangled, unintelligible words emerged in gasps. Charlie lunged up out of the chair with a kind of groan that seemed to be part of the movement and seized him. He staggered heavily and almost brought them both crashing to the floor. He recovered his footing somehow. Peter's body went limp against his, shaken by sobs. He crushed it to him, wanting to crush the sobs from it. "Oh, God, Christ dammit. I love you. Is that what you want? As if you don't know. I love you. It's driving me crazy. I sit at the office and think about you, about all of you, yes, about having your cock in my mouth. Do you understand? You don't know what it does to me when you come like that. As if you were giving me your life to swallow. I never liked it before. No, it's you. It's all you. All right, goddamn it, I have a big cock, but it would have to be twice as big for me to have all I want of you. When I'm inside of you, I want more and more. I know where to touch you to make you laugh. I know where to touch you so you moan with just sheer goddamn happiness. I know how to make you growl. And I want more. Always more. It drives me crazy. It's been like that ever since I first looked at you in the car. I couldn't believe my eyes. I measured you like a silly high-school kid, and you let me have you. You let me have you, all of you. All beauty. And ever since, you've turned me upside down. I don't know what I am anymore. I've fought it, I've tried to make sense. But it's all just you. Always you. All summer long and here still. Watching you. Looking at you naked. Seeing the incredible things that go on in your eyes when you look at me. Oh, Christ. I love you, goddamn you."

Peter was motionless in his arms. "Come to bed, darling," he murmured.

Charlie pushed him from him and gripped his wrists hard and fell back into a chair and pulled him to his knees in front of him. He ran his fingers through his hair and jerked his head back roughly so that his mouth fell open. "There. Where is it? If I could find it, I'd smash it." His whiskey-laden breath was hot in Peter's face. His meticulously groomed fair hair was disheveled. His aloofly smiling mask was contorted by rage and rapture. His eyes looked almost glazed in their fury of concentration. He withdrew one hand from Peter's hair and put his fingers on his face and began to model it as if it were clay. He drew thumb and forefinger, one at the hairline, the other along the eyebrows, across his forehead. "That plane." He placed his palm flat on his brow. "That's part of it. You have to have hair just that golden and growing the way it does." He stroked it briefly. He worked his fingers around the sockets of the eyes. "Look at them. A mile apart and the lashes all furry on your cheeks." He ran his forefinger down his nose and framed his partly open mouth, thumb on one side, fingers flattened on the other. "And that. Oh, Christ." He fingered the lips, spreading and lifting them at the corners. "Here's your smile, but I can't make it work. It's inside somewhere." He shaped the chin with his thumb and gripped his neck and placed his thumb on the windpipe and pressed. "That would stop it. Where would it all go then?" He suddenly released his neck and brought the sides of his hands slicing down on his shoulders. Peter swayed, but recovered his balance and remained kneeling before his love, his eyes wide on the intent face. Charlie's eyes moved from hand to hand, studying the space between them. Then he twisted the tie out of the way and began to pull at the buttons of the shirt, ripping it open. He thrust his hands within and tangled his fingers in the silken curls of the armpits. He placed the tips of his fingers at the point where muscle was joined to arms and traced the line of his breast. He took a deep shuddering breath and ran his hands down the ribs and thrust his fingers just inside the top of the trousers. "That's where I stopped measuring. From here on was where it all happened." He withdrew his hands from inside the shirt and circled his waist. He grappled with belt and buttons and cloth in an impossible striving for knowledge. He ran his hands down over the buttocks and held them. He rested his forehead on Peter's shoulder. "And here. Oh, here. Praxiteles — all those flabby bottoms — he was thinking of girls. Michelangelo was kidding with those great hunks of shapeless flesh. I've known a boy. I've measured beauty. What more do I want?"

Peter feared the brutality he felt in the searching hands, he feared to make a move of his own. "Please come to bed, my darling," he begged.

Charlie lifted his head. "Nothing," he shouted into Peter's face. "Not anything more from anybody. Beauty. Love. Fucking shit." He flung Peter from him, and he toppled back against the hassock. Charlie slid off the chair onto his knees and lifted his arms as if he were being crucified. "See? Here I am groveling at your goddamn feet. Is this the way you want me? Let me go. For Christ's sake, let me go." He bent over and pounded his thighs with his fists. Then he sprang up and careened over to the wall and pushed himself off it and disappeared into the kitchen.

Peter lay sprawled against the hassock, his head back, his hair on end, his tie over his shoulder, his shirt ripped, his belt undone, his fly open. He was utterly spent, incapable of thought, even less capable of feeling. In a little while, he heard Charlie return. He opened his eyes with an effort and saw him slumped against the wall, holding a glass, looking down at him. His face had changed shape with drink.

"What the hell are you lying there for?" he demanded. "Why aren't you up finishing your packing?"

Peter didn't move except to shift his gaze to the ceiling. "It's a little late for that, isn't it? If I'm queer, you are too. Why don't we start with that and work something out from there?"

"You want me to beat the shit out of you as a farewell present?"

"It wouldn't be farewell. I'm not going. I can't. I just haven't got the strength. Why don't we go to bed? We can figure it out in the morning."

"Oh, no. You know damn well what would happen if we went to bed. I'm not taking any chances. That's all over. Finished."

Peter shifted his eyes back to Charlie. "You said things just now I'd never dare say, even though I've thought them a thousand times. What are we supposed to make of that?"

"I don't know what I said. Who cares? You'd never understand anyway."

"What about what you've just done to me?"

"What've I done to you?"

"I don't know. Raped me? Destroyed what little sanity I had left? I don't know. All I know is that nothing will ever be the same again."

"What won't be the same?"

"Anything. Most of all my paying any attention to you when you tell me to leave."

"Goddamn it, you're getting out of here. If you want to lie there, I'll drag you out into the hall and leave you."

Peter rolled his head on the hassock. "I've thought I was losing *my* mind. Maybe you already have. You're asking me to kill myself. I've been thinking about doing just that. I guess I'm not the type. It all seems all right up to the point where I pull the trigger or jump or whatever, and then I know I couldn't do it. I certainly couldn't do it as long as I know you want me."

"Want you! I want to kill you. Are you going to get up?"

"If you'll come to bed with me."

"Well, I won't, goddamn it. Never again."

"Then I'll stay here for a while."

Charlie lurched forward and grabbed his arm. For a moment, he teetered and almost fell but he managed to straighten himself and began to pull. From where it rested on the hassock, Peter's head thumped onto the floor.

"Stop it," he commanded.

Charlie obeyed, swaying over him. "Are you going to get up?"

"Do you want another slugging match? You wouldn't have much of a chance this time. You're stinking drunk."

"I'm drunk, am I? We'll see about that." He began to pull on the arm again. Peter yanked it away, and he staggered back and banged against the wall.

"Now just leave me alone." Peter closed his eyes.

"You're getting *out* of here." It was a wail of frustration. Peter heard him coming at him again. Charlie kicked him hard in the ribs. Peter struggled into a sitting position.

"You're really going to push this as far as it'll go, aren't you? I won't hit you. I probably ought to. I probably ought to knock you cold and get it over with. I can't stand hurting you." There was silence, except for Charlie's heavy breathing, as Peter slowly rearranged his clothes. He pulled out his wallet and extracted a card and studied it. "All right. Let's see how sad and disgusting we can make it. A bit more or less won't make any difference in the morning." He pulled himself to his feet and squared his shoulders and threw back his head and took a deep breath. He went to the telephone and, holding the card in front of him, dialed a number.

"Mr. Whitethorne please. Oh, Tommy? Hi. This is Peter Martin ... Yeah, the one and only. Can I come see you in a little while? ... No, no trouble. You said to call you and — well, I'm calling you. I haven't had a chance before ... Oh, maybe a half an hour or so ... Fine. If anything turns up, I'll call you back." He hung up thoughtfully.

Charlie was leaning against the wall, a sneer on his face. "The Congressman's boy? What's wrong with the Congressman?"

"He's probably in Washington."

"You planning to go to bed with him?"

"The way he's been looking at me at C.B.'s for the last few months, I don't see how I can avoid it. I'll probably get laid by every man in New York. That's one thing you've taught me how to do."

Charlie's mouth clamped shut. The muscles of his neck swelled. He lifted his fists to his face. His control broke. A sob escaped through clenched teeth. He covered his face with his hands and repressed sobs shook him.

Peter stared at him, appalled. "Oh, no. No, don't, please don't. You've never cried before. I swore I'd never let you." He went to him and put his arms around him and led him to a chair and put him into it. He knelt beside him and smoothed his hair. "Please, my darling. Don't cry. You *can't* cry. It's just not like you."

"I've — wanted to — often enough," Charlie gasped between sobs.

"Oh, my darling. My own love. I'll go if you stop it. I'll go if you want me to. I won't see Tommy if that's wrong. It just doesn't seem to matter much what I do if I'm not here with you. Please, sweetheart. Please, my dearest. I guess I understand. There're a lot of things you want to do in life. You can't have me hanging around your neck all the time. I just want you. I guess I am a silly little queen. You'll be fine without me. You'll probably get married and have lots of babies. I've never dared tell you how much I've wished I could do that — have your babies. Lots of little Charlies. God, what heaven. You don't have to worry about me. I'll be OK, I guess. It seems people get over everything. I won't get over you because I don't want to, but I'll be OK. It must count for something to start life with what I've had. So much happiness. So goddamn much happiness. More than most people have in a whole lifetime, I'll bet. Please don't, darling. Everything's going to be OK. You're going to be a big star, and I'll come see you and tell all my friends that I was yours and always will be. Or I won't say anything, if you don't want me to. But I'll know. God, will I know. Please, darling. Please."

The sobs gradually subsided as Peter continued to stroke his hair. At last, Charlie rubbed his eyes with the flat of his hands and put an arm around Peter and hugged him close. He rested his head against the golden hair.

"God, baby. You're so good." His body heaved with a long sigh. "Why does this happen if it's so wrong? That's what I'd like to know."

"Who says it's wrong?"

"It is. It must be. We can't be the only two people in the world who're right. OK, maybe I'm queer, too. At least, a lot of me is. But I'm not going to be. You'll see. It could only have happened with you. You're the only one. You always will be. My boy. My baby. I swear to that."

"I'm glad. But don't say any more, please, or you'll get me going again. I feel as if there isn't a tear left in me. I probably will have stored up plenty by tomorrow." He disengaged himself and stood abruptly and went into the alcove. Charlie found an unfinished drink beside him and drank it. He was aware of Peter moving about nearby, but he couldn't look at him. He heaved himself out of the chair with difficulty and weaved his way into the kitchen and replenished his drink. It seemed to him that he had barely done so when Peter dropped both bags in the hall and was standing in the doorway. He had combed his hair and was wearing a fresh shirt. Even in his drunkenness, something happened in Charlie's chest as the impact of his beauty struck him.

"Well, out into the cold, cold world," Peter said. "You can keep the rug. Mother will kill me."

"What are you going to do?"

"That's a hell of a question to ask a silly queen at nine-thirty on a winter night. How should I know? I want to find out what everything's all about."

"Will you go on with school?"

"I don't know. No. There's too much I have to learn."

"Do you have enough money?"

"Oh, money. I haven't figured out yet why people make such a fuss about it. Anyway, I've got plenty."

"Will you let me know where you are?"

"Sure. If I am anywhere. I know none of this is really happening, I'll wake up and we'll be in each other's arms with great hard-ons, the way we always are."

"Oh, Christ." Charlie swayed toward him, and Peter stepped forward quickly and caught him. Their mouths met and opened to each other. Their kiss was drowned in tears. They laid their heads together and clung to each other.

"OK, OK, OK," Peter whispered. "You're probably right, darling. I guess it was too soon." He withdrew carefully, holding Charlie's swaying body, and took his hands and placed them gently on the counter. "There. Got it? Hang on. Go to—" His voice caught. He thrust his hand into his pocket and slapped metal onto the counter. "The keys." He turned and pulled open the apartment door and shoved his bags into the outer hall. He looked back from the threshold. "Go to — bed, darling." He pulled the door closed behind him. Charlie looked at his hands where Peter had put them. He lifted one and grasped the almost empty bottle and poured himself a drink. He wasn't even aware that he was crying. He felt fine.

He woke up the next morning fully dressed on the bed. He had such a hangover that at first he didn't remember what had happened. It wasn't until he had showered and shaved and was fumbling about in the kitchen at the unfamiliar chore of getting himself breakfast that it hit him. He slumped over the kitchen table with his head on his arms and wept.

W HAT HAPPENS NEXT is incomprehensible in retrospect unless we adjust time to youth's rhythm. It seems too compressed, too dense for its chronological dimension. The crowded hour is both the privilege and the burden of the young. Minutes drag as experience accumulates — an afternoon, an evening can contain the foundations of a life; a day is a sufficient span of time to break a life in two. Later, when all experience has lost its novelty and the years flash by, a decade may offer not a single memorable event. Looking back on the crucial epoch of discovery, we say, "Good heavens, did all that happen in only one short winter?" While it's happening we say, "Dear God, will this never end?" or, "This eternity is not enough."

It was a day for telephone calls. Charlie called C.B. from the office and told her not to write Peter's mother. "I don't think you completely understood what he was trying to tell you yesterday. Anyway, I packed him off last night. He'll write his family himself. He's going to live with some friends from school." Being able to talk to her with nothing to hide made him feel as if this must be what it had been all about, that he had won the right to deal with her as an equal. Life held no more schoolboy secrets.

Later, his mother called from Philadelphia and asked him to have lunch with her the next day at a sort of tea shop where nobody he knew ever went. "You needn't tell Mother I'm coming," she said. It was the only odd note struck in an otherwise ordinary conversation.

At the end of the morning, unable to restrain himself any longer, he called Tommy Whitethorne. "Did Peter turn up last night?" he asked.

"Oh, yes. I more or less expected to hear from you. I think we'd better be careful what we say on the telephone."

Charlie suddenly felt an imposed intimacy with Tommy Whitethorne that he very much disliked. "I just wanted to know if he's all right," he said coldly.

"Yes and no. Yes, I guess, in the way you mean. I understand better than he does the position he's put you in. I'm sorry. I don't think you should see him for the time being."

"I have no intention of doing so."

"Oh. Well, if we can get off in a corner at C.B.'s on Sunday, I'll be able to tell you more."

"Thanks," Charlie said, and hung up.

He called Hattie and arranged for her to cook dinner for him that evening.

They arrived at the apartment within minutes of each other, which was what Charlie had been counting on. Once she was there, chattering and crowing with laughter, the place felt quite safe and normal.

After dinner, they went through their scene several times, making nothing of the kiss. Eventually, Hattie said, "I suppose it's about time for Peter to show up. Let's go to Leary's for a drink."

Charlie looked at the rug. "He's gone," he said. He jumped to his feet and hurried out of the room and shut himself in the bathroom. He braced himself at the sink as his shoulders heaved with his silent tears. When he had himself under control, he returned to her.

"You all right?" she asked, her bulging eyes surveying him.

"Sure. I just had a funny sort of cramp in my stomach. It's passed."

"Compliments of the chef. What do you mean, Peter's gone?"

"He moved out yesterday."

"Awfully sudden, wasn't it? Lovers' quarrel?"

"How did you guess? As a matter of fact, he's moved in with some kids at school, which is what he was planning to do all along. This place is too small."

"Rather cramped, I would've thought. A perfect place for passes now."

"Ideal. Shall I make one at you?"

Her great, mocking eyes bored into his. "Don't bother. If you want me to go to bed with you, just say so. I don't want you to think I'm like those other girls you mentioned."

"What're we waiting for?"

"*I've* been waiting to lure Peter into a sack and drop him into the East River."

"You really mean it? You really want to go to bed?" It seemed enormously important to him that it should be right. No nonsense, no hasty retreats. He liked her a lot, and the thought of going to bed with her made him feel that he loved her. It didn't matter whether C.B. liked her or not; there was nothing suspect about marriage if it came to that.

She laughed at him. "Don't tell me I'm going to have to talk you into it."

"I just want to be sure you know what you're doing. I don't like all the teasing and heavy breathing and the rest of it. I've had enough of that."

"Aren't we masterful. You'd better be good." She laughed at him again. "Don't worry. I know what I'm doing. I just happen to be madly in love with you."

Their eyes met and dueled with each other. He smiled with satisfaction as hers turned defenseless with desire.

"Come on," he said gently, generous in victory. Her look was deeply exciting. He felt himself stirring with it. He stood and held out his hand to her. She shook her head.

"Let me get undressed. Women look so silly getting out of their harness."

He moved away from her with a gesture toward the alcove. "Help yourself. Call me when you're ready." He went to the bathroom and took off his clothes. In spite of his excitement, he was relaxed and completely self-possessed. This was the way he had always hoped it would be with a girl; easy, voluntary, civilized. He stood in the bathroom doorway, idly stroking himself. "How you doing?" he asked, raising his voice only slightly to carry around the corner.

"Just a second. All right."

"Do you mind if I'm naked?"

"I hardly expected you in full evening dress."

He laughed as he came out, his sex swaying heavily. It rose into full erection as he approached her. Her eyes were wide on it.

"Well, well, well," she said. "I feel as if I ought to stand up and salute. You mean to say there are girls who've turned that down? They must've been stuffed with sawdust." She was lying on the bed under the sheet. She pulled it off. She could have been a skinny boy hiding his sex between his legs, narrow of shoulder and hip. Her breasts were unexpected, gently swelling with enormous nipples that stared at him like insentient eyes. He lingered over her a moment, displaying himself. Her eyes didn't waver. "Come on down here where I can get at you," she said. He sat on the edge of the bed and put a hand on a breast and covered the hard nipple.

"Do you do this with anybody that comes along?" he asked, piqued at her clear-eyed composure.

"Don't get smart. I told you I'm in love with you. That doesn't happen to me every day. I'm not a virgin, in case that matters to you.

He stretched out beside her and gathered her in his arms. There was very little of her. Her body felt as if it could be demolished by the act of love. The thought brought him a new excitement. She took his sex in her hand and felt all the length of it.

"So this is the way boys are built. The others — well, only two when you get right down to it — must've been undernourished. I'll admit it doesn't come as a complete surprise. I've been doing some discreet crotch-gazing." She laughed as he performed what he supposed were the essential preliminaries. He put his hand between her legs and fingered her. He took her nipples in his mouth. He lifted his head and put his mouth on hers. As their tongues met, her composure vanished. Her nails dug into his back, her body writhed beneath him, her breasts began to heave. He lifted himself and guided his sex to hers and entered her. She tore her mouth from his and uttered a wordless shout. "Oh, no. No. No," she cried. Whatever the negative referred to, it was clearly not intended to arrest him. She grasped his buttocks and pulled him to her. His sex thrust deep within her. Her face dissolved into a look of animal hunger, rapt and possessed. "Oh, God. No," she crooned. "It's not possible. I'm yours. Charlie. I'm yours."

He felt intensely the truth of it. His sex possessed her, feeling immense in her slight body. He was filled with a lust for procreation. This was the way it was supposed to be, his taking this panting, writhing creature and giving her life. There was no question of holding back. She drove him furiously, her hands working his buttocks to move his sex all through her, her hips thrust up and rotating in a passion to enjoy all of him. His orgasm came quickly. He uttered a series of great shouts as he felt himself exploding within her. "Oh, God. Oh, God. Oh, God," she cried in unison with him as he collapsed, heaving, on top of her. She seized his head by the hair and put his mouth on hers.

When their breathing was steady, she lifted his head, still holding it by the hair, and looked searchingly into his eyes. "Was it good?" she demanded.

138

"Mmm," he murmured drowsily. He was unprepared for her clown's face. He was lost in a sensual dream of Peter: his arms held his big, smooth, richly fleshed body; his rapturous laughter sang in his ears; he saw his replete smile after they had been overwhelmed by shared orgasms. Recalled by Hattie, he resolutely closed his mind to Peter.

"I could die when I think of all the time we've wasted," she said. "I feel as if you'd made about ten babies all at once. What bliss." She released his hair and ran her hands down his back and over his buttocks. She slipped one hand down between his legs and fondled his balls. His whole body jerked in response, and his sex began to grow inside her. She swivelled her hips slowly, and her face was once more blotted out by animal hunger. "You're going to do it again," she gloated.

"Sure."

She continued to fondle his balls. "Lovely. Oh, yes. What a guy. More and more. God, yes. Take me, dammit, take me. I'm all yours."

His second orgasm came almost as quickly as his first. When he was done, she disengaged herself. "That's enough of *that,*" she said, "or I really will have ten babies. I feel as if you'd reduced my little gadget to shreds."

"What little gadget?"

"The thing I wear, silly. So I won't have babies."

"Oh. Do you wear it all the time?"

"Always when I'm going to see you. I'm an optimist. How right I was." She rose and left him. He noted as she left that the hips were just too wide for plastic tension; the buttocks looked slightly sprung. He closed his eyes and drifted, luxuriating in the freedom of not having to run off to the bathroom himself. He felt a sense — if not of joy — of at least a job well done. He could give her what she wanted as well as anybody. And there was no doubt that she wanted it. That was exciting. Her frail body seemed totally consumed by him. It was thrilling. What if she did have a baby? That would be rather exciting, too. It had been exciting to think of this power in him when he was inside her. They'd have to get married. He would have achieved man's estate. It was a reassuring thought. There was no room for strain or conflict between them. It was so straightforward — her wanting him, his taking her. And aside from that, she was a lot of fun. If he were married, there would be a reason for staying on at the job. He knew he was a success at the office; there were already hints of promotion. Perhaps it was silly to knock himself out in the theater. He heard her returning and half opened his eyes for a glimpse of her breasts and closed them again. She lay down beside him. He put his arm around her and drew her to him, but remained indolently on his back.

"Fancy us," she said with laughter. "What a gorgeous way to spend an evening. Why haven't you done this to me before? It must've been obvious I was a pushover."

"No opportunity."

"And all this time I've been thinking you didn't really like girls."

"Satisfied now?"

"My, oh, my. I'll tell you a secret. I don't know as much about it all as I pretended. The first time was when I was still at school. At a dance. He must have been a very wicked boy because he had me before I knew what was happening. The other wasn't so long ago. I was touring in *Our Town*. Well, last spring. I told you. I met this divine man out of town. I fell in love on the spot. Well, perhaps not quite like you, but it was the first time I really knew what it felt like. That's terribly important for an actress. It wasn't much of an affair. He was married and was nervous about me being emotionally involved. I'm afraid he rather ditched me. Agony. Tell me about you."

"Oh, only three or four times, really. I told you. They never seemed to know what they wanted. It always spoiled it."

"You can't say that about me." She laughed and fondled his sex. It responded lazily.

"No. You're perfect."

"Fascinating. Your cock, I mean. I've never had a chance to see how they work. It goes on getting bigger. What does it feel like when it's getting hard like this?"

"I don't know. Like I want to have you."

"Like you want to fuck me?"

"Sure. Like I want to fuck you."

"Does it ever get hard when you're out? I mean, in public?"

"Sometimes."

"How too utterly embarrassing. I've watched it a lot. Crotch gazing. It sometimes looks enormous."

He chuckled a trifle self-consciously. "I guess that's when I wanted to fuck you."

"I'm glad you waited, really. It feels so natural now. I guess because I've imagined it so often. Even when I thought you never

140

would, it was such divinely agonizing suspense. What bliss for it to've actually happened. This is really you I'm holding. Amazing. You feel as if you want to fuck me again. It gets so hard. It's incredible. Fuck me again, lover. I have to go soon."

"What do you mean, you have to go?" He opened his eyes at last and looked at her.

"Of course I have to go. You don't think I'm going to stay here all night, do you?"

"You certainly are."

"Oh, no. I live with my family, remember."

"What difference does that make?"

"They leave me alone if I stick to the rules. One of them is not sleeping out."

"But you've *got* to stay."

"If you only knew how I want to. Don't talk about it now. Here. Let me put it in. There. Oh, there." All he could think of was her leaving. He couldn't face a night alone. It was too late to get drunk. She had to stay. He was scarcely aware of the act he was performing. Slowly he realized that his orgasm wouldn't be quick this time. He wanted to postpone it as long as he could. Anything to keep her here. He left the active role to her. He took a deep breath and thought about being alone and felt the orgasm receding further. He became aware of an increasing intensity in her activity. He moved his head and looked at her. Her eyes were rolling, drugged with wonder. The hunger in her face was mingled with incredulity.

"Something's happening," she gasped. "I don't know what. I've never had anything like it. It's fantastic. Charlie. Oh, Charlie." She flung her legs up and wrapped them around him. She bit his shoulder. She sank her teeth into his neck. She let go to roll her head wildly on the pillow. "Oh, God. Oh, Charlie. Fuck me. Fuck me. Don't come. More. More. Please. Christ. Oh, yes. All of it. Please don't come." She unwrapped her legs and beat on his buttocks with her heels. Her hips writhed frantically. She began to croon as he took control. He drove into her in long thrusts. He felt complete mastery of himself and her. He was on the edge of orgasm, but he was able to withhold it as he awaited the climax of her extraordinary frenzy. Her crooning became a shrill ululation. Her fingers were tangled in his hair. Her mouth was all over his shoulders and chest, biting hard. Her knees clung to his flanks, moving to his rhythm. She screamed. Her body was convulsed by

141

a long shudder, and she burst into sobbing laughter as he felt himself streaming into her.

He lay on her, dozing. He didn't know how long he had been there when she stirred and pushed at him feebly. "Let me up," she said. He rolled over onto his back, but she didn't move. "I guess that's what sex must be all about. Coming together. It's never happened to me before."

He didn't quite grasp the significance of what she was saying, but it appeared to score in his favor. He felt for her hand. "You're not leaving?"

"Of course I am, silly. I have to. What would my family think if I came traipsing in in the morning? Well, they'd be right. What would the servants say? It would cause the most frightful row."

"I'm not going to let you go."

"What difference does it make? You'll go to sleep. You can't go on fucking me all night."

"Who says I can't?"

"I understand boys have their limits. I know a girl who says it happened to her nine times in one night. She seemed to consider it a record."

"All right. Six more times and I'll let you go."

She put her hand on his sex. "Boasting. It gets so much smaller. That's what I don't understand. Where does it all come from?"

"Leave your hand there and you'll soon find out."

She removed it. "No. Please. I *have* to go. It's horrid of you to make it more difficult."

"I want you here in the morning."

"That would be bliss, wouldn't it? Maybe over the weekend. I could make up some story."

"What if we were married?"

"What do you mean, 'married'?"

"I mean, if you told them in the morning you're going to get married, there wouldn't be any row."

"Oh, wouldn't there be." She hooted with laughter. "Married! Are you serious?"

"Of course. Why shouldn't we get married? The amount of time we spend together, we might as well be. And now there's this."

"Do you love me?"

"Of course."

"Then why haven't you said so?"

"What've I been *doing* all evening?"

"There is that. But a girl likes to hear it just the same."

"All right. I love you."

She laughed at him. "You're more convincing when you're acting it out. I doubt if you know anything about love. You probably never will."

He lifted his hand and put the back of it over his eyes. For a moment, he couldn't hear her words, although he knew she was still speaking. Then she was saying, "—in love with you. I suppose I might as well consider myself. We'd better have a drink."

He pulled himself up instantly and sprang out of bed. That was just what he wanted. He went to the kitchen and mixed two strong ones. Maybe it would put her to sleep. Noticing an odd musky smell about himself, he washed his sex at the kitchen sink. Stroking it with a towel brought it back to life. Her eyes went to it as be returned with the drinks.

"It never really gets all that small, does it?" She propped herself up in bed and took her glass. He moved in beside her. He was amazed that a girl could be so unselfconsciously naked with him. She might as well have been clanking with all her fancy jewelry for all the difference it seemed to make. She took a swallow of her drink and choked. "Good God. Did you put the whole bottle in?"

"I've got the same. We need it. So what about it?"

"About getting married? Oh, I admit I've thought about it. I suppose a girl does. Ever since I first feasted my stunned eyes on you. Of course, I'll get married dozens of times. Actresses always do. It's the life, I suppose. The need to constantly renew oneself emotionally. But you'd make a lovely first husband. I can put a glamorous picture of you in my autobiography. Can you afford to get married?"

"I don't make very much, but C.B. gives me an allowance. It's been plenty for—" He took a quick gulp of his drink. "Peter and me" remained unspoken. "It's been plenty so far."

"But you're not going on with that sickening job, are you?"

"Hell, no. It's just till I get a break in the theater. The trouble is, if I become an actor, C.B. will probably stop my allowance."

"What do you mean, *if* you become an actor? I'm not going to marry some little publisher's clerk."

"I'm not a clerk. Anyway, I'd quit tomorrow if anything turned up."

143

"Nothing ever will turn up if you're not out looking for it. I'm not going to marry a man who's tied up in an office. At least, not till I'm a star. The hours wouldn't work. You're always having to think about going to sleep just when it's time to go out and make the rounds and see the people who count. No, that's out."

"All right. All right. We'll get married and as soon as we see how things are going, I'll quit."

"I have some money of my own. It's not much. It comes to a few hundred a month."

"A few hundred a month! Well, hell, what are we worrying about?"

"I don't think my family will be beastly about you. You *are* in the *Social Register,* aren't you?"

"Sure. In Philadelphia."

"And you're C.B.'s grandson. It's really quite dismally respectable. They probably expect me to run off with some nigger jazz player. They might even be pleased."

"Then it's all right? You're not going to go?" He spoke with such insistence that she studied him for a moment, the mockery in her eyes softening with defenselessness again.

"You're sweet. Maybe you really do love me. There's still an awful lot to decide."

"I'm going to have another drink to celebrate." Her glass was still quite full so he took his own and refilled it and returned to her. Everything was going to be all right now. It was marvelous to have the whole night ahead of them, drinking and talking, and comfortably naked together. He had never had drinks in bed before. The apartment felt agreeably inhabited, leaving no room for ghosts. He kissed the side of her mouth in a burst of high spirits. "Well, then. How do we go about it?" he demanded.

"Well, of course it's got to be a deep dark secret until it's done. I won't have my family turning it into a circus. I'll call home in the morning and say I had to stay overnight with a girlfriend. They won't believe me, of course, but by the time they get around to grilling me, we should be Mr. and Mrs. I have a cousin who's very big in city politics. President of something or other. I'll find out all about it from him. He's a pal. He won't rat on us. I know we have to have Wassermanns."

"What about all the people who run off and get married overnight?"

"That's in other states. It's different here. Oh, my God. Birth certificates. How too utterly complicated it all is."

"I've got a passport. That ought to do."

"Of course. How clever of you. So've I. Sam will be able to fix everything. I'll take care of it in the morning."

"I'll have to tell C.B."

"Oh, no you don't. It's a secret from everyone. I know families. Yours is no different from mine. You let me handle this."

He knew that C.B. couldn't possibly object, but for some reason he wasn't particularly looking forward to telling her, either before or after. He decided not to push his point.

"I'm afraid I'm not going to be much help, anyway," he said. "My mother is coming in for lunch."

"Your mother? You never talk about her. What for?"

"I don't know. Shopping, I guess."

"Well, you'd better get rid of her quickly. And you'd better tell your office you're not coming back after lunch. I'll need you."

"You mean you think we can do it tomorrow?"

"Absolutely. That's the whole point. If we can't do it quickly, I won't do it at all. And now I *have* to do it. Look at me. Spending the night with a man. I've never done it before, but you're practically my husband." She crowed with laughter. "What're you like in the morning?"

"The same. Irresistible."

"I might make your breakfast, just to see what it's like. But don't count on it in the future. Let me out. I've got things to do." She crawled over him and left him.

He stayed where he was, finishing his drink. She was gone a long time. He found that he was almost asleep. He pulled himself up and heard her still splashing about in the bathroom. He went to the kitchen and fixed himself a nightcap. He had almost finished it when she came out. He held her briefly, feeling vague and disconnected.

"Go to bed. I'll be right there," he said. He went through his nightly routine in the bathroom. A quick shower woke him up. The thought of her lying there waiting to be quickened into life by him aroused him. He came out and snapped off lights, feeling her eyes on him. He imagined her legs parting, her hips lifting with need of him. It aroused him further, so that his sex jutted forward in a heavy curve, not yet quite erect. She stared at it as he approached the bed.

145

"It *is* fascinating," she said dreamily. "It's always different. I'm glad girls don't have them. I wouldn't know what to expect from one minute to the next."

He staggered slightly as he got into bed. He stretched out and took her to him, counting on the contact to bring him into full erection. His sex was bulky between them, but failed to react as vigorously as he had expected. He put his mouth on hers and stroked her back, waiting for the final surge that would permit him to mount her. He found himself getting drowsy. Too much to drink, he reassured himself. It had happened before, but it had never mattered. Peter would always do something about it. Peter's miraculous mouth. To give himself time, he feigned sleep. He let his head slide back and pulled himself up with a start.

"You're sleepy, lover. So am I." She reached behind him and snapped off the light. "Kiss me good night and hold me. What bliss."

He lay outraged in the dark. Why had she let it go at that? Did she think he couldn't get it up? She hadn't even felt it to see. That would have been all he needed. His sex ached. He felt incomplete and frustrated. It was always the same. Girls just didn't understand. Her loss. Let it go. He drifted off, resentment lodged in some layer of his consciousness.

It was still there when he woke up, his morning erection lying across her belly. He took her quickly and thought only of himself, straddling her, with his body propped above her on his arms, a smile of private satisfaction playing about his lips at the hunger he saw in her sleep-drugged face and at the longing that was still in it when he left her.

"That's quite a way to wake a girl up," she said as she stumbled around the kitchen in one of his dressing gowns. "I mean, it really gets the day off to a flying start. Are all boys like that in the morning, like bulls?"

"I wouldn't know." He liked the image. She'd find out whether or not he could get it up.

"I just want to know what to expect. It's certainly more fun than an alarm clock."

They made arrangements to keep in touch during the day, and kissed, and he was off. She called at noon, crowing at him over the phone, to tell him that it was all settled. She would meet him after lunch to take him to have his Wassermann and they would be

146

married later in the day. Her cousin had apparently swept aside various tiresome delays and formalities.

His mother was waiting for him at her tea shop, wearing a rather fussy suit that bore no relationship to the rough tweed coat she carried over her arm. Her hair was in gentle disarray under a sensible hat, her habitually worried look slightly more pronounced than he remembered it. She moved in an air of small crises that seemed about to overwhelm her. She had her usual effect of making him feel tired. They kissed perfunctorily and settled themselves in a little booth.

After they had ordered unappetizing food, he smiled at her dutifully, wondering as always how she could possibly be C.B.'s daughter, and asked, "How's everything at home?" He wanted a drink desperately.

"Oh, very well, thank you. Yes, I think so. We miss you always, but we've had plenty of time to get used to that, haven't we? You look a bit haggard, dear."

He had never known her to find him looking well. He shrugged. "I'm fine. How did you happen to come over?"

"Oh, well, I thought it would be nice. I haven't been since the spring."

"Are you staying over?" he asked, prepared to rattle off a list of urgent business that would engage him for the next twenty-four hours if she were.

"No, I shouldn't think so. You didn't tell Mother I was coming?"

"No. You said not to. You mean, you've come over just for lunch?"

"Well, not exactly. I did want to see you." Her worried look intensified.

"Well, here I am. Was it about anything in particular?"

"No, not really. That is, I understand there's been some sort of trouble with Peter Martin."

So that was it. He blushed and dropped his eyes, but he wasn't really concerned. He knew how to handle her. "Trouble? Not at all. He's moved, that's all."

"Oh, has he? Oh, I see. Well, you see dear, Mother called the other day — day before yesterday, was it? — and seemed to be in one of her states. We love you very much, you know. We want you to know that if you're in any sort of trouble, we're prepared to stand by you."

"Well, thanks. But—" Food was brought to the table, and they remained silent while it was put before them. It was typical of her

147

to assume that he was in trouble, unlike C.B., who assumed when trouble came that it was somebody else's fault. He looked at her and smiled reassuringly. She continued to look worried. "I don't know what it's all about. Did C.B. put you up to this?"

"Oh, good heavens, no. On the contrary. But you know, dear, much as I admire Mother, I don't think she's always the best person in a jam. She's inclined to go too far. I understand she's refused to receive Peter."

"Yes, she has." He looked at her levelly.

"And she's told you why?" She returned his look with unusual directness. Thank God for Hattie, he thought. Without her, this might have been fairly disagreeable.

"Of course," he said.

"You see, dear, when we're young all sorts of odd things happen to us. Especially when the affections are involved. I know you're very highly strung. I talked to Cousin Sarah yesterday. You know all the trouble she's had. She's quite well now. She hasn't had to be put away for several years. She says that psychiatry has made tremendous strides in all sorts of fields that we never even used to mention."

He almost laughed in her face. He felt so safe that he was beginning to enjoy himself. He was tempted to lead her on just to see how far she was willing to go. "You mean Peter should go to a psychiatrist?"

"Well, maybe he should, but he can't really be my concern. I want you to know that if you've been troubled in any way, if anything's happened that's put you under a strain — I want you to feel free to talk about it, either to me or your father. I know Mother has much more influence over you than we have, but you mustn't think she's the only person who loves you."

He was unexpectedly touched. So this was the way it would have been if Peter had got them into a real mess. He no longer felt like teasing her. "Thanks, Ma. But you really don't have to worry. I'm not troubled in the least. I've written you about Hattie Donaldson. I've been seeing a lot of her recently. As a matter of fact, we're going to get married."

"Why, how very nice." She looked enormously relieved, although the air of worry never completely left her. "Married. Well, of course, you can't think of that for a long time. But how nice you have a girl. I want very much to meet her. She must be lovely.

Now, you will promise not to rush into anything, won't you? It would be a great mistake. You've never had a real girl before. I was so hoping you would. You must bring her home for a weekend. I'm afraid you won't be able to afford marriage for quite some time."

"Well, maybe not. We're—"

"And all this about Peter — why was Mother so upset?"

"Oh, maybe he had some sort of crush on me. He's just a kid. It happens all the time. C.B. exaggerated it out of all proportion."

"She distresses me. I'm afraid she's growing more unbalanced with the years. She's always been given to extremes. It made it very difficult for my father. He was such a gentle soul."

"Gentle? He beat you."

"Oh dear, did she tell you that?" She shook her head with a worried little frown. He felt himself being trapped in the pattern that imposed itself on all their meetings. He let himself be drawn to her and then was engulfed in her constant nagging worries. She was never angry or indignant or gay. Just worried. She reduced life to a single thin note, endlessly struck. "He may have slapped me once a little too hard when I was naughty. He was under a constant strain. She loved him with such unbalanced passion."

"But she hated him."

"Hated him? I remember when he died. She screamed and tore her hair and kept calling to him to come back to her. It was terribly sad."

Of course, she was wrong. She always arranged facts to suit herself. "What did he die of?" he asked with odd reluctance.

She looked around her vaguely. "I don't think I've ever known exactly. I was just a child. Some sort of accident, of course. We were living on the plantation at the time. I'll never forget when they brought him in. The darkies were standing around with their eyes rolling. Mother was screaming and asking him to forgive her and begging him not to die. It was most distressing. I don't think she's ever been quite normal since."

He firmly rejected this version of C.B.'s tragedy. Why should she beg forgiveness of a "drunkard and a beast"? Those had surely been her words. She wasn't a liar, or insane. "I'll have to speak to her about this," he muttered to himself.

"Now that you're in love — I mean, that's why you spoke of marriage, isn't it? You are in love, aren't you, dear?"

149

"Sure, I guess so," he admitted, as Peter, unbidden, filled his mind's eye.

"You'll find it's not always easy to be reasonable. Love is a very difficult emotion. That's why control is so important. Remember that. Try always to exercise control. We can make such terrible mistakes if we let love get out of control."

He shifted restlessly in his seat. He knew about control. He knew too damn much about control. The single thin note jangled in his ear.

He left her with a huge question crowding into the center of his life. Of course, Peter's attitude toward C.B. made no sense. His mother was always wrong about everything. The question remained: Was it right to entrust his life to C.B.? He knew that that was what it amounted to. Everything that he was doing was for her: Peter's departure, the impending marriage, even though she might not be wholly pleased with it at first, were offerings on the altar of her approval. Why should he question her now? Because of a slight discrepancy in two versions of an event that had happened long ago? His mother had been a child and was never a reliable witness. The recompense for his decisions would be immediate and considerable: freedom from emotional torment, socially acceptable married status, Hattie's challenging companionship. There was no time for questions.

Another telephone call revealed that Hattie was in full command of the marriage plans. By five o'clock that afternoon, Charles Mills and Harriet Donaldson were man and wife. They parted immediately, Hattie to announce the news to her family and pack a bag, Charlie to see C.B. They arranged to meet at his apartment as close to seven as possible. He didn't know what he was going to say to his mother when she discovered that she had had lunch with him on his wedding day.

C.B. put aside a book and greeted him. "I'm so glad to see you. I've been so looking forward to hearing the end of Peter's sad story. Is it too early for a drink? Of course not. How dashing you're looking. I'm quite sure you're the most attractive man in the city." She returned to her seat and pressed a bell. "Now tell me everything."

"About Peter? There's not much to tell. He admitted that living together the way we were, he was beginning to get a funny feeling about me. He said he knew that that sort of thing could happen between men, and he agreed right away to move in with some friends he's made at school. We didn't talk much about it. He was pretty embarrassed."

"I see." A maid appeared and C.B. ordered ice. She rose and went to the bar cabinet and began to prepare drinks. "Well, if you're satisfied, I must be, too. He apparently got a grip on himself after he left me."

Just being with her dispelled any questions lingering in his mind. She always said the right thing, adopted the most accommodating attitude. Ice was brought, and he had no further excuse for postponing his announcement. He rose and took a few uncertain paces in her direction. She turned and held out his drink. He went to her and took it. "Listen." He took a gulp of the drink. "I've got some pretty sensational news for you. You'll probably think I'm crazy. Well, as a matter of fact, we got married today."

"Really, my dearest? As far as I know, I haven't been out of the house since yesterday. Perhaps you'd better tell me who 'we' is."

He threw his head back and laughed with nervous relief. "I guess I'm not making much sense. Hattie, of course. Hattie and I got married about an hour ago."

Her expression didn't change. She reached out and took his glass from him and left both their drinks on the bar. She crossed the room and pressed the bell. She remained with her back to him until the maid reappeared. He stood rooted to the spot, barely able to breathe. Surely she couldn't disapprove to the point of refusing to speak to him.

"A bottle of the Moët et Chandon, please," she said. "In an ice bucket." She turned and held her arms out to him, a smile beginning to play around her eyes. He stared at her and roared with laughter again and hurried to her. She kissed him on both cheeks and stood back and looked at him. "It was very naughty of you not to tell me, but I suppose that was Hattie's doing."

"Well, yes. She didn't want anybody to know until it was done."

"I quite understand. She was afraid that tiresome family of hers would make a display of you. There's nothing more barbaric than long engagements. When did you decide?"

"Only yesterday. We've been seeing so much of each other that it seemed the only sensible thing to do. And then, with Peter gone, it was possible for her to move into the place with me."

The maid entered with the champagne, and C.B. went to it and expertly uncorked it. She filled a glass and turned and held it up. "Here's to you, my dearest. I wish you so much happiness." She drank and then filled a glass for him and gave it to him. He felt like crying with gratitude and admiration and love. She was perfect. Who else could have taken the news without batting an eye, without a hint of reproach at its suddenness?

"You're marvelous, C.B." He lifted his glass to her. "Here's to you."

"Oh, my dearest, I hope this will be the happiest day of all our lives. It's so thoughtful of you — both of you — to've come by yourself. It's my last chance to be alone with you. From now on, you'll be Hattie's. I do want to enjoy this moment. Fill my glass. I should think we might get a bit tipsy." She crossed the room and sat. Charlie brought the bottle in the ice bucket and put it beside them. They looked at each other and laughed. "I want to hear all about it," she said. "When did you know you were in love? Of course, Hattie's been in love with you right from the start. I saw that the first day you brought her."

"So she says. I guess it took me a little longer."

"I think that's normal in a man. Women know their minds better about such things. How does her career progress? Will she go on with it?"

"Oh, yes. People say she's good, you know. She's waiting to hear about several possibilities."

"Did I tell you I had a note from Sapphire? She's invited me to her opening night, if you please. She has the last laugh. Thank heavens I didn't try to keep her on here. Won't it be a bit difficult for you if Hattie does find work?"

"How so?"

"The theater's such a disorderly life. Up all night and sleeping all day. Oh well, perhaps she'll give it up as she settles down. I'm sure she'll find it much more satisfying being your wife than an actress."

"I doubt it. She's mad about the theater."

"Of course, she's not really part of it yet. As she goes along, she'll doubtless find that it's really too disreputable. Nobody can have anything to do with it without being soiled by it, though I'm sure Hattie would prove an exception. I suppose you'll be looking for a bigger apartment."

"No, we haven't thought about it."

"But you must, my dearest. You must consider Hattie. The place isn't suitable for a couple. A woman needs some modicum of privacy."

Charlie thought of Hattie last night and almost laughed. What would she need privacy for? "Well, we'll see. She hasn't moved in yet, naturally. She's home now packing a bag. She won't bring all her stuff until tomorrow."

"I see. Well, I'm sure you'll find that I'm right. You be the one to suggest it. Don't make her feel that she's being difficult. It would've been perfectly normal for her to refuse to marry you until you found something bigger."

"OK, I'll ask her, but I don't think she really cares."

"Nonsense. Let's see. I suppose I'll have to stop your allowance. I know you wouldn't accept it now."

"Why not?" he exclaimed. She couldn't mean it. She must know that he really needed it now, as he hadn't before. Hattie was a free spender; he couldn't have thought of marrying her if it hadn't been for the allowance.

"But you're a married man, my dearest. It wouldn't be right for you to be in any way dependent on me, much as I might like you to be. I'm sure Hattie wouldn't want it. Women like to have their men all to themselves, even to the exclusion of harmless old grandmothers. You must have gone over your finances together. You surely didn't expect the allowance to go on indefinitely. Perhaps Hattie has some money of her own."

"A little, I think," he admitted unhappily. She was obviously right. He ought to be ashamed of himself for having counted on her help.

"Well, there you are, you see. We must think of a splendid wedding present. Money? It's so cold-blooded. Perhaps you'll let me furnish your new apartment. Some really good things. A charming setting is so important."

"What if we don't move?" Money, rather than furniture, was very much on his mind.

"There is that. Well, now that you're safely married, I think you'll agree we have time to see how everything works out."

"Oh, sure."

"You know all I have is for you. Your mother will get nothing, nor your brother. I wish there were some way for you to have your money when you need it, now, while you're young, but I'm afraid you'll have to be patient, my dearest. I can't last forever."

153

"Don't be silly, C.B. I don't want anything. You're not even old yet."

"I don't feel old, thanks to you. It's been such a delight watching you grow up, developing into the man I hoped you would be. And now it's done. Married. I don't suppose any female relative is ever really quite prepared for that. The next thing I know, you'll have turned me into a *great*-grandmother. How ghastly."

"You'd love it. I must say, I would too."

Her eyes slid past him and focused on something in space. "Tell her to call me. Perhaps she can have lunch with me tomorrow. You're not invited, my dearest. I hardly know her. You really hadn't prepared me for this."

"I can't believe it yet, myself."

"What about your parents? Will you deign to tell them?"

They laughed and drank their champagne. Parties were discussed. She would make something special of the coming Sunday. Later, there would be dinners.

When he left her, in spite of the champagne and her ready acceptance, he was vaguely dissatisfied with the big event of the day. She had made him feel somehow that life was over. Money. No more allowance. He couldn't possibly quit his job now until something very sure came along. He didn't mind too terribly, but Hattie would. C.B. had generously excluded Hattie from her general condemnation of the theater, but there was something in what she said. He thought of Meyer Rapper and of how tempted he would have been if he had been approached differently. Hattie's insistence on her nightly round of the bars was faintly whorish. Life wasn't over; it was just beginning and it promised to be far from simple. He thought of Hattie moving in. He quickened his pace. It wasn't seven yet. He wanted to get home before she did.

He found the place empty. He went immediately to the drawer where his drawings were hidden, under shirts and a sheet of lining paper. Once Hattie was installed, there was no knowing how completely she would take possession. He didn't want to keep them, anyway. He drew them out and shuffled through them without looking at them squarely. Destroying them would destroy the pain he felt simply holding them. C.B. was right as usual. He must never again allow himself to get so involved with anybody. He saw that his self-portrait and a particularly explicit one of Peter were missing. He tore them into small pieces and realized that the fragments were still too compromising to throw away. He went to the kitchen and put them in a pot and set fire to them, listening for Hattie all the while. They made a brief, alarming blaze. When it had subsided, he took the pot to the bathroom and emptied it into the toilet and flushed. Dead and buried. Now if Hattie would get here quickly, it would be all right. Keep busy, be with people — that was the solution. It was bound to pass. It had to. He didn't see how he could go on living if it didn't.

The apartment was filled with an acrid smell of burned paper. He opened the kitchen window and fixed himself a drink. When he heard her coming down the hall, he closed the window and opened the door for her. She entered with a suitcase and a bag of groceries and the air of a conquering hero. She stopped in the hall and wrinkled her absurd nose.

"Do they burn rubbish in the backyard?"

"Not often."

"What a stench." She dropped her suitcase and took the groceries to the kitchen. "A drink. My God, a drink. And please address me only as Mrs. Mills. I have to keep being reminded I'm married. I don't feel any different than I did last night. I mean, *after.* I've been thinking of that all day."

"Shall we go to bed and celebrate?"

"What a dreadful waste of all the lovely food I've bought." She looked at him and laughed. "What's it doing now? Is it getting hard for me?"

"You can find out for yourself anytime you feel like it."

"That sounds like being married. That's better than being called Mrs. Mills. I've got a man." She went to him, and he put his arms around her and they kissed. She thrust her hips up hard against him. "Mmm. It's up to its usual tricks. Shall we forget about food? No, it's legal now. We can wait." Accustomed to embraces being followed by active loveplay, he was unprepared for her to break from him and take her drink into the living room. She left him aroused and belligerent. He was damn well going to teach her to consider his needs. He followed her and found her peering pensively into the alcove. "Where am I going to put everything? I took a look at my closets and almost fainted. Where did I get so much junk?"

"C.B. says we should find a bigger place," he said, making it sound like a reproach.

"Oh, no. She's not going to turn me into a housewife. This is quite big enough. I'll jam everything in somehow."

He smiled in spite of himself. There was no denying that she was fun. "How did it go? Is your family still speaking to you?"

"They tried to look disapproving, but I was right. They never believed their nutty daughter would settle for anybody so presentable. Are you ever in for it. We're going to be up to our ears in family for weeks. Now that it's done, they're going to pretend they planned it this way. Of course, they were sure I was pregnant, but once I convinced them I wasn't, they actually smiled."

"How do you know you're not?"

"What do you think I've got my gadget for? If anything goes wrong with that, Margaret Sanger will wish she'd never been born. No babies for at least ten years. If then. How was C.B.?"

"Wonderful. Really marvelous. She acted as if it was the most natural thing in the world. Almost as if she expected it. She wants you to have lunch with her tomorrow. She's got parties on the brain, too. Of course, she's stopping my allowance."

"The bitch." Her eyes bulged with indignation. "What do you mean, 'of course'? Oh, I knew it. I knew she wouldn't let her precious Charlie go without a struggle. Why do you think I wanted to get it over with quickly? I don't give a damn about my family, but I knew C.B. would fix us if she could. Stopping your allowance. As if that'll satisfy her. I can't wait to see what she tries next."

"Don't be so ridiculous." This was a legitimate excuse for attack. He would make it clear right from the start that he wouldn't take any nonsense from her. "The allowance was just to help me get started. She said herself it wouldn't be right for me to be in any way dependent on her."

"Ha, ha, ha. Did you tell her you were going to quit that lousy job?"

"No, I didn't. I don't have to tell her everything I do."

"Like being an actor, for instance. You wouldn't want to tell her that, would you?"

"She knows it's a possibility."

"And she's just waiting to give you all the help and encouragement you need?"

"I don't need her help. About anything. She knows it as well as I do. I don't know why everybody has the idea that she rules my life."

"Who's 'everybody'?"

"Well, you, for one. You might as well accept the fact that I'm damned fond of her and I won't allow you to knock her."

"Oh, now we're going to be told what's allowed, are we?"

"You're damn right." He looked at her, at the huge eyes, the comic nose, the stubborn little chin, and wondered why he bothered to shout at her. Her will was iron, but it couldn't affect him. No matter what she did, she couldn't hurt him. He shrugged. "Any objections?" he added with a smile.

"Ohhh." She made an exasperated noise in her throat. "Maybe we should go to bed, after all. At least you don't talk when you're doing that."

He could tell by the look in her eye that it was more than an idle suggestion. "No. You said later. You'd better get over the idea that I'm some sort of machine you can turn on and off whenever you want. What about all that magnificent food you were going to fix us?"

He was comfortably aware of having won a skirmish. She became all bright solicitude; she wooed him with laughter. They had more drinks while she prepared one of her elaborate meals. What with the wine and the brandy afterwards, they both got hilariously drunk and the next morning neither was very clear about how the evening had ended.

Hattie called C.B. and accepted her invitation to lunch in a few hours. It went more smoothly than either of them had expected. C.B. deployed all her charms, and although Hattie was prepared to be aggressive, she found no occasion for it. She had even thought of exposing Charlie's theatrical ambitions just to prove that she knew him better than C.B., but she ended by respecting his wish for secrecy.

"You know, of course, I'd love you simply for being Charlie's wife, even if you weren't such a delicious creature." C.B. put an arm around her waist as she led her from the dining room to the small library for coffee.

"You're so sweet. I thought you'd hate me."

"Because of your doing it so suddenly? Not at all, my dear. I quite understand. Marriage is such a private matter."

"I never really thought he'd ask me. When he did, I thought we'd better do it quickly before he changed his mind." She hooted at herself.

"Had you known each other long before? Physically, I mean."

The distaste with which she pronounced the word was lost on Hattie.

"No. I'm virtue incarnate, even though nobody would believe it. Just the night before, when we were deciding to get married. Night before last, actually. How amazing."

"He must be an exquisite lover, even though I know he's had little or no experience."

"Sensational. Exquisite's hardly the word." Hattie looked at her with something approaching a leer and laughed softly in her throat. Since C.B. had raised the question, she could allow herself to gloat a bit. He was, after all, hers now.

C.B. responded with a worldly smile. "You're a very fortunate child. There is one thing, however, that I must tell you. This may come as a great blow to you. I'm sorry, but it's my duty to speak. You must never bear him children."

"Children?" She crowed with laughter. "I should hope not. I'll probably marry several more times before I even think of that. But what do you mean, 'never'?"

"There are certain things one doesn't discuss except in the strict confines of one's family. I would have been obliged to speak to Charlie if he'd given me any warning. Of course, you are family now but very newly so. Are you quite sure you know what you're saying? In my experience, when a girl is in love, the first thing she thinks about is having a child by the man she loves."

"Not me. Don't worry. If anything went wrong, I'd have an abortion."

"I see." C.B. appeared to be in no way discomfited, though there was perhaps a trace of regret in her voice as she added, "In that case, there's no need to pursue the subject."

"How fascinating. Is there a lot of madness in your family?"

C.B. waved her hand dismissively. "I don't always understand you modern young people. You don't consider your marriage to Charlie permanent?"

"Good heavens, no. I'm madly in love with him now, but an actress can't shut herself off from new experiences. I don't think Charlie would want to stay married if I were unfaithful to him."

"I should think not. How extraordinary. Aren't you being rather heartless?"

"Heartless? You mean by talking about being unfaithful to him? Married couples are always unfaithful, aren't they? I just know that when it happens, I won't make any pretense about it. I've told Charlie I expect to have at least four or five husbands."

"I see. And what did he say?"

"Oh, he doesn't listen to half the things I say. He's terribly removed, you know."

"No doubt. Well, I confess I find this conversation unusual, but I think we'll be friends, my dear. If you change your mind in the future, come to me. Meanwhile, I shouldn't discuss with Charlie what I've referred to. He knows nothing."

"You're so gorgeously mysterious, C.B. I absolutely adore you. I thought we were going to be enemies."

"I see no need for that, my dear."

THE NEXT WEEKS were filled with family, both Millses and Donaldsons, although the latter had a vast numerical superiority. Since Christmas was coming, there appeared to be no end to it. There were cocktail parties and dinner parties and over the weekends there were parties all day. One of the first was C.B.'s Sunday affair, filled out for the occasion with unaccustomed females. Charlie had no difficulty in having a private word with Tommy Whitethorne.

"Now that you're married, I don't know whether you're interested, but I might as well tell you all I know," Tommy murmured. "In case you're wondering, to begin with, the answer is no. When he called, I assumed that all those insidious looks I'd been giving him here were paying off, but it was no go. He said he wouldn't do it with anybody you knew. He's such a sweet guy that I didn't insist. It's not like me, I can assure you."

"Where is he?"

"He left me a couple of days ago. He was going to the YMCA. I warned him what to expect. He'll be torn to pieces. I think that's really what he wants. He hopes he'll forget you that way, poor kid. He's dropping Columbia. I wouldn't be surprised if he's quit his job by now. He was planning to."

"What's he intend to do for money?"

"He doesn't think about it. He'll probably get away with it, too. He's the sort people fall for hard. I did, God knows. Just having him around the house was better than any lay. I'd have kept him with pleasure without asking anything in return. Well, maybe that's going a bit far, but I thought about it. Are you in the clear with C.B.?"

"Certainly."

"And now you're married. That's the safest way. I'm planning to do the same thing myself. Anyway, our friend will keep in touch with me. He wants you to be able to find him in case you want him. Of course, I wasn't supposed to tell you that, just drop a hint."

"Thanks."

"Well, happy marriage. It's lousy, isn't it? I mean not being able to come right out and live the way you want to. That's what he just can't understand. I tried to make him see it our way, but it's like speaking a foreign language to him."

"Thanks again." Charlie turned away, not caring whether he was rude or not. Tommy Whitethorne took much too much for granted. Charlie got himself a fresh drink and went and stood beside Hattie.

It was a pose that was to become familiar over the weeks, drink in hand, Hattie at his side. The drinks were consumed in large quantities. His capacity grew so that he was drunk a large part of the time, but rarely noticeably so. He got very little sleep. He postponed a decision about his job from day to day, but he insisted on making the rounds of her theatrical haunts whenever they could get away from a party early enough. She couldn't accuse him of neglecting their careers. As he never had with Peter, he also felt obliged to make a daily affirmation of his potency. That, after all, was what marriage was to a great extent about. By the time they got to bed, he was usually too dazed with alcohol and fatigue to care about anything, but in the morning he could count on performing quickly and efficiently. His awareness that she always had her diaphragm in place robbed the act of its initial joy of procreation; it was as sterile as any of his play with boys, but nobody could accuse him of being an inactive husband.

A selfish one, perhaps. On one of the few evenings when they stayed at home, Hattie made just such an accusation. He had had less to drink than usual, but by now he was accustomed to having a drink in his hand during all his leisure hours, so he was far from sober when she suggested going to bed. She was already in it when he had finished in the bathroom and snapped out the living-room lights. Her eyes held a speculative look as she watched him approach.

"There's no denying it's a compelling apparatus," she said, with laughter breaking through the words. "I just wonder if we're

160

realizing its maximum potential. There must be a way for us to keep it operational longer."

"What's that supposed to be all about?" he demanded, sitting on the edge of the bed.

"Girls like to have orgasms too, you know. At the beginning, the average was a bit better, but in the last three weeks I've come exactly twice. Bang, bang, bang, and it's all over."

"Why do you take so long? Has it occurred to you that you might be frigid?" His sex, which had been extended in the preliminaries of erection, began to shrink as he realized its performance was being criticized.

"Me? Frigid?" She crowed at him. "It's a well-known fact that most girls do take longer. There are books about it. Maybe you should read one. *Marriage Can Be Fun* and things like that. You see them in all the Broadway drugstores."

His sex shrank still further. "Oh, for God's sake. Are you trying to suggest that I'm not good in bed?" His tone was incredulous; his prowess had never been questioned.

"Good heavens, no. You're so good that one wants more. Perhaps I'm doing something wrong;" She reached out and put her hand on his diminished sex. He pushed it angrily away. "Oh dear, now I've hurt your feelings. You're no good to me at all like that. Forget everything I said."

"Forget it? Maybe you should read one of those books yourself." The confidence he had acquired over the last weeks, the conviction that he was a success in his marital role, was rudely shaken. His sex was useless; his mind was clogged with rage. "Goddamn you," he shouted. "Just when I'm about to fuck you, you start a discussion of orgasms. Don't you understand anything about the way a man is made? By God, I'll show you some things." He leaped up and charged into the bathroom. He scattered her cosmetics as he fumbled about and found the tube of lubricant where it had been left weeks earlier. He applied it to himself, swaying slightly and deeply absorbed. Associations crowded in on him. His sex reared up and grew under his knowledgeable touch and locked into rigidity. He grabbed a towel and lunged back into the alcove. "There, goddammit. Take a good look. Is there anything wrong with that? Now turn over."

"What do you mean?"

"You heard me. Turn over. On your stomach."

She stared at him and then did as she was told. "So now we begin the fancy games. I'm warning you, I probably won't like this."

"Why shouldn't you? Lots of people do." He straddled her and applied the lubricant roughly. He took her hips and lifted them and drew them to him. He guided his sex between her buttocks and shifted her hips and entered her. She screamed. "Shut up and relax, goddammit." He continued his penetration.

She cried out again. "Oh, no. Oh, God, no. Please Charlie. Don't. Stop it. You're too big. I can't take it."

"Why can't you? Plenty of others have." He held her hips firmly and forced his way slowly into her. His chest was heaving as if he had run a race. She whimpered, she cried out, she cursed him through sobs. As he completed the long, inexorable penetration, he reached around instinctively between her legs to grasp what wasn't there. His hand remained to caress what was. Her body shuddered, and she began to respond with cautiously gyrating hips. She sobbed and crooned and cursed him some more. Her movements became freer and more agitated. Her hair fell over her face, her breasts swayed from her chest, she hung on his sex as she struggled for satisfaction. He felt moisture accumulating as her excitement mounted. He laughed. She looked so like a little animal, abject, totally subjugated. Her crooning rose to a wail. At last, it was broken by a succession of strange barking coughs. Her body was shaken by spasms, and he drove his orgasm into her as she collapsed beneath him. She burst into tears as he lay on top of her.

"Stop it, goddammit," he commanded when he could speak. "You came, didn't you? Isn't that what you wanted?"

"Yes."

"Then what are you crying about? You like it."

"Get out. Get out of me. You've ripped me apart."

He withdrew slowly and wrapped himself in a towel and lay beside her. "What's all the fuss about? You liked it. Why not admit it?"

She rolled over onto her back, and her weeping abated. She wiped her eyes with her hands. "I'm in love with you, you lousy shit. I'd probably like it if you nailed me to the wall and threw darts at me. Don't push it. That's all. Just don't push it."

He laughed at her warning. There was a brief silence.

"You said plenty of others," she said more calmly. "Since when have there been plenty? Is that what you did with those three or four girls?"

162

"Don't be silly. Haven't you ever heard about boys in school?"

"Is that what you did with Peter?"

"Yes, dammit, if you're so damned anxious to know. That's what I did with Peter."

"You son of a bitch."

"He also liked to suck my cock, in case you're looking for ideas. Why not try it all, since you're not interested in having babies?" He laughed again. Let her know everything. What difference did it make? He felt free at last for the first time in months.

"Goddamn you. You bastard. You can't have babies, anyway. C.B. says so."

His laughter died, and he stared at her heavily. "What are you talking about?"

"Something about your family. I don't know what. The Mills Madness. She told me weeks ago."

"You're out of your mind."

"Ask her yourself, if you don't believe me. She said I must never bear your children. As if I ever intended to."

He lurched up out of bed and careened back to the bathroom to wash. He couldn't seem to make his mind work properly. Couldn't have children? It didn't make any sense. People were always making up these idiotic stories about C.B. Hattie was just trying to unload onto him some of the blame for her own decision to remain childless. He damn well would put it to C.B., except that it wasn't something he would like to talk to her about. Maybe an opportunity would turn up when he could touch on it naturally. It obviously didn't matter as far as Hattie was concerned.

His sense of freedom was fleeting. Christmas came and went, and he felt more and more trapped, trapped in the endless round of office and parties and bed, trapped by her clothes, which were everywhere so that he could never find anything of his own, trapped by the bills that now began to come flooding in. He could make no sense with her about money.

She had only a vague idea about how much she had and when she received it. Even though their expenses for food and drink were minimal, she could go through his salary in an hour of shopping "to keep the house stocked," as she put it. He couldn't imagine how they would manage when the parties stopped, although the parties carried built-in expenses of their own. She took it for granted that their hosts must be thanked with gifts; flowers, candies, exotic fruits,

163

or bottles of fine wine were dispatched to all but her immediate family.

"Listen, I know we have to do something about the Jamiesons," he remonstrated after they had been to a flower shop together one evening, "but does it always have to be dozens of roses? What was the matter with that plant?"

"Oh, God, are you going to start whining about money again? It's mine, isn't it?"

"How should I know? We've got bills right now for over four hundred dollars and you haven't got twenty-five in your account. Who takes care of the balance?"

"I've got credit in this town. The Donaldsons are good for four hundred dollars."

"The bills are addressed to Mrs. Charles Mills."

"Well, why don't you go out and do something about it if you don't like it? No, you'll go grubbing along at that office just so you can count your pitiful little earnings at the end of the week. You're not even a clerk. You're an accountant. Imagine adding up all those bills." She laughed at him and swung forward on his arm and looked up at him teasingly. "I know somebody who needs a drink."

H E WAS THINKING about a drink on his way home one dark winter afternoon when he stopped for a look at Bergdorf's windows. He had come to the last one and was about to go on when he became aware of a man moving in close beside him. He froze, keeping his eyes fixed in front of him so as not to give any hint of interest.

"Doing anything this evening?" a voice murmured close to his ear. A rude dismissal sprang to his lip in the instant before he realized who it was. He turned slowly, not knowing what was happening to his face, knowing only that he was totally unprepared for the encounter. Peter threw his head back and laughed.

"How's my best boyfriend? I told you I'd follow you if I saw you in the street. This was bound to happen sooner or later. I thought I might as well get it over with."

Charlie looked at him. His beauty was as troubling as a half-remembered dream. He was dazzling. He wore a handsome over-

164

coat flung picturesquely over his shoulders like a cloak. There was an air of expensive carelessness about all his dress. His skin, which had long retained the ruddiness of the summer tan, now was pale and luminous. The golden hair was ruffled by the wind. Charlie was speechless. With embarrassment? With delight? Because there was simply nothing more to say? He didn't know.

"You all right, honey?" Peter's eyes filled with solicitude. "You don't look too hot."

Charlie glanced about him nervously. "Hey, take it easy," he said, finding his voice.

Peter laughed. "Still worried somebody'll get ideas? Listen, champ, New York is teeming with faggots. One more or less won't frighten the horses." He gave an effeminate flip of his hand. "All right. I'll try to stay within a foot or two of the ground. Are you on your way home to the little wife?"

"You heard about that, of course. You're looking wonderful."

"Your sister manages. Come on, let me buy you a drink. You look as if you could use one."

Charlie looked at his watch to give himself something to do. He knew he should get away as fast as he could. There was a hollowness in the pit of his stomach. His chest ached with the beating of his heart. He felt dangerously close to tears. "It'll have to be quick," he muttered.

Peter gave a hitch to his coat, and they fell into step beside each other. "It's amazing running into you like this," he said in a breezy chatty tone that was new to Charlie. "I mean, right now, of all things. You'll never guess who I'm going to see in a little while. Sapphire."

"You're kidding." The summer was evoked. Charlie found conversation possible. "I'll be damned. I read all the reviews, of course. She's made quite a hit. C.B. went to the first night. I must say she's eaten all her words very handsomely. Have you seen the show? "

"Not yet. There's this party up in Harlem that Hughie Hayes asked me to. She's going to be there before the theater. Golly, I wish you could come. How about this joint?" They turned into a bar. A blowsy hatcheck girl was crowded in behind a little counter in the entrance. Peter shrugged off his coat and laid it before her. The girl looked at him and smiled appreciatively.

"My, my, a real beauty. What're you doing later, beautiful?"

"I won't tell." He grinned and added a suggestion of a lisp. "As you see, I'm with this gentleman for the moment."

She laughed. "Wouldn't you know. Us girls don't stand a chance these days."

"Oh, come on. There's plenty for all of us."

"I guess that's the truth." She laughed again. Charlie's face was burning as he handed over his coat. The girl was looking after Peter and chuckling.

They sat on stools at the bar. A bartender came lumbering over to them. "Two whiskies, please," Peter ordered. "And don't you eye me like that, you brute."

After a startled moment, the bartender rested his arm on the bar and laughed and shook his head. "That's a good one. That sure is a good one." He heaved himself up and went off to get the drinks. Charlie didn't know where to look. His face was burning more fiercely than ever. The bartender returned with the drinks and leaned across the bar confidentially to Peter. "I slipped a little extra in yours, sonny." He laughed and shook his head again. "'You brute.' That sure is a good one." He went off down the bar.

"Don't you ever get into trouble?" Charlie demanded in a muted voice.

"Why should I?" He laughed and lifted his glass to Charlie and drank.

Charlie took a thirsty gulp and began to feel less conspicuous.

"What are you doing now?" he asked.

"The street. I guess that's about as close to it as you could come. It's a very high-class street, though."

"Don't talk such nonsense."

Peter looked at him with clear, untroubled eyes. "It's not nonsense, champ. I don't take money, if that's what you mean. People give me things. I sell them when I have to. Watches. I could open a goddamn watch shop. It turns out I'm a perfect thirty-nine. I guess you are too. It's amazing how many peoples' clothes I can wear. What more does a kid want?"

"Plenty. How long do you think you can keep this up?"

"That's no problem. There's a war on. I won't be around much longer. Maybe the Army will make a man of me. Or maybe I'll make the Army." He giggled.

"Stop talking like that. It's disgusting."

"Oh, darling — hey, who do you think you're talking to?" A grimace of pain crossed his face, and then he leaned over his drink and launched into a rapid, mumbled, semicoherent little monologue. "Now, now, now. We've been through all that. Enough. Enough of this. Come on. Up. Up, Pete. Up. That'll do. You see? You can do it if you put your mind to it. There. Now. One, two, three, and—" He took a deep breath and straightened. "Sorry. Where were we? Oh, yes. Nowhere. Hell, champ, I'm just having fun, sort of. The talk is part of the act. Pay no attention."

"I don't like it. Why do you have to have an act?"

"Why do—? Oh, come on, that's not fair. Leave your little sister be. Tell me things. What've you been doing?"

A battle was raging within Charlie. He was shocked and repelled, drawn, held. He felt as if he had been touched by magic. He would have welcomed resentment, bitterness, recriminations. Sunny sweetness flowed out to him like a healing balm. Was this what it had been like all those months they had been together? A memory of happiness came to him as if from some former existence, known but not quite his own. His sex stirred even as he rejected him with contempt. So they had had a great time together in bed; that might happen with anybody. He was forgetting everything that really counted. Peter was nothing but a silly fairy. His stomach churned at the thought of him handling, being handled by, other men. He knew he ought to go, but he gestured to the barman for another round. "This one's on me."

"Come on. Tell me things."

"Oh, well, getting married's taken a hell of a lot of time. Everybody wants to celebrate. Hattie has an awful lot of family."

"She's fine?"

"Sure, great."

"And what about all the little Charlies?"

"She doesn't want any for a long time. Her career and all."

"Is anything happening in the theater for you?"

"Not yet. We're working on a possibility now. There might be something in it for both of us. It's not much of a play, but I might have one of the leads."

"Hey, wonderful. We've got Sapphire all set. It's your turn now. I was glad Meyer Rapper's play flopped."

"Yeah. Virtue rewarded."

"I really ought to leave in a few minutes, dammit. I don't want to miss Sapphire. Now that we've finally run into each other, it'll probably happen every five minutes. This is a crazy town."

Charlie suddenly knew that he couldn't leave him now. It was finished, there was no question about that, but he had to catch a glimpse of his world, he had to see him with his friends simply to reassure himself that he was well out of it. The sweetness that radiated from him was a trick of personality, hiding God knows what sickness and corruption. Peter had obviously surrendered to the worst in himself, yet Charlie felt in him an inviolable purity, manifested even in his making no move to touch him. Even here at the bar, he had kept his legs carefully to himself. It made Charlie feel lonely. "Listen, did you mean it about taking me to this party?"

"You mean you'd come?" Peter's face lighted up.

"What the hell. Hattie will kill me, but I want to see Sapphire too."

A doubt crept into Peter's eyes. "It'd be wonderful but — Well, I don't know who all's going to be there, but there'll probably be plenty of other faggots, You've never been to that kind of party. If you think I'm bad, wait'll you see some of the others. You sure you won't mind?"

"I'll try not to. Who knows? Maybe I'll let my hair down too, for once."

"You?" Peter laughed, but there was pain again in the set of his mouth and behind his eyes.

Charlie went off to find a telephone and returned in a few minutes. "She's wild. I'd forgotten we were having dinner with her parents."

"What did you tell her?"

"The truth for once. I've told her all about us."

"You have? Golly. You know, it's amazing. I used to sit around wondering what you were doing, who you were seeing. Now somebody else is waiting, and I'm out on the town with you. We've never done anything like this before."

"Well, here we go." They looked into each other's eyes, and Charlie looked hastily away.

They took an uptown double-decker bus on Fifth Avenue and climbed to the top. Crowded together on the narrow seat, there was no way of not touching. Even though they were insulated from each other by heavy coats, Charlie found their proximity deeply troubling as they swayed and braced themselves against each other with the lurching of the bus. He could see in his mind's eye every muscle working in the known, loved body. He wouldn't stay at the party long; just long enough to say hello to Sapphire. Even if there were an opportunity for a private moment with Peter, he wouldn't take advantage of it. He would definitely keep his promise to Hattie to meet her at her parents' house by eight-thirty.

They walked up a brightly lighted, crowded, derelict Harlem street, Peter's coat swinging rakishly from his shoulders.

"I've never been up here before," Charlie said, feeling foreign and ill at ease among the milling black faces.

"I've been a few times. There's something about it. There're some crazy places."

"Who did you say is giving the party?"

"Hughie Hayes."

"He's a Negro?"

"Hughie Hayes? Come on, you dope. The piano player. He's just opened a place in the Village. He was in Paris for years."

"You're making me feel like a hick. I don't get around in your colorful circles."

Peter was watching the street numbers. He turned in at a great crumbling pile of blackened masonry. They found themselves in an ill-lighted, malodorous lobby, with cracked and peeling walls. As they mounted sagging stairs, the smell became overpowering.

"What does he live in a dump like this for?" Charlie asked. "You sure you got the address right?"

"I've seen some pretty bad places up here. I guess it's hard to find anything decent." They mounted two flights and turned down a high, wide, dark corridor.

"God, it stinks. I don't think I can stand it."

"Maybe it's better inside."

"You know this guy well?"

"No, I've just seen him a couple of times at his club."

They came to a door at the end of the corridor, and Peter pushed a button. The sound of music came to them faintly. In a moment, the door swung open heavily, the music swelled, and Peter was greeted by a slender, attractive, youngish brown man. He made an impression of great elegance.

"Well, here's my angel baby." He drew Peter in, and kissed him lightly on the mouth. "How's my baby?" For a moment, his eyes were only for Peter, and then the latter drew back and with obvious embarrassment managed to introduce Charlie.

"He knows Sapphire too. I thought it'd be all right to bring him."

Charlie held himself stiffly, rigid with rage, but Hughie Hayes made no attempt to kiss him. "You can bring all your friends, baby.

169

Especially if they're young and handsome. She's here. Throw your things anywhere and come on in." There were remnants of the South in his speech, overlaid by Paris and London.

He ushered them into a large, immaculate, ornately furnished room filled with people, for the most part seated. They seemed to be conversing seriously; there was none of the high-pitched chatter and laughter Charlie was accustomed to on this sort of occasion. He breathed deeply and realized the smell had been overcome. The gathering was mixed, black and white, men and women, with men in the majority. In the center of one small group was Sapphire, looking very much as she had in C.B.'s kitchen — small and round-faced and shy. She beamed when she saw Peter.

"Hello, Petey honey. I'm glad you came. Why Mr. Charlie! What a nice surprise. Your granny told me you're married and all. Congratulations." She rose as Hughie led Peter away.

"I'm the one who ought to be doing the congratulating. We've all been talking about Sapphire. You're a big success."

"Well, I can sing, even if your granny didn't believe me." She put her hand over her mouth and giggled. "She is a one, your granny. She came to my opening, and she sailed into my dressing room and took me in her arms. Right in front of everybody. Lawdy."

"She says you were wonderful. I've got to come see you."

"You do that. You ought to come with Petey. That's one lovely boy. He just dotes on you, Mr. Charlie. Of course, he has his ways that some folks don't understand, but I don't know. I say, if it's love, the Lord won't mind. There's enough hate in the world. Now you're married, he's a pretty lonely boy."

Charlie was blushing furiously. He had no taste for intimacy with Sapphire; the company made him sufficiently self-conscious. He had come persuaded that he had no racial feelings. Theory was no aid to practice. There was something about these whites and blacks sitting around together that made his skin crawl. The kiss had seared his mind. He heard himself laugh pointlessly. "Oh well, he'll be getting married himself one day soon." He was appalled by the idiocy of the remark. "I'd better get myself a drink."

"Now, you let me get you one, Mr. Charlie."

"No, you stay here. I'll be right back." He escaped and looked around for a bar. He saw Peter sitting on a bench at the piano with Hughie Hayes. Lonely? He'd take anything so long as it was wearing pants. He spotted a table with bottles on it and made for it. He was pouring himself a stiff whiskey when a strikingly handsome, dark, white youth sauntered up to him.

"Hi. I'm Whit Bailey. You came with the Growler, didn't you?"

Charlie took a long swallow. His eyes automatically assessed the youth: hands, crotch, mouth. Damned attractive. Once upon a time, he would have been ready and willing, but that phase was finished now, done with, almost forgotten. "Did I?" he asked, lowering his glass.

"Sure. I saw you come in together."

"You mean Peter Martin?"

"Yeah. The Growler. You mean, you haven't had it?"

"Yes, I've had it."

"Well, then."

"I don't get it. Why do you call him the Growler?"

"Well, everybody does. Don't you get around? When he growls, you know you're all set. Didn't he growl at you?"

"Yes, as a matter fact, he did."

"He's sensational, isn't he? I bet you're pretty sensational yourself. You look sort of like him."

"So I've heard."

"How about going someplace after this?"

"Such as?"

"Well, we can go to my place or yours. Whichever you prefer."

"Not my place. I have a wife."

Confusion clouded Whit Bailey's face. "Oh." A light dawned in his eyes. "Good lord. Is your name Charlie? Holy mackerel. You mean I've hit the jackpot? Well, how about it? We're wasting our time here. Let's go to my place."

Charlie considered throwing his drink in his face and decided against it. He glanced in Peter's direction just in time to catch his eye on him. Peter turned hastily back to Hughie. Good. Let him sweat this one out. He smiled encouragingly at Whit Bailey. "What makes you think I'd dump the Growler?"

"He never does it more than once with anyone, does he? Oh yes, of course. You're Charlie. I'm a bit confused."

"Don't be. Just carry on from where you left off. Persuade me. I might dump all sorts of people for you."

"You're dangerous, aren't you? It's exciting. Look at me. I'm beginning to get the shakes."

Peter turned hastily back to Hughie. He had known it was going to be all wrong from the moment Hughie kissed him. But what could he do? Slap him in the face? A kiss didn't mean anything. And now Whit. Whit was one of the few of his ex-lovers he remembered. A beauty. He had broken his once-only rule a couple of times — had lived with one guy a week, with another for three — but he had made a particular point of his rule with Whit simply because he had wanted so badly to break it. If he had been enormously attracted to Whit, why wouldn't Charlie be too? They were practically the same person. Bringing him here had been a gamble; he had known that, but he had thought there was little to lose. He knew better now. Charlie with Hattie was bearable. Charlie with another boy would really finish him off. Maybe it was just as well. The hour he had spent with Charlie had pretty much finished him off anyway, every minute of it telling him how much he had lost.

Hughie ran his hands over the keyboard and worked his way into a blues. "Still carrying the torch, aren't you, baby?"

"You know about it?"

"I guess everybody in town knows about the Growler. Any chance of me hearing that famous growl? Je t'aime, tu sais."

"I don't know, Hughie. It just happens. I'm not in much of a growling mood tonight."

"Why don't you go break it up, baby?"

"No use. And I guess you'd better stop calling me baby."

"Oh. Sorry. Anything you say, sweetheart."

"I want to go talk to Sapphire before she leaves."

"Stick around, will you, ducks? The squares will be leaving soon, and then we'll have a ball. The club's closed tonight. I've got a mess of food in the kitchen. We're ready for a siege."

Peter went and talked to Sapphire, keeping his back turned to the bar table. He talked to the famous blues singer he hadn't seen when he came in. He talked to the famous expatriate white novelist, who had been cast up on his native shores by the war. Charlie was suddenly at his side.

"I'm getting out of here. You were right. I can't take it." His face was rigid with fury.

"Anything wrong, champ?"

"Wrong? No. I see what you really are, that's all."

Peter looked at his feet. "Yeah. Well, I guess that's the way it is, darling. See you around." He turned away and crossed the room to a window and stood looking out. He talked to himself under his breath while silent tears slid down his face. When he was able to turn back to the party he saw that Whit Bailey was still there. A good many others had left. The decrease in numbers made the room noisier. Everybody seemed to be laughing. Hughie was letting loose at the piano. Peter went and stood beside him. Hughie looked up and smiled.

"Toujours cafardeux, ducks? Why don't you have a drink?"

"I've had a couple. I don't drink much. I'm fine."

Whit joined them. "That's a charming friend you have, Charlie Whoever. He was making a big play for me, and then all of a sudden he called me a dirty little faggot and walked out. What in God's name does he think *he* is?"

"He wants to be straight. Did he really make a play for you?"

"That's what I thought it was. I guess he was just leading me on. He didn't have to try very hard. He reminded me of you." Whit lifted a cigarette between thumb and forefinger and, holding his lips apart, inhaled deeply.

"What are you doing that for?"

Whit held his breath a moment before answering. "It's a reefer. Marijuana. Haven't you ever smoked it?"

"No, what's it do to you?"

"Makes you feel great. Sexy, too. Want to try it? Come on."

Peter followed him over to a group surrounding an ugly, very black little monkey of a man who was sitting on the floor. "Hey Freddy, you got another one of these things for the Growler?" Whit asked.

"I got one all marked and set aside for the Growler." He handed up a cigarette. "Just take it nice 'n' easy."

Peter took it, and Whit gave him a light. "Are you supposed to hold it the way you did?"

"Yeah. Pull it way in and hold it as long as you can."

Peter experimented. Aside from a slight giddiness from inhaling so much air, he felt nothing. He grew bolder, drawing the smoke deep into his lungs. He had heard only vaguely of marijuana and wondered if it would be habit-forming. A bit late to worry about that.

Whit was watching him closely. He giggled as Peter held his breath. "If it makes you feel sexy, you know who's waiting for you."

Peter exhaled. "I don't feel anything yet."

"You will. Boy, it's really getting to me now." He giggled again.

Peter lifted his hand for another puff. It seemed to take a very long time for the cigarette to reach his mouth. He finally took a puff. The room swayed slightly and then receded. "That's funny," he said when he had exhaled. He lifted his free hand and found that he was stroking the back of Whit's head. "You know something? You're one of the prettiest guys I've ever known." His voice didn't sound like his own. He hadn't even intended to speak. He laughed. He went on laughing. He felt as if he had been laughing forever. Eventually he took another puff of the cigarette. The room seemed very big, the people in it all crowded together on top of him. Everybody was laughing. His hand wasn't on Whit's neck. It was on Hughie's shoulder. Hughie stood in front of him smiling.

"You riding high, duckie? You feel all right?"

"I feel wonderful."

Hughie's smile broadened. His teeth were strong and white in the dark honey-brown of his face. His eyes were kind and gentle. They seemed to swim into Peter's. Peter growled.

"Oh, lordy, chéri angel. Did I hear my ears correctly? I want it. I want it bad. We'll get rid of these people soon." His mouth was on Peter's. His lips were soft and full. They kissed for a long time. Peter wondered if everybody was watching. It didn't matter. He was lying on the floor. Better this way. His rigid sex felt as if it would burst his trousers. He wriggled about to get it more comfortable. "Man, this white boy is really flying," an unknown voice said. "Man, he is *built.*" Peter laughed. His head was in somebody's lap. There was a great crowd of people far above him. They were talking very loud, but the piano drowned out what they were saying. A hand smoothed his trousers, shaping his sex. "Leave that alone, Siddy baby." Hughie's voice sounded quite close. "I want that for myself."

"Boy, you don't know what you're getting," Whit said. "If anybody can do anything with what you've got, he is the one who can." Peter laughed. It felt good to laugh. He laughed some more.

He woke up naked in a wide, elaborate bed. He seemed to be surrounded by a great deal of drapery. He had no idea where he was. He didn't know what day it was or whether, in fact, it was day or night. His sex was aching with an erection that felt as if it had been there forever. He lay without moving as his eyes explored his surroundings. He was alone on the wide bed with nothing over him. Lights were on. Looking across his feet, he saw an open door and the shine of tile. A bathroom. He reached down and pulled at his sex to ease it. Memory stirred. A party. Charlie. Hughie. Whit. Had he broken his rule and gone home with Whit? No, he had never been in this room before. Then it must be ... As he picked through his sluggish brain, Hughie entered soundlessly from the bathroom. Rather, Peter's vision was filled with a monumental dark phallus with Hughie somewhere in the background. His eyes widened as they measured it. Then he rolled over onto his stomach, a cry of agony already gathering in his throat.

Hughie was wearing a dressing gown when he woke him. He was stroking his bottom. Peter opened his eyes slowly and saw him and smiled.

"Hi," he said.

"Come on, sweetheart angel. It's getting late."

Peter's smile turned into a little spurt of laughter. "Hey, how about me?"

"That's just it. How about you. You're dynamite, angel. You scare me."

Peter wriggled down in the bed so that his head was in Hughie's lap, his arms around his hips. "Don't you want it again?"

"Listen, chéri. Are you awake? I don't want anything to do with love. 'Specially with a golden boy like you. You're just about the whitest white boy I've ever seen. You've got me headed right over the deep end. I've got to stop while I still can. I'm going to give you some breakfast, if we can call it that, and then I'll take you for drinks at Walter Pitney's. I'd love it if you'd have supper with me at the club, and then we say good-bye. It's going to be the old sad story for me, but that's the way it's got to be."

Peter pushed the dressing gown out of the way with the side of his head and kissed the dark sleeping sex. Then he straightened out and lay back with his head on the pillow. "Sure. I understand. Anybody would be nuts to fall in love with me. I'm dead as a doornail. All the same, it was fantastic."

"Same here, angel. Je t'adore, mon amour. After I've cried over you a little while, I hope we see each other a lot. If there's ever anything I can do for you, you let me know, hear? It's all yours, angel. Voilà. Un point, c'est tout."

Peter had heard of Walter Pitney often; it was one of the few major addresses on the homosexual circuit where he hadn't been. The fact that Pitney was one of the richest men in the city didn't particularly interest him. The opportunity to add a new meeting place to his list did. Hughie gave him a fresh shirt and a pair of gold cuff links and they set off just twenty-four hours after Peter had arrived. They held hands in the taxi going downtown.

"Listen, angel," Hughie said, "when we get there, I'll go in first. Just give me a few seconds, and then come along."

"Why?"

"It's better for Walter. It doesn't look good for a black boy and white boy to go in together."

When they stopped on Park Avenue, Hughie handed him a five-dollar bill for the taxi and left him. Peter paid and collected the change and followed. A manservant admitted him to Walter Pitney's apartment. He was confronted by a Renoir as he handed over his coat in the hall. When he saw that it was real and not a print, he gave his tie an extra little tug. The manservant bowed him toward the living room. As he entered, his eyes made a quick survey, doing his usual head count. He had been to bed with all but four or five of the exclusively male, exquisitely tailored group. Two new faces briefly caught his attention and then Hughie was introducing him to his host.

"This is the Growler, Walter. He's the loveliest boy in New York, bar none."

"I have eyes, Hughie. Anybody can see that." Walter Pitney took his hand and gave him an expansive friendly smile. He was wearing very thick horn-rimmed glasses that absorbed all his features except for his smile. He was a solidly built man with gray hair. Peter judged him to be fairly old, surely over forty-five. "I've heard so much about you. I've asked everybody I know to bring you. Have you stayed away on purpose?"

"Hughie's the first person that suggested it, and here I am."

"I'm so glad. What will you have to drink?"

Peter looked at Hughie and laughed. "What's good for what ails me?"

"Champagne. It's the only thing this early in the day." They looked at each other and laughed together.

"So that's the way it is, is it?" Walter Pitney gave the order to another manservant, who had appeared at his side. "I like to see people having a good time. That's my philosophy. We've had some times together, haven't we, Hughie?"

"Paris was the place for it. That's the truth, Walter."

176

The champagne was brought. Peter took a glass and drank. He sighed happily. "Golly, that's good."

Walter beamed. "What a delightful chappie. Nobody ever tells me anything is good around here. Do you want me to introduce you to everybody?"

"I think I know most of them."

"Well, don't let me keep you from your friends. Enjoy yourself. That's the main thing. Just ask for anything you want."

Peter glanced at Hughie, who winked at him, and went on into the room.

"Doll! Come here and give your sister a kiss."

"Look out, girls, Here comes the Growler. Get her — she's drinking champagne."

"Hello, beautiful. When are you going to growl at me again?"

"Aren't you going to speak to your old mother? That's better. Oh, those lips."

"Darling. You look divine. How you manage when you lead such a wicked life I'll never understand."

"Hello, sweetheart. I'm not about to forget the other night. Call me, damn you."

It was the conventional exchange of the world he had adopted and although he found it silly, he had learned to accept it. He was introduced to a film star. He was introduced to Meyer Rapper.

"So you're the bastard. I've been waiting to sock you in the nose."

"Dear me." Meyer Rapper offered him his charming smile. "Right now? Or will you wait till I'm ready to leave?"

"It doesn't matter anymore. Your play was a flop."

"One of my many well-wishers, I see. How odd. You're a most extraordinary-looking creature, and yet you remind me of somebody. Who could it be?"

"Charlie Mills."

"Charlie Mills? Charles Mills. Ah, yes. You're quite right. How did you know?"

"Because that's who I look like."

"I see. The way you say that, I very much wish I were Charlie Mills."

"The way *you* say that, I do, too."

"What an extraordinary young man. Are you interested in the theater?"

177

"Not remotely."

"How splendid. I've fallen in love with you on the spot. What are you doing for dinner?"

"Busy."

"I'll bet you are. Ah, well, life doesn't distribute its rewards as easily as all that. My psychiatrist is going to have a difficult hour tomorrow."

The manservant appeared before Peter and filled his glass. He found himself gazing at a Rouault. He shifted his gaze and saw five Matisses in a row. It had never occurred to him that people actually owned such things. A little shiver ran down his spine. Walter Pitney approached and beamed at him.

"You have everything you want?"

"Yes, thank you. This is a fabulous place."

"You like it?" He looked as pleased as a child. "Ah, there, Meyer. You know this delightful chappie?"

"I've had the alloyed pleasure."

"Come along then," Walter said to Peter. "There's a very attractive lad who's dying to meet you. If nothing more exciting turns up, perhaps you'll stay and have a quiet dinner with me."

"Thanks a lot, but I'm supposed to go on with Hughie."

"I've had a word with him, I don't think he'll mind. But don't commit yourself. Somebody else may carry you off. I like to see people enjoying themselves."

"This is going to sound corny, but I'd love to have a chance to really look at your pictures."

"Would you? How delightful. Nobody ever pays any attention to them. I'm very fond of them myself. But they'll be here. I hope you'll come often. Ah, here you are, Tim. This is Peter."

Peter found himself looking up into one of the new faces. It was a broad, open, rugged face, a farmboy's face, topped by a tousle of fair hair. Their eyes met and held. The face broke into a broad grin. Peter growled softly in the back of his throat. Tim laughed, big male laughter.

"I've heard a lot about you," he said, his eyes holding Peter's. His voice was soft and lazy. "I've gotta catch a train in an hour. I wanted to meet you before I left. I'll be back in two days."

"Does it have to be that long?"

Tim laughed again and put a great paw of a hand on Peter's shoulder and gave it a squeeze. "That's the way I feel." They stood looking into each other's eyes. Peter finally took a deep breath that caught in his chest and shook his head.

"Good lord," he said incredulously. "This wasn't in the program at all."

"I knew it the minute you came in."

"You saw that awful performance? God, I'm going to kill myself. I'm sort of a tramp, you know."

"I doubt it. I know all about you. I thought you did it kinda cutely."

Peter's eyes melted into Tim's again. They were blue and smiling, not the deep purplish blue of Charlie's, but bright and clear, like a sunny lake. After a moment, they both burst out laughing. "Where's the man with the champagne? An hour, did you say? Who are you, for God's sake?"

"I'm Timothy Thornton and you're Peter Martin and I'm a lawyer. Well, I'm a messenger boy, really, but I have the right to call myself a lawyer. I'm going to Washington in fifty minutes and I'll be back day after tomorrow and, boy, you're going to be waiting for me."

"Boy, am I ever. Unless I come to Washington with you. I've done stupider things in my life."

"Don't think I haven't thought of that. Except that I'm meeting my boss on the train. There's no way of working it."

"Are you old enough to be a lawyer?"

"I'm older than I look, I guess."

The servant came and filled Peter's glass. He presented Tim with a fresh drink. Their eyes searched deep into each other as this was taking place. Their faces set with rapt absorption, and their lips parted as their breathing accelerated. Peter made an almost imperceptible negative motion with his head.

"Fifty minutes wouldn't be enough," he said.

"Not by a long shot. Anyway, I have to leave here in twenty. Fifteen." He looked at his watch.

Details began to fix themselves in Peter's mind. The eyes and hands he knew now: the eyes that accepted and reassured him, the strong grip of the big hands. The mouth was broad and grinned beautifully. He was tall, but his heavy shoulders stooped slightly, which brought him down within reach. His size made him a protective presence. Peter had never felt protected before.

"What am I supposed to do until day after tomorrow?" he asked. "Walter's asked me for dinner. Does that mean the usual? Do you know him?"

"Know him? Lord, he's an old friend of the family. He brought me out, as it happens. Walter is — well, you'll probably find out. Anything you do with Walter is all right with me. He's got his quirks like everybody, but he's a nice man. Just remember that."

"I don't quite understand. I was only talking about having dinner with him, but it doesn't matter. How much time?"

Tim looked at his watch. "Not enough to matter a damn. You call me Thursday afternoon, see. After four. We'll have all Thursday night." He took out a wallet and gave Peter a card.

"Thursday night and Friday night and any other night you say."

Tim's eyes were smiling at him. "I thought you were strictly for one-night stands."

"You know that? Well, then, you must know that rule is permanently suspended for you."

"Yeah. I guess I know. Come on." He put an arm across Peter's shoulder and gripped the base of his neck. Peter felt a thrill to the soles of his feet. "Let's get out of here for a minute, and then I'll have to go."

Peter moved in close to him, seeking shelter in the big body. They crossed the room together, oblivious of the people they passed. By the time they were in the hall, they were in each other's arms. Their tongues roamed each other's mouths. Peter hung on Tim's neck. Tim's hands ran down Peter's back and planted themselves on his buttocks and pulled his hips in hard against his own. A servant coughed discreetly as he passed, but neither heard. Peter felt engulfed and contained. Their mouths parted.

"Oh golly," Peter murmured, "do I ever want you. Come back, for God's sake."

"Don't you worry. You can count on that." Tim lifted a hand to Peter's face and gave his cheek a little pat. His eyes searched from mouth to hair and back to the mouth, his own mouth working, opening and closing, as if he were trying to decide where to sink his teeth. He ran his hand down Peter's nose and gave it a little tweak. His eyes sought Peter's. "Unnnh. Talk about growling. Yeah. You're it." They laughed softly as their bodies spoke for them.

"You'd better go now," Peter said. "I'm apt to start tearing your clothes off." They laughed and broke apart, and Tim strode over to a chair where a hat and coat were laid out beside a small suitcase. He gathered them up. "Tim," Peter said as a statement of fact. He turned, poised for departure. "Nothing. I just wanted to say your name." He went to him and put his hand under his arm, and Tim hugged it to him as they went to the door. Peter opened it.

"Thursday."

"Thursday." Peter's eyes held a dazzle of blue as he closed the door. He stood without moving, realizing that he was going to be unfaithful to Charlie at last; he had never allowed the others to count. Tears came to his eyes as he felt Charlie's hold slipping. He had built his life, such as it was, around this empty commitment; it would be strange to be without it. He was not yet released from the prison to which he had condemned himself, but he was no longer sealed off beyond reach or hope. He felt intimations of freedom. Perhaps Tim would complete the miracle on Thursday. He adjusted his clothes and pushed at his hair, waiting for everything to subside and return to normal. Then he went back to the party and retrieved his glass where he had left it in passing and found the servant to replenish it. Walter Pitney joined him.

"There you are, laddie. For a moment, I thought some lucky devil had spirited you away. You hit it off with Tim?"

"Golly, did we ever."

"I'm so glad. It's a shame he had to go off just now, but he'll be back in no time. Anticipation sometimes adds a touch of zest." His shining thick-rimmed glasses and his genial smile gave him an air of benevolence. The cheerful banality of everything he said was benevolent too, like blessings recited from a book. All his movements were firm and precise, which lent him authority, the aura of a man who knew what he wanted and would probably get it. Peter thought of what Tim had said about him and felt agreeably like part of the family.

"Is that dinner invitation still on? I want to hear all about Tim."

"I thought you two would have something for each other. I'm delighted you discovered it so quickly."

Peter laughed with happy release. "I'll say. I think I'm going to be out of circulation for a while. I'd better go speak to Hughie."

"He's right over there." Walter nodded and smiled. Peter crossed the room.

Hughie smiled at him secretly when he saw him. "Find something big, chéri?"

"Big, all right."

"That's good, chéri. That'll make it possible for me to hate you a little bit. Not very much. Just enough to make it easier."

Peter put his hand on his shoulder and rocked him gently. He held out the change from the taxi. "Here's your money. You're a great guy, Hughie."

"You too, chéri. Put that chicken feed away. You going to stay for dinner with His Highness? That's good, too. He's a nice man, Walter."

Peter looked him in the eye. "Thanks for last night."

Hughie laughed with a flash of white teeth. "Ooo-eee. You white boy."

The party broke up slowly. Peter was the object of much furtive ribaldry when it was learned that he was staying on. There were references to a massage machine, which Peter assumed had something to do with a joke he hadn't heard. He went through a few self-conscious moments when he was finally alone with his host. Now was the time for a hand to be placed insinuatingly on arm or shoulder, even an attempt at a kiss. Nothing of the sort occurred. Walter made no attempt to close in on him.

"I'm delighted you stayed. An unexpected pleasure." He beamed benevolently. "Will you stick to wine, or would you like something stronger before dinner?" He went to a table and pressed a bell.

"Maybe a whiskey to settle everything. I guess I'm getting a bit drunk."

Walter smiled approvingly. "Enjoy yourself. I do like to see people enjoying themselves." A manservant entered and fixed a whiskey for Peter and began clearing away glasses and bottles. Peter felt as if he were hermetically sealed into a world of silent opulence that had no connection with the city as he knew it.

"Have you noticed the Soutine over the fireplace?" Walter asked. "It's one of my favorites."

"Is that who it is? I wasn't sure. It's a beauty. Everything you have is fabulous."

"I'm so glad you appreciate them. Collecting means a great deal to me. There's a lot more scattered about. I'll show you all of it, later, or some other day. Daylight is really more satisfactory. Come look at this Cézanne. That's the prize of the lot."

They moved about the room together, their attention fixed on the paintings. Walter took no advantage of the many opportunities he had to put his hands on Peter.

They had dinner in a dining room dominated by a gorgeous Blue Period Picasso that Peter had often seen reproduced. The meal was excellent, served with excellent wines, and Peter particularly enjoyed it because he was able to turn the conversation to Tim. He learned that he had been a brilliant law student, that he had had several unhappy love affairs, that except for Walter's place, he avoided the "gay rounds," as Walter called it.

They moved for coffee to a small study, where they were greeted by a half dozen sunny Bonnards. Peter swirled his brandy in a great balloon of a glass and sighed. He had reached the point where he couldn't concentrate on anything for very long. His thoughts ran into each other, but he was pervaded by a sense of glowing well-being. Better drunk than high on marijuana. Not so crazy.

"This is the greatest evening I've had in a long time," he said. "You're a lucky guy."

"Well, yes, I guess I am. When I meet a charming person like you and am able to give them pleasure, I feel it very strongly. It doesn't happen very often. Let me give you another spot of brandy."

They inhaled their brandy, which made Peter's head reel, while Walter told stories about how he had acquired various items in his collection. "I have some rather extraordinary things in the bedroom," he said eventually. "I'm sure you'll appreciate them. Let's take the brandy."

"Well, I—"

"Oh, of course. I see what you're thinking. I assure you I have no intention of touching you."

"No, I didn't mean—"

"I have a very good idea of what it must be like for somebody with your looks, being mauled constantly. It must get very tiresome. I don't like that sort of thing at all. Shall we go?"

"Yes. Sure." He was still a bit dubious, but he reminded himself of Tim's reassurances. He rose with some difficulty, but once on his feet, he felt fine. Walter took the bottle and led the way down a long corridor to a big, darkly elegant bedroom. He flicked a switch. One whole wall was covered with drawings of male nudes, all of them museum pieces.

"Golly," Peter gasped.

"They're very fine, aren't they? Take your time."

Peter wandered along them. Walter made an occasional comment when he lingered in front of one. He imagined Charlie's drawings hanging here and found that they stood up surprisingly well under the comparison. He turned back to his host.

"Wonderful." He laughed, at ease now that Walter had offered further evidence of his good intentions. "Quite a crowd to sleep with."

"I would so love to see you naked beside them. The three-dimensional model, so to speak, and the artists' idealizations."

"I'm much skinnier than these guys. I'm more like him." He pointed to a delicate Donatello.

"Charming. I do wish you'd show me."

"Are you kidding?"

"Of course not. I'm not going to lay a finger on you, you know."

Peter had had enough to drink so that the idea of taking his clothes off seemed rather a lark. He thought of Tim's words. Walter had been very nice. If that was the way he got his kicks, what difference did it make? He shrugged and laughed. "OK, if you really want me to."

"How delightful. Go in there. You'll find hangers and everything." He indicated a door that Peter discovered led to a spacious dressing room. When he had stripped and hung his clothes up, he stretched and ran his hand over his chest and stomach. Nakedness had become his natural state; he felt no self-consciousness. He returned and found Walter stretched out on the bed wearing a dressing gown. His eyes were immediately riveted to a small hand massage machine on the table beside him. He didn't know what it was all about, but his only thought was to get out. He wondered how he could do it without making a scene.

Walter's level, unemphatic voice was soothing. "How lovely. It's just what I had hoped for. The purity of the body's line when there's no hair is incredible. You're one of the loveliest boys I've ever seen. Come stand over there." He indicated a place at the foot of the bed. Peter approached warily. "Yes. You move beautifully. You can't imagine what a pleasure it is to watch you. Wouldn't you like to do yourself?"

"Do myself? "

"Think of somebody you like very much and jerk yourself off. It would give me great pleasure."

Peter stared and blushed and burst into uncomfortable laughter. "I thought I'd done just about everything, but this is the nuttiest — I couldn't possibly."

"I'm sure you could." Walter's voice was unruffled. "There's no need to be embarrassed. Think only of your own pleasure. Pretend

I'm not here. Imagine you're at home alone and wishing very badly for somebody." Walter's voice was smooth and hypnotic.

Peter's hand went to his sex in an almost protective gesture. "But I can't—"

"Of course you can. You're embarrassed to let your hand do the natural thing. Don't be. Think of the pleasure you can give yourself. Caress it the way you would if you were alone. There, you see? It must feel very pleasant. Just relax completely with yourself."

Peter's eyes had closed. He drifted in an alcoholic mist. He thought of Tim as he slowly stroked himself erect. He heard the click of a switch, and an angry little buzz filled the room. The voice droned on above it.

"There's so much of it. A regular homewrecker. I would never have guessed. Take your hand away for just a moment. Yes. Superb. With all that, I should think you'd use both hands. Haven't you tried that? I think you'd enjoy it. Yes, like that. When you come, don't worry about where it goes. Just think of pleasing yourself. Are you thinking of Tim? He has a splendid body, you know. I imagine you've guessed. Not at all like yours. Big and sturdy and muscular, Michelangelo, with marvelous, curly, golden hair, almost as golden as your pubic hair. As for the principal instrument, I know you'll be delighted with that. It's not quite as long as yours, but much thicker, very powerful. The plowboy, I used to call him. That's what it makes you think of. Strong and solid and hard, plowing and sowing. Yes. Ah, yes."

Peter uttered a brief cry as he achieved his orgasm. His hips worked; he spilled himself across the bed. His knees buckled and almost gave way. He heard a grunt, and the buzz stopped with a click.

"Here, laddie. Use this." He opened his eyes and saw a towel being offered him. He took it and wiped himself in silence. He looked around him without looking at Walter and saw a wastebasket and went and dropped the towel in it. He stood with his back to the bed.

"I shouldn't have done that."

"Of course you should have. You surely enjoyed it, and it gave me enormous pleasure. It was very beautiful."

"I'm sort of mixed up. Tim said anything I did with you was all right."

"I'm sure he did. He knew I wouldn't touch you."

185

"I'll have to think about it. I must be drunker than I thought."

"Do you mind wearing one of my dressing gowns? I like to see a young man wandering around in a dressing gown." Walter brought him a dressing gown, and Peter took it and put it on. "Have some more brandy. I'd like to have a talk with you."

Peter took the brandy. Walter waved him to a chair. He sat, and Walter pushed up a chair for himself. Peter felt not so much ashamed as oddly shy at having performed such an intimate act before a witness. Accustomed to being honest with himself, he knew that he had briefly enjoyed it, in a way; it was the way that bothered him. It was a show-off sort of thing that went against his nature. He didn't want Tim to know about it, but he knew he would have to tell him.

"You must know by now that you're a very fascinating and a very beautiful person," Walter said. "I'm very much taken with you. Very much, indeed. More than I have been by anybody for many years. Are you satisfied with where you're living?"

For a moment, Peter couldn't remember in which of a succession of shabby rooms he had left his bags. "Oh, yes. Sure. It's fine."

"I ask because I keep another apartment in this building. It's quite small, but I'm pleased with the way it's furnished. It's free. If you can use it, I'd like very much for you have it."

Peter was finally able to look at him. The glasses glinted at him. The smile was benevolently undemanding. He looked authoritative and very nice. "Listen, Walter. I don't think you understand. I'm probably about to get involved in a pretty important affair with Tim."

"I very much hope you are. He needs you. All the more reason why you should have a nice place where you can be together. It won't always be convenient for him to have you at his place. A certain amount of independence is very important if you want these things to last."

"I have an idea I will. As long as Tim does." It was all so new to him. If Tim would want him to have a decent place of his own, Walter's offer was not to be brushed aside. "What if I do take the place? What would Tim think?"

"I'm sure he'd be very pleased. Do you have a bank account?"

Peter laughed. "What for?"

"There's a branch of Chase just around the corner. I'll open an account for you tomorrow. You might stop by in the afternoon and give them your signature and so forth."

186

"What am I supposed to do with it? You know I don't have a job, don't you?"

"Neither do I, but we both need money."

Peter threw his head back and roared. "You're a very funny man. But come on, be serious. I don't take money."

"Of course you don't. If you did, I'd give you a ten-dollar bill and say good night. You let me handle this."

"I guess I'm getting drunker by the minute. None of it's making any sense."

"I'm sure it will tomorrow." He rose and went to a handsome desk and pushed about in a drawer. He returned with a set of keys and handed them to Peter. "Eight-C. You're probably tired. Do you want a bite to eat? Well, then, why don't you go up and take a look at the place? You can spend the night if you want and move in tomorrow. Everything's there. If you need anything, there's a house phone that connects with me here. I can always send up Laszlo. I can't tell you what a delightful day this has been for me."

Peter rose, swaying slightly on his feet. "It's been quite an amazing evening. You're a great guy, even if I don't know what it's all about."

"I think I've explained it, but we can talk about it some more tomorrow. Come by when you've finished at the bank. I'll be home all afternoon. If you're at loose ends until Tim comes back, perhaps you'll have dinner with me."

"I'd love to. Only, what if I don't want to — to do that nutty business again?"

"It's entirely up to you, laddie. Don't commit yourself, in any case. Something more exciting might turn up during the day. There *is* one more great favor you can do me if you care to. Give me back my dressing gown now."

Peter smiled and peeled it off and handed it to him. The glasses cast off reflections as his head moved in a long scrutiny of his body. "One of the loveliest? Perhaps the loveliest. Perfect skin. You and Tim are going to be very beautiful together. You can go ahead and get dressed now." Peter turned and started for the dressing room. "There's no question that your bottom without any exception is the loveliest I've ever seen."

Peter laughed. "No fair talking behind my back."

187

HE STOOD IN THE MIDDLE of the living room and looked around him. It was furnished like the one below on a more modest scale, dark, opulent, with the curious hermetic atmosphere that made him feel totally cut off from the city outside. With Tim here, he would be enclosed in a rich, secret intimacy, the thought of which almost took his breath away. Rebellion stirred in him, mingling with the excitement he felt at the prospect. His life was being taken away from him. He thought of Charlie's parting words last night. Face it: there was nothing more to hope for there. Think of the future. No more shabby transient rooms. No more chance, unpredictable encounters. No more watches to sell. That was a problem. He wasn't sure he was ready for any of it. He was being pushed into Tim's arms before he had really made a choice. He thought of smiling blue eyes, of the big lazy grin. No, he was pretty sure of that. That was still his. Stunned astonishment remained. None of it was real. None of it was happening to him. He shed his clothes around the room to take possession of it. Naked, he crossed the small entrance hall to the bedroom, which was largely filled with an enormous bed covered in antique brocade. The love nest, he thought with inner laughter. They'd never find each other in that great expanse of mattress. He went on into the luxurious bathroom, where he found a cabinet filled with useful things, all new and wrapped and bearing expensive labels: toothbrushes, soap, toothpaste, two very fancy-looking razors, shaving cream, cologne, the familiar lubricant. Very thoughtful. Perhaps it would all be gone when he woke up in the morning.

It wasn't, nor was there time for his astonishment to pass. He went uptown to the room he had left two days before and packed his bags and paid the rest of the week he owed. This left him with very little cash. He reminded himself to sell something so that he could get in some provisions for tomorrow. He settled himself into his new quarters and spooned some baked beans directly from the can into his mouth and set off for the bank. There, an armed guard made a telephone call in response to his inquiry. He was ushered into a managerial office. There were a good many smiles and bows. If Mr. Martin would just take a seat. He was still unaccustomed to this adult form of address and had to suppress a giggle. There were forms to sign and checkbooks to choose. He was handed a deposit book.

He had fifty thousand dollars.

The book slipped out of his hands, and he had to retrieve it. He held it tight and stared at the zeroes, searching for blemishing decimal points. His voice broke into a squeak when he tried to speak.

"Look, there must be some mistake," he finally managed.

The official chuckled. "I don't think so, Mr. Martin. If we made mistakes with sums like that, we wouldn't be in business very long, would we?"

He was out in the street and walking fast, occasionally breaking into a run, to his new Park Avenue address. He stormed into Walter's study, to which a servant had directed him. Walter looked up from his desk.

"Now listen," he said, breathing hard. "What is all this? Are you a nut or something?"

Walter beamed at him. "How charming you look. All glowing and wind-blown."

"Come on, now. Do you have keepers or guardians or something? They'll probably have me put in jail."

"Sit down, laddie. Cool off." He sat back and looked at Peter and shook briefly with silent laughter. "It's worth it just to see you looking the way you do. Now *you* listen, laddie. It may seem an extravagant gesture, but I think you'll find that people who are used to handling money are more practical than those who aren't. I thought very carefully before deciding on the amount. Look at it from your point of view, which is what I did. Wisely invested, it could bring you about fifty dollars a week. That's a good deal more, I agree, than you could hope to earn for some time to come, but hardly enough to kill your incentive if and when you decide what you want to do. It's certainly enough to take care of you if you want to leave. As long as you're living upstairs rent-free and perhaps allowing me to provide some of your food and drink, you should be extremely comfortable. If, instead of capital, I'd offered you fifty dollars a week, I'd've been inviting a poke in the nose. It's as simple as that. The money means nothing to me. I often pay a great deal more for one of my pictures."

Peter noted the possessive pronoun and his classification among Walter's collection. "What am I supposed to *do* for it?" he demanded.

"Nothing you don't want to do. You can be very sure of that. It would perhaps be easier to understand if I said I'd fallen in love with you, but I'm reticent about certain things and people mean so many different things when they say that. Let me put it this way: If I had a son, I'd want him to be you. If I had a lover in the usual sense, I'd want him to be you. I want you to be part of my life, as Tim is in a lesser way. I want to think of you upstairs having an important affair. I want you to come and go, I want you to have meals with me when you have nothing better to do, I want to talk to you about my pictures, I want to look at you. If from time to time you care to indulge my whims, I'd be very happy, but that isn't essential. I may as well tell you I'll have others. I'm sometimes attracted to boys who will do it for money. I suppose I strike you as odd, but I've never enjoyed the struggling and grappling of making love. I'm a purely visual person. I've never liked the look of my own body and prefer not to expose it. There are bound to be awkward moments in the act of love. I wouldn't even want to watch you and Tim performing it, beautiful though you may be together. So much for that part of it. I want you to be free to live with me in the way I suggest."

"But what if I decide to clear out?"

"Exactly. That's really the point of what I'm saying. I found out very early that the more you want to hold people the more they want to be free. So I decided to do things my way. It once brought me eight years of great happiness. That's not a bad return on an investment. You now have money to lead whatever life you choose. I won't give you any more. If you spend it all next week, it will simply mean that you're not the person I think you are, and I will have made a rather expensive mistake. I don't often make mistakes about people. I've only felt what I feel about you twice before in my life, and I was right both times. You completely enchant me. I do hope you'll give me the pleasure of watching you live."

"Wow." Peter took a deep breath and swallowed to clear the lump in his throat. "You've got to admit it's pretty overwhelming. I've got to have time to think. I want to talk to Tim about it."

"That's very sweet. You value friendship. You're a very good person. I wouldn't do what I've done if you weren't."

"You certainly have a way of leaving a guy speechless. I haven't even thanked you."

"I think we can let time take care of that."

They agreed to spend the evening together, and Peter returned to what he was beginning to think of as his own apartment and selected a watch he thought would bring a good price and went out and sold it. He bought provisions and returned to the apartment and burrowed through his clothes and brought out the heavy cardboard folder in which he kept Charlie's drawings. His throat ached as he held it. If escape was within his reach, this was the point of departure. He mustn't go on treasuring these things as the promise of a return to the ecstatic happiness in which they had been created. Face it: the past was a dream ended. One of the drawings he could never part with; the other was simply a prized possession that he could offer for another's enjoyment.

He sat with the folder in front of him for a long time trying to think his way through the situation. No matter how persuasive Walter might be, he had to be sure that he wasn't selling himself in some way. Even such a simple act as giving him a drawing he would like might have unpleasant implications. The pose was provocative. Would he be using his body to tantalize him, to exploit his peculiar tastes? No, he had no interest in exploiting him. He hadn't accepted the money yet. He wouldn't feel it was his until he had talked to Tim. He didn't even know what his feelings for Tim were, but he knew he felt something for the first time in months. It was there within him, glowing, stirring him to life, stretching his nerves with anticipation. If it was going to lead to something, it would have to start with everything clear between them. Just don't build it up in your mind, his inner voice warned. He felt very young and inexperienced. Silly little faggot, he told himself. You're in pretty deep. Make sure you don't do anything that'll louse up your life.

When it was time to join Walter, he withdrew the drawing of himself from the folder without looking at the other and went downstairs. Walter was waiting for him in the living room with drinks set out.

"I want to give you something," he said without any preliminaries. "I think you'll like it, but I don't want you to get me wrong. You'll see what I mean when you look at it." He handed over the drawing.

Walter studied it for several minutes in silence. "Extraordinary," he said finally. "It's very lovely. Quite aside from the subject, it's beautiful. Beautiful work."

"That's what I hoped you'd think. I didn't want you to get the idea that I went around handing out pictures of myself with a hard-on. I mean, well, it's a picture, not a proposition."

"Of course, laddie. I understand the point you're trying to make. I'm very proud you're willing to let me have it. It means a great deal. But tell me about it. Who did it?"

"Charlie." He paused, waiting for the pain to cut into him. He thought of Tim and assured himself stubbornly that he would no longer be alone and found he could go on without wanting to burst into tears. He went on at length, telling the story of his life, which was simply the story of Charlie.

"You're still very much in love with him, aren't you, laddie?"

"I don't know. Maybe I always will be, but I don't see what good it'll do me. Tim did something to me. We just looked at each other, and it happened. That's why I'm so excited about it. Except that they're both sort of blond, he's not at all like Charlie, so it can't be transference or whatever you call it. I've sometimes thought I'm a sex fiend, but Tim makes me realize I'm not really. I'm going out of my mind wanting to go to bed with him, but it's more than that. I don't know how many guys I've done it with in the last few months, but I've never really wanted any of them more than once. It's not like that with Tim. I guess I must be in love with him, or at least beginning to be."

"You're full of love, laddie. Tim will be very lucky if you offer him some part of it. I'm sorry your friend isn't going on with his art. He has a great talent. I'll have it framed. It's good enough to hang with the others, if you don't mind."

"I don't mind if Tim doesn't. You'd better ask him. I honestly don't know anything about anything for the moment. I won't until tomorrow night."

They had an excellent meal and a pleasant evening with the pictures. When Peter went back to his place, he hid the drawing of Charlie away. He still didn't trust himself to look at it. Maybe he would with Tim someday.

The next day was simply feverish waiting. He drowsed in bed as late as he could. He spent a long time in the bathroom, grooming himself. He went out and bought food and wine and flowers. The flowers took up quite a lot of time. He fussed about in the kitchen, making sure that everything was in order for dinner. It was time at last to call. His voice trembled when he pronounced Tim's name to the girl who answered the phone. Then Tim was on the line sounding astonishingly familiar.

"Is that you? Thank God. This is getting out of control. Where can I meet you?"

192

His voice trembled again as he replied, "I'm in Walter's small apartment. You know the one."

"You are? I'll be damned. That's fine. I'll be there by six."

"Is it all right?"

"Is what all right? It was all wrong being away."

"I'll say. I meant about the apartment."

"It's perfect. It's been empty for I don't know how long. Listen, if I go on talking, something's going to give. I'm going to hang up now." He did.

Peter sat staring at the phone, thinking of all the things he wished he had said. He hoped he hadn't sounded cold. Tim had managed to say so much in a few words. Getting out of control. All wrong being away. Something's going to give. He lay back in the chair and laughed. Tim had it bad, too. Exciting and wonderful. He hadn't made it all up in his mind. He sprang up and tore off his clothes and took another shower. He considered not dressing but decided it would look tartish if he was sitting around all ready to go to bed. Tim would be dressed. He should be, too. He gave dressing his careful attention, choosing things he thought he looked his best in. He got out ice and bottles. He adjusted the flowers. He tried to keep his mind a blank. After an eternity of silence, the bell rang. He rushed to the door and flung it open. For an instant, his eyes were bathed in blue, then Tim was inside. He put down a small suitcase and flung off his hat and coat all in one movement and took Peter in his arms. He moaned as their mouths met. They kissed for a long moment. Their heads parted, and they leaned a little away from each other, their arms crooked, holding each other by the elbows, their hips thrust forward and touching, swaying slightly as their erect sexes played with each other through layers of cloth.

"Clothes. Hell. I thought you'd be ready for me."

"I thought of it. I decided I ought to be respectable. There're things I've got to tell you. It's really all right my being here?"

"Why're you looking so worried? He gave it to you because he's stuck on you. So what? I knew he would be."

"It's more than that. He's given me fifty thousand dollars."

"Good God." Tim stared, motionless with astonishment. A grin slowly spread across his face. "That's fabulous. You've driven him mad. Not that that's really big money to him. He can spare it."

"I haven't accepted it yet. I had to talk to you. What am I supposed to do?"

"Listen, we can talk about it later. I can't think straight now. Let's go to bed. Please. You don't know what it's been like. I've been going crazy thinking about you."

"Me too. But I had to tell you first. I want everything to be the way you want it."

"Well, then, come on. I want to see what I'm getting that's worth fifty thousand bucks."

"Tim."

"Yeah?"

"This means something, doesn't it? It's not just going to be a quick lay?"

"Are you crazy? For two days I haven't been making any sense at all. I don't know why I wasn't fired. I wouldn't have cared. Hell, I would've been glad. I could've got back here that much sooner. This is the biggest thing that's happened to me — I don't know, maybe in my whole life. You knew that when I left."

"I hoped so. That's why Walter and this place bothered me. We can leave it till later so long as you know I want so much to be everything you want me to be."

"I don't think you'll have to try very hard. But please, please. For the love of God have mercy on my aching cock. I want you in bed."

"That, sure lord, is where I want to be."

"Well, come on."

"We'll have to let go of each other if we expect to go anywhere."

"I know. That's the hard part."

"When it happens like this, it certainly makes everything else seem pretty crappy."

Tim gripped his arms hard. "Come on."

There was no time for sophisticated lovemaking. Peter knew that he could never get through the preparations necessary to his particular desires. It was all done in minutes with hands and grappling bodies. They spilled themselves onto each other.

They lay together afterward, Tim propped on an elbow, a big hand toying with Peter's hair. "You're it. You're really it, Skeezix. I've been waiting so damn long for you. I don't mean two days. I mean years. I was beginning to think you'd never turn up. You're mine now. The Growler. Who would ever have guessed it?"

"I would have, if anybody had told me about you. And how about dropping that name? The Growler's dead. It was a pretty good joke while it lasted." He was memorizing Tim's face: the fair hair

194

falling over the heavy brow, the wide-set eyes, the high, rather massive cheekbones, the strong jut of the nose, the curve of the big, firmly modeled mouth. There was nothing subtle or elusive about it. It was all honest and straight and easy to read. What he read now was love. He was moved and grateful. He snuggled in closer and ran his hand over the cloud of blond hair on his chest and put a finger in his ear. "You're staying the night, aren't you? I mean, that's the way it's going to be, isn't it?"

"Are you kidding? Try to get me out."

"And tomorrow night?"

"You're damn right."

"That's enough to look forward to really. Are we more or less going to live together?"

"What do you mean, more or less? You're mine now."

"I'm glad. It's nice to know. I want you to fuck me, you know."

"How do you mean?"

"Really fuck me. You know. You inside me."

Tim's eyes were grave. "You do? That's something I've never done."

"It's amazing how many guys haven't. Just wait. Then I'll really be yours." Tim's sex stiffened against his leg. Peter laughed. "I don't mean necessarily right now, unless you really want to. Don't you want me to cook you some dinner?"

"I guess so, if it won't take too long."

Peter pulled his head down and they kissed. The kiss deepened as their hands explored each other, finding new places. Peter was overwhelmed by his size: heavy shoulders, big arms, deep chest, great columns of legs, the thick sex like a club. He wanted him badly in the way he liked best. He wanted to be his. He felt protected again. He wanted to hide in his chest. Tim drew his head back and looked at him and began to laugh. "You really are something, aren't you, Skeezix?" His laughter was filled with delight and amazement. "I knew you were beautiful, but I never guessed the half of it."

Peter smiled and opened his mouth and snapped it shut with a click of teeth. He growled. "Shall we go on from here, or dinner?"

"You can do anything you want with me. You say."

"Then let's get the damn food over with so we can concentrate on things that matter."

"I'm not so sure I'll let you go. You can do anything you want except get out of this bed."

Peter put the heels of his hands in the hollows of Tim's cheeks and pressed gently. "I don't want to go anywhere."

"If you're sure that's true, then I guess it's all right." He disentangled himself. Peter slid over to the edge of the bed and stood. Tim scrambled after him and put his arm around his waist and turned him. He kissed his rigid sex with his open mouth and ran his tongue along it. "Where did you get all this? It's amazing on such a skinny little guy."

Peter ran his hand through the fair hair and pressed his head against his stomach. "It seems to be bigger than usual today. That's what you do to it."

Tim swung his legs over the side of the bed and stood. Peter took his hand and held him, and they remained motionless as they studied each other's bodies. Walter's description had been accurate. Peter ached inside with wanting him. He shifted his hips so that their sexes met and crossed. He looked up and their eyes met and they laughed.

"Do you suppose we're going to stay like this all through dinner?" Peter asked.

"I wouldn't be at all surprised. The way you make me feel, I'll probably be like this for the next month."

They moved apart reluctantly, and Peter put on a dressing gown. Tim went to the entrance hall and opened his bag and pulled a robe out for himself. Peter fixed them drinks in the living room. They looked at each other's lifted dressing gowns and rocked with laughter.

"Do you suppose this could mean we want to make love with each other?" Peter asked.

"Don't be ridiculous. We're both guys."

"So it would appear. Maybe slaving over a hot stove will have some effect." They laughed some more.

Tim followed him into the kitchen. He sat at the table while Peter turned his back to him and busied himself with a meal he'd kept simple on purpose.

"How's yours?" Peter asked with a giggle after a few minutes.

"The same."

"So's mine. It's going to get in the soup." They shouted with laughter. Peter collapsed over the sink. "This is ridiculous. Suppose we have to go around like this for the rest of our lives."

"It'll ruin my career. No jury would take me seriously." They howled.

196

"That's better," Peter said while he caught his breath. "At least, it's not so much in the way."

"Yeah. Sex is no laughing matter." They continued to be shaken by little bursts of giggles.

"God, I love you, big boy," Peter said. "You're so damn silly."

"Yeah, I know. That's what everybody says."

Peter set the table and put the food on it and poured out wine. "Now listen," he said when they had started eating. "We've got to get this Walter business straight. You know what happened, don't you?"

"Sure. Hell, I was there before you. I'm too old for him now. He likes 'em young."

"You don't mind?"

"I told you anything you did was OK. I wasn't crazy about the idea of his seeing you before I did, but we'd hardly met. I didn't have the right to start laying down the law. Now that you're mine, now that we have each other, what difference does it make?"

"Well, what do you want me to do about the money?"

"Take it, for God's sakes. You're worth every penny of it. There aren't any strings attached, are there?"

"No. So he says. Except that I know he's going to want me to strip sometimes."

"I don't see what harm that can do you."

"You wouldn't mind if I did?"

"Why should I? I wouldn't mind if you took a shower in a gym. Plenty of guys would stare at you there. That's really all it amounts to. As far as I'm concerned, we can ask the whole town in to look at you. You're so damn beautiful. *Look.* Not touch. I'll kill anybody who tries that. I'm not kidding. As for the other part of it, so long as you think of me, that doesn't matter much either."

"I'm not so sure. That's the trouble. It wasn't the same as doing it by myself. I was awfully drunk and thinking about you, but I don't know. You seem to get involved somehow with the person who's watching. That's what bothers me. I'm no exhibitionist, but in a way I sort of liked it. Something really wonderful had just happened to me, you'd just been there and kissed me, and I was doing something I didn't want you to know about. That's the bad part. I agree with you, otherwise. It doesn't mean a thing. I don't mind taking my clothes off if I like somebody and they really want to look at me."

"Are you saying you're seriously considering turning him down?"

"I want you to tell me. There can't be anything even a little bad between us."

"You're incredible." He put his hand out and touched Peter's. "How've you been getting by, Skeezix?"

"Sleeping around. I haven't been a whore, but I want you to know all about me. People give me things. I sell them. I've never done it with anybody I didn't want to. That was the point of the Growler routine."

"Yeah, but as you say, the Growler's dead. I want to give you lots of things, but I'd want you to keep them."

"I'd never sell anything you gave me. I can get a job."

"Sure. You'll probably want to anyway. But fifty thousand dollars! Why don't you explain it to Walter the way you have to me? I think he'd understand."

"He probably would, and then I'd feel lousy for not being willing to do such a little thing for him when he'd done so much for me."

"Maybe you'd better be a lawyer. You're really picking over the fine print. Look, I've known Walter a long time. I performed for him dozens of times. I know what you mean. I got to sort of enjoy it in a peculiar sort of way. But honestly, it doesn't mean anything finally."

"I wouldn't want you to do it."

"Well, we can't be each other, Skeezix. We've got to accept that, right from the start. But let me finish. I know why he's given you the money. He must've told you. You can give him so damn much, even if you feel you shouldn't take your clothes off. He had a very sweet guy with him for years. He was killed a couple of years ago. He's been very lonely ever since. He just wants your time. I won't be able to be with you always. He's obviously fallen for you. Who wouldn't? If you like him, what's wrong with giving him an interest in life besides his pictures?"

"I don't know. Maybe you're right. So long as he understands I may not do my act for him again. So much depends on what happens to us. Are we going to be faithful to each other?"

"The minute we're not we might as well call it off."

"That's good. That's the way I want it. Do you think two guys can make this sort of thing work? I mean, are you thinking about the next few weeks or for real?"

198

"For real, Skeezix. It couldn't be anything else with you. Not the way I feel. I've always felt like a damn fool telling a guy I'm in love with him, but with you I think it'll be different. I don't see how I can hold off much longer."

"We don't have to tell each other things."

"There's somebody else, isn't there?"

"You said you knew all about me. I guess you must know about that. I'll tell you about it, but I'm not sure tonight's a good time unless you insist. It was easy to talk about it when I wanted to explain to people — you know, guys I really liked — why they shouldn't let themselves get serious about me. That's hardly the case with you. I want you to be serious about me. I'm serious about you. That's for sure." Their eyes met and probed into each other. After a moment, Peter's breath caught and he inhaled deeply to ease his chest. Tim's regard was calm and level.

"I'm in love with you, Peter." He broke into a broad grin. "There. I don't care whether I sounded like a damn fool or not. It's the truth."

"You didn't sound like a damn fool. You sounded beautiful." Peter exploded with laughter. "Three guesses what's going on under the table."

Tim laughed with him. "Same here. Maybe we ought to see a doctor."

"Come on. Let's get back in bed where we belong, even if we are both boys."

They rose and laughed again as their condition was revealed. They held each other's sexes as they crossed the apartment to the bedroom. They threw off their dressing gowns, and Tim made a dive for the bed.

"Wait a second, big boy. I'll be right there." Peter went to the bathroom and applied the lubricant to himself and returned with the tube and a towel. He squeezed the tube into his hand and stroked it onto Tim's heavy sex. He looked into his eyes. "I want this so badly. If you've never done it, you can't imagine. I'll be yours, big boy. I'll really be yours." He spread out the towel and lay on his stomach beside Tim. "Go ahead. Just take it easy at first. When you're all inside me, then — well, then fuck me." As Tim moved into position, he backed up onto his knees and reached behind him for the sex and guided it to him. "Just let me show you at first. There. Oh, yes ... Easy ... God, you're a big one ... Yes, almost ... Just a little — yes ... Oh, God ... Now. I can take it all."

"Good sweet Jesus," Tim gasped.

Peter uttered shaky little sobbing laughter. "Oh, God, beautiful. So beautiful. Fuck me, beautiful." He growled as he began the movement with his buttocks and hips to ease the sex within him and make it part of him. He felt Tim's big hands gripping his haunches. The sex swelled and penetrated deeper into him. He laughed as he welcomed it and surrendered to it. After the months of passionless intercourse, his whole being thrilled to the hard flesh that filled and possessed him. He began to tremble all over as he felt the love in the possession and in his submission to it. He wanted to give all of himself and to have all of himself taken, used, known, consumed. The sex moved within him, withdrew, drove hard into him. Yes, take me, he prayed, and groaned with ecstasy.

"Dear sweet mother of God," Tim gasped. "It's not — Holy Jesus. I can't — Oh, please. Peter, goddamn it. No. Oh Christ. No." He ended with a shout, and Peter felt the flood surging into him as the great body collapsed on top of him. "No. No. No. Not without you," he insisted angrily as the orgasm shook his body.

"Hush." Peter found his face and stroked it with the tips of his fingers. "Be quiet, big boy. I'm glad you came so quickly. That must mean I'm right for you, thank God. Next time, you'll do what you want with me. Now I've got you all inside of me. I belong to you, big boy."

"Christ Almighty. I wanted it to go on forever. I can't believe it." He laughed unsteadily. "All I can think of is I want to marry you."

"Hey, I've got myself a husband. It's about time. I pronounce us man and something-or-other. We're married, big boy."

"You're so right. You're really mine now. Next time, I'll do it right so you'll come with me. That must be something. Imagine a little squirt like you teaching me a thing like that."

"I still have some things to teach you. There're other ways of doing it. We'll find the way you like best."

"We've found it. I'm really going to fuck you. You want me to, don't you, sweetheart?"

"Want you to? Golly. All day and all night, without stopping."

"I mean, we're not supposed to take turns or anything?"

"Are you kidding? What do you think I've got myself a husband for? Now, just a second." He shifted slightly and the sex slipped from him. "Just lie on your back and don't move." He jumped up and went to the bathroom and washed himself. He came back with a washcloth and washed Tim carefully and dried him. He could feel Tim's eyes on him as he performed the chore. He threw the washcloth into the tub and returned and started to get into bed.

"Wait a minute. Let me look at all of you. You're Peter. I'm so in love with you, Peter. It sounds perfectly reasonable when I say it to you. I'm in love with Peter. Peter's getting a hard-on. So am I. Come here, sweetheart."

Peter scrambled into bed and was gathered into strong arms.

PETER QUICKLY FOUND that he was more mistress than wife. After some thought, he decided that it was probably better that way. Their relationship was passionate but mirthful. He didn't doubt that Tim was genuinely in love with him, but he was also ambitious and a lawyer. Peter adored him, but the feeling lacked the obsessive quality which he associated with being in love. He would probably never feel that way again about anybody. If there had been a real question of marriage, he would have accepted, but there would have been some small hesitation in the back of his mind. He wasn't sure that he would have wanted Tim's babies. It was the only way he could express it to himself. The picture of Tim settled into a successful law career was slightly oppressive; but Tim as a lover was a complete delight. They called each other constantly during the day to laugh and exchange nonsense. They spent many evenings and many nights together, but Tim had an extensive social life connected with his work, and from that, of course, Peter was excluded. He spent at least one or two nights a week in his own place, which Peter never saw. Their own social life was largely confined to Walter's gatherings, where they were known and accepted as a couple. Peter liked that very much. He loved Tim most when he took his hand or put his arm around him or kissed his ear when they were with other people. He stood within the protection of the big body, and his heart felt as if it would burst with pride and happiness.

He spent a great deal of time with Walter, out at galleries and dealers tracking down a new acquisition, at the apartment for meals, even discussing his business affairs. Walter advised him about investing his money, and an interest in finance was born in him. His life took on direction. He decided that in the fall he would enroll at Columbia as a full-time student. He wanted to take art and business courses. He thought he would probably become an art dealer if he escaped the war. Walter was delighted with this development. To please him, Peter often invented an excuse to take a shower in his bathroom and wandered around naked in front of him, but the massage machine never appeared again. Walter apparently understood and had either renounced his whim or was biding his time. Peter had the satisfaction of knowing that he never regretted his investment.

One blustery late-winter morning when Tim hadn't spent the night with him and he was having breakfast alone, his attention was caught by an item on the *Times* theatrical page. A new play called *Bumblebee* was about to go into rehearsal. Among the cast were Harriet Donaldson and Charles Mills. He was strongly tempted to call and congratulate them, but decided it was better to leave it alone. He was enormously pleased. He looked forward to seeing them on the stage. He and Tim would go together. Tim knew all about Charlie.

THE MILLSES' ENGAGEMENT for *Bumblebee* was Hattie's particular triumph. Ever since the New Year, when she had first heard of the project, she had hounded the director, a friend of hers named Andy Mars. He agreed that he could probably use her in a small part. He admitted that Charlie might be right for one of the leads, but would commit himself no further.

"What makes you think the guy can act?"

"I just happen to know, that's all. We've worked up a scene together. Let us do it for you."

"I haven't got time. Maybe later. Even if the guy's Barrymore, I'm not sure I'd use him. He gets on my nerves."

"Try to be a little professional, for Heaven's sake."

Charlie was less than enthusiastic about the whole idea. When Hattie managed to wangle a copy of the play, he found it a silly trifle. There were to be no glamorous stars. It was being done on a shoestring. When Hattie found out that Andy Mars was having trouble raising money for the production, she extracted a thousand dollars from a cousin who dabbled in the theater. This assured her a part and Charlie a reading. The antipathy that Andy Mars felt for Charlie was reciprocal. He was a brash, hard-driving young man, barely out of the amateur class. He had done some professional work in summer stock, which didn't give him the right, as far as Charlie was concerned, to act as if he'd invented the theater, especially since all he had to offer was *Bumblebee.*

"Who cares if it's any good?" Hattie demanded. "We'll be seen. It's bound to get you a good job in stock this summer."

"What if we can't get jobs in the same company?"

"Then we'll have to be apart for a few months."

"I see. A devoted wife."

"Who ever said anything about being a devoted wife? I'm an actress, goddamn it. Even so, you're not doing too badly. It's not every girl who'd fall for you the way I did. You and your Peter."

"Let's leave him out of it, shall we?"

"Gladly. Why can't you? Why do you have to go running off to Harlem with him?"

"Oh, God. That was weeks ago. Haven't we had enough of that?"

"I didn't like it then, and I don't like it now. How am I supposed to know what went on between you?"

Charlie smiled at her. "You can't possibly know, can you?"

"Ohhhh. I just wish you cared as much about being an actor as you do about sex. You and your great cock."

"Don't knock it, baby. I might not let you have it." He laughed at her.

Bumblebee slowly passed from the talking stage to a firm reality. All the money was finally raised. A theater was booked. A date was fixed for the start of rehearsals. Charlie was called for a reading. Hattie went with him and sat in the auditorium with Andy Mars. When Charlie had finished, she looked at Mars. He was chewing gum fast. He jerked his head up and down several times.

"OK, you may be right. He's pretty good. He'd give the play some class. I've got to see a couple of other guys, but I think he might be it. He can come again tomorrow and read for the goddamn author." Hattie crowed with laughter and gathered up her things and ran down the aisle to Charlie.

Charlie had a second reading and was told he could have the part. He had two weeks to quit his job and break the news to C.B. He and Hattie went to a dingy little office on West Forty-sixth Street to sign their contracts, both for the same minimum salary despite the disparity of their parts. Everything about it struck him as terribly shoddy. He had never believed in the production, and now he was actually caught up in it. Of course, Hattie was right. It was what it could lead to that counted. He was on his way at last.

He went to see C.B. on the way home after giving notice at the office. Trying to prepare himself, he was appalled that he had committed himself so deeply without at least discussing it with her first, giving her some hint of what was in the wind. There was nothing to mitigate the blow. When he had imagined this happening, he had always assumed that there would be names to drop, a star, a writer, a director, something to provide some glamour to titillate her. This was simply shabby, a third-rate little enterprise that would sink without a trace within days of its opening. He couldn't blame her if she never forgave him.

She received him with her usual delight. "You're looking so well again. For a while, you were getting a rather worn look. All those parties must have been exhausting. The Donaldsons always overdo everything. So attractive." She gave his hand a little squeeze and went to her bar cabinet and fixed drinks. "How's Hattie?"

"She's fine. She's got a job."

"How splendid. A play?" She returned with the drinks and sat with her feet tucked together under her.

"Yes, it's not a big part, but it's wonderful for her. I'm not so sure about the play."

"The theater is such a gamble. Up one minute and down the next. Still, I'm terribly pleased for her."

"I've got some more news. Pretty big news." He had to sound pleased himself if he hoped to win her over. "I've got one of the leads in it."

"In the play?" She looked at him and lifted her hands and let them drop into her lap. Her face was drained of expression. "So it has come at last. I knew it was inevitable. Oh, my dearest, you do distress me."

"Please, C.B. The theater isn't the way you think it is anymore. I mean, lots of perfectly decent people go into it these days. Jimmy Stewart was at Princeton. There's a whole bunch of people coming up now that all worked together. Margaret Sullavan. Henry Fonda. Lots of them."

"I know, my dearest. The world's changing. But I can't bear to see you do this to yourself. Of course, you'll be a star." She said this in such lugubrious tones that Charlie managed to laugh.

"Wouldn't you like that? Everybody's always said I should be a success at it."

"I've said so, too. That doesn't make it any easier. You say the play's not very good. What will you do if it closes?"

"Summer will be coming soon. There're always a lot of jobs in stock. It's a big part. Even if it only runs a week, everybody will see me. I mean, all the theater people."

"Yes, of course. Well, what can I do to stop you? I don't like to rattle my will, but of course it will make a difference. I'll have to take you out of it, my dearest."

"Oh, C.B., I don't want your money. I'll probably make tons anyway. I just want you to live forever."

"It's a kind thought, but I don't imagine I will. So you spurn my money? You'd be quite tolerably rich, you know."

"I can't back out of it now," he said, almost wishing that he could. "I told them at the office today."

"I suppose Hattie is behind this. I'm afraid I shall come to hate her."

"Come on, C.B. Please don't make it sound as if I were doing something awful to you."

"No, no, it's what you're doing to yourself that distresses me. Of course, that's selfish too. You've always been such a joy to me. Now I shall have to watch you coarsen yourself, adapt yourself to the mob's taste. I'm delighted about poor little Sapphire, but do you want to put yourself on an equal footing with her? You have such exquisite sensibilities. You'll have to root them out or be trampled under. You've always responded to everything that's fine and beautiful in life. I would never allow myself to imagine you committing a gross or ugly act. Do you really believe such qualities have a place in the jungle of the theater? You've always been such a superior creature, such a true gentleman. What is to become of all that? No, I'm afraid this is a little bit good-bye, my dearest. I'm very sad." She held up the image of himself to which she had taught him to cling and smashed it before his eyes. The shock left him bereft, much more so than the threat of disinheritance. He must remain in her eyes all that she imagined him to be.

"I didn't have to do anything gross or ugly to get this part," he said, thinking of Meyer Rapper. "Honestly. You're exaggerating. Please tell me you understand my wanting to try it."

"I daresay I'll recover. I try to keep my life full of interests. I've been seeing a great deal recently of a most extraordinary young man. Very handsome. Stanley Price. I haven't had a chance to tell you about him. There's so much I want to do for him. Perhaps I'll feel free now to nibble a bit at capital. I've been guarding it so zealously for you. Of course, Harold has been very pleased with your work for the firm. Too bad. He was planning some interesting things for you after you'd been there a year. We've even talked a bit about my investing in the business. No matter. If the theater is to be your fate, so be it."

"But C.B., there must be something to be said for using whatever talents you have." He didn't want to hear any more about the unknown young man, and he was genuinely bored by his future in the publishing house.

"You know what I think about that. The greatest talent lies in making a rich, well-rounded life for oneself. However, you have your Hattie. She doubtless feels you'd drift apart more and more if she went on in the theater alone."

"We haven't been drifting apart. It hasn't got anything to do with her. You said yourself that you've known it was inevitable."

"Yes. As so many sad things are inevitable. Well, I suppose I must drink to your success." She picked up her glass and did so. He stayed on much longer than he had intended, trying to win an approving smile, trying to provoke her to argument so that he could at least fight back. Her cheerless resignation was worse than angry opposition; it lay on him like a sentence against which there was no appeal. He prayed for the unlikely fluke of success; even she would find some compensating excitement in that.

REHEARSALS STARTED on a blustery day in late winter. The cast, the director, the producer, the author, and a dozen or so nondescript, rather shabby people (Hattie and Charlie were dazzling exceptions) gathered in a peculiar hall in the Times Square area. Charlie couldn't imagine what it could have been originally intended for. It retained traces of an attempt at grandeur, some curlicues painted on the walls, a dusty glass-and-metal chandelier, but it was inconceivable that any festivities could have been contemplated in it. It was long and tall and badly lighted. It was full of chairs. They all sat in a row with Andy Mars by himself in front of them and read through the play. This group effort did nothing to brighten the material. Hattie had one reading that made everybody stir slightly with sounds of amusement. Charlie found that the girl he was supposed to be in love with was a mousy little thing with a singularly grating voice. When they had finished, they all stood up and wandered about. Andy Mars approached Charlie.

"Have you started learning your lines yet, Mills?" he demanded, snapping his chewing gum.

"Yes. As soon as we go through it a couple of times so I can get an idea of what the others are like, I probably won't need my sides."

"I just asked a question. You don't have to make a speech. Your reading's OK, but it's a reading. I want to see you put some life into it."

"Sure. Just as soon as we get on our feet," Charlie said, but Andy Mars had already turned away and was talking to somebody else. Charlie decided there was no need to take offense. He probably had a lot on his mind. Andy Mars began pushing chairs around. These three chairs were a sofa. Two chairs a few feet apart were a door or a window. He chalked off the limits of the stage on the floor.

"OK, everybody. Let's get going."

People made entrances and read lines. Mars gave them directions. Charlie made his first entrance and read a line. Mars gave him a direction. Charlie moved accordingly and read another line. Mars gave him another direction. Charlie read another line. Mars interrupted him.

"Listen, take notes, will you? I don't want to give you this stuff twice."

"I don't have to take notes. I can remember."

"I said, take notes."

Charlie looked at him. Anger stirred in him. He didn't like his looks or anything else about him. Take it easy, he told himself. "Look, you want me to get rid of my sides. What's the point of marking them?"

"I didn't say anything about getting rid of your sides. I said I wanted you to speak like a human being. This isn't goddamn

Shakespeare." There was a murmur of amusement around them. "Let's just cut the crap and do what I say."

Charlie continued to look at him, allowing disdain to creep into his expression. "Make up your mind. One or the other."

Mars's eyes glinted. "All right, smart ass. Do you want to be in this show or don't you?"

"You're holding things up. I'm not."

Mars turned abruptly away. Charlie smiled to himself as the rehearsal resumed. By evening when there was a break for food, Charlie was desperate for a drink. Mars was obviously determined to provoke him to the limits of his control. He had adopted "smart ass" as a permanent form of address. He interrupted constantly. He sneered at Charlie's readings. Yet there was an indirection in it, a failure to meet Charlie's eye, that made it possible for Charlie to take it. Mars seemed almost to be addressing some inner devil.

"Christ, what a shit," Charlie exploded as he and Hattie hurried down the street to a bar.

"He may think he'll get a better performance out of you if he gets you worked up. You do have such a grand manner, darling. He's probably using psychology."

"Some psychology."

He had three drinks while she had one, and began to calm down. "Hell, I don't care," he said with a shrug. "It just makes it awfully hard to concentrate."

She laughed. "Poor Andy. He looks like a tough little tug bumping its nose against a luxury liner. He'll probably get tired of it in a few days."

"If I don't let him have it before then."

"I think I know what he means about your reading. We can go over it later. I'll show you."

"I don't need to be shown anything." Mars was bad enough. He wasn't going to be patronized by Hattie. "I haven't had time to get started. I'm ready now, goddamn it." He had time for a fourth drink before they went back to work.

The drinks were a help. He breezed through his lines with ease and authority. Even Mars seemed impressed; at least he devoted some attention to other members of the cast.

The duel wasn't over, however. It started again the next day.

Charlie had just launched into one of his more important scenes. After a few moments Mars stopped him. "All right, smart ass. I gave you a movement on that line. I told you I wasn't going to block everything twice."

"You don't have to. I know what you gave me. It doesn't feel right. It's more natural on the next line."

"You'll damn well make it feel right. Who's directing this play, you or me?"

"Oh, you are. I wouldn't be bothered, myself."

There was a shocked murmur around them. Mars stood looking at the floor. Counting to ten? He turned back to his chair. "All right, David Belasco. Let's see what you've worked up for yourself."

The exchange set the tone for the day. Charlie met Mars's slashing attack with insolence. He managed to maintain an unruffled exterior, but the effort worked at his nerves. He needed a drink. He seized a moment to rush out and have one during the afternoon. It simply made him want another. In the evening break, he tossed back five while Hattie watched with speculative, protuberant eyes.

"You may have found the right way to handle him," she said. "I think you have him on the run. But be careful, for God's sake. You're playing a tricky game."

"It's all so damn silly," Charlie said, feeling the alcohol loosening his taut nerves. "If he'd leave me alone and do his job right, we might make something of this ridiculous play."

The next day, he carried a briefcase to the rehearsal hall. There was a bottle of whiskey in it. He left it in the small anteroom. Whenever he had a free moment, he went out and took a quick swallow. It made everything much easier. Mars's attack simply bounced off him. He let himself be bullied and insulted. He laughed cheerfully in the director's face. He caught Mars's suspicious eyes on him several times when he thought Charlie wasn't looking. The day passed much more quickly than usual.

He had his briefcase with him the next day. Mars came up to him as soon as he arrived. "All right, smart ass. You said you wanted to get used to working with the others. Is three days enough? I'm trying to be patient, but when are we going to be favored with this great display of histrionic ability?"

"What's the matter now?"

"Plenty. The comedy scenes aren't bad, but your love scenes stink. Couldn't you possibly give the impression of at least being alive?"

"It takes two to make a love scene."

"Oh, God. Wouldn't you know. I'll take care of Stella. I'm talking about you."

"OK. Let's work on it. Just tell me what you want."

"Don't worry. Meanwhile, you might find time to go over that scene in Act Two with Stella. You seem to like it out there in the hall. Take her with you."

The day's work began. His access to the bottle limited by Mars's instructions, Charlie found it dragging painfully. He went over the scene with the girl in the anteroom, eyeing the briefcase all the while. Mars began to load him with small extra business to strengthen the relationship with the girl. It was nagging and painstaking work. The afternoon was coming to an end when they got to the scene in Act Two. They started into it. Before they were halfway through, Mars leaped up out of his chair.

"Good sweet Jesus. You're in love with her. You think she's going off with another guy." He shoved Charlie roughly out of the way and rattled off his lines with ludicrous intensity. "There. I know this makes demands on your imagination. She's a girl. You're supposed to like her. Christ, these Park Avenue faggots. You're—"

Charlie took a quick step forward and swung his fist. Andy Mars dropped in a gratifying heap at his feet. He rose slowly, rubbing his chin. He stood uncertainly for a moment and then withdrew to a safe distance.

"All right, Mills. Get out. Get out and stay out."

"Who the hell do you think you are? I've got a contract."

"Then why don't you go home and read it? Everybody here is on trial until the end of the fifth day of rehearsal. That's tomorrow."

Charlie had vaguely heard of such a clause, but it had never occurred to him that it would ever be invoked. He couldn't imagine being fired. "Fine," he said with an admirable show of insouciance. "I never wanted to be in your idiotic play anyway."

"Or in any other, I hope, for your sake. Equity will have a report of this. Drunk at rehearsals — I know what's in that briefcase — assaulting the director. I don't think you're going to be deluged with offers."

"You terrify me. Just watch who you call a faggot. Equity would be interested in that, too."

"All right. Enough of this chitchat. Out. You're holding up my rehearsal."

Charlie turned to Hattie. "Are you coming?"

Her eyes blazed at him. "Are you out of your mind? I'm working."

He turned on his heel and left. It was inconceivable. Here he was out in the street without a job. His theatrical career had come to a premature and at least temporary end. Of course, he hadn't really been fired; hitting Mars had been one way of saying that he had had enough. He was glad to be out of it, he assured himself, swinging his briefcase. A ninth-rate tank-town production. It probably wouldn't run for more than one night. Poor Hattie. She'd go on grubbing away at it, nursing her dream of stardom. It was all so pathetic, really. Not worth a moment's regret. Panic crept under his guards. He quickened his pace. He wanted to get home and wash away the grime of that awful rehearsal hall and forget it.

Once home, a drink seemed more urgent than a shower. He had several and began to feel safer. At least he could examine his circumstances with a certain degree of detachment. His life seemed to be falling apart. He had quit what had been about to turn into a very interesting job, he had no money, their debts were still piling up. The season was just about over; there was little hope for anything in the theater till summer. How were they supposed to get through the next two months? He'd missed only a few days at the office. Perhaps he could go and explain that he'd made a mistake and was ready to return; they'd been sorry to see him go. Except that Hattie would never speak to him again, or become so insufferable at his immediate capitulation that they wouldn't be able to go on living together. C.B. had been right again; the theater was pretty nasty. First Meyer Rapper. Now this. How could anybody with a shred of self-respect work with a cheap little bastard like Mars? Yet he was generally regarded as a bright new talent. Cheap and shoddy. He stood up abruptly and poured himself another drink and took a long swallow of it. Better. Look at it in perspective. That was important. It was all Hattie's doing. There was no doubt of that. Hattie, who had come between him and Peter, Hattie, who had talked him into quitting his job, Hattie, who had finally alienated C.B., Hattie's debts, Hattie's litter that made it impossible for him to be comfortable in his own place, the smell of Hattie those ghastly days every month when he felt he would choke on it. He drained off his glass and poured another drink. What was he going to do about it? Do about what? Forget it. He was safely beyond panic now. He could contemplate being penniless for two months, being unemployed, even being unable to get a job in summer stock with complete indifference. What did any of it matter? Nothing in life was worth making a fuss about. Wisdom at last. He would talk it all over with C.B. and let her straighten it out. He ate odds and ends from the refrigerator and continued to drink. He settled in the living room with a bottle at his side. He dozed.

Suddenly Hattie was upon him, a clanking blaze of indignation in the middle of the living room. "Great. Really great. I can see you're going to have a brilliant career."

"Oh, forget it," he growled.

"Jack Dempsey himself. I talked Andy out of taking it to Equity, but a fat lot of good that's going to do. We mustn't speak rudely to the great Mr. Mills. We mustn't criticize the great Mr. Mills. If the great Mr. Mills is displeased he walks out." She was a mocking clown's face, looming over him, grimacing obscenely.

"Can it, will you? I'm not interested."

"Of course not. You can go to bed with Peter, but you can't go to bed with Meyer Rapper when you have a chance at the biggest break you'll ever get."

"No, I can't," he shouted.

"Andy's right. You are a faggot. Not a plain, ordinary faggot, but a dedicated faggot. You can't have a roll in the hay for fun or profit. You've got to have the boy of your dreams. Any real man would've let Rapper have him and gotten on with the job."

"You slut. You filthy slut." He reared up out of the chair.

Hattie stood her ground. "Fine. Now I suppose you're going to knock *me* out. Why don't you take up prizefighting?"

"You'd let yourself get laid by anybody, wouldn't you, if you thought it might help you get a job."

"Considering what most of the men in the theater are like, I don't think it's apt to be a problem. But yes, goddamn it, I would. I'm going to be a success. I'm not afraid to work at it in any way I can."

"You're nothing but a whore. A dirty goddamn whore. Maybe I *will* give you a good sock."

"I'm not afraid of you," she crowed at him. "At least I've got you out of that pitiful little commuter's job. You'll have time now to get out and do something. If it means sleeping with somebody, you'd better think twice before you turn it down. Your fancy boy's not going to be much help to you."

"You're really dirty, aren't you? Dirty and stupid. You'd like to turn me into a whore, too, wouldn't you? We'd make a fine pair. Well,

212

you're not going to, you understand? I'm going to take every penny I can get my hands on, including your parents' wedding present, and pay off the bills. I should've done it weeks ago. I may even sell a few of your more valuable trinkets. Once we've got all that cleared up, we can sit back and starve together."

"You shit. You try any tricks like that, and you'll really be in trouble. It's my money, remember."

"I hear a lot about your money, but it never seems to pay for anything. Anyway, your father gave it to me to take care of, so you can kiss it good-bye."

"I warn you, Charlie Mills. I have my own plans for that money. God, you've got such a dull conventional little mind. Paying bills!"

"Ridiculous, isn't it? Like trying to live on the money you really have. I can't wait for you to see what it's like. Sure, quit your job. Be an actor. Christ, I'll bet you don't make one full week's salary out of this great production. You're not even a well-paid whore."

"Oh, God, deliver me. If you go on screaming about money, you're going to be sorry."

"Am I? What're you going to do about it?"

"Don't you wish you knew. Just don't try anything smart with my money, that's all. I'm warning you."

"All right, you've warned me. Now run along, will you? You make me sick." He slumped back into his chair and poured himself another drink.

She stood in front of him, breathing hard. With studied deliberation she removed a great deal of jewelry and dropped it in a clattering pile on the desk. He could feel the animosity running hard and strong between them. All his drinks had put him at a disadvantage; he hadn't quite succeeded in gaining the upper hand.

She left the room. He interpreted it as a retreat. She couldn't stand up to him for long, but circumstances had given her a new weapon. He thought of the weeks to come, of her going off triumphantly to work every day, of her inevitable endless taunts as he fruitlessly went the rounds of the theatrical offices. By God, he wouldn't take it. He really would use her wedding present. That would drive her wild. He'd fix it so that she was thrown out of the damn play, too. Faggot. She would pay for that.

She returned, bringing the animosity with her, and lolled before him, wearing a loose dressing gown. "Still sulking? Oh, well, don't let me interrupt you. You're too drunk to be worth much as a fuck."

"Am I? We'll see about that." He heaved himself out the chair and staggered slightly and began pulling off his clothes. "God knows, a fuck is all you're good for." He grappled with his shoes and peeled off his socks and brushed past her as he dropped his trousers. He careened into the bathroom and began to fling her cosmetics about as he searched for the lubricant. He hadn't used it with her a second time, but he had to have it now. He'd make her grovel. He wanted to see her writhing beneath him, grunting and panting like a little beast. He felt his sex stiffen and lift with a lust for hurting her. He found the tube and lunged out of the bathroom. She was naked in bed. He stood swaying over her.

"All right. Turn over," he ordered.

She looked up at him with a mocking smile. Her eyes dropped to his sex. "The great Mr. Mills. When all else fails, he always has that to wave around." She lifted herself into a kneeling position and sat back on her heels. "If this is going to be one of our fun nights, why don't we try something new? A blow job, I believe it's called."

"Sure. Go ahead. I thought you'd get around to it sooner or later."

"Yes, we mustn't let Peter have all the fun."

"I just hope you do it half as well."

She glanced up at him, and her eyes went blank and steely. She leaned forward and took the sex in one hand and opened her mouth and clamped her teeth into it.

He roared with rage and pain. "Stop," he shouted.

She ground her teeth into him. He felt as if he were being ripped to shreds. The pain became a ravaging instant of hate. His fists doubled. He tried to pull away but he was gripped in a vise of pain. He seized her hair and yanked. Her teeth tore him. A sob of pain caught in his throat. "Oh Christ—" He lifted his fist and smashed it into the side of her face. Instinct tempered the force of the first blow, but as her teeth continued to tear into him he struck again and yet again, his muscles driving with all his strength. It became a frenzied intoxication of destruction. Destroy her. Destroy their life together. Recapture the happiness she had destroyed. For an instant, Peter flashed into his mind like a beacon lighting the way out of black horror.

He went on hitting her after her teeth had lost their grip. He was on the bed, straddling her, beating her with both fists. His chest heaved. His breath came in wheezing gasps. When the veil of rage lifted from his eyes, he saw blood everywhere. There was blood on

214

her face and breasts, blood on his sex and thighs. His hands were bloody. He remained poised over her for a stunned instant and then scrambled out of the bed. He backed away from it. She lay inert and motionless. The room was filled with a thin muted scream. He realized that the noise was coming from his own throat. He turned and ran into the bathroom and turned on water. He couldn't look at his torn and throbbing sex. He swabbed at himself with a washcloth and wrapped himself in a small towel. He stumbled back into the living room, without looking toward the bed, and gathered up clothes from where he had thrown them. He pulled them on, looking only at his hands as they performed their necessary chores.

The trousers chafed his sex. Every move hurt. He adopted a slight crouch and sidled to the door with a hand in his pocket to hold his sex immobile. He opened the door with care and slipped out and closed it gently behind him, as if he were afraid of waking her. Walking as fast and straight as he could, he went up Lexington Avenue till he found a drugstore and entered the telephone booth. He had to see C.B. She would take charge of everything. But he couldn't see her or call her in the state he was in now. He called Tommy Whitethorne.

"Tommy? Listen, do you know where Peter is?" He spoke in a mumbled undertone as if he might be overheard.

"What's the matter? Speak up. Did you say Peter? What's going on?"

"Please. I can't talk now. Do you know where he is? It's important."

"Sure. I've got his number here. Just a second. I might as well warn you he's shacked up in fairly ornate style."

Charlie waited only to get the number and hung up. His hands were shaking as he dialed again. In a moment, he heard the familiar voice.

"Oh, Jesus, thank God," he almost sobbed into the phone. "Listen, I've got to see you. Can I come right away?"

There was a pause and then Peter's voice seemed to come from very far away. "Charlie?"

"Yes. I've got to see you right away."

"You sound funny. Is something the matter?"

"Yes. Everything. Listen, don't make me talk now. Just give me your address."

"Sure, but — well, it just isn't convenient now. Can't we make it tomorrow?"

"No. That's what I'm trying to tell you. Oh, God, baby, you've got to help me."

"Well, in that case. Can't I come meet you someplace?"

"No, it's got to be there. You'll see why. This is serious. You've got to believe me."

"I see. Just give me a little time to think. No. All right. Of course you can come. Only, I couldn't do this for anybody but you. Understand? You really mean it's serious? It'd be a hell of a lot better for me to meet you out someplace."

"It just isn't possible. Please, baby. Please believe me."

"Sure. I do. OK." He gave him the address and hung up slowly. He had been taking off his jacket when the telephone rang, and he had it with him on his lap. He put it on again as he went back to the bedroom where Tim was just hanging up his. Tim turned and glanced at him questioningly. Peter went to him and stood looking up into his deep-set eyes. "Damn. Oh, damn. This is rotten. I can't stand it. I'm going to have to ask you to leave, big boy."

"Leave? Now?"

Peter nodded. "It was Charlie. He sounded awful. He has to see me right away."

"Can't you go meet him somewhere?"

"That's what I wanted to do. He said it had to be here. I can't imagine what it is. He really scared me."

Tim laid his hand on Peter's cheek and looked at him. "Don't you think maybe I should stay?"

"I thought of that. I certainly don't want any secrets. But from the way he sounded, I think it may be something pretty bad. It wouldn't be fair to him until I've found out what it's all about."

"I see." He turned back to the closet and took the jacket off the hanger and put it on. He put both hands on Peter's shoulders and grinned. "I'll go quietly." The grin faded, and his eyes looked gravely into Peter's. "There's just one thing I want you to tell me. Is there any chance of this leading to bed?"

"With Charlie? Good lord, no. No. I'm yours, big boy. You know that."

The big hands gripped Peter's shoulders hard. "You're mine, all right. I don't know what I'd do if I lost you. I love you, squirt."

"I love you. So damn much."

Tim leaned over and kissed his mouth. He straightened and looked down at him with smiling eyes. "You never say you're in love me with, do you? I'm on to your tricks, but I don't mind. I'm sure as hell in love with you. If you only knew how much I wanted to lock you in and not let you see him. I've never felt anything like it."

Peter moved in close to Tim and dropped his forehead against his shoulder. "I have to see him. He asked me to help him. You do understand, don't you?"

"Sure. I trust you, Skeezix. I know anything you feel you have to do is right. You're so damned straight." He put his arms around Peter and held him close.

"It's lousy. This is the first time I've ever done anything that's kept us apart for a night. Or even five minutes, as far as that goes. It really bothers me."

"And I do it all the time, don't I? I'm going to have to do it again tomorrow. That damned Chrysler thing. How about a quickie if I can get away from the office early? We've never done that."

Peter lifted his head, and they looked at each other and laughed. "That'd be pretty racy. I'll be lying around in something sexy waiting for you."

"OK. We'll talk first thing in the morning. I hope it isn't anything too bad."

"I hope so too. I'll call you in a little while if it's anything I think you'd want to know. Thanks, big boy. Big lover boy."

They held each other and exchanged a long kiss and Tim gave Peter's nose a little tweak and was gone. Peter looked at his watch. Five minutes. Charlie would be here any moment now. He searched his mind for some explanation for the strange call. The only reason he could think of for Charlie turning to him was that it must have something to do with his special world. Had he got into trouble in a bar? It frightened him. If it had anything to do with the police, his coming here would risk involving Walter and even Tim. He warned himself not to be snowed under by Charlie, the way he always had been. Keep cool. Try to think straight. There was too much at stake. The doorbell rang, a jangling intrusion on the silence. Peter started and then hurried to the door and opened it. Charlie lurched in and sagged against the wall. Peter's heart turned over.

"Good God Almighty," he gasped. "What's the matter?"

Charlie passed a hand over his eyes and shook his head. "Thank God you're here. Is there anyone else? If I can just get out of these clothes, I'll be better."

Peter looked at the slack face, the sagging body. Obviously dead drunk. He saw the dark stain at the crotch, and his blood froze. "Come on," he said. He kept a careful distance even though he longed to help him when he saw the difficulty with which he walked. He led the way into the bedroom and turned away as Charlie began to drop his trousers. He went to the closet and took out a dressing gown, moving slowly to fill up time. He dreaded seeing Charlie naked; he held the dressing gown up so that he would be ready to cover him as quickly as possible, and turned back. Charlie was cautiously removing a blood-soaked towel from his sex. Peter stood transfixed. His stomach heaved, there was a prickling all through his arms and legs. "Oh, Christ," he murmured. He sprang forward and threw the dressing gown over Charlie's shoulders. "For God's sake, go into the bathroom and take care of it. There's stuff there if it's still bleeding. I'll call a doctor." Charlie started to move away. "Have you — Did some guy—"

"Hattie."

"Hattie! Oh, Jesus." He turned and sprinted for the telephone. She had ripped his cock to pieces. He would kill her. Of course, it could be fixed. It had to be. Even though it would never be his again, the thought that Charlie's body might be permanently damaged filled him with a desolation like death. He dialed a number.

"Hello, Phil? It's Peter. I'm sorry to call so late, but you've got to get over here ... No, I mean right now ... You know I wouldn't ask you to if it wasn't serious ... Well, somebody's cock is all torn up ... Yeah, thanks, honey." He hung up and returned to the bedroom. He heard water running. In a few moments, Charlie came out, moving more naturally now, wearing the dressing gown. Peter's breath caught at the glory of the beloved body beneath the loosely flowing silk. He couldn't help it; all the last months were obliterated by this form, this flesh, this longed-for presence. He wanted to hold him and care for him. There was something very wrong with his face. Pain? He turned his eyes from him with an effort.

"The doctor's coming. Come on out, and I'll give you a drink." He moved quickly ahead into the living room. Charlie followed and slumped into a chair. Peter brought a drink and held it out to him. He shook his head without looking up.

"Oh, God, I'm in such a mess. I don't know what I would've done if you hadn't been here."

Peter put the drink beside him. "You'd better tell me."

"She did this with her teeth." His shoulders contracted, and he covered his face with his hands. He uttered a groan that became a whimper. His shoulders heaved with a deep difficult breath. He dropped his hands and looked at Peter with staring eyes that were filled with terror. "I beat her." His voice came out in a hoarse whisper. He looked down at the hands resting on his knees and doubled them convulsively into fists. "I beat her as hard as I could. I may've — I don't know. I may've killed her."

Peter's scalp crawled. "What do you mean, you may have killed her? God, you must've been drunk. What are you talking about? Where is she?"

"She's there. I ran. I had to get away. I had to find you."

"Oh, darling." It was said as a protest, yet his heart filled with gratitude at this declaration of a need. They stared into each other's eyes. Charlie's face was distorted by a grimace, and his fingers tore at his hair as he swayed and choked in an agonizing effort to suppress the terror within him. Peter clenched his jaw. His whole body began to tremble. "No. No. Don't. We've got to do something. She may need help. She may be dying while we're sitting here. You must be out of your mind." He sprang at the telephone and dialed their number with violently shaking hands. He let it ring as long as he could stand it and then flung the instrument down. "I've got to get over there. Have you got the keys? I'll take care of everything. You just stay here and wait for the doctor. Don't answer the phone if it rings. Where're the keys?"

Charlie was sitting doubled over, his head on his arms. He lifted a ravaged face and looked at Peter sightlessly. His throat worked. "I'll get them," he said, without moving.

"No, don't bother. Just tell me where they are. Are they in your jacket?"

Charlie nodded. Peter rushed back to the bedroom and found the jacket and fumbled through the pockets. He retrieved the keys. His scalp crawled again as he thought of entering the apartment. He moved jerkily as he went and stood in the entrance to the living room. Charlie sat all gathered in on himself, staring at the floor.

"OK, I'll go now." His voice was shaky. "Don't do anything. The doctor'll be here soon. Don't answer the phone. Have you thought what you'll tell the police if they get into it?"

Charlie looked up. "She did this to me. She had her teeth in me and wouldn't let go. What else could I do? That's self-defense, isn't it? Oh, God, baby. I'm so scared. I knew you'd help. Don't tell her where I am. There was so much blood everywhere."

"Don't worry about anything. It's got to be all right." He hesitated a moment, fighting down fear, and then turned and left. He grabbed a taxi and had himself dropped on the corner within sight of El Morocco's lights. He was already thinking about being an accessory after the fact or whatever it was called. Tim would know. What would he do if he found a corpse? No, it just couldn't happen. Charlie was in a state of shock. He'd been too drunk to know what he was doing. He'd probably just hit her a couple of times, maybe knocked her out, and then panicked. His hands were trembling as he paid the driver. He clung to shadows as he made for the truss shop. As he reached it, there was the sound of car doors slamming next door and a burst of laughter. His heart was beating fast as he entered the dingy building. He remembered about fingerprints. At the end of the hall, he stood at the door, listening. He heard nothing. He made a supreme effort to get a grip on his nerves and muscles and inserted the key noiselessly. Then, covering the knob with the flap of his jacket, he turned it and gently pushed the door open. It made a small sighing sound. He stood just inside the doorway, his heart pounding against the side of his chest, his knees trembling, listening. Silence. Then a dragging sound that made his breath catch, and a thump, and he heard Hattie cursing in a tearful voice. Relief made his head swim. Should he go to her? It would probably only make matters worse. If she could move and curse, she was able to go to the phone and call for help. He prayed for her to do it now so that he could be sure. There were other, unidentifiable sounds. She was there, a few feet from him, moving around. At any moment, she might come out to go to the bathroom or kitchen. No, she mustn't find him here. He took two infinitely careful steps back into the hall and pulled the door to behind him. It made a faint click. He heard her muffled voice call, "Charlie." He scuttled down the hall and let himself out. He stood among the garbage pails and took a long breath. His heart was still pounding, his knees trembled beneath him, but he was filled with a wild elation. She was all right. She wouldn't have called out, she couldn't have heard the door click, if she weren't in full possession of her senses. She could take care of herself. He sprang

220

forward and hailed a taxi that had discharged passengers in front of the nightclub.

He burst into his apartment and was confronted by Phil emerging from the bedroom.

"Hi, honey. Kiss." The doctor gave him a peck. He was a cheerful-looking young man. He jerked his head toward the bedroom. "Nasty. Like everything, it could've been worse. Is it true about its being his wife?"

Peter nodded. "Just a minute." He went to the bedroom door. Charlie was getting up from the bed. They looked at each other, and Peter nodded. "She's all right." Charlie sank back onto the bed. Peter turned again to the doctor. "It isn't serious?"

"Serious enough to call me. You were right about that, snooks. The bleeding's just about stopped. She really got her teeth into him. God. Women are queerer than anybody. It'll be in working order again in a week or two. I wouldn't mind having another look at it when it's healed." He winked at Peter. "I've got to run."

"You don't want a drink? Listen, thanks a hell of a lot. I'm sorry about its being so late, honey."

"For you, anytime. Love to Tim and Walter." He gave Peter a pat on the behind as he went out. Peter returned to the bedroom.

Charlie looked up at him. "You saw her?"

"No, but it's all right. I need a drink now. Come on, I'll tell you." It made him uncomfortable for Charlie to be in the bedroom; he didn't think Tim would like it. He waited for him to rise and preceded him to the other room. Charlie's untouched drink was still on the table where he had left it. He put some more ice in it and fixed himself one. Charlie stood watching him.

"It feels better?" Peter asked.

"Yes. Much. Tell me, for God's sake."

Peter told him. Charlie sank into a chair and put his head in his hands, pressing his temples.

"Thank God. Oh, thank God. I really thought I might've killed her. I don't know what I was thinking while it was going on. I was so drunk, maybe I wasn't thinking anything. I probably really wanted to kill her. I know I thought about you. Jesus." He lay back in the chair and closed his eyes. "What's going to happen now? Everything's been so awful. All of it. Oh, God, baby. Why haven't we been together?" Tears spilled from his eyes and rolled silently down his cheeks.

Peter's hand clenched his glass. He looked into it and swirled its contents around. "Please don't. Things just happen, that's all." There was a long silence.

"Can I stay here tonight?" Charlie asked.

"No." Peter was barely able to get the word out.

Charlie lifted his head and rubbed his hand across his eyes and looked up. "What is this place? Is somebody keeping you?"

Peter turned away and took a swallow of his drink. He opened his mouth to speak but couldn't. He waited a moment for the knot of hurt to dissolve. "I don't much like that question. You have no right to ask it, but no, as a matter of fact. This was lent me by a friend."

"Well, what are we going to do?"

Peter's body stiffened. He closed his eyes briefly and took a deep breath. "'We'?"

"I can't go back there. You know that. I'll never see her again. Oh, God, baby, I'm counting on you so completely. I've got to. I can't go to C.B. like this. You've got to help me."

Peter swallowed hard. Tears sprang into his eyes and he shook them away. "Please. Please," he begged. "There's a lot you don't know about. I'll do everything I can. You know that. But there're certain things I just can't do anything about. How can I help?"

"We've got to find someplace for me to stay. Hattie's capable of anything. She might go to the police. She could charge me with assault and battery or attempted manslaughter or God knows what. She'd do it if she sets her mind to it. The scandal wouldn't stop her. Maybe I ought to get away somewhere until we see how things stand. I can't think straight. Tell me what to do."

Faced with practical decisions, Peter felt more safely under control. "I see what you mean. Maybe you should clear out for a few days. I'll do just about anything for you, but I can't let you stay here. There's somebody else involved. Besides, I'm not too difficult to find in this town. If Hattie wants you, I'd probably be the first person she'd think of. No, we've got to think of something better. The trouble is, with that thing you can't go just anywhere. It has to be taken care of." There was no solution that wouldn't involve him. He resisted the responsibility even as he welcomed it. Charlie had come to him; he wouldn't have wanted it otherwise. This was something he was going to have to fight his way through within himself, alone. It was worse than anything he had feared, but he had to face it for his own sake. He had to face it for Tim's sake. Tears flooded up behind his eyes. He took a long swallow of his drink and put it down. "All right. I have an idea. Let's give it a try." He went to the telephone and dialed a number. A sleepy voice answered. "Hello, Whit honey? Peter. Did I wake you up?"

"Not exactly, if you get what I mean. It's lovely. What's going on?"

"I'm in sort of a mess. Do you still have your car?"

"Sure. You want it, sweetheart?"

"Could I borrow it for a couple of days?"

"Sure. You want it now? It's in that garage on Third. You remember? You damn well should."

Peter laughed. "I remember."

"I'll call and tell them you can have it. You'd better take some identification."

"You're a chum, honey. I'm sorry if I interrupted something."

"You didn't interrupt. It's divine. 'Bye."

Peter hung up. "Well, that's that," he said without looking at Charlie. "I'll pack a bag. You can wear something of mine."

"Where're we going?"

"I don't know. Connecticut, I guess. It's the easiest. I was up at Stamford a few weeks ago. It's a pretty big town. There'll be a hotel."

"I haven't got any money."

"That's the least of our worries. Just a minute. I've got to make another call." He returned thoughtfully to the bedroom and picked up the house phone that connected with Walter. "Hello, old pal," he said when Walter answered. "You're not asleep?"

"No, indeed. It's always a pleasure to talk to you."

"Well, listen. This is sort of crazy. I'm going away for a day or two. Charlie's in some pretty bad trouble."

"I see. Are you with him, laddie?"

"Yes. Tim knows. The thing is, will you call him first thing in the morning? I might not be able to and anyway, he'll ask a lot of questions I can't answer yet. Don't tell him I said that."

"I understand, laddie."

"Tell him I may not be here tomorrow evening. He's busy anyway. Tell him I'll be back for sure the next day. What day's that? Oh, God, Thursday. Tell him I'll see him Thursday."

"I will. Is there anything I can do to help?"

"No. Tell him I love him, will you? I do, you know."

"Of course you do, laddie. Something like this was bound to turn up sooner or later. Try to keep your head screwed on the right way."

"Yes. I'm going to have to. Thanks, Walter."

"Good night, laddie. Call me if you need anything."

Peter hung up and brushed tears from his eyes and squared his shoulders. He went to the door and called, "Come on, champ. We're going to hit the road."

CHARLIE LAY SLUMPED over on his side of the car where Peter had pushed him, asleep. Peter concentrated on driving. There had been the terrible moment when Charlie had settled serenely against his shoulder, and the heartbreaking moment when he had pushed him resolutely from him. Packing, picking up the car, getting through the city's traffic had all been safe, impersonal occupations. Now Charlie was asleep. He hoped he stayed asleep. Sleep. That's what they both needed. There had been enough for one day. Tomorrow everything would be different. Just think about driving. Don't think about anything else. No.

When they reached Stamford, he woke Charlie up and drove around the deserted town until he found a policeman. He asked for the best hotel. It turned out to be an impressive establishment, and when they had aroused the personnel, Peter took two rooms.

"Wouldn't it have been cheaper to take a double?" Charlie asked on the way to the elevator.

"It's all the same. Coming in at this hour, it looks better this way.

The rooms were across a hall from each other. Peter opened the bag in Charlie's room and took out the things he had brought for him.

"OK," he said briskly. "What you need is sleep. We'll figure things out in the morning. How's your — how does your cock feel?"

"It hurts. I'm supposed to change the bandage in the morning."

"Well, get a good sleep. Good night." He snapped the bag shut and picked it up and marched out of the room, without ever quite looking at Charlie.

He lay in bed, slowly relaxing. So far so good. See? Here I am alone, big boy, thinking about you. I know I don't deserve any medals for being alone. There wasn't much choice. But I'd have

224

been alone, anyway. He thought of Charlie sleeping a few yards away, and a tender smile crept over his lips without his knowing it. He slept.

When he woke up, it took him a moment to figure out where he was. Then a singing filled his whole being that brought him leaping out of bed. He was with Charlie. It was a brief euphoric moment that had passed by the time he was on his feet. Had he dreamed it, or had the few little things Charlie had said meant that he expected them to be together again? Not that he had really known what he was saying; he had been half-crazy with drink and exhaustion and terror. Peter wondered if he could seriously consider abandoning Tim. He wondered, too, where he would find the strength to reject Charlie. He was pretty sure that he was going to be faced with some enormous decisions. There wasn't anybody around to help. He called down for breakfast and went into the bathroom. When he had eaten and dressed, he called Charlie.

"You awake? Good morning."

"Same to you, baby. I just woke up. God, it's wonderful. I mean our being here. Why don't you come over?"

"No. You have breakfast and get dressed. I want to get the papers, just in case."

"Yeah, I suppose that's a good idea."

"How do you feel?"

"Much better. It hurts a lot less."

"I'm glad. Listen, hotels give me the creeps. We've got things to talk about. Let's drive out in the country somewhere. It looks like a marvelous day."

"Wonderful. Just give me half an hour."

"Right. Meet me downstairs. Hurry up."

He put the phone down slowly. Another hurdle cleared. He was sure it was too soon for anything to be in the papers, if there was going to be anything, but he went down and picked them up anyway. When he had assured himself that he was right, he devoted himself to a study of the stock market. He was so absorbed in it that he was unprepared for Charlie. Something distracted his attention from the paper, he glanced up and saw him coming, and sprang to his feet to greet him. His knees almost gave way. He had never known what he looked at when he looked at Charlie: the face that was a little like looking into a mirror, the set of the neck and shoulders, the tapered torso, the way he moved, the long big-knuck-

225

led hands, the crotch. He took it in all at once before their eyes met. All the bleariness of the night before had gone from his face, and the agony that had marked his features. He looked fresh and confident and beautiful. They stood looking into each other's eyes for a long moment. For Charlie, it was a moment of homecoming, warm and consoling. After the new and alien channels into which he had tried to steer his life, he sensed that he had found his true course again.

"Oh, God," Peter whispered.

Charlie moved in beside him and took his arm and squeezed it. "Come on."

They went out like that, Charlie holding him close in public. The sweetness of it was almost more than he could bear. He couldn't feel the ground under his feet, only the hand that gripped his arm.

"You want to drive?" he asked as they reached the car. He knew it was a mistake as soon as the contact was broken and he was getting in on the other side. He mustn't let Charlie take control. He mustn't revert to what he had been last summer, a silly helpless lovesick kid. He watched Charlie settle behind the wheel and felt doomed.

They drove out into the country, neither of them knowing where they were or where they were going. It was a brisk sunny day with a strong hint of spring in it. Peter breathed deeply and felt sanity returning.

"This is real country," he said appreciatively. "Look. Stop. Turn in here." It was a country lane that wound off from the main road through trees. Charlie turned into it, and they drove on slowly and came to a wooden bridge over a stream. Peter stopped them again.

"Let's park here. I want to get out. I want to sit on that bridge. It reminds me of Virginia."

Charlie did as he was told. They went and sat in the sun on the bridge, dangling their legs over the meandering stream. Peter resolutely pushed his happiness from him. "Now listen, I've been thinking," he began, getting down to business. "It seems to me that what we've got to do right away is figure out how to get in touch with Hattie. I suppose you don't have a lawyer? Well, I do, but I can't ask him to handle this. I guess *I'll* have to do it somehow. Hey, wait a minute. Isn't she in a play? Aren't you both supposed to be rehearsing a play?"

"I was until yesterday. I had a fight with the director, and he kicked me out. That's part of the whole story."

"Do you think you hit her hard enough so she won't be able to work today?"

"Oh, God, baby. I'm afraid I did. It's all such a nightmare. Last night and everything that's happened since last fall — since — since the night I made you leave. I don't know how I did it. I don't know what I was thinking of. I've been such a damn fool. I say fool, but I mean much worse. Wicked. Cowardly. Selfish. Everything in the book. I'm not just saying it. I know it. Never again, God help me, never again."

"What are you going to do? I mean, you've got to finish things with Hattie, of course. But then what? Are you going on in the theater?"

"Hell, no. That's no life for us."

Peter gripped the planks beneath him. His nails dug into them. "'Us'?"

"We've got to be together, baby. I'm nothing without you. You said it, but I wouldn't listen. I need you, baby."

"But you don't understand," Peter burst out. "I've got another guy. I love him, dammit."

"You mean—"

"I don't know what I mean." The tears he had been struggling against since the night before welled up once more. Once more, he struggled against them, and this time he lost. They gushed from him. He clung to the planks of the bridge and arched his neck back and opened his mouth and gave vent to the torment within him. He felt Charlie's arm around him. He felt his mouth on his hair. He was seized with a fit of trembling that shook him from head to foot. He bowed his head and choked and gasped. Slowly his body went slack as Charlie held him with both arms, pressing him close, spreading kisses through his hair.

"I'm a silly little faggot," Peter gasped when he could speak. A little spurt of laughter burst from him. "What'll people think?"

"I don't care if the whole world sees. I love you."

"Oh, God, why couldn't this have happened two months ago? When we went to Harlem would — could something have happened then?"

"I don't know, baby. I was going crazy being with you again and then we got there and that colored guy kissed you and I saw how much at home you were with all those people. I guess I'd never really been jealous before in my life."

Peter wiped his face with his hands and pulled himself straight. One of Charlie's arms released him, but the other remained around his shoulders. He looked down into the moving water below. "I met Tim the next day."

"Is that his name? He can't have you, baby. I don't care how rich and beautiful he is." Charlie's arm tightened around his shoulder.

"He isn't rich."

"I don't know anything about any of it. All I know is, we belong to each other. You said so, and for always. I wouldn't listen, but I must've known it all along, baby."

"You call me that all the time."

"You used to like it."

"You don't know what you're doing to me. You're tearing me apart. You always have." He shook off Charlie's arm and scrambled to his feet and stood, looking out along the stream. "I have a guy. I love him. I really do. I have a life. It's good. No, it's more than that. It's exciting. It's going somewhere. I can't throw all that away. It would hurt too many people. And for what? So you can go on fighting me because you're not queer? You're having a bad time so you think you need me. What happens when it's over? You won't need me then. You won't let yourself need anybody. You never have and you never will."

Charlie circled his ankle with his hand and rested his head against the side of his knee. "Please, baby. I don't mind your saying all the bad things I am. But don't say things you know aren't true. All right about the queer part. I've lied to myself and you. I'm as queer as a coot. I found that out with Hattie. I'm a silly faggot, just like you. Now that we've got that straight, what's the next step? You know I need you. It isn't just now. It was when I first saw you and year after next and always. You said it, and it's true. Does Tim need you that way?"

"Yes."

"Do you need him?"

"No," Peter shouted to the fields and the stream. "No, goddamn me, I don't."

"And you don't need me."

"I've got by. For a while there, I never thought I'd make it, but I've survived."

228

"Christ, if Hattie hadn't done this to me, if we could be together and hold each other, there wouldn't be any more questions."

"What Hattie's done at least makes us think for a change. Otherwise, I'd be in bed with you by now and then nobody would be making any sense."

"All right. Will you answer one more question? I don't want it to sound as if I were so damn sure of myself because God knows I'm not. Still, I can't help seeing the way you look at me. Do' you love him the way you love me?"

"God, you really want it all, don't you? All right. You must remember some of the things I said that memorable night last fall. I wasn't just making it up. I fell in love with you. I fell in love with you with all of me, with my eyes and with what little sense I have, and my cock, and my goddamn ass, every silly ounce of me, inside and out. Do you think that happens twice? I was in love with you then and I'm in love with you now and it hurts. Christ, it hurts. I've done the most terrible thing I could ever do. I tried to be happy without you. I took advantage of somebody else to do it. I should've known better. I should've known if I couldn't be with you, I couldn't be with anybody. And I've been happy, dammit. I haven't been reeling around in any goddamn state of bliss, but I've been happy, thanks to him. Do you think I can leave him after that?"

Charlie's hand fell away from his ankle, and he hunched his shoulders and bowed his head. They didn't speak for a long time, while the sun shone on them.

Finally, Charlie grunted and lifted his head. "No. I don't know what to say. Talk about havoc. I've really done a good job of it, haven't I? If this stream were deeper, I wouldn't mind jumping in and floating away. I'll clear out if you tell me to. Everything you say about what I've done is true, but I'm almost sure you're wrong about one thing. I think we both could fall in love again." Charlie paused and looked up. Peter met his eye and looked away and then squatted down on his haunches beside him. Charlie went on, "The thing we have is in us. It's not something we spend like money until it's all gone. It grows. If we don't have each other, we're both bound to find somebody we'll want to give it to. You've got to see that. You see everything so clearly. The one thing we both must've learned is that it's wrong to try to settle for substitutes. You've told me Tim is a substitute. Sooner or later, you're bound to find somebody you'll want to give it all to, the real thing. Is that fair to him? Wouldn't it be better — leave me out of it — to break now when it's still at the beginning than to go on letting him think it's something solid? That's the thing. There's every reason for you not to want to have anything more to do with me. It wouldn't be like that with somebody new."

Peter had shifted so that their arms were touching. He exerted a slight pressure now. "You're right about Tim. I've already thought about it. That's what's so bad. I don't see how I could ever forgive myself if I left him."

"Well, if I clear out, we'll have three miserable people, if that makes you feel any better. And it'll all be my fault. I know that. But Jesus, baby, I'm ready now to give my whole life to you. Everything. At least with Hattie I found out what it means to really live with somebody. That's the way I want it to be with us — like you said, as if we were married. I'd give my soul for the chance to make you happy for a change. You. Goddamn it."

"Could I call you darling whenever I wanted?" Peter asked with a giggle.

"Oh, God." He opened his mouth and took a deep breath and shook his head. "You're so wonderful. Even now, when I feel as if I'd die if I don't make love to you, and can't, when you're making me see what a shit I've been, it doesn't matter. I'm with you. I've always fought everything. There's no fight left in me now. You decide, baby." He lifted his knees and put his arms around them and rested his head on them. "Please take me." He had penetrated at last to the core of himself. Awareness had been slowly filling him. Last night, even when he had been paralyzed by fear, he had taken Peter for granted. Since then, layers of the fabrication on which he had built his personality had been stripped away until he had reached this ultimate exposure. Pride, assurance, self-sufficiency — all were gone. He was this little thing crying for acceptance. He was ready to build afresh from there. He felt Peter shifting around beside him so that he was sitting once more with his legs dangling over the side, but close against him, offering him the comfort of his body.

"I've been praying you could make it right," Peter said slowly. He knew that there was a great deal that wasn't right yet but he knew, too, that he was powerless to resist Charlie's appeal. This was the moment he had longed for and dreaded. It was done. There could be no going back. It was a time for fireworks and rocketing emotions, yet he felt primarily a quiet sense of something known and expected and needed. Tim had fallen away into the past. There

230

was nothing anybody could do about it. The rugged farmboy face filled his mind's vision as he said good-bye. He went on, "I couldn't see how there could be any hope for us. I hoped just the same. I think I see now. It's not going to be easy. The only thing that'll keep me from feeling guilty for the rest of my life is if we make it really right."

"Oh, my darling baby." Their arms were around each other. They hugged each other to their sides.

"Come on, darling," Peter said. "We really will frighten the horses. We've got an awful lot to decide still. We'd better get back where there're telephones."

They rose and straightened their clothes and went to the car. As if by mutual agreement, Peter took the wheel. He drove until he found a place to turn. On their way back, when they reached the bridge again, he slowed.

"I'll always remember this bridge. Golly, do you suppose it's symbolic or something? Well, let's cross it." He took Charlie's hand and speeded up, and they headed back toward town. "I suppose we should've burned it behind us. Listen. We've got to find Hattie. I'll call our place and if there's no answer, we'll call the producer of that play. At least, we'll know if she's working."

"If you can spare the money, I'd like to call C.B., too. If Hattie goes to her, God knows what she'll say. I've got to prepare her."

Peter braked and pulled over to the side of the road. He should have known it; he was behaving like the lovesick kid he had warned himself against. He should have known that happy endings don't happen all that easily. Would Charlie ever understand what together meant in the way he thought of it? "That's another thing," he said, risking his whole hand on one play. "C.B. Are you ready to tell her we're together, that we're a pair?"

"But, baby, I can't do—"

"Then I don't want you to see her again. I've done things in the last few months that lots of people would think are pretty disgusting, but I haven't wanted to murder anybody. And that's because I've found out things. I've found out that I can't fake with anything that's so important to me. I won't insist on holding hands with you in restaurants, but that's about it. I love my mother, but if she wants to have anything to do with me, she's going to have to accept you as the man I live with. That goes for everybody."

"But C.B. is different. She's—"

"Oh, no, she isn't. She'll know we're living together. That's not going to be a secret from anybody. If you can't tell her, she's out. Or else the whole thing is off."

Charlie knew that he couldn't possibly tell C.B., but he also knew that Peter was right. He felt as if he were cutting into some vital part of himself as he spoke. "All right. I'll tell her," he said.

Peter started up the car again, and they returned to the hotel. They went to Charlie's room and put in some calls. The apartment didn't answer. At the producer's office, they learned that Hattie was no longer associated with the production of *Bumblebee*.

"We can't have this hanging over us," Peter said. "After lunch, I'll have to go back to the city and see what I can find out."

"I'll go with you."

"No, darling. That long drive wouldn't be good for you. I want your cock to heal."

"Oh, God, so do I. I can't stand it much longer. I want your cock. It's not just sex. I've got to know we belong to each other again. I could have you — you know — in my mouth."

"But you can't. It'll make you—"

"Oh, baby. I start to get a hard-on every time I look at you, but it hurts so much it goes away. It's been like that ever since last night when I was still bleeding and I thought I was about to be hauled off by the police."

Peter knelt between Charlie's knees and kissed him. "Please don't want it until we can have it all together. It's never been the same with anybody else. I don't want just part of it. It would drive me crazy for us not to be really together."

"I know. You're right. I just wanted to blot everything else out. Everything I've done, everything you've done. We're back where we belong now. I know it, but it's such hell not to be able to do anything about it." There was so much he wanted to give some firm expression to. Yesterday he had had a wife, a budding career, a life. Today it was all gone. After he had talked to her about Peter, C.B. would probably be gone too, although he was already trying to hit on a way to deal with her so that a break could be avoided. Peter was all he could be sure of and yet his life felt fuller and richer than it ever had before. It should be frightening; this beloved creature kneeling before him was all that tied him to life, but he wasn't really frightened. Peter had accepted him. He didn't have to pretend anymore. He could look into Peter's wide, accepting eyes

232

and wonder what Peter saw reflected in his and shape himself as he found the answers. That was what life was going to be: a shaping of himself in the mirror of Peter's eyes. He was astonished at his acknowledgment of his homosexuality and still not totally convinced of it; to the extent that it was true, it applied only to Peter. Whatever problems they faced, infidelity would not be one of them. There was only one body in the world he wanted; the fact that it was male seemed unimportant. It was Peter, which made it right.

Already he felt himself growing into himself, into a self he had only occasionally glimpsed through Peter, into a self that could exist only in Peter. Pleasure was an inadequate word for the way he wanted Peter in his mouth and the flow of his body's essence into him; it was a rite, a manifestation of his dependence, a demonstration of his need to honor and cherish him.

Peter ran his fingers over Charlie's face and held it briefly between his hands and stood up. "Lunch. Let's have it up here, shall we?"

"Sure. Aren't you being awfully free with your money?"

"Well, that's another thing. I've got quite a lot of it. Fifty-six thousand, five hundred, and some-odd dollars. I've made a bit in the last couple of weeks."

Charlie threw his head back and laughed. "Made a bit? What in God's name are you talking about?"

"Well, I only started with fifty. It's going to be a bit difficult to explain. We'd better order."

They did so, and Peter told him about Walter while they waited. "That's going to be another big blowup, of course," he ended. "I feel like hell about that, too. He's such a sweet guy. I'd better get through it all this afternoon. I won't have time to pack up the apartment. I seem to've accumulated an awful lot of junk in the past couple of months. Well, junk maybe isn't the right word. As you see, my life hasn't been exactly simple. Maybe if the coast is clear, we can go in tomorrow and do it together."

Lunch was rolled in on a table, and they sat and ate and built the future.

"I've been thinking," Peter said. "I told you I want to go back to school in the fall. Not necessarily for a degree. I know the courses I want to take. What about your painting? If the theater's out, wouldn't you like to really get to work on that?"

"It's the thing I'd like most," Charlie said, realizing suddenly that with Peter, work could become a vocation. "But there's no point in being a Sunday painter. I've got to find a job."

"Now listen, you've thought like that for too long. C.B. again. Isn't painting a job?"

"Well, sure, a hell of a tough one. But what am I supposed to live on?"

"We've got the money, for God's sake. The income isn't much, but we can get by. Until we both get started, it won't do any harm to take a little capital when we need it."

"Are you sure it's all right for you to keep me?"

"No, I couldn't keep you. Any more than you'd keep me. We're each other. Anything we have is ours. That's the way it's going to be. If you don't feel that way, the hell with it."

"Golly, to borrow an expression. You're quite a guy, aren't you?" His mind was saying Peter, Peter, Peter, wonder and delight growing with every repetition.

"Whatever I am, I'm it with you," Peter said. "I'm just beginning to feel it. Holy cow, this is exciting. I'm in love. Big news. I'm with the guy I love. At last. I'm going to live again with the guy I've always loved." He jumped up and circled the table and put his arms around Charlie from behind and nuzzled his ear. "Oh, God, darling. This was worth waiting for. We'll make it now, won't we?"

"You're damn right, darling. Darling baby. Don't make me cry into these chops."

"No more crying. We've done more than our share of that. We really are silly faggots — bursting into tears every few seconds." He went back and sat down. "Where were we? Oh, yes. Should you go to school or something, or do you just paint?"

"There're people in the city I'd like to study under, but first I'd like to get back to it on my own."

"Well, how about this? What if we find someplace out around here, really in the country, and rent it for the summer? Just us, and you could start painting again and we'd fuck a lot and all that sort of thing. Then we could get down to business in the fall. How would that be?"

"That would be just about heaven, baby."

"All right. That's settled. Now I really ought to get the hell into the city. Swallow whatever you're chewing. I'm going to give you the biggest, wettest kiss you've ever had in your life, and then I'll

234

go." He rose and went to Charlie and squatted beside him. They kissed at length. He dropped his head back, and they looked at each other.

"I don't want you to go without me," Charlie said. "Actually, it doesn't make sense. I can't just call C.B. I'm going to have to see her. If possible, I want her on my side if Hattie decides to blow the works. I've got to go with you."

Peter rose, looking thoughtful. "I don't quite see *how* we should work it. Hattie. I'll start at the apartment, if it's not surrounded by the police. I might even have to call her parents. The thing is, C.B. may already know things I ought to know. Yes, you'd better call her now and see what happens."

"OK." Charlie rose from the table and placed the call and waited tensely. The plans Peter was elaborating with such confidence would make it even more difficult to deal with her. The two of them living conspicuously in the country. His painting. Living on Peter's money. He braced himself to face some hint from C.B. of a scandal brewing with Hattie. First things first.

He got one of the maids, who told him placidly that C.B. was expected back after lunch. Nothing in her manner suggested crisis. He left word that he would stop by in an hour or two. He hung up and turned to Peter. "It sounds all quiet there."

"Good. Now the problem is how we're going to keep in touch. I may find out things you ought to know immediately, especially if the police are in it. I don't particularly want to call you at C.B.'s. You have my number. I'll try to do everything from there. If I absolutely have to, I'll call you. Otherwise, I'll wait for you to finish with her." He approached Charlie and stood in front of him and looked him gravely in the eye. "Now listen. I don't care what you tell her so long as you don't cheat on how I figure in what you're going to do. I mean this. I'm all yours and I'm totally in love with you and always will be, but she can still kill it if you let her. She's going to try."

"She can't succeed. I worship you. I mean that literally. Down on my knees."

Peter touched his arm. His eyes lingered in Charlie's another moment, and then he turned away. "Well, we'd better get going. We'll have to come back here tonight. I won't be able to use the apartment after this afternoon."

They drove into the city, talking in bursts, interspersed with thoughtful silences. Peter drew up in front of C.B.'s building. "If you don't hear from me," he said, "don't worry. It'll mean everything is all right. Just come to me as soon as you can. If I'm not there, I guess you'll have to wait."

Their hands reached out and gripped each other hard for a moment. Then Charlie let himself out, and Peter slipped quickly into gear and drove away.

He parked the car opposite El Morocco. He took a deep breath and crossed the street and rang the bell marked "Mills." He was tense and keyed up, but he had rehearsed what he would say to Hattie, so he was almost disappointed when there was no response. He wanted to get it over with. After he had rung several times and waited, he put the key in the lock and entered. At the end of the hall, he listened at the door before cautiously opening it. He went in on tiptoe and peered into the living room. Nothing. He edged forward until he could see into the alcove. He exhaled and relaxed and looked around him. The place looked very tidy. He had been prepared for pools of blood, but the bed was made and there was no trace of violence. He looked around the living room. There was a sheet of paper on the desk and even from where he stood he could see that it was addressed in large letters to "YOU SHIT." He went over and picked it up.

YOU SHIT,

If you dare come back here, you'll see I've had all my things taken away. You better make sure I never see you again. I was going to turn you over to the police, but my family swore they'd never have anything more to do with me. As if I care, except I happen to need them. You'll be delighted to hear that I have to spend the next few weeks in the hospital having my face fixed up. Don't you feel manly? You shitty faggot. I'd be happy to go around for the rest of my life looking like Frankenstein if I could see you locked up where you belong, but I've got to think of my career. Thanks for fixing it so I had to quit the play. I hope I've fixed you for life. Maybe you bled to death. It's too much to hope for. Just watch out.

There was no signature. Peter folded the sheet and put it in his pocket. All their planning and worry was for nothing. It was wonderful, they had only themselves to consider now, but it rather took the wind out of his sails. He had seen himself rushing about, perhaps dodging the police, conferring with lawyers. It had turned out to be what he had hoped it was last night — an ugly ending to a situation that could have been tragic. He was left with nothing of any real importance to do except to wait for Charlie to extricate himself from C.B. He had tried not to let his thoughts dwell on the interview, but he was far from tranquil about its outcome. He knew C.B. as an adversary, and he knew that this was an occasion for her to draw on all her reserves of coercion. Charlie had seemed awfully sure of himself this morning, but he knew the hold she had on him and understood it. He wished he hadn't had to challenge it.

He approached the telephone and looked at it for a long hesitant moment. He was playing for his life now. He picked it up and dialed C.B.'s number.

When it was answered by a familiar Negro voice, he hardened his accent and asked for Mr. Mills. In a moment, Charlie was on the line.

"I'm sorry to interrupt, darling," he said. "It's all right. I was thinking of how worried you must be and I couldn't see why you shouldn't know — it's all right."

"Oh, fine," Charlie said in the careful neutral tone he had always used with him on the telephone. "Could you explain a little more what you mean?"

"She's back with her family, and she isn't going to make any trouble. I'm here at our place. It's all OK. I'll go on home now and wait for you there. I love you."

"Same here. Thanks for calling. You'll be hearing from me."

Peter hung up. It was as straight now as he wanted it. The crisis was over; Charlie didn't need him anymore. Whatever he said to C.B. would be what he wanted to say.

He took another look around the little apartment, remembering the day they had arrived. He felt curiously removed from everything that had happened here. He had been another person. It would all be different now, if it was going to be anything at all. He tossed the keys in the air and caught them and slammed the door behind him when he went out.

His own place still felt like Tim. This evening he had been coming for a "quickie." Sweet big boy. Hell and damn. Yesterday, he had held Tim and been held and loved it. Today, he wouldn't let him touch him. It didn't make much sense. He had never knowingly hurt anybody before. It must take a lot of guts. He hoped he had enough. He went to the house phone and pressed the button. Walter answered.

"Hi. Listen, I might as well get this over with. I'm running out on you. I guess I was an expensive mistake."

"Ah? Where're you going, laddie?"

"I don't know. Nowhere. I took Charlie out to Stamford last night. It was the only place I could think of because of those pictures we went to look at the other day."

"Well, that's not very far. Why do you say you're running out?"

"Well, because I am. I know I ought to give the loot back, but I just can't. We need time so badly. Later, I'll pay it back. I swear to God I will."

"The money? That's yours. There's no question of giving it back. You say 'we.' I assume Charlie's come back to you."

"Yes, he has. Oh, God, yes, has he ever. That's just it."

"Are you going to settle in Stamford?"

"No, of course not. I mean, I thought we might find someplace in the country to rent for the summer. He wants to get back to his painting."

"How splendid. It's not unusual for people to go away for the summer. But won't you have to have a place in the fall?"

"Well, sure. But—"

"I still don't quite understand what you mean by running out."

"But I've told you. I have to break with Tim."

"Of course you do. Poor Tim. I'm very sorry for him. It's going to be a terrible blow. But surely you and Charlie will be quite comfortable upstairs there where you are."

"You mean you don't think I'm a louse for doing this?"

"Good heavens, laddie. I'd have been very disappointed in you if you hadn't. We've all known about Charlie. I even took the liberty of warning Tim at the beginning, but he's in love with you and quite rightly disregarded me. You're in love with Charlie. Nobody could guess that he'd be free again. If he is, of course you must be with him. You've done nothing underhanded."

"Oh, my God." Peter sank onto the bed. "You mean, you want me to stay? You want me to bring Charlie here?"

"Of course, laddie. I sometimes think you don't understand me very well. I've told you it gives me great pleasure to watch you live. What could give me greater pleasure than to see you with

238

the person you really love? It's haunted you all these months. I could see that. You've been very brave. I'm looking forward to meeting Charlie. I know I'll be very fond of anybody you care for so much."

"I understand you all right, but I can't always believe it. You're fantastic. Listen, what am I going to do about Tim? I can't stand doing this to him. It's happened to me. I know what it's like. It's the worst thing I've ever done to anybody in my life."

"You mustn't think of it like that, laddie. These things happen. It's nobody's fault. As you say, you've been through it. He's a man. It's part of life. He'll have to accept it."

"But what'll I do? I can't call him at the office. What did he say when you told him I was leaving town?"

"He didn't take it very well. He said you had no right to. I had a sharp word with him. I think you'd better let me handle this, laddie. Perhaps I'll ask him to come see me after his dinner tonight. I'll have to think about it."

"I'll see him, of course, if he wants me to, but I don't see what good it'll do. He said if I was ever unfaithful to him, that would be the end of it. Well, I have been. Do you think it would help him to know that? I mean, if he hates me, maybe that would be better than what I've been through."

"It's very sweet of you to care so much about his feelings. Happiness often makes us rather cruel. I don't know. I'll have to see how it goes. What are your plans?"

"Well, I thought you'd want me to pack up and leave. I've borrowed a car I have to give back tomorrow. I'll bring Charlie back here. Golly, how wonderful. I want so much for you to meet him. We can think about finding something for the summer over the weekend or sometime."

"That sounds sensible, laddie. I'll have to speak to Tim immediately. We don't want to risk having him turn up there. Would you like to have dinner with me tomorrow, or do you want to have a first evening together?"

"No, we'd love to. God, I'm so happy, Walter. I wish everybody in the world could feel like this."

"You're very sweet, laddie. I'm terribly happy for you. I wish you could hear your voice. It's ecstatic."

Peter laughed. "I don't see how it could help being. Thanks for everything, old pal. It doesn't do him much good, but I love Tim

239

such a hell of a lot. Please try to make it easy for him. It's hell, isn't it?"

"It may be, laddie, but you've got to think of Charlie now. These things so rarely work out right. You've got to prove that they can."

"Boy, we will. Don't worry about that. Just give us the next fifty years."

He had scarcely hung up when he heard a key in the lock and the front door opening. He sprang up from the bed and took a few steps toward the door. Tim filled it. In the instant, he knew that this was inevitable, that he couldn't have left it for Walter to handle. He saw joy and relief flood Tim's face; the blue of his eyes filled his own with love. "Skeezix! Oh, Christ. Thank God, you're here. Walter said not to expect you till tomorrow."

"Then how come you're here?" Peter asked.

"I couldn't work. I told them I was sick. I had to come here to feel near you. That's what you do to me. I've been so damned worried." He started forward. Peter stopped him with a look.

"Please, Tim. I'm not staying."

"Oh, no you don't." Tim's happy grin widened and he moved forward again with confidence. "I've got you now. Where've you been?"

Peter stood his ground, but shook his head slowly. "Please. You don't understand. I'm trying to tell you. He's coming here in a little while and then we're going. Together."

The grin faded. "Then I'm staying. I've had enough of this. What's it all about?" He stood close to Peter, his face earnest, but love still shining in his eyes.

Peter looked into them without flinching, steeling himself for what his next words would do to them. "It's about everything. Our lives, everything. It's no good. There's nothing I can do about it. I'm going back to him. For good." He saw all the features contract, he saw the fist lifting, he felt its impact on his chin. His head snapped back, and he staggered and fell. For a moment, he was close to unconsciousness. Then his reeling head steadied, and he put his hand over his eyes and shook his head slightly. He worked his jaw.

"You little shit," Tim said.

Peter dropped his hand and looked up. Tim was sitting in a chair, rubbing his hand. His eyes were on him, hard and dangerous. The sheer bulk of him imposed itself on Peter's consciousness. Despite the blow, he felt safe and protected and oddly at peace. He knew he would never feel any of these things with Charlie; ecstasy, tension, challenge, conflict, and total commitment were what he had chosen. He gathered himself together and pulled himself to his feet. "I deserved that," he said. "If it would do any good for you to beat me up, I'd let you. I really would. There's no point asking you to forgive me because I can't forgive myself. I know how bad this is. I can't help it."

"I'm yours. That's what you said, isn't it? You seem to've forgotten."

"How could I forget? It was true. How could anybody know this was going to happen?"

"Nothing's happened, as far as I'm concerned."

"Oh, for God's sake. I'm telling you. He's left Hattie. He wants me back. I'm going to him."

"You're not going anywhere," Tim said quietly. His body was all held taut, ready to spring.

Peter looked into the hard, unyielding eyes. "Now listen, you're a hell of a lot bigger than I am, but when I get worked up I can fight. I don't care what you do to me, I'm going to him."

"That's what you think. You must be nuts. He dumps you. He dumps his wife. How long do you think it'll be before he dumps you a second time?"

"That's my problem, isn't it? You know what you said about our being faithful to each other. Well, it's finished with us, that part of it."

"You've been to bed with him?"

"Yes."

Tim stood abruptly and started for the door. He stopped before he reached it and turned back slowly. Peter's heart contracted when he saw his face. His eyes had deepened into pools of hurt and bewilderment.

"No. I guess it's not as simple as that," he said haltingly. "Oh, darling. My Peter. What's happened to you? I trusted you so completely."

Peter swallowed hard. This is where the guts come in, he told himself. He mustered all his strength to meet the stricken eyes. "I guess you shouldn't have. All I can say is, there haven't been any secrets."

"Oh, Christ, have your goddamn secrets if you've got to. Sleep with him, if that's what it's all about. You can't leave me. We've gone too far."

"I know. That's what I can't forgive myself."

"Then don't do it. Look, Skeezix. I know it hasn't always been perfect. I don't know. I thought you were happy. It'll be just us from now on. The hell with everything else. Come here."

"No." Cut it. Cut it clean, he urged himself. That's all he could do for him. "Don't you understand? I couldn't let you touch me ever again. You're right. I've been a shit. Let's leave it at that."

Tim looked at him with eyes that were drowned in hurt. His chest heaved once. "I just don't believe it," he said.

Peter longed to hold him and comfort him as best he could, but he knew it would be false comfort. He wanted to tell him how happy he had been, how very nearly perfect it had seemed, how much he loved him, but he knew that to say anything would be only an attempt at self-justification. His whole being bled with the wounds he had inflicted, the wounds that had once been inflicted upon him.

"You'd better be going, Tim," he said.

"I'm sorry I hit you. Did it hurt?"

"Quite a bit. Not as much as all the rest of it."

"I'm so in love with you. You never said you were in love with me. I've got to remember that. If you had, I'd kill you now. I still can't believe it. God, I've had fun with you."

"Please, Tim. Please don't make me say anything. It's all piling up inside me and it wouldn't be fair to you. I know."

"Well, I guess this is it. Before I go, I wish you'd call me by my right name."

"I've wanted to, big boy."

"Yeah." A ghost of a smile lifted the corners of his lips as his eyes dwelled deeply in Peter's. He closed them suddenly and turned and went. "You can throw out anything I've left behind," he called from the hall, his voice sounding strained and high-pitched. "I don't want any of it."

Peter heard the door close and his mouth opened and he inhaled a deep, strangled breath. He stood where Tim had left him, staring at nothing, waiting for the pain to ease. All he needed now was to learn that C.B. had proved too much for Charlie, and he would be left in the ruins of what had seemed until yesterday a good and satisfying life.

CHARLIE REACHED C.B.'s apartment just after she had returned from lunch. She was still dressed in smart street clothes and wore a dashing hat. She was moving about the big living room, pulling off gloves and adjusting a flower arrangement. He thought only of the news that would please her and he felt good to be with her, even though the impossible subject Peter expected him to broach to her loomed ahead of him like a foreseen disaster.

"Ah, my dearest." She greeted him with the trace of coolness she had allowed to shade her manner toward him since he had decided to go on the stage. "Tessa said you'd called. What an odd time to come visiting. But then I suppose I must adjust to your theatrical hours from now on."

He went to her and leaned over and kissed her, keeping at arm's length. "No. I don't think you'll have to do that. Forget about theatrical hours. I'm going to sound like an awful ass, but I think you'll be pleased. I quit the play yesterday. You were right. I couldn't ever work in the theater. The people *are* pretty awful." He was counting on this opening to restore her to him, and he watched with a deep stirring of relief as it happened. It didn't make any sense to be at odds with her. Her eyes brightened. She lifted her head and clapped her hands and stretched them out to him. He took them happily.

"Oh, my dearest. Oh, dear, I feel almost sad for you. What a terrible disappointment it must be. Bear with it. I know you'll never regret this decision. How superb you're looking. You know, in another ten years you're going to be most distinguished. It would've been wasted on the stage." She tucked her arm under his and led him toward chairs. "You can't know what this does for me. I feel as if we're waking up from a bad dream. You mean it? It's really over?"

"Definitely," Charlie said as he seated himself cautiously. "I'm afraid it's not all pleasant, though. Hattie was furious. She went out of her mind. I know you don't want to hear all the details, but she got so violent that I had to use force on her."

"You mean you struck her?"

Charlie caught a throb of exultation in her voice and studied her with curiosity. "Well, not exactly. She turned into such a madwoman that I'm afraid she got hurt."

"My poor dearest. How unbalanced she must be to provoke you to that degree. One sees it in her. Her passion for the theater. It's all part of it. It's what I tried to tell you. Is she still angry with you?"

Charlie looked at the floor to make sure he knew exactly what he was going to say next and looked back at her. "It's finished. I couldn't stand it and cleared out. I haven't been back. I don't intend to see her again. The point is, I don't know what she's apt to do next. I thought she might've already tried to make trouble with you. She was in such a state that she might claim I beat her or I don't know what. She's capable of anything."

"We'll forestall her." She moved forward to the edge of her seat, a fire of excitement in her eyes. "You must see a lawyer. I know just the man. I'll arrange for you to see him tomorrow morning. You must tell him the whole story. If she dares make charges, we'll be forearmed. I know the Donaldsons. They're drunk with the illusion of power. If they're foolhardy enough to make a move, we'll smash them. Hattie has said enough to disqualify any claims she might make as a wife." Her rich voice shook as she demolished them. She reached out to him, and he gave her his hand as she settled back in her chair. "This does mean divorce, I assume. Poor dearest, experience is falling on you rather heavily very early in life. Perhaps it's just as well. You'll know better for the future. I warned you you could never depend on people. You'll find they're generally made of coarser stuff than you're accustomed to."

His palm was sweating, and he extricated his hand to wipe it on a handkerchief. "Hattie's changing. It's what you said, this thing she has about the theater. Nothing else finally counts for her."

"Ah, well, I knew from the first she would never do for you, though I did my best to befriend her. Better for her to go quickly than allow her to poison your life. You mustn't worry about this, my dearest. See the lawyer. I'll take care of the rest. He'll send the bills to me, of course."

"I don't see how I'll ever make it all up to you, C.B." She was being superb. She was outdoing herself; if the situation were as simple as he was presenting it, he could sit back and let her handle everything, as she always had, but the more she said the more impossible it became for him to hint at Peter.

She continued to weave her spell: "You've always made it up to me for any poor thing I may have done for you, my dearest. After all, what else am I here for? I can't tell you how thrilled I am to have you back, free of the theater, free of Hattie. I feel as if we were starting life all over again. There are so many things I have to tell

244

you about — people I've been seeing, things I've been doing. We've been rather cut off, as always happens when a man marries. I'll start your allowance again, of course. How lucky I haven't signed the new will. I'll tell the lawyers to destroy it. We'll have such an exciting time together. Will you want to go back to your job? It could doubtless be arranged. Harold was terribly upset to see you go."

"No, that's one thing I'm sure of now." He began to feel the beating of his heart, but he was confident that he could work his way around the subject somehow. "At least, not yet. You see, anything I do is bound to be temporary, anyway. I'm going to get caught by the war any day now. Whatever time I have left, I've decided I want to see if I can really do something with painting."

"I see. Well, I won't oppose you. I simply don't see how you can manage from a practical point of view."

"Well, there are various possibilities." His palms were sweating freely now, and he was gripping the handkerchief in his hands. He tried to look at her directly but didn't quite succeed. He heard the distant ringing of the telephone and no longer knew what he was trying to say. He tugged at the handkerchief and felt it give.

The maid stood in the doorway. "Telephone for Mr. Charlie," she said.

A cry of alarm almost escaped him. Peter had said he wouldn't call unless it was bad. Did this mean the end of everything? Don't panic. C.B. would manage. He had got to her in time. She was prepared for battle.

He rose carefully with a muttered "Excuse me" and went out to the telephone. When he came back, there was a new spring in his step. They smiled at each other as he resumed his seat.

"Good news?" she asked.

"Oh, no. Nothing—" Just that he was really free at last.

"Good heavens. Forgive me. I didn't intend to pry. I've been thinking about what you said. Don't you think it would be a good idea to have a talk with Harold and perhaps work out some sort of leave?"

With Peter's eager, devoted voice still ringing in his ears, he felt a great urge to say his name, to sketch the life they were planning together. "Oh, well. Maybe," he said.

"You mentioned various possibilities."

"Various possibilities? Oh, yes. About painting. Well, actually, I saw Peter last night. I—"

"Peter? That's a name I hadn't expected to hear again." She straightened in her seat. "You've been seeing him?"

"Of course not." He was able to meet her eye as he spoke this truth. "It was just that I needed help last night. I don't want to explain it all to you. I couldn't let any of our real friends get mixed up in it. He was the only person I could think of. He was very good about it. I know you're wrong about him, C.B. Whatever that fuss was all about last fall, it was mostly just a misunderstanding."

"So you've suggested." She sat very still and straight, her eyes unblinking, waiting.

"I know what I'm talking about. Anyway, it turns out he's inherited quite a lot of money. He has an apartment on Park Avenue, and he was talking about renting a place in the country."

"Strange. I should think I would have heard about it from his family."

"You probably will. It's fairly recent, I think. Some distant relative he didn't even know. Anyway, the country would be fine for work. I thought I might go out there for the next month or two, however long it is, and really get at it. He'll eventually be taken by the Army, too."

"You seem to have had an opportunity for quite a long talk. Did you discuss finances? Is he to pay all your expenses?"

"Of course not. It wouldn't cost anything, anyway. I haven't had time to really think about it, but if you approve — that is, if you're willing to give me the allowance — there wouldn't be any problem."

She stirred slightly and shifted her eyes from him, and he breathed more easily. She seemed to be giving the matter serious thought. He congratulated himself for having got through it so convincingly.

"I think I have a better suggestion," she said finally, and her voice held the smooth, indulgent resonance with which she usually addressed him. "I think you must admit that you've been unhappy in your relationships with others, my dearest. Why risk another disappointment? Perhaps you should have the opportunity to test your gift. I'm prepared to give you your allowance and add to it the amount of the salary you've been earning for whatever length of time you think reasonable. If the apartment is too small, we could find something more suitable, some sort of studio. You could always have the house in Rumson if you feel the need for country, though I have the impression that many artists prefer the city for work."

246

"But C.B., I couldn't let you do all that," he stammered. He was unprepared for this, and yet it was so like her, offering him everything, suspending her judgment in his favor. He didn't see how he could refuse. And why should he? The country didn't matter; she needn't know he was with Peter. No, that was what Peter insisted she must know.

"Since when have I stinted in helping you when I could see my way clear to do it?" she asked, putting her hand out to him again. He didn't take it.

"Oh, never. Of course not. You've always been fabulous. But this is different. Well, you've said yourself I couldn't accept your help if I was doing something you didn't approve of."

"But I do approve. You've presented a very persuasive case. The war does change things."

"But it's too much. I thought I might just do this on the little money I've saved. Being a guest and everything."

"Precisely. Why put yourself under such an obligation? Surely I'm closer to you than Peter."

"Of course. Peter is just a possibility. We've always gotten along pretty well together. I thought it would be sort of fun to do it with him. You know — being alone — painting can be pretty grim."

There was a long instant of silence. Her body sagged slightly. Her eyes were full on him. "I've been waiting for you to betray yourself," she said with terrible precision. "I'm afraid you have, at last."

All of his body went cold. The skin of his face seemed to stretch taut so that he had trouble making his lips work. "But C.B.—"

"I'm not a fool, nor a complete innocent." Her voice sank to a dark rumble of revulsion. "Do you think I don't know that you've held him in your arms and succumbed to your unspeakable passion? Do you think I don't know that you've debauched your art in the service of your obsession? I let it go on under my roof because I was determined to save you. I will not allow you to debase your body further. I've watched you grow up into beauty. I will not permit you any longer to abandon yourself to bestiality."

He passed a trembling hand over his eyes. It couldn't really be she speaking. She couldn't know. He felt all of himself disintegrating, his body moving toward total collapse. "How can you say these things?" he demanded in a barely articulated murmur.

"I will say a great deal more, yet not one word in total condemnation of you." The dark voice throbbed in his ears. "The taint is in your blood. Can you have any idea of what my life has been? Married, with a small child and a drunken incompetent husband, living with this knowledge in the back country, miles from anyone, in a hideous house, surrounded by darkies and animals." She paused and looked beyond him, and her voice hardened and began to throb with power. "I saved your mother's life once. Your grandfather was riding somewhere about the property. I was in the front of the house, dealing with some household problem. I heard something, a shout from the darkies' quarters I think, I've never been quite sure. I looked out and saw a man running along the road in front of the house. As I watched, he turned in and headed straight for the front door and I saw him — a huge buck nigra, stark naked, his feet pounding the ground. I knew immediately that he had run amok. Your mother was romping on the veranda, heedless, directly in his path. I had only seconds to act. I rushed to the door, and out, and ran to her. She thought it was some game and laughed and tried to escape. I could feel the earth shake under his pounding feet. I seized her and dragged her to the door. She began to cry. He was almost upon us. The stench of him filled my nostrils. The air moved around me with the rush of his approach. I flung her into the house and grabbed the door and turned. He was a magnificent creature, his teeth flashing in an insane grin, his black skin glistening with sweat, his muscles swelling. He was aroused, terrifying with potency, a huge black appendage quite rigid. I slammed the door and shot the bolt just as he flung himself upon it, beating it so that the whole house shook. That is the beast that is in me and that I have always fought. It is in you too, and we must fight it."

She stared straight ahead of her. Even after she had stopped, her voice continued to sweep over Charlie, submerging him in its mesmeric rhythms. He opened his mouth and closed it again. His heart was pounding in response to the fierce passions that beat in her words. It was as shattering and meaningless as a nightmare. Peter had forced this on him; he should never have spoken his name. He would never pronounce it in her presence again.

"I don't understand," he murmured at last.

"You shall." Her voice sank again, as if she could barely bring herself to speak. "My mother was a vile and evil woman. My father was a Negro."

She took a deep breath and closed her eyes. Silence held them motionless as the word bored into his mind. He realized that his mouth was hanging open with slack astonishment and closed it and swallowed with difficulty. It had nothing to do with him. Yet here was C.B. a few feet from him, part of him, the foundation of his life, branded with the word. He thought of an ornate room in Harlem, of a dark face pressed to Peter's, of an army of monkey-faced servants, children, animals. The word linked him to all of that. His instincts recoiled with distaste. His stomach felt queasy as he saw that she was going to speak again. He didn't want to hear any more.

"There's no need to tell you how I learned it," she said in a spent voice. "My mother was very rich. The man I called my father allowed himself to be used by her, but the secret wasn't kept. When I found out, your mother was already born and it was too late. I very nearly opened my veins and let the blood run from them. I would never let any man touch me again. Your grandfather died for failing to respect that resolution."

"You killed him?" Charlie gasped.

"If you wish to know, I'll tell you, as I've always told you everything, though no other living soul knows the truth. We were driving home in the buggy. We'd been to the village for some business transaction. After we'd turned in to the plantation road, your grandfather grew amorous. He'd been drinking as usual. When he persisted, I thrust him from me and whipped the horse. Perhaps I used more strength than I had intended. I suspect drink had more to do with it. As the horse bolted, your grandfather toppled over and fell out. His foot caught somehow in the step of the buggy. The horse was a skittish mare called Miranda. There was no holding her, although there were those who found this difficult to believe. She made a dash for home. Your grandfather was dragged for two miles over a rough road. There was nothing I could do to save him. I was prepared then, and still am, to go to any lengths to defend myself from the beast. It's what you must learn. Your mother should never have married. She knew it, but she was willful and obstinate. By a miracle, neither you nor your brother were visibly marked."

A chill ran through Charlie at the violence in all her words, but the revelation of her parentage began to acquire some proportion for him. A thousand thoughts flew through his mind; curiosity predominated. It was all so remote. It didn't really change anything. He was still so shaken by her performance that he couldn't even quite grasp why she was making these points now. "Did you tell Hattie I shouldn't have children?" he asked.

"She told me she had no intention of having any. I urged her never to change her mind."

"Why? Because of color? What about my brother?"

"He is your mother's child. She must do as she thinks fit."

"I can't understand why you haven't told me any of this sooner."

"You gave me no warning of your marriage. You had had no serious involvement with a girl thus far. I had hoped you had triumphed over your baser nature."

"Then how could you think all those incredible things about me? The things you said about an obsession."

"Incredible? Yes. I brought you Peter with the hope that you would find love in friendship. Great men have done so. I couldn't know that the love I saw in him was the mask of corruption. Only the knowledge of your heritage saved me from turning from you with loathing."

It finally came clear to him that she was preserving in him her illusion of perfection. It was gallant and touching, but it also horrified him. Any wrong he committed would, in her eyes, be sanctioned by blood. His sleeping with Peter or beating up Hattie were manifestations of the beast. She offered him everything, not just financial security but a life free of all strain or challenge. For the first time in his life, he was conscious of the power he had over her; he could make any demands, except one. He saw himself this morning hunched over on the bridge, unguarded and exposed. Please take me. Abject and pathetic? He had felt more truly himself than ever before, strong with the knowledge of his need. He was emboldened to test the limits of her indulgence. "Even if everything you think were true," he said, "wouldn't that be better than risking having a family?"

She lifted a hand and brushed his words away. "Do you wish me to believe that you have a warped and twisted nature? It isn't true. You were the victim of a treacherous and insidious passion, but you had the strength to overcome it. You must cultivate that strength. It's a necessity imposed on you by blood. You've had your Hattie. Knowing what you do, you doubtless won't want to marry again. I offer you the life I've always seen for you and planned for. We can achieve it together."

He saw himself leading a life of fastidious celibacy, at least in appearance. What would happen when he roamed the streets at night? Dr. Jekyll and Mr. Hyde. The beast at large. He spoke hastily as he realized where these thoughts were leading him. "Yes, C.B. I'll have to think about it." He thought of Peter waiting in the apartment he scarcely remembered from last night and stole a hasty glance at his watch. He should go soon, but he was no closer to meeting Peter's demands. C.B.'s revelation had taken precedence; he would seize the next opening.

"I've always believed in independence for a man, as you know, but I'd be willing for you to stay here while you're getting things sorted out if you think it would be agreeable."

The beast caged. Rather limiting for Mr. Hyde. Watch it, he warned himself. He was aware of the extreme uncertainty of his control. Something was about to give. "Well, I—" he began, but it was too late. A picture of them living here together sprang into his mind, he aging and distinguished, an elegant couple denying all passion, immaculately white in defiance of their dark forebear. He threw his head back and uttered a shout of laughter. He doubled over and laughed until tears came and his sides and stomach ached. He didn't quite know what he was laughing at, which made him laugh even harder. There was an edge of hysteria in it, but this passed in a clean sweep of laughter. He laughed as all fear and shame and inhibition were lifted from him. She had offered him her last and greatest gift — release. He laughed as he welcomed it. His sex began to hurt with his convulsions, and he struggled to master them. He felt her eyes blazing at him, and he finally subsided with a burst of giggles.

C.B. sat motionless, staring at him. "Get a grip on yourself." Her voice was icy with command. "I can forgive you anything but this."

"I'm sorry. I don't know what possessed me." He glanced at his watch again and pulled himself up on shaky legs, hoping he wouldn't collapse with laughter again. "I really ought to go. I have things to do."

"Then you wish me to call you at home later about the lawyer? Has Hattie left?"

"No. Well, yes. You see, Peter has—"

"I don't wish to hear that name again."

"Don't be silly, C.B." He spoke lightly and with affection. "I've been trying to tell you. We're going to live together."

She sprang up and was on him. She seized his hands and pressed them to her breasts. Her body swayed against him and she held him to her despite his wince of pain. "I will not permit you to do this."

Her voice was hoarse with fury. "You've sent him away once. It must not start again. It is too vile."

"Please, C.B. I—"

"I will not permit you to defile yourself again. You drag me through your filth."

"I don't think you should talk about things you know nothing about."

"Know nothing about? I know your body as if it were my own. I've saved you once, but at what cost to myself? All through the summer I suffered in my own flesh as you surrendered to unnameable depravity above my head." Again there was the exultant note in her voice. She crowded against him, hurting his sex, and he thought of the times when he had found her caresses troubling. He knew it was impossible, but he felt it now as a sexual assault. He held her firmly away from him.

"Just because two men live together, it doesn't mean it's depravity," he said with finality. "It was your idea in the first place."

"I closed my eyes until he left me no choice. I have made every allowance, and for good reason, but if you give way once more to this disgusting sickness, I could never face you again."

Charlie looked at her levelly. She knew everything, and the heavens hadn't fallen. There was no point in beating around the bush any longer. He thought of Peter's faith in him and found that it wasn't difficult to speak the truth. "I love him, C.B. He explained it to you. How did he say it? 'I love him in every possible way, the way men love women.' I don't know how it happened, but I wouldn't want it any different." Unknown to him, a joyful grin began to spread across his face at finally sharing with her some truth about himself.

It faded quickly as she flung his hands from her and backed away. Her face was contorted into a face he had never known. It hurt him to look at her. "Go. Go. Go," she repeated with whispered abhorrence.

"Please, C.B."

She lifted her hand palm outward and moved it back and forth in front of her, exorcising him. He dropped his eyes in pity. "I'll call you," he said, and turned and left her.

He fled as fast as he could, through long halls, down in the elevator, and out into the street. He couldn't take the time to make a phone call. He hailed a cab and gave Peter's address. He rang

Peter's bell, and in a moment the door opened. He stepped quickly inside and Peter closed the door and took him carefully in his arms so as not to hurt him. They stood close together, their heads resting against each other, simply savoring each other's physical presence.

"At least you're here," Peter said. "That's all that matters."

"Where else would I be, my baby?" He felt all of Peter's healing sweetness flooding out to him and was proud that he was at last in some small way worthy of it.

"I might as well admit I was ready for anything. Is this it? You're here now? Good lord. I was frightened."

"Frightened? Don't ever be frightened again, baby. It's really all right about Hattie? We can relax?"

"Yes. I'll show you." They drew apart and Peter gave him Hattie's letter. They moved into the living room while Charlie read it.

Charlie shoved it into his pocket and shook his head. "Jesus. What a lovely couple we made. I must've been out of my mind."

"What about C.B.?"

Charlie looked at him and shook his head again. "I'll tell you, but it's a whole book. All I can say is, I feel as if we were the two most normal people in the world after that."

"Hell, darling. I'm sorry." Peter went to him, and they stood with their hands on each other's waists. Charlie smiled.

"Don't be. I guess it had to happen. The big news is, I'm a queer nigger."

"You're what?"

"Yeah. It seems C.B.'s father was a black. She was very much worked up about it. It's supposed to make me give up sex." They looked at each other and burst out laughing.

"Oh, darling, how marvelous. That must be why you smell so funny. But what's it all about? Is she afraid I'll have little black babies?"

They shook with laughter until Charlie's hands were so full of the feel of Peter's convulsed body that a shiver ran down his spine and his breath caught and he instantly sobered. "God, I wish you could. You were right about her. As always. She really wants me all to herself."

"But do you suppose it's true?"

"About her father?" He realized immediately that the question should have occurred to him. Not that it mattered. What mattered was the new knowledge that she was capable of fabricating the story

253

if she thought it would suit her purpose. True or false, he was beginning to rather like the idea. If he was going to be an outcast, he might as well be a thorough one. A bit of black blood was the final touch. He looked into Peter's dancing eyes. "I don't care, so long as you don't mind my touching you. Jesus. To think I was in a state about your being kissed by a Negro." Their eyes were filled with memories of cruelty and hurt, and of lost, now recaptured ecstasy. Charlie took a deep breath and ran his tongue over his lips. "You're such a goddamn miracle. When I think I actually did everything I could to fuck this up I feel like — I don't know what. Down on my knees again. Worship isn't enough."

Peter leaned forward and rubbed his forehead against Charlie's. "I'm going to like this," he murmured. "Daily services. Hourly services. Golly, I wish they could begin right now. Come on. We might as well get going." He drew his head back and looked around him. "Good lord, what am I talking about? I'm nuts. We don't have to go anywhere. This is ours. That's something I have to tell *you*. I'll call that hotel and tell them we'll pick up the bag in a week or so. We'll go look at houses when your cock has healed. Go on. Take those lousy pants off and put on a robe. No more clothes until it's all well again. We've got to have a drink. There's so damn much to celebrate. Is it too early? No. Champagne. That's the thing. I'll phone for some. There's so much to talk about."

They stood with their arms around each other while Peter called a nearby liquor shop and ordered bottles of iced champagne. He hung up and put his hands on Charlie's face and ran them through his hair. He growled.

"You're sexier than anybody, even with your cock in a bandage. I wish something was the matter with mine. It feels as if it's going to go right up through the ceiling. Enough of that. Come here." He took his hand and led him to the desk, where he had placed a cardboard folder. "I've planned a kind of ceremony. It's sort of weird, but it means a lot to me." He opened the folder and took out Charlie's self-portrait. "I know you've never liked it, and I can see now that it isn't as good as what you can do. I don't need it anymore. I want you to tear it up."

Charlie took it from him and studied it, holding his hand over it at various angles. "No, it's not good. True, though. The artist greeting Peter Martin." They laughed. "Where's the other one you stole? The one of yourself."

254

"It's hanging in pretty good company — Michelangelo, Leonardo, Donatello, all those kids."

"Did you donate it to a museum?"

"Practically. It's downstairs. You'll see it tomorrow."

"Oh, yes. Walter. OK, you ready?" He held the drawing out and tore it in two.

"Ouch. That hurt. That was pretty final. Well, that's what I wanted it to be. You realize what you've done, don't you? That makes it official. You can't leave me or kick me out again, ever. I haven't got anything to take your place now."

Charlie looked at him, and his eyes widened as he stared. They turned liquid with tears. He shook his head incredulously. "You're not true. I've measured everything, but there's so much more. You go on and on and on. I'll never get to the end of you. I'm going to try, darling. Just give me a lifetime to try."

He was still staring when there was a knock on the door. Neither of them moved to admit the champagne.

I T'S A SHAME epilogues are no longer in fashion: Jane Austen would have had a field day with all that's left over. We could shift about in time: twenty years, thirty years. Thirty years would project us slightly into the future, which is perfectly all right with me. There would be my modestly successful career as a painter. (I can emerge from my third-person anonymity; nothing very discreditable happened after Stamford.) There would be Peter's quite extraordinary success as a financier, if that's what you call somebody who makes money out of nothing; he was able to give Walter a fifty-thousand-dollar picture years ago. Always there would be Peter and Charlie, surviving the separation of war, against exotic backgrounds, passion intact if tempered by the years, experiencing daily happiness that plunges sometimes into despair, since it is man's nature to be easily surfeited with happiness. There would be very little new to record, for they have developed within the circle of their preoccupation with each other, a limitation that all intense relationships impose. Peter and Charlie. Peter has always been one for public declarations. I can't do better than this.